WICKED WISHES

A FICTION-ATLAS PRESS ANTHOLOGY

C.L. CANNON   K. MATT   JO HOLLOWAY   R.A. LEWIS

ADAM GAFFEN   ERIN CASEY

BAREND NIEUWSTRATEN III   L.R. BRADEN

JOELLE NICHOLE   J.M. RHINEHEART   S. BREAKER

VIOLA TEMPEST   DELIARIA DAVIS   PAUL EAGLE

MELISSA E. BECKWITH

FICTION-ATLAS
PRESS LLC

Thank you for supporting The World Literacy Foundation!

100% of all proceeds from the sale of this book will be donated to the **World Literacy Foundation**, which is a global not-for-profit that works to lift young people out of poverty through literacy. The World Literacy Foundation operates on the principle that education is a basic human right.

MEET ME AT THE CROSSROADS
BY C.L. CANNON

They say death is the greatest adventure—the first step into the unknown. For some, it can be a welcomed reunion with loved ones or even their creator. For others, the mere thought sends a shiver down their spine. Causes their heart to race. Makes them willing to do anything to beat the reaper. Anything to live forever…

As it turns out, immortality wasn't all I wished it to be, and death became a mistress I passed in the night but could never know. If only I could do it all over again, what different choices I would make.

***

Death wasn't something I thought too much about in my youth. Children need not worry about such things when the threat of their ends were percived to be at least a lifetime away. The young already believed themselves to be immortal.

I was fourteen before I really had a close experience with mortality. My father had been away for nearly a year, fighting a war for men who wouldn't allow him to lick their boot, much less shake his hand. We learned of his demise a whole season after he had passed from this life.

A ceremony was hastily arranged but no body was ever returned to us. The loss felt close and distant all at once. Almost like a dream I might one day wake up from. A few months later, my youngest sister succumbed to a violent fever that burned her from the inside out in a matter of days. A week later, it also claimed my brother.

The light in my mother's eyes left her that night. She was haunted and fearful. Every cough, every scraped knee sent her into a protective fit. My sister and I were her willing prisoners, doing our best to placate her fears. Eventually, she became a shut-in, scared of her own shadow at times. Unaware that the real monster had sprung from her own womb and would one day return to torment her.

When death finally came for me, I was twenty. I stood with a thick rope wrapped around my neck for a crime I, incidentally, hadn't committed. They executed criminals at crossroads in those days—no need to sully a lord's land with the bodies of low lives. As our last moments approached, the man hanging beside me was read his last rites as well as his sentence and began to weep loudly. He begged God for mercy, for refuge, and finally, forgiveness. He was given none of these things as far as I could tell. The board beneath his feet gave way, plunging him toward his fate. His neck made a resounding snap, and suddenly, there was only the quiet stillness of waiting. I'd lost my use for a god long ago, and he didn't seem very interested in winning me back. As the priest began to administer my last rites, a thought planted itself in my mind and began to grow until, finally, it burst from my lips.

"No, no. I am not dying today!" I wailed. "Please, someone, anyone, help me!"

"Shut it, prisoner," the hangman grunted, dealing a swift kick to my legs. The board beneath me wobbled, and I squeezed my eyes tight, expecting the end, but to my surprise, it never came.

When I opened my eyes, time seemed to have stopped completely.

The priest was frozen in place, hand outstretched in prayer. The hangman's foot had yet to fall back to the ground. They stared blankly ahead but drew no breath. The only movement came in the form of a wispy gray fog darting this way and that, growing in size, until finally, it dissipated, leaving a beautiful woman in its wake. She wore a long billowing black dress, her hair a wild tangle behind her.

With a snap of the woman's fingers, the noose disappeared from my neck, and I found myself standing in the road beside her.

My hand rubbed my chaffed neck, and I managed to whimper, "Who, who are you?"

A smile lit up the woman's face as she turned to me. "Why, Desmond, don't you know? I'm your salvation. I heard you call for me."

There was something unsettling about her voice. Like a long-forgotten melody sung in the wrong key.

"Are you a witch?" I asked.

She seemed mildly offended. "Hardly, though many of them call to me, just as you did. I can help you, Desmond. I want to help you. I can make this all go away. You need only tell me what you desire most in the world, and it will be yours."

I was a foolish young man but not naive enough to trust someone being so intentionally deceptive, especially when my life hung in the balance.

"And what's the price, demon? There's always a price."

"Well, that depends on the wish, doesn't it? One can hardly set terms without knowing the details."

I didn't need long to make my decision. Death had touched so many in my life, and only moments before, I'd felt its cold hands wrap around my own neck. "I want to live forever. Never to die. Now, tell me your price."

"So demanding," the woman cooed. "I like a man who knows what he wants."

"Can you do it or not?" My chest tightened, fear and anticipation stealing my breath.

"Of course I can, and all I require are a few pesky souls in return."

"Souls?"

"Yes, you will never die, and in exchange, once a year, on the anniversary of this gift, you will bring me a soul," the woman explained.

"You want me to kill people for you?"

"Oh, no, you can't kill them. How would I acquire their soul? No, I need the near-dead. The desperate. I'll provide you everything you need to deliver them to me."

"I won't harm innocent people. There must be something else you want," I pleaded.

The woman's cool and seductive persona fell away, leaving cold indifference in its place.

"If you don't want it, I can always leave you where you were," she said, gesturing to the lifeless body still hanging beside me.

I wasn't ready to die then, though I've wished for it many times in the days since.

"Can it be anyone? Criminals? Murderers?"

The woman's eyes seemed to ignite like crimson fire as she assured me. "Anyone."

What choice did I have? If I said no, I was dead. If I said yes, well, at least then I'd be alive. With forever to think about it, perhaps one day, I could find a way out of the agreement. I closed my eyes and swallowed the lump in my throat. "Do it. Make me immortal."

"As you wish," the woman said. A triumphant smirk spread across her beautiful face. She'd won. She'd always known she would. She was a spider, and I was the fly caught in her web. There was no turning back now.

The woman stepped closer, stealing my last living breath as her mouth captured mine.

The world went black for a moment, and then came the pain. My nerves felt as if they'd been set afire, and my chest ached with the acute absence of oxygen. Splinters seemed to shoot through my gums as long fangs emerged, piercing my bottom lip. And that smell, that smell was intoxicating. I felt the world shift around me as time resumed its previous path. My ears bled with the sound of a booming prayer, an earth-shattering thud as a boot connected with the wooden platform. And then, only instinct remained. Quick as lightning, I snapped the priest's neck and sank my fangs into him, draining the man dry. The executioner managed a strangled cry before I tore his throat out, not stopping until I'd suckled every last drop of his lifeforce.

"Oh, my, what a ferocious beastie you are, and such a mess," the woman admonished.

"What have you done to me?" Anger and confusion consumed me. I sprinted with inhuman speed to stand before her.

Her eyes betrayed her indifference. "Only what you asked, dear Desmond. You're neither dead nor alive. You cannot be killed, and you're well equipped to decimate anyone or anything that tries. This is what you wanted."

"No, this is not what I asked for," I spat. "I never wanted to be this thing, this creature."

"As you said so wisely before, there's always a price. You never made clear how you'd like to be immortal, only that it was your desire to do so. My methods have accomplished the task, and as such, this deal is now binding."

The woman in black spun on her heel and began walking back into the gray mist.

"You tricked me," I accused.

"Oh, Desmond, humans are so easy to manipulate, you'll see. You can hardly blame yourself. Now, go, enjoy your eternity. I'll see you in one year's time." By the time she'd uttered the last words, the fog had swallowed her up, leaving me alone with nothing but corpses for company.

***

At first, the hunger seemed to be endless. The mere proximity of a human set my instincts in motion. I avoided the main roads and settlements for this reason. I even tried some alternatives. Surely if the blood of a human could sustain me, an animal could do the same. A slaughtered deer, a few hares, and some violent vomiting later, I concluded animals were incompatible with my diet.

I managed to live off random travelers and vagrants for a time and eventually began trusting myself in small townships. As time passed, my resistance became easier. I learned to trust my senses and lure my prey into seclusion rather than ambush them in plain sight. Thieves and prostitutes were easy enough to target—people who wouldn't be missed. People I could convince myself might deserve such a fate or perhaps a rescue from the cruelty of life. It was the worst of criminals I brought to the lady in black. Serial murders, gang members, rapists. Each time the lady took them with a smile, dragging their addled bodies into the mist, never to be seen again.

I intentionally avoided my own village. Temptations loomed there. The man who sent me to the gallows for a simple misunderstanding. The girl who kissed me beneath an elm tree. The mother and sister who still mourned my untimely death. Finally, in the tenth year of my immortality, I convinced myself that I had gained enough control over my emotions. What harm could a short visit impose? I would stay in the shadows, never revealing myself. It was only the sight of my family that I craved, blood be damned. I told myself my feelings wouldn't put them in harm's way. But feelings aren't choices we make, and we cannot banish them so easily. When you're a vampire, your senses and emotions are magnified tenfold. Feelings overwhelm you no matter how you try to fight them. Pleasure, pain, desire, hunger, they're insatiable. The only thing more overwhelming is regret—disappointment in your lack of restraint.

Imagine my surprise when upon visiting my childhood home, the very man who had damned me to this fate ate at my mother's table as my sister sat lovingly by his side. And the children, children sat at their feet laughing. The man who wrought my destruction had stolen more than my reputation. He'd stolen my family. White-hot rage consumed me as the sound of blood pounded in my ears and assaulted my nose with its sweet smell. The monster took over, leaving death and destruction in its wake. My sister answered the door first, her face a mix of elation and confusion. My fangs easily tore through her skin, draining our shared blood. My strong hands crushed her neck, eliciting a strangled cry and then a sickening crack as I left her in a bloody heap at the threshold. The children screamed and sobbed but, ultimately, succumbed to my wrath. And then there was the man, the man who'd stolen my life. He stared up at me as if seeing a ghost.

"You're, you're d-d-dead," he stammered. "This isn't real. You can't be here!"

"Oh, I am real, and you will pay dearly for what you've done to me."

Before I could advance upon him, a voice called from the far end of the room.

"Desmond? My boy? My boy, you've returned!"

My mother, ever my protector, hobbled to stand between me and the object of all my life's torment. She was much older looking than I remembered. The ten years since I had last seen her had weathered her features harshly.

"I knew you would come back," she crooned, stepping close enough to embrace me before fully drawing back to fully take in my appearance.

"Why, my boy, are you hurt?"

It was only a fraction of a second, but somehow, she managed to bring me back to myself, to the horror of bodies and blood. It was then that my foe began his retreat, and the old woman who had raised me and so lovingly taken care of me became merely an obstacle between me and my vengeance. Her small head easily dislocated from her body, and I tossed it aside before pinning the horrified man to the wall.

"You're crazy. You're a demon!" he wailed.

And oh, how right he was. Only a demon could commit such atrocities. Only a man without consequence, who answered to no one, save the lady of the crossroads.

And that was precisely what this man deserved. He deserved to be consumed by pure evil, and I knew just where to go.

The mist rolled in, and with it, the lady.

"Oh, Desmond, what have you done?" she asked. Mock concern laced her unearthly voice.

"You did this to me, demon. When will it be enough? When will your lust for these souls end? When will I be free?" I raged, tossing my foe at her feet.

"Free? That was never part of the deal," she tsked. "You wanted forever, and that's exactly what I've provided."

"Just kill me," I begged, voice drunk with sorrow, body covered in innocent blood. What was left to live for? Every person I had ever loved, or who had ever loved me, was gone, the most beloved by my own hand.

"I'm sorry, Desmond, I couldn't kill you if I wanted to. You made sure of that when you accepted my help."

"I wish, I wish I'd never met you," I whispered.

The lady's mouth twisted into a frown. "Now, don't be rude. After all, you'd be dead if it wasn't for me, and wasn't death your greatest fear?"

"It was," I began, "but not anymore. Now I just fear the day I'm as cold and ruthless as you."

"Well, you have a millennia to try," she said, dragging the bleeding man behind her into the mist. His screams for mercy were cut short by a squelching suck before the mist faded completely.

The revenge I sought was short-lived, replaced instead by grief. I returned to the scene of my crimes, disgusted with my so-called control. I buried what was left of my family and vowed never to love a human again. I didn't belong to the mortal world anymore. And so, I sought out others like me.

In the meantime, I decided to test my limits. She was right. Nothing could kill me. I tried fire, starvation, and drowning. I even tried cutting off my own head once, but the blade was never sharp enough to leave a mark. It was as if an invisible surrounded my body, preventing every attempt to change. There would be no further progression, no aging, no harm, only stagnation.

Fifty years later, I met more of my kind, though their origins were much different than my own. They could be killed, though the task was far from easy. Sunlight weakened them, and certain herbs had the power to repel them. They could also pass their affliction to others, a feat I hadn't been able to manage successfully. I learned a great deal about myself from their friendship, but they never quite filled the hole in my existence. Every decade I spent with them, the more I resented their differences. The more I yearned for change. I began spending more time in solitude, going out only when the need to feed was unbearable, or my yearly offering was due. Time went on, and the world changed, but we did not. The lady was immovable. Every year it was the same. A new soul, a new plea for it to just end until, eventually, I stopped asking. Time has a way of healing wounds, blunting pain, tricking us into normalcy. Repetition can make anything seem normal.

***

"And so, you see, here we are," I say, pulling my SUV to the side of the small country road.

A muffled sob comes from the passenger's seat. I remove the scarf from the young woman's mouth, dragging her from the vehicle and squarely into the middle of the crossroads. The motions are like muscle memory after all this time.

"Why are you telling me this? Are you some sort of crazy person?" the girl cries. "Please, just let me go."

Black streaks of mascara slide down her cheeks as she begs for her life. They always beg, especially the young ones. They have so much to live for, just as I did once. The least I can do is give them an explanation.

"It's been six hundred years, and I figure someone should know the story, even if it's for only a moment. Besides, it's cheaper than a therapist."

My teeth sink into the tender flesh of the girl's neck, and I drink in one long, deep gulp until her heart slows to a murmur. I've gotten good at making it painless over the years. One quick slip into a sleep I hope she'll never wake from.

Wisps of familiar gray mist swirl around me, and time once again stands still.

"Still playing the victim after all these years, Desmond? It's been over a century since you've brought me even a sniff of an adulterer, much less someone truly evil."

"Oh, I figured that one out years ago," I tell the lady in black. "See, you like the evil ones, and I'm not about to give you one ounce of happiness after all you've stolen from me."

Her face twists, mulling over my declaration. "My, what an imagination you've cultivated over the years. Does it make you feel better? Does it make the truth go down easier? You did this to yourself."

"I'm not interested in the truth, and neither are you. It's the lies that really sate your hunger. That's the whole reason you came to me. You knew I'd fall for the lie just to survive. You were counting on it. One day, lady, I'll unravel your lies. Until then, I'll spend the rest of my existence watching you choke on the purest of the pure. Enjoy your dinner."

The lady in black shakes her head, grabs her offering by a strand of long golden hair, and walks once again into the mist. "Poor, Desmond, you never learn, do you? You'll never be free," she calls over her shoulder.

"Maybe not, but I'll never stop trying."

The End

ABOUT C.L. CANNON

C.L. Cannon is a USA Today Bestselling Author, publisher, publicist, editor, designer, and lots of other occupations with the -er sound at the end! She is a woman of many talents who never gives up or stops improving. She enjoys writing about love and friendship. She loves it even more when she can add fantasy and science fiction aspects to those themes! She's a self-proclaimed Harry Potter freak (Slytherin Pride people), lover of anything Joss Whedon (Spuffy forever), Tolkien fiend (who enjoys second breakfast), and addict of classic literature

(Social class struggles turn me on… literally ;) yah see what I did there?) She spends her days trying to #bookstagram/#booktok (and probably failing), helping other authors grow and succeed (I love my job), and loving on her two babes (velociraptors), Seth and Petey.

You can find her basically everywhere on the net (man I just aged myself). Visit her website, join her street team, or stalk her on her socials for more content!

Website

clcannon.net

Fan Group

facebook.com/groups/clcannon

Everything Else

lnk.bio/clcannon

tiktok.com/@clcannonauthor

instagram.com/cl_cannon

facebook.com/clcannonauthor

goodreads.com/clcannon

THE INFLUENCER
BY VIOLA TEMPEST

"If you're seeing this, it means we should be friends. So, like my page!"

Alexis Day frowned and let out an annoyed growl, swiping to delete the voice recording. It wouldn't do. She didn't sound… cheerful enough. She stared at her cell as the video played again, smiling to herself. She looked good, her makeup looking *just* right; she'd made an effort, but it didn't *look* like she'd made an effort. The T-shirt she wore was a size too small for her frame, revealing just enough of her figure without being too much. Perfect for Shutter, the world's most popular social media platform and, really, the only one that mattered anymore.

Alexis just couldn't get the voice right. She sounded too desperate, and in fact, she was.

She hadn't jumped on the Shutter phenomenon quickly enough, sticking to her previous haunts, ones where she knew exactly how the algorithms worked and thought people would never abandon for way too long.

People hadn't deserted the likes of Click, Flash, and Chatter completely; she still got decent traction on her profiles when she turned her attention to them, but they were an afterthought. Shutter mattered. That's where the influencers hung out; that's where the money was made; that's where she belonged.

Alexis just had to figure it all out, and her frustration with the platform increased each day.

No, not with the platform. She loved it and marveled at its perfection. Alexis just hadn't stumbled on the magic formula, the way to turn her videos viral, going from a thousand views to millions.

The previous night, Alexis couldn't sleep. She'd aggressively swiped through her cell, studying the most popular videos, watching "How To" videos on Chatter, reading endless blogs, and found nothing to help her. She'd done *everything*. Tried it all, but nothing worked. Finally crying herself to sleep, Alexis had concluded that she just didn't have *it*, so she'd have to change herself.

She woke up with a plan. With her first profile, Alexis had tried to be herself too much, revealing more of the mid-twenties, single, bookish, and opinionated woman she was. That wasn't Shutter. Skimming through the videos she'd uploaded, she realized she'd plunged in too hard at chasing those trending videos instead of starting off small and building the perfect Shutter personality.

So, she deleted her first profile. It caused a stabbing pain in her heart at first. Her palms grew sweaty when she pressed confirmed when Shutter asked if she *really* wanted to go through with erasing her handle and all her videos. Alexis almost said no. Almost. Even though it made her neck muscles tighten, her mouth go drier than the Sahara Desert, she pressed yes, and let her phone fall onto the bed. She'd curled up into a ball then, sobbing over the wasted past months and thousands of lost followers.

But she had to do it. They'd come back, plus more.

Alexis then went to work, cleaning the tears from her face, showering, carefully selecting her too-small T-shirt and tight leather pants. They had to be the right color, the correct shape. She spent an hour in front of her mirror, getting her makeup just right, her hair stylish and messy but suggestive. Then, she got on her bed, lying on her stomach, working to find the perfect angle.

Smiling, she reviewed the video one more time, forgetting how many takes she'd burned through before settling on the perfect one. Alexis smirked back at her reflection, brown eyes twinkling, feet up in the air as she lay on her belly. That pose seemed to attract thousands of viewers without a problem. Sex sells.

"Okay, let's try this again," Alexis told herself, waiting for the recording to play through once more. "Bright, cheerful. Spontaneous. You've got this."

Holding record, Alexis took a deep breath, suppressing the butterflies in her stomach, and matched the smile in the recording.

"If you're seeing this, it means we should be friends. So, give me a like!"

Falling back onto the mattress, Alexis laughed, listening to her voice repeating the words. That last-minute change worked. *Give me a like*. Not desperate at all.

"Perfect," Alexis grinned, fingers flying across her screen as she added a few worthwhile hashtags. "I've got this."

<hr>

Pangs of pain shot through Alexis' stomach as she reached for her phone. She'd stuffed it under her pillow after hitting publish, resisting the urge to stare at it as the notifications flooded in.

Or so she had hoped.

It's why she had thrust it to where she couldn't see it and went on her laptop instead, responding to comments on her other social media, flooding her posts with *LOLs* and a healthy modicum of emojis. The love her activity received definitely helped boost her ego. Her experience with Shutter so far has really knocked it out of the park, and Alexis reflected on the strength it had taken to delete her old profile.

She'd never erased a handle before. Never. In truth, she'd never needed to; she had the social media knack so many others strived for. Before the rise of Shutter, people recognized her on the streets a few times a week while she went out for a simple cup of coffee or while she was out looking for that perfect photo opportunity. Of course, she posed for selfies with her followers; they helped her handles spread across the world, reaching new followers to love her.

But Shutter didn't work that way.

Taking a deep breath and ignoring the pain piercing her stomach, she reached out with a trembling hand, plunging her fingers beneath the pillow and almost shuddering when they came into contact with the cool, smooth plastic and glass of her phone.

Closing her eyes, she pulled it free, her fingerprint unlocking the screen without her looking. A tear trickled down her cheek. *This is too much; I can't do this. What if no one liked it? What if no one's commented? Worse, what if I get a handful of pity emojis?*

Her breath came fast. Even with her eyes closed, the room seemed to spin. The pain in her stomach increased, a constant stabbing as it tried to flip around, battling with her intestines to escape through her throat.

"No," she whispered, her voice shaking. "I can do this. I can!"

Opening her eyes, Alexis opened the Shutter app and laughed. Tears flowed from her eyes, and she scrubbed them away so she could see her notifications better, laughing again.

She'd only posted the video half an hour ago, but it already had 2,432 views, 500 likes, a bunch of comments... and she'd gained followers! Just 700 so far, but she crushed the disappointment; it *had* only been thirty minutes!

Laughing, she liked all the comments, chatting to her new friends, striking while the iron was still hot. All the blogs she'd read said to comment, to like, to interact, all to help the video spread and gain more traffic.

Alexis laughed as an idea popped into her head and typed a comment onto her own post for others to see. "Hey! I'm new here, so would you share my video, too? You're the best. Love you!!"

"Okay," she breathed, placing her precious device down on the mattress. "I think my stomach will finally let me have some coffee, maybe some fruit, and then?" She grinned, glancing at her phone as more notifications swept in. "More videos!"

Alexis wiped the streaky mascara from her cheeks, her trembling hands smearing it further as she stared in the mirror.

"Hideous," she told herself. "Loser with no talent. No one cares about you! No one!"

She tried to sigh, but a wet sob sounded instead, followed by more tears. In the corner of her room, where it sat on a charger, her phone pinged. Even though the noise made her heart skip a beat, she ignored it. It hadn't made a noise in well over an hour. Stifling her tears, she waited, fixed on a point in her mirror where she couldn't see herself *or* the phone.

"Maybe it's just something with the time zones," Alexis whispered, nodding as she spoke. "I'm on the East Coast, after all. Maybe I need to upload my videos later on in the day to capture LA and the rest of California."

But her cell remained silent, the deluge of notifications refusing to sweep in. Alexis sobbed again and leaned forward, her head touching the glass. "Why? Why can't I get it right?"

It had all started so well. Her new profile gained a steady stream of followers, her videos a healthy number of daily likes and comments, and recent uploads brought views in for her old work, too.

But then the raging river of notifications dried up. Her clips, still pulling off that look of a cute, girl-next-door sexy style she aimed for, stopped gaining views. Alexis tried more provocative clothes, jumped on the spicy trends, and went on following sprees of her own, hoping the profiles would follow back, but nothing helped. Every day, each new video pulled in a lower number until the one that morning finally broke her.

Alexis had worn her lowest cut top. Her shortest shorts. She'd flirted outrageously with the camera, performing take after take until she had it *just* right. It was her magnum opus, the greatest Shutter clip anyone could ever take.

In the four hours since she posted it, the video boasted less than a hundred views and a handful of likes, with even fewer comments.

She'd torn through the trending clips on Shutter, rage building, breath harder to come by, frustration making her chest tight as she poured over videos inferior to hers, created by users with less talent and looks than her.

Or so her anger told her. When the tears broke her rising hostility, Alexis realized the truth. All the other Shutter creators had more talent than her and looked better than her. Were better than her.

"Why won't they, why can't they, see the thought and effort I put into all this?" Makeup ran down her face, black tears running away from her red-ringed eyes. "Why can't they just feel sorry for me and like my videos?"

Her sobs faltered. Pity. That was it! A last resort, sure, but it could work! Alexis tapped a finger against her lip, studying her reflection. A mess stared back, but she could fix it a little, so it still appeared genuine but presentable. Dabbing at her face with some tissues had the desired effect, cleaning the worst of the wreck of blacks, blues, and reds on her face.

She hesitated, turning around in her chair, eyeing her maddeningly silent cell. Making people like her because they felt sorry for her... It was desperate.

Alexis smiled. "A pity follow is still a follow!"

She jumped to her feet, a bounce in her step she hadn't had since her Shutter triumph two days before, and grabbed her phone, yanking it free from its charger. She took in the notifications it had blared, a follow, like, comment, and private message from a user called Dream-ComeTrue, and hit the create icon. Taking a deep breath, she started to record.

"Life is just so hard, right?" Alexis wailed, putting enough of her true feelings into her voice. "Just nothing ever goes the way I want it to. I'm not pretty enough, so no boyfriend. Not rich enough, so I can't get the things I want. Now, no one will even leave me a like or a follow?" She let a sob leak from her mouth, and she didn't have to try all too hard to make it sound real. "What do I have to do? Please, tell me. Please!"

Bottom lip trembling, Alexis hit publish. No hashtags, no witty, suggestive comment. She sent it out into the digital world, and as she did, her stomach flipped.

Did I just make a mistake? Oh, no, I did, didn't I?

Bile flooded her throat. Sweat surged through her skin, making her palms slick. Her head pounded.

"Oh, God," Alexis wailed, trying to breathe normal breaths. "I'm having a panic attack."

Vision swimming, neck muscles tight, she glanced around the room, looking for anything to distract herself. Her eyes fell to her screen, the Shutter app still open, the private message from Dream-ComeTrue still waiting for her.

"That'll do!"

"I've seen your profile," the message from the anonymous profile read. "You've got talent, but you need luck to cut it online these days. I can help you."

Alexis bit her lip, the waves of panic subsiding a little as she focused on her cell. About to message back, the typing icon appeared below the message. DreamComeTrue was writing!

She jumped when her cell pinged.

"I'd delete that clip if I were you," the new message read, "though I get what you're going through. Users will just laugh at you, but I won't. I want to help, and I know I can. You listen to me, and you'll have all the followers you want. You'll be FAMOUS."

Famous. What Alexis had always dreamt about. People loved celebrities, obsessed over them, hung onto every word they typed, studied every photo and video they uploaded.

Alexis read the messages again. DreamComeTrue had it right; people *would* laugh at her clip. She pulled it up, wincing as her high-pitched whine of a voice disturbed the silence, her stomach flipping again as she stared at her tear-streaked, makeup ruined face and hit delete.

Tight muscles relaxed in an instance.

Returning to the private messages, she typed into her cell.

"Tell me more."

Alexis sat in a darkened booth of a local bar, The Exchange, a place only a few blocks from her apartment. A flicker of doubt had gnawed at her when she realized DreamComeTrue lived in the same city as her, but so did another twenty million people or so.

She didn't really go to bars, but this one opened early, and there weren't many people around. Jazz music thumped at an acceptable level, though it still made the booth's table vibrate. Despite being inside, and the bar's gloomy setting, Alexis wore her oversized sunglasses, and the hood of her pullover covered her hair and forehead. She didn't know why, but she'd done it on instinct. DreamCome-True knew what she looked like; he'd seen her clips on Shutter. Sighing, she glanced at the time on her phone. The guy still had a minute to show. Any later than that, she'd leave. Doubt crept into her stomach again and whispered to her anxiety.

Alexis bit at her fingernails, the varnish chipping. She'd read about meeting followers, and every blog said not to do it. Any clip she found warned her against it. Stalkers. Obsessed weirdos. They preyed on the influencers, couldn't get enough of them, re-watching their videos, commenting with their demands, and searched the towns and cities they lived in for a glimpse of them.

What am I doing? I've come out here, alone, to meet a creepy weirdo called DreamComeTrue who says he can help me. Have I lost my mind?

"That's a nasty habit, you know? Biting your nails."

Alexis almost leapt out of the booth as her heart tried to escape through her chest. A man stood before her, grinning. Slim and average height, he wore a plain brown sweatshirt, faded-denim jeans, and white sneakers. His hair was slicked back, an expensive cut made to look accessible, and the faint smell of rich aftershave swam into her nostrils. His mesmerizing green eyes twinkled despite the gloom.

The guy screamed money.

"DreamComeTrue?" Alexis breathed, her hammering heart settling down.

"Call me Kel," he replied with a smirk and pointed at the booth. "Mind if I sit down?"

Alexis nodded, eyeing her cell. He'd arrived right on time. Kel glanced around, caught the eye of a passing bartender, and raised a hand.

"They don't do table service here," Alexis murmured as the worker approached.

Kel shrugged.

"Hey, how's your day, man?" Kel asked, raising his eyebrows and smiling.

Alexis stared at his perfect white teeth and his gleaming skin and wondered why she'd never seen such a beautiful face before on Shutter. A man like him would easily get millions of views with every upload.

"Good," the bartender replied, eyes shining. Kel obviously had the same effect on him as he had on Alexis. "What can I get you?"

Kel glanced at Alexis, then winked at the man. "Now, I've never been here before, so sorry about this, but I didn't realize you don't do table service... But could you get me an Americano and a Skinny Almond Milk Decaf Latte for the lady?"

He knows my drink... He knows my drink! Wait, how? Did I upload a video about it? I must have... Haven't I?

The bartender grinned. "Yeah, no problem. I'll make them myself."

Kel watched him leave, then turned his grin onto Alexis. She never wanted that smile to go away.

"So... You said you can help me?"

He sat back, crossing his arms, head cocked to the side. "Straight to business, eh? Being famous really matters to you, doesn't it?"

"Of course, it does." Alexis frowned. "I mean, look at you. You've got everything."

Kel laughed. "I'm not famous."

"You must be!" Alexis leaned forward. "You've got money for the most expensive clothes, you know, the ones that don't *look* expensive, but they really are. Your teeth are the whitest I've ever seen. Your skin doesn't have a single blemish. You can charm people into doing whatever you want… You *must* be famous."

The bartender returned, carrying the drinks and setting them down without taking his eyes off Kel, who beamed back.

"They're on the house," the man said, cheeks turning red.

"Ah, thanks," Kel replied, pulling out his phone. A high-end phone, just released. "Can I leave you a tip, though? It's only fair." The man nodded. "How much do you make an hour?"

"Ten dollars," he replied, pulling out an e-reader for payment.

Kel typed on his phone, then tapped it against the reader. "There you go. Have a nice day, my good sir."

"A hundred dollars?" the man cried, eyebrows shooting up his forehead. "I can't accept this."

"You can, and you will," Kel replied, his voice and eyes a little rougher than before. "Now, have a nice day."

He sipped at his Americano as the man staggered off, dazed by his good fortune, and winked at Alexis.

"See," she said, "you *are* famous. The way you tipped him and sent him on his way."

"Being famous doesn't bother me." Kel smiled, putting his coffee down. "Helping people does. So, tell me this; why do *you* want to be famous?"

"I want people to love me." Alexis didn't even need to think about it; the desire was seared into her soul ever since she grew up watching influencers living their best lives on Chatter. "I want to matter to people."

"And being famous makes that happen?"

Alexis stared at him. Didn't he understand? "Of course it does!

Being famous is the best thing you can hope for. Why bother doing anything if people aren't going to notice?"

Kel tapped a finger against his lip, the shadow of a smile on his face. Alexis blinked. The light surrounding him appeared darker than before, his green eyes brighter. She blinked again and shook her head, the man opposite her suddenly normal again—*just a trick of the light.*

He reached into his pocket and withdrew a small vial. Glancing around, he placed it on the table, letting it stand between them. A glittery gold liquid filled it; one Alexis couldn't pull her eyes away from.

"One sip of this will see your luck turn. Just a few drops onto your tongue, and your next Shutter clip will get millions of views. You'll get hundreds of thousands of followers. Loyal ones."

"Really?" Alexis asked, raising an eyebrow. She *wanted* to believe. The liquid glittered and swirled just so…

"Really."

She met his eyes. "What do you want for it? I've got money, but I won't do anything else, not until I know you better anyway, and that isn't a—"

"I don't want anything." Kel leaned back. His head cocked to the side again. "It's yours. My payment comes in ways you wouldn't understand."

I wouldn't understand? This is too weird. A magic potion? But what if it works… Alexis studied the liquid, the bar's lowlight playing off the glitter, soothing her. She reached forward, her fingers twitching. It could be the answer to all her problems.

"I can just… take it?"

Kel snatched it away from her grasp at the last moment. Rage bubbled in Alexis' chest as he held it just out of her grasp.

"Just a few drops at a time. That's all you need. Say it."

Breathing in, she let out a calming breath. It didn't work; her fingers still stretched for it. "Just a few drops."

"Remember that." Kel leaned forward and pushed the vial onto her palm. "This is potent stuff. Have fun now."

Kel climbed to his feet and walked off without a backward glance;

he didn't even finish his coffee. The bartender looked hopefully in his direction and half-raised a hand, one that Kel ignored.

Alexis stuffed the vial into her pocket and snatched up her phone. It hadn't cost her anything, and just a drop of the liquid wouldn't hurt. Would it?

⸻

Weeks later, Alexis wondered what would have happened if she'd followed Kel's advice and taken just a few drops of the liquid. She hadn't heard from him since, though her private messages were hard to keep up with these days.

She hadn't followed his advice. Instead, she'd downed the entire vial in one go. Better safe than sorry.

Her limbs had trembled when the liquid slid down her throat, her stomach warm as it settled there, its sweet, peach-like taste lingering in her mouth as she smiled at herself in the mirror. Grabbing her cell, she put Kel's potion to the test and piggybacked on one of Shutter's latest trends. In all honesty, she hadn't expected much and tried to kid herself into nonchalance when she hit publish and set her phone back down onto the mattress.

The number of notifications she received drained her battery life within an hour.

Since then, she'd had to get multiple devices. Chargers hung out of every socket in her room, and Alexis pondered hiring a personal assistant to carry out all the pesky demands of being an influencer. It wasn't just on Shutter where her popularity had bloomed. Her presence across all her social media had exploded, and the advertisement money she'd made on Chatter would set her up for life within a month or two.

Grinning and leaning back against her new, expensive, and highly comfortable office chair, Alexis reviewed her follower statistics, pausing as she studied her Shutter profile. That had been the golden goose, the one that mattered more than any other. Before she met Kel and drank his formula, she had a measly three thousand followers. Now, she had twelve million people behind her, with thousands more rolling in by the second. By the end of the month, she'd be the number one profile on the app. People loved her. They hung off her every clip, imitating her, buying the products she suggested—which made her team of sponsors admire her even more—and creating clips in her honor, hoping, wishing, that Alexis would return the favor with a tiny like.

"Dreams *can* come true after all."

Glancing around, she picked up her burner cell, one with private profiles for her apps, one designed for her to take with her when she went out and about, a quiet cell that would keep her connected with the social world but not inundated with notifications. "I think I deserve a coffee today."

Getting to her feet and stretching, her eyes caught a new notification sliding into her DMs. Without thinking, she opened it, then scowled.

"Can we meet? Please."

It came from a profile called ShutterFlutter065. She'd already blocked ShutterFlutter001 through 064, the guy — and it just had to be a man — always asking the same thing.

The only drawback of fame, aside from the constant barrage of followers demanding attention, were the obsessives. *At least I was never that bad.* Hitting the block button and tossing her phone aside, Alexis pulled on a wide-brimmed hat and shades before leaving for her treat.

"Oh, my God… It's you, isn't it?"

Behind her oversized sunglasses, Alexis blinked at the barista who'd taken her order at Café Moon, her favorite local coffee shop. The girl's lips trembled, her hands shaking as she attempted to scrawl the fake name Alexis had given her onto the paper cup. *She must be new, never seen her in here before.*

"Who?" Alexis muttered, forcing her voice to sound deeper and huskier.

"Alexis Day, from Shutter!" the barista squealed, her wide eyes shining with unshed tears. "I knew you lived around here and hoped you might come in one day. I saw a Café Moon cup in one of your clips."

Alexis' eyes rolled before she could stop them, and she hoped the lenses of her sunglasses hid them enough. Anything could spark anger in an obsessive, their undying love switching to hatred in a matter of seconds. She'd seen other influencers talk about it before, the experience forcing them to tears while they recorded their clips, their loving followers sending them love to heal from the experience. Alexis had suffered it herself. On one of her rare recent excursions to the mall, she stopped to sign autographs in a shoe store. When she tried to leave as the crowd built, a young blonde-haired girl with big brown eyes hurled a swarm of abuse at her, calling her ignorant and accusing her of betraying the followers who made her who she is.

That reaction video still got millions of views a week.

Frowning, Alexis peered at the girl. She looked familiar, but she couldn't place her, though the barista's roots distracted her. The blonde showed through from her poor dye job. *Probably did it herself.*

"Sorry, I don't know who you're talking about. How much for the coffee?"

The girl's face turned to stone. *See, a crazy obsessive. I knew it. Sometimes I wonder if this fame is worth it... Ah, who am I kidding? Of course, it is.*

"Three-fifty."

Smiling, Alexis recalled Kel's way with the bartender back at The Exchange. It felt like a lifetime ago. "Hey, how much do you make an hour?"

The barista's mouth twisted. "Eight dollars."

Alexis' eyebrows climbed her forehead as she pulled out her burner, typing away into it, then presented it for payment. "There you go, a little tip."

The girl took the cell, fumbled around with it as she grabbed the e-reader, then handed it back without a smile. "Your coffee will be ready at the end of the counter. Have a nice day."

Alexis' jaw almost fell open. She'd tipped the girl a hundred and fifty dollars! Fury welling in her chest, she almost pulled off her shades to reveal who she really was but thought better of it. People stood around her, waiting to order, cellphones in hand. A 'Do you know who I am?' meltdown would be all over Shutter within minutes.

Nodding, Alexis moved to the counter's end, her coffee appearing like clockwork. Grabbing it, cell glued to her face, she left, taking the long way home as she sipped at her drink, flicking through her apps, planning her new clips for the day, and wondering if she could somehow mention ungrateful retail workers. Sighing, she looked up, finding herself in a part of the city she didn't recognize.

Crap.

Her cell pinged. Frowning, she came to a stop. This cell never got any notifications. Glancing at it, her heart and stomach fluttered as one. It came from DreamComeTrue.

How?

"I warned you," it read, anxiety creeping from Alexis' gut. "An entire bottle at once is too much for anyone."

She glanced around. Did Kel follow her? The sun seemed darker, the shadows longer, the streets emptier. Pulling her hat lower, Alexis moved, head down, hoping she'd find somewhere she recognized.

Her cell pinged again. The anxiety worked its way into her chest.

"You should be nicer," ShutterFlutter066 had typed. "You mean an awful lot to me. To all of us."

Alexis' coffee crashed down to the ground and exploded onto the concrete as she ran. She didn't know where; she didn't care. Her body told her to flee, and her limbs agreed. Alexis ran, her phone pinging and pinging as notifications continued to flood in, chasing her all the way back home.

Under her covers, Alexis trembled and sobbed, clutching her closed laptop, twitching as every one of her cells pinged and chirped. She'd turned them all off, but somehow, they powered back up and cried for her attention. ShutterFlutter's last DM, from one number 147 now, told her that she knew how she liked her coffee.

The barista.

Alexis wasn't safe.

Throwing open her laptop, she turned on some music — she didn't care what, anything to drown out the pinging — and gasped. Messages flooded the screen. Clicking into another browser changed nothing, changing apps didn't stop it, and the computer wouldn't turn off.

"I'm going insane!" Alexis laughed, tears streaming down her face, the constant pinging building into a hellish electronic cacophony. "I'm going insane!"

"Where are you, Alexis?"

"We miss you!"

"How's your day today, Alexis? You're my favorite influencer."

"I know where you live."

"Be careful next time you leave your house."

"I HATE YOU."

Outside Alexis' apartment, Kel shook his head and put his phone away.

"They never listen," he whispered, though he didn't feel sorry for her. He never did. "Enjoy the rest of your fame. I hope it's everything you ever wanted."

He melted into the shadows, the faint pinging of an army of cellphones sounding in his wake.

ABOUT VIOLA TEMPEST

Viola Tempest is a dystopian fantasy and paranormal romance author who yearns to expose the truth of those in the modern world: the good, the bad, and the ugly. Her inspiration primarily stems from life experiences, those who annoy her, ex-boyfriends, and the crazy dreams that pop into her head every once in a while.

Find out more at: violatempest.com

facebook.com/authorviolatempest

instagram.com/author_violatempest

goodreads.com/goodreadscomviolatempest

MUSICAL MEALS
BY ERIN CASEY

Scales? Fangs? An insatiable appetite? When I made my idiotic wish, this wasn't exactly what I'd had in mind.

But I'm getting ahead of myself.

Rejection has always been a part of my life. A father who left me when I was born. An absentee mom who spent more time pining for a new boyfriend than taking care of her daughter. A best friend who stole my boyfriend. A girlfriend who decided we should see other people. So, I came to expect rejections as I looked for vocal coaches or a studio that would take a chance on a budding artist like me, but they didn't hurt any less.

Limerick's Pub was a good place to escape to when you received bad news, and in the last week, I'd gotten a tsunami of it. I chose my typical table near the stage where the newest indie singing sensation would entertain the crowd. I swiped through yet another email with the opening lines, "We regret to inform you," words I'd become so familiar with, they'd begun haunting my dreams.

I flipped my phone over with a snort, just shy of shattering the screen, and threw back another Silver Bullet.

"Whoa, that's your third one, Katrina. Maybe you should slow down."

I leaned my head toward my waitress, Shae, a beautiful, thick, curvaceous woman with bright green eyes, curly copper hair, and *very* kissable lips. "You're counting now?"

"Considering I had to order you an Uber the last time? Yeah." She slid into the seat across from me. "What's wrong, hon?"

"I'll need another shot for that."

"Rin...."

"Fine, fine." I ran my fingers through my black hair, entered my password, and handed her my phone. "Another rejection."

Shae sighed as she read through it. "I'm sorry. I was really sure about this one."

"Yeah, well, with all the singing contests and people going viral on TikTok, it's hard to compete." I rolled my eyes and tapped on the cursed app. "My last video didn't even break two-thousand views."

Shae patted my hand. She'd, unofficially, become my go-to therapist when I got bad news. I was one of the regulars who frequented her table, first off. Second, one evening we got to talking, and after staying past closing and sharing some personal conversations, we ended up having a one-night stand. *I* wanted it to be more than that, but she said she didn't think she was a good person to date. Something about family drama and a past bad breakup. Most people might have never gone back to the pub after that, but I valued our talks and friendship too much.

And maybe I held a tiny sliver of hope that she'd be ready to date again one day.

Like I said, I'm used to rejection.

"So, what's our lineup tonight?" I asked, glancing at the stage.

"The usual," Shae replied. She cocked her head when the door opened, and by the look on her face, I knew I'd be left alone shortly. "But we got a huge surprise at the last minute. Vanya asked to join the roster."

I gaped in surprise. "*The* Vanya?" Talk about an up-and-coming TikToker! That woman had gone viral overnight. Limerick's Pub was a great spot for brand new artists, which she technically was, but I would have expected an influencer of her caliber to frequent more popular bars. "Did she offer to do a crowd talk after her session?"

"Yep. I was going to text you to come tonight, but when you said you were on the way, well, I thought I'd surprise you. Cheer up. Maybe you'll get lucky."

I smirked and wiggled my eyebrows suggestively.

Shae blushed as she swatted me with her order pad. "Not like that!"

"Heh, jealous?"

"Hmph, just enjoy the show. I'll get you a water and something to eat to soak up those shots. Jalapeno poppers?"

"Oh yeah, with extra berry sauce, don't forget!"

"Do I ever?" Shae smiled then disappeared into the growing crowd.

I leaned back, admiring her from behind. If we didn't end up together, whoever got the honor of dating her would be very lucky.

By the time I had my drink and food, every table had filled to capacity. I started to dread that someone would sit with me, but Shae steered them away, probably so she'd have a spot once the show started. The thought made me a little giddy.

The room was packed, mostly with regulars, but there were quite a few new folks who'd likely heard about Vanya's upcoming performance. I eyed the new occupants curiously, catching sight of a woman flipping tarot cards across from a lonely-looking man. Beside her, a spoon twirled in her tea without anything touching it.

Witch.

News had broken out across the city several years ago about cryptids existing. I'd seen a few in passing, usually witches near the park or a werewolf out for a run in the local forest preserve, but they often kept to themselves. Some were brave enough to do things in public, like the tarot witch. Sometimes it was still hard for me to believe they were real. And if werewolves, witches, and vampires existed, what else was out there?

Shaking my head, I turned my eyes back to the stage as the first performer appeared.

I spent the opening act listening to the singer and looking through my phone at other prospects on my coach wish list. Maybe Vanya had advice on who to apply to next. Or tips on TikTok set up or how to get such a huge following to notice me. I didn't proclaim myself to be the most amazing singer, but I had talent. The nights *I* sang at the pub told me as much.

As the act wrapped up, I clapped, making sure to follow the singer on social media to show my support. It was a competitive world, but it was important to support fellow singers. Enough douche nozzles already plagued the streets; I didn't need to be one of them.

The lights dimmed, and the crowd quieted as a single spotlight illuminated the stage. I heard the click of heeled boots before Vanya stepped into view. Heat rushed through my cheeks and ears. Vanya was gorgeous. Her tall frame commanded attention. Luscious purple ombre hair swept around her shoulders and down her back—a few beaded strands, her signature look, dangled by her cheeks, matching her necklace. Vanya smiled charmingly, lips full and also purple, a cool contrast to her warm amber skin. She wore an iridescent corset with a violet jacket and skirt. Black boots ended mid-calf with a small heel, not that she needed more height.

"Good evening, Limerick Pub!" Vanya shouted and waved. "Let's hear it for Garrett! He was amazing!" She gestured to the opening singer. He turned crimson with embarrassment and delight at being noticed. "I think a collab is in order," Vanya added with a wink. She walked around the stage, one hand sweeping through her hair. "My name is Vanya, and I'll be your main act for the night. So, sit back, relax, and don't be afraid to give requests," she said, pointing to a jar at the end of the stage. "Stick around at 11 p.m. when I host a Q&A. Enjoy the show!"

Vanya launched into her first song. The clarity and depth of her voice sent chills down my spine. I melted into my chair and couldn't take my eyes off her. Neither could anyone else in the room. Normally, there was an undercurrent of chatter during performances, but not tonight. Pool and dart games halted. The witch put her cards away. All I could do was stare and listen, captivated by Vanya's siren song.

"Isn't she incredible?" Shae asked.

I gave a start and looked across the table. At some point, Shae had joined me, and I'd never even noticed. "Breathtaking," I whispered back and slowly bit into my now cold jalapeno popper. Everything about Vanya swept me away into another world. Her fluid dancing, her song, a flick of the wrist on beat. In the brief moment her eyes met mine, it was like she was singing to *me*, and only me. I wanted to climb onto that stage and do whatever she ordered me to do. Never before had such a primal instinct to *follow* come over me.

"Thank you, thank you!" Vanya shouted, breaking the spell.

I gave myself a shake and rubbed my head. I hadn't even noticed her song end. Had I dozed off? Spaced out? "When did she—" I started to ask before I realized Shae was no longer sitting with me. I glanced around and spotted her cleaning a table. Huh, she hadn't even said goodbye. Maybe she hadn't wanted to disturb me.

Vanya waved as people rose, clapping and cheering. "You're too kind. I was going to take a break, buuut, let's get this Q&A rolling! You've been such a great audience."

I scurried toward the front of the stage along with a couple dozen other people. We jostled each other, bumping shoulders and spilling drinks. In the back of my mind, I laughed at how absurd it was, but I couldn't ignore the impulse to get closer and learn Vanya's secrets.

Vanya perched on the edge of a stool, eyes alight. "Who's got a question?"

Hands shot up, mine included, and a jolt of jealousy ran through me as she called on someone else. The questions were pretty typical. When did she start singing? When she was a child. Where did she study? With an at-home tutor. Could she sign something? Yes, of course. And on and on they went. She called on everyone except for me. Just when her eyes met mine again, a well-dressed man stepped onto the stage. He whispered into Vanya's ear, causing the woman to sigh.

"I'm so sorry, everyone," Vanya said. "That's all for tonight. You asked great questions, and I had a wonderful time. I'll return soon!"

I ground my teeth in frustration. No! This was the closest I'd gotten to her, and I thought I was next. There had to be a way to talk to her!

"Vanya, wait!" I called before I could stop myself.

She looked back at me, as did the man, likely her coach or manager or something. The man frowned and touched Vanya's arm, but she waved him away lightly as she strode toward me. "Hey, I'm sorry I didn't have time to answer your question."

"Please," I begged. "I've never met another singer like you. I've been trying for years to get a break, but no luck. Do you have any advice? *Anything* that can help?"

Vanya gave me a pitying look that both sparked hope and anger inside of me. I didn't need pity. I wanted advice. Was she looking down on me like some sort of peon, someone beneath her, incapable of ever reaching her status?

I flushed. "Sorry," I mumbled. I was making an idiot out of myself. How many starving artists ran up and asked her to toss them a bone? I wasn't anything special.

"Wait." Vanya pulled something out of her jacket pocket. "I've seen some of your TikTok videos. Katrina Mitchell, right?"

My mouth dropped in shock. She knew me? Vanya *knew* me? "I… uh…yeah, I uh…whoa." I puffed my cheeks like a bloated chipmunk and tried to control myself. "Yeah, that's me. You've seen them?"

"Yes! You're really good. Here." She held out a card. "If you've got time, stop by my houseboat in, say, an hour. I'm happy to talk with you. It'll just be easier without the crowd," she said, gesturing to the lingering group of people. "I'm sorry it's so late. I'm booked the rest of this week, and I'd really like to help."

I couldn't believe my luck. Vanya was going to talk to *me*? My inner child screeched like a banshee and did a cartwheel. "Y-yeah! That'd be great!"

Vanya flicked her hair back and winked. "See you soon. Oh, and please don't bring a crowd. This is just for you." With a wave, she reached for the man's arm, and they walked off the stage together.

I expected to wake up from a dream. Or for the floor to open up and swallow me whole. This was *not* happening. Had I finally caught a break? Holy hell! I looked at the card and ran my thumb over the embossed golden print.

A hand caught my arm. "Hey," Shae said. "Did she answer your... why does your face look like that?"

I rotated on my foot and practically shoved the card into Shae's face. "She offered to talk to me tonight, personally! She even gave me a card to meet up with her. Pinch me. I'm dreaming, right? I'm dreaming?"

"Rin–"

"Forget it. I'll pinch myself, ow!" Nope, not dreaming.

Shae didn't share my enthusiasm. "Katrina, are you sure about this? I mean, you don't even know her, and you're going to meet her somewhere alone at this hour? That's got red flags all over it. And the town's gotten more dangerous lately. Women have been attacked or abducted. Plus, you know certain cryptids like to roam at night."

My excitement deflated, but only a touch. "Oh, come on, the pub let her sing here. And it's not like she whispered her address in secret to me. She has it on a card so I can show it to anyone and let them know where I'm going. I'll be fine, Shae, don't worry so much."

But Shae took my hands and held them tightly. A strange troubled look crossed her face that I'd never seen before. "Rin, I really don't have a good feeling about this."

I frowned. Shae was a pretty good judge of character. She'd been fine with Vanya up until now. Maybe she was jealous? I pulled back a little, keeping the card tucked close. "I'm a grown woman. I'll text you when I get there and when I arrive home."

Shae tightened her hold. "Katrina, *please*."

"This might be my one chance," I argued and pulled my hands away. "Stop mothering me. I can take care of myself." And before Shae could argue, I hurried off to pay my tab (and leave a nice tip even if Shae had pissed me off), then slipped out the front door with the rest of the crowd.

Cool wind bit my cheeks as I walked briskly along the sidewalk. I pulled my jacket closer and climbed into my car, plugging the address into my GPS. About twenty minutes later, I pulled up along the docks to find a few houseboats floating lazily on the water. I searched through them until I spotted Vanya's number. The house was modest in size and painted beautiful shades of purple, white, and green. I looked around, expecting to see another fan or two she might have also invited, but nope, I was the only one.

I slid out of my car and went up the ramp to the front door. Before I could knock, a voice called out.

"Over here!"

I found Vanya sitting near the bow. She'd pulled up another chair. Both were covered in blankets to stave off the chilly air. She'd changed into a hoodie with a front pocket and a comfortable pair of yoga pants. "Hey, I hope you don't mind us meeting outside. Privacy and all," Vanya said.

I shook my head and sat down. "I appreciate you meeting with me at all."

"We singers have to help each other out, right?" She tucked her hands in her hoodie. "What do you want to ask me?"

I leaned back in the chair and looked at the sky. Thousands of questions rushed through my head. How could I ask her just one? "How did you know?"

"Know what?"

"That you were good enough to make it? I'm supposed to be a singer, I feel it in my gut, but I get afraid I'm not good enough. If I'm talented, why hasn't anyone taken me on?"

Vanya gave a knowing nod. "It's a competitive world, unfortunately.

You have to find what sets you apart from the other singers and show-case that. Otherwise, you're just another fish in a school."

I snorted lightly at the analogy. She had a point, though. I couldn't pinpoint anything extraordinary about me. I was just *me.* Who would want to take a chance on a plain Jane?

"For what it's worth," Vanya went on, "I think you have a beautiful voice, and any coach or group would be lucky to have you."

I rolled my head toward her and chuckled. "I'm guessing you don't have room for a protege?"

Vanya laughed. "Oh honey, I have a hard enough time keeping my own career going." She pressed her lips together and offered a sad smile. "You really want this, don't you?"

I looked at the card in my hands, imagining what it would be like to see my name on there instead. "More than anything. It's stupid, but even now, when I blow out birthday candles, I still wish to be a famous singer. I'd give anything to live that dream, to feel like I'm worth something."

"That's not stupid," Vanya murmured. She stared at me for a long moment. I found myself lost again in her dark eyes, trusting her to have the answer I couldn't find. She moved her hands around in her pocket and stood up. "Let me show you something."

Without hesitation, I followed her. We walked to the tip of the bow and looked out across the dark waters. They washed against the boat in soothing whooshing sounds. I gripped the railing and gazed down at them. Vanya leaned beside me.

"I'm going to give you a single piece of advice that will help your wish come true."

I snapped my head toward her. Was she serious or just making fun of me? By the look on her face, it was the former. I faced her eagerly. "Yeah? What's that?"

Vanya moved closer.

Pain exploded in my neck. My eyes darted to the side, taking in a strange, twisted knife shoved into my throat, Vanya's amber hand wrapped around the hilt. My mouth opened in a soundless gasp. I was too shocked to do or say anything.

Vanya leaned forward and kissed me deeply. Something sharp pierced my lip, and I tasted both blood and an odd salty liquid that burned my tongue. As our lips parted, she whispered, *"Breathe,"* then shoved me over the side of the boat.

Icy waves wrapped around me, clawing my chest and stealing my breath in an instant. I failed my arms and tried to reach the surface, but either the shock of cold or the gaping hole in my neck made my body lock up. The starry sky above blurred as the water pulled me down into a dark abyss. I tried to hold my breath, but Vanya's voice kept echoing in my ears.

Breathe. Breathe. Breathe.

I didn't want to breathe.

Breathing meant choking.

It meant drowning.

Meant *dying*.

But as my lungs burned and my vision faded, all I could do was release a cloud of bubbles with my dying breath.

<hr>

Light.

Air.

Voices squeaked and moaned.

I opened my eyes to a world I'd never seen before. I floated, my arms outstretched and my body feeling weightless. I could see through the water surrounding me as if I wore goggles. But no, it was with far more clarity than that. My ears thrummed to strange noises…beats…tempos. I could hear things speaking.

I'm dead. I have to be dead, I thought. But didn't thinking mean I was still alive?

I pulled my hand toward my face and stared at the strange webbing between my fingers. Specks of green and white scales dotted my arms and—

Wait…*scales*?!

I lurched forward, somehow, in the water and looked down at myself. I still had my shirt on, but below that, my pants…I didn't have pants. I didn't have LEGS! An iridescent white and green fishtail greeted me instead.

"What the hell!" I shouted. I grappled at my face and pulled at my hair which twisted around my hands in green-tinted ringlets. My fingers brushed over my face and along my throat, and there I felt slits in my skin, helping me breathe, keeping me alive. Right where Vanya had stabbed me. "What the hell?" I whispered this time.

"Don't be afraid."

I floundered and spun in two circles before stopping in front of another figure in front of me. An elegant ombre purple tail graced her body. Her hair and lips looked the same as they had on stage, but gills split her throat, and her eyes glowed white in the water.

"Vanya? You're…I'm…what the hell? You're…I…we're *mermaids*?"

"Sirens, actually," Vanya said. "We're far better singers."

"What happened to me?" I shrieked.

Vanya only smiled and swam closer. She placed a cool, comforting hand against my cheek and rubbed it. "I granted your wish and turned you into what you wanted, a singer no one can deny."

I jerked free of her hand. "I have to be dreaming. Okay, Katrina, wake up. This is not funny!"

"You know it's not a dream." Vanya circled me and grabbed my wrist. "I saw it in your eyes when you watched me sing. Everyone was drawn to me because of my siren song. But you…I've never felt such a pull from someone. You were meant to be this."

"I wanted to be a singer, not some kind of fish!" I shoved her roughly and looked down at myself, mind and heart racing. This was the stuff of fairytales, not real life! What was I supposed to do now? "I can't be this. This…this is wrong. This isn't real!"

Vanya's face twisted into something ugly. She grabbed me before I could stop her and jerked me toward the surface. I tried to fight her off, but her grip was inexorable. I shut my eyes, fearing her next heinous plan.

Water broke around us, and air rushed across my face. I felt myself being thrown and landed with a painful thud on something hard. I cried out and flailed like…well, a fish out of water. Breathing grew harder until the gills closed, and I could gasp in the fresh air. The moment I could breathe normally, a change came over my body. I watched in wonder as the webbing sucked back into my fingers. My tail rippled and split apart, leaving two pale naked legs covered in goosebumps behind. I couldn't stop myself from crying in relief.

Vanya pulled herself out of the water and sat on the edge of her boat like a queen. Though she breathed fresh air, her tail remained. "Better?" she asked in a dark tone.

I looked around frantically and reached for a blanket, yanking it over my waist. "What did you do?"

"I made you a siren," Vanya said like it was the most obvious thing in the world. "That dagger is magical, as was my kiss. It forced the change. You just had to, well, *breathe* in the transformation."

"You mean die. You killed me. You killed me and made me *this*. How are you even real?" I sputtered.

Vanya grinned, revealing sharp fangs. Well, that explained the pain when she kissed me. "Oh, honey. Cryptids live right beneath your nose. Are you really shocked that sirens exist too? This," she gestured to the two of us, "is a *blessing*. You can make anyone fall in love with your voice. No more failure. No more rejections. Now you're worthy."

"I wanted to do all that with talent, not as some kind of creature!" I shuddered and staggered to my feet, keeping the blanket wrapped around me. "Change me back."

"I can't," Vanya said, lifting her chin proudly. "Once the transformation is complete, there's no going back."

I stared at her in horror. "You didn't even ask if I wanted this!"

"Would you have believed me?" Vanya shook her head and placed her hand over her heart. "You have the soul of a siren. I could see it in your eyes and in the way you were called to me. We can help you, show you what it means to be one of us."

"*We?*"

"My pod," Vanya said, gesturing to the houseboats around her. "The bigger our pod, the stronger we are, and the easier it is to feed."

I froze, not liking the way she said that. "Feed?"

Vanya showed off her fangs even more, reminding me of a cheesy vampire villain. "What do you think these are for?"

"I don't know! I haven't exactly had much time to think." I reached up to my mouth and gasped. Sure enough, sharp fangs protruded from my gums. No, no, no, no. "So, so what, we eat fish or something?"

"Do you not know siren lore?" Vanya asked with an air of disappointment. "Sirens sing sailors to their doom and then…." She gestured to me, and I felt my blood run cold.

"You're not saying we…."

"Eat people? Oh, they're delicious."

"I'm going to be sick."

Sirens. Tails. Scales. Eating people. It was just one nightmare after another. I leaned over the edge of the boat, convinced I was going to hurl, but by some miracle, I held it in. "You're crazy," I muttered. "I'm not eating people. I refuse to be this *thing*. I just won't change. I'll stay human." Because clearly, we could be both human and siren; how else could Vanya sing on stage?

Vanya shook her head. "It's not that simple. Too much water can change a new siren. You need time to train, to learn control. And flesh is the only thing that sustains us. Regular food alone won't work anymore. If you don't eat it, you'll die." She moved, and with the same grace she'd had on the stage, her body changed back into her human form. Unlike me, she managed to keep her pants on. Another part of the magic? Vanya came to my side, but I held up a hand, warning her away. "Let me help you, Katrina. My pod has been suffering, dying because of fights with other pods and cryptids. I won't let my family vanish without a fight. We need more strong souls. And besides, now you have your wish."

I glared. "This isn't what I wanted."

"You said you'd give anything to be a famous singer, didn't you?" Vanya leaned in, her breath caressing my skin. "Face it, Katrina. You need me, and I want to help."

I bristled and whirled on her, getting in her face despite her dangerous fangs and the fact she might still have that damn dagger on her. "You think I'll trust you after this? No. You don't get to help me. You don't get to call me family. I'll figure this out on my own, without you. And without eating people." I shoved past her and tightened the hold on my blanket. "And I'm taking this with me."

Vanya didn't try to stop me as I stormed down the plank. But I heard her feet slap the deck as she followed me. "You'll be back," Vanya called. "And I'll be waiting."

I gave her a hearty middle finger and hobbled to my car. My body ached from the shock and transformation. And my mouth still tasted disgusting from the kiss. As I settled into the driver's seat and turned up the heat, the gravity of my situation crashed down on my shoulders.

I was a siren, a creature of myth. And according to Vanya, if I wanted to survive, I had to turn into a cannibal.

Tears welled in my eyes, and between swearing and striking my steering wheel in anger and grief, I broke down in tears.

Sleep eluded me that night. I tossed and turned in bed, trying to convince myself this was a nightmare or a trick. But no matter how many times I pinched myself or punched the wall—because that was a bright thing to do—the nightmare stayed real.

I pressed my hands to my face before crawling out of bed. If I wasn't going to sleep, maybe a shower would help me feel better. At the very least, it'd get the stench of fish off me.

I turned the shower on as hot as I could stand and stepped inside. Water rushed over my face and drowned out the noises in my head, albeit briefly. Showers always helped clear my troubled mind. I breathed in and out deeply to calm myself and reached for the shampoo.

Webbing appeared between my fingers. It was my only warning before my legs wobbled and fused together. I toppled with a cry, taking shampoo, soap, and a green loofah with me. I ended up on my back, tail arched in the air over me, my loofah-covered head ringing from smacking it against the side of the tub.

Son of a...

With a groan, I struggled to right myself and stared at my glistening tail. For what it was worth, my tail was gorgeous, the fins elegant like a betta fish. The scales ended right beneath my navel, leaving my torso bare. My normally black hair had regained its siren green, though now I noticed some black streaks in it as well.

Vanya's warning rushed back to me. *"Too much water can change a new siren."*

"Balls!" I flopped back down and draped my arms over my face. What the hell was I going to do?

I wallowed in my own self-pity and despair until the water got cold. After turning the shower off, I grabbed a towel and did my best to dry myself. Vanya had changed so effortlessly, but here I was, stuck with a tail. When the towel didn't work, I grabbed onto the tub and hoisted myself out, thinking getting away from the residual water would help.

An ungraceful bellyflop later, and I landed in a heap on the floor with the towel over my head. A slew of curses left my lips as I resumed drying off. I imagined my legs returning and the tail vanishing as I got the last drops off my body. I don't know if it was the drying or thinking happy thoughts that did it, but my tail trembled and transformed back into my legs.

My relieved sigh was immediately drowned out by my snarling stomach.

Great...of course, I was hungry.

Once dressed, I dragged myself to the kitchen, Vanya's warning loud in my head. I'd prove her wrong. I was going to eat regular food and to hell with the siren rules.

A mild bowl of oatmeal and nuts seemed like a good place to start. I settled at the kitchen counter with my food and pulled out my phone. Thankfully I'd left it in my car when I visited Vanya and hadn't taken it for a swim. My screen lit up with several texts and missed calls from Shae with varying degrees of worry. I played back the most recent call.

"Rin, please pick up the phone. Tell me you're okay. You're freaking me out. I don't care what time it is. Call me."

I bit my lip. Normally, I would have called her instantly, but what was I supposed to say? "Oh, hey, guess what, you were right. I shouldn't have gone because Vanya turned out to be a man-eating siren and turned me into one too! Fun, eh?"

Heh, yeah, that'd go over well.

I couldn't keep ignoring her, though. I sent a simple, *"I'm home safe. Sorry, phone died,"* and took a bite of oatmeal.

Putrid mush filled my mouth. I gagged and spat the oatmeal across the counter, expecting it to be moldy or covered in maggots. But no, it looked like regular oatmeal and smelled like it too. Panicked, I ripped open my cupboard and tried some crackers, then beef jerky, then chocolate.

All of it ended up in a saliva-filled mess in the trash can.

Part of me wanted to curl up in a ball and cry, but the stubborn side said screw it. I grabbed a paper towel and shoved pieces into my nose to dull the taste. And then I forced myself to eat my oatmeal. Not all of it made it down, but in the end, I got through about half a bowl.

My stomach continued its complaining.

I pinched my eyes in frustration. This was messed up—all of it. And I needed a distraction.

If I was going to be forced to be a siren because of an idiotic wish, I might as well see if I could put the damn thing to good use. I was not going to let this control me. I would find a way to live my life, even if it meant plugging my nose and forcing myself to eat awful food.

I set up my phone in my office and picked a song I'd been writing for a while. Might as well see if I could catch someone's attention. I settled in at my keyboard and recorded a TikTok of myself singing and playing. I didn't sound any different to my ear, but the music came easier than I was used to. I didn't have any trouble hitting the notes. I just sang what was in my heart.

I played the video back a few times. I sounded good, but again, not much different from the norm. "Well, might as well test it out," I muttered. I flopped onto the couch and added a few hashtags before I posted it. Usually, my videos got a couple likes early on, so the initial dings didn't surprise me.

Exhaustion from last night's ordeal, the fall in the shower, lack of sleep, and my food issue weighed down on me, and I eventually fell asleep.

A cacophony of bings roused me. I opened my eyes and reached for my phone, thinking I'd only dozed off for a few minutes, but it had been a couple hours. I swiped to my video and damn near dropped my phone on my face.

I had hundreds of thousands of views, likes, comments, and new followers. I shot up and looked at the video in shock. Each refresh brought more interaction, the likes of which I'd never seen before. And the comments! They were filled with adoration and excitement.

"How have I never heard of you before? You're amazing!"

"ON FIRE!"

"YES QUEEN!"

"Do you have an album? I want it now!"

My mouth dropped. They were talking about me. They…they were talking about *me*!

I fell against the couch with a laugh and ran my hand across my forehead. It had to be a fluke, right? Just a lucky hit on the For You Page.

So, I recorded another TikTok and posted it. And just like the first, it flooded with views and likes instantly.

Amidst scrolling through the comments, my phone lit up with another text from Shae. *"Are you sure you're okay? Can I come over?"*

I tensed. I didn't want her to see me right now. I wasn't sure what I'd say to her after last night. And what if I accidentally turned again? I had to get this under control before I could trust myself to be around people, especially Shae. *"I'm really busy today. We'll talk soon, okay?"*

DMs filled my inbox, mostly from fans admiring me, but then I noticed a few vocal coaches commenting. I read through them all, marveling at their praise. Two even asked if I wanted to collaborate.

Right, collab when I wasn't sure when I'd grow a tail again.

I glanced at my legs and rubbed them ruefully, then swiped to the next message.

Vanya's name appeared in my DMs. I hesitated, panic sweeping through me, before clicking it.

"You sound incredible. I see you're putting your new abilities to good use. Let me know when you're ready to talk."

I narrowed my eyes and responded with a middle finger emoji and blocked her.

***

I spent the next couple days at home recording TikToks and trying to get this siren business under control. Showers were a no-go since I kept changing while standing, which almost led to a broken arm. I settled for baths instead. It felt like nothing I did helped me control the siren side. Whenever I was in water, I changed. Even washing the dishes had dropped me on my face and left me with a bloody lip.

Eating didn't get better. Water was okay, so protein shakes helped, but everything tasted terrible. I'd ordered delivery and tried varieties of meat and fish. None of it helped. The worst part about it was each time someone came to my door, I could *smell* them, and they smelled delicious. Like the juiciest steak, I'd ever had. Their scent tempted me and made my mouth water. And sometimes, when I brushed their hand to take my bag, I felt scales form on my arms.

I decided asking them to leave my order at the door was a better idea. Because of everything that had happened with Covid, no one questioned me.

No matter how much food I put in my body, I was never satisfied. And it started to show on my face. Despite using beauty filters to hide how I was feeling, comments flooded in asking if something was wrong. They still praised my singing, but their worry for my health was obvious. I assured them I was fine and going through a juice cleanse (it was the only thing I could think of).

By the fourth day, I was ravenous. I hadn't yet left my apartment for fear of changing in front of someone. I ignored Shae's calls and texts. Since I had a work-from-home job, no one in the office noticed an issue, except when we had to have our cameras on. Then I got the questions about how I was feeling.

I opted to take a couple of days off to focus on my health.

I was wasting away before my very own eyes. And when I changed, scales flaked off my tail. The green and white had dulled. I went so far as to look up my symptoms, like I was a fish, and found that I was showing signs of starvation and possible fin rot.

I was dying. I was sure of it.

And the only person I could talk to was the same one I never wanted to see again. So that meant either I needed to suck it up and contact Vanya, or I was going to go belly up.

I languished on the couch, exhausted, struggling to stay awake, and trying to ignore the stench of my trash building up in the kitchen. I really needed to take it out before the cockroaches joined my pity party.

Suddenly, I heard a knock on my door. Had I ordered food and forgotten? Maybe it was an Amazon package. I waited, afraid that if I opened that door and smelled someone, I'd actually throw myself at them like my own personal buffet. Maybe they'd go away.

But the knocking continued, growing more insistent. I looked up at the ceiling and clenched my hands. I could do this. I could stay in control.

I rolled off the couch and held my stomach as I lumbered across the room, cursing my landlord again for not inserting a peephole. I inched the door open, keeping the chain in place.

"Katrina?" Shae's worried face poked between the crack. A floral scent assailed my nose, and I almost gagged. She held a vase of flowers in her hands. "Can I come in?"

"I'm not feeling up to company," I said, trying to hide my anxiety. I couldn't smell Katrina yet, probably because of the flowers, but what would I do if I actually *did* smell her? "And you didn't have to bring me flowers."

"I didn't. Someone left them for you."

I frowned. Who the hell would leave me flowers? And who knew where I lived besides some friends and family? Maybe they'd seen my worsening condition on TikTok. Who knew? I pressed my head to the door, then slowly opened it so I could accept the gift.

Big mistake.

Shae's eyes widened at the sight of me. "God, Katrina. What's going on?" she asked and stepped inside, looking me up and down.

"I look that terrible, huh?" I said with a joking smile that didn't quite reach my eyes.

"Let me help you sit."

I shook my head and held out my hand to stop her from coming further inside and tempting me. Thank God for the flowers. "I don't want you to catch whatever it is I have. Thanks for stopping by, though."

Shae flushed. "I'm not going to leave you here like this. Let me help you! You know you can talk to me about anything."

Not this, I thought demurely. Shae wouldn't understand. She might even have me committed. And yet, I wanted so badly to confide in someone. Tears stung my eyes, and I looked away as I tried to close the door. "I gotta get some rest."

"No!" Shae shouted. "This isn't fair, Katrina. You keep ignoring my texts and my calls. I know we're not dating, but if you're punishing me for that–"

"What? Oh God, no," I said, alarmed. "I can be an ass, but I wouldn't manipulate you into a relationship like that. I didn't mean to give that impression. I care about you. I do. And if you felt ready, then I'd welcome you with open arms, but right now, I'm serious. I don't know what's wrong, and I don't want you to get sick, so *please*, will you leave? I'll keep you updated better; I promise. I've been sleeping a lot, that's all."

"Not long enough that you haven't been able to make TikToks," Shae argued. "You aren't…Katrina, you aren't trying to make yourself thinner, are you? You look like you're starving yourself, and if you have an eating disorder, I want to help. I know what it's like to want a smaller body." Shae reached out and cupped my cheek. The warmth and comfort made it harder to hold back my tears. "I don't want anything to happen to you."

I leaned into her hand and stood there, savoring her touch. It was the first loving touch I'd felt from someone since the night at the pub. I breathed her in against my better judgment, but nothing triggered me. Was I finally starting to resist the smell? Did the flowers have something to do with it?

I didn't want to test my theory on Shae. "It's not an ED. I'm getting checked by the doctor tomorrow, and I'll give you an update," I lied. Yeah, last thing I needed to do was go to a doctor's office and get penned in by people and blood.

Shae didn't look satisfied. "I could stay the night and drive you."

"Shae…." I sighed and reached for the flowers. I wanted to be touched by her concern, but all I could do was fear sinking my fangs into her. I pulled the vase from her hands and rubbed her arm. "I'll call soon." I closed the door and locked it.

I leaned against it while Shae banged and begged me to let her in. At least I'd made it clear I wasn't trying to guilt-trip or gaslight her into a relationship. Geeze, that was the last thing I wanted. I slid down the door and held the flowers, thick tears rolling down my cheeks. I didn't move, not even when I heard her resigned sigh and her retreating footsteps.

I closed my eyes and must have fallen asleep, because when I next woke up, the vase of flowers was lying on its side, water covering my... tail. I'd transformed again. I moaned and reached for the letter left behind in the bouquet. My name was on the front in delicate pen strokes. I opened it and wilted.

"Katrina, you need help. You're fading quickly. Let me in. Let me save you. This isn't a game, and I don't want you to die. Call me or come find me. - Vanya."

Her number and address were in the letter. She probably assumed I threw away her card. How did she know I was getting so bad? I'd blocked her on TikTok! Though knowing her, she would have created a fake account.

I crumpled the letter and threw it.

I rolled out of the water and lay on the floor until I dried enough to get my legs back. Unfortunately, it put me close to my kitchen trash, so I got to enjoy that putrid stench for a good twenty minutes before I was able to stand up. It was awful. I could at least take it outside to the dumpster. This late at night, I doubted anyone would be around to bug me.

With shaky hands, I tied up the bag, slid my feet into shoes, and went out the backdoor. I kept a firm grip on the railing so I wouldn't fall. The wooden boards creaked beneath my feet as I headed toward the dark alley behind the apartment. The light fixture had burnt out months ago, so I usually only took my trash out during the day. I was too tired to care now.

I opened the lid and tossed the garbage in. The fresh air felt good, even if it still smelled nasty. I looked up at the faint outline of the moon and stars behind the city smog. At least it was a nice night.

A sweaty hand clamped around my mouth as I was shoved violently into the wall next to the dumpster. Another hand pinned my wrists to the small of my back. "What do we have here?" a voice sneered into my ear. Beer and stale popcorn wafted on his breath. And with it came the smell of his skin, and oh how good did it smell.

I struggled, tugging at my arms, but he had a good grip on me. Suddenly, he jerked me around and banged my head into the wall.

Dazed, I wobbled and felt him cover my mouth again and slip his hand under my shirt. *That* snapped me back to attention.

I opened my eyes and saw the drunken hunger in his gaze. I knew what he was going to do, what he wanted. His body was so close, his smell overwhelming my sense of fear and igniting my own hunger. My terror faded, and I moved my mouth enough to let my fangs slip out. He tried to get a firmer grip, but I sank my fangs deeply into his hand.

Delicious, salty blood flowed into my mouth before he jerked his hand back with a yelp. The taste overtook me, filling me with a euphoria I hadn't felt in ages. My stomach rumbled in anticipation of a meal, and no matter how hard I told myself to stop, I couldn't resist. The blood had awoken the siren in me. Sharp claws formed on my fingers. I looked up as he raised his fist to punch me, likely to pay me back for the bite.

I swiped my claws across his throat first. The man gurgled, grabbing his bleeding neck, but I didn't give him a chance to staunch it. I jumped on him, slashing him with my claws, and brought my fangs down on the side of his neck that he didn't have covered. I drank deeply and tore his flesh away, devouring it like a rare piece of meat.

I lost myself. The world turned red, and my hands and mouth moved of their own will. All I knew was my stomach, for the first time in days, felt satisfied. My body, so fragile and weak minutes ago, throbbed with a newfound strength. I savored every moment, every bite, until the red ebbed, and real-life returned to me.

My vision pulsed as I glanced down. Blood coated my webbed and clawed hands. I looked frantically at my legs, which shockingly hadn't turned into a tail. But I was covered in crimson. I licked my lips and followed the trail of blood to what was left of my attacker.

I cried out in shock as I scrambled away from his remains. There was really nothing left to identify him. I'd devoured almost everything, even bones. How had I eaten *bones*? He was dead…my assailant was dead, and I'd killed him.

He deserved it. You knew what he was going to do! I tried to reason.

But not like this! I argued back.

Yeah, the asshole had it coming, but to get eaten like an animal? I wanted to throw up, but I stopped myself both because I didn't want to see *him* come back up and because I finally felt full.

I took off my shirt, leaving me in a bra, and tried to wipe the blood off my face and hands. The moment someone found his meager remains, they'd question the tenants. I couldn't hide my clothing easily. Oh God, what did I do? Would Vanya know? How had she and her pod not been caught?

The horrible realization almost made me cry.

I had no choice. I had to find Vanya.

I took off my bloodied shoes and held them close. I wrapped a clean part of my shirt around my free hand and rushed up the stairs. I moved with a speed I hadn't had before my feast. I yanked open the door and locked it behind me, then grabbed a trash bag and shoved all of my bloody clothing and shoes inside. I didn't want to get wet and risk turning into a siren again, so I used wipes to clean up myself as best as I could. Then I pulled on clothing, stuck the garbage bag into another bag, and went out the front door to get to my car.

People's scents still caught my attention, but not so much now that I wasn't hungry. Small mercies. I didn't need to take out someone else on my way to Vanya. I got into my car and practically sped to the houseboat.

I cried. I cried because of what I was. I cried for what I'd done to the man, even though he deserved it. And I cried because I'd failed to survive as a siren on my terms. I'd have to appeal to Vanya...I had no other choice.

As I pulled up to the docks, a familiar car was already sitting in front of Vanya's houseboat. It had to be a coincidence, someone with the same car. But when I parked, I saw the person sitting in the vehicle beside me. She looked at me, and we both gasped in surprise.

"Shae?" I whispered. What the hell was she doing here? Had Vanya targeted her too? I scrambled out of the car and heard her door slam. "Shae, what are you doing here? You can't go in there!"

Shae ran up to me and grabbed my arms. She looked me up and

down, and I expected her to scream because she'd found blood or something on me. Instead, she grasped my cheeks and yanked me to her chest.

She kissed me.

I almost expected another dagger to the throat, but instead, I felt fangs click against my own.

Wait…fangs?

I pulled back from the kiss and stared at Shae in shock as her eyes took on a whitish glow, similar to Vanya's. Her beautiful copper hair turned ombre as colorful as the sun. And as if to make sure I knew what I was looking at, she lifted her hand and showed the webbing between her fingers.

"You're a siren?" My shoulders instantly fell. "She got you too? Shae…Shit, Shae, I should have warned you. I should have–"

"I already knew," Shae said quietly and cupped my face. "I was turned into a siren long before we met. This…this is my pod." She nodded to the boats and then looked at me sadly. "I never meant for you to find out or for this to happen. When Vanya asked you to meet her…I was just afraid you were going to find out about me. I didn't think she'd actually turn you into a siren! But watching your videos, the way you changed, I was afraid. That's why I came today to check on you, to see for myself."

"Why didn't you say anything?" I asked.

"Because I wasn't sure. And I wanted to give you the chance to tell me first in case I was wrong. When I realized later that I couldn't smell you at the door, I knew you had to be one of us. Sirens don't smell 'good enough to eat' like humans do. I'm so sorry, Katrina." She wrapped her arms around me and pulled me close. I wanted to be mad, but as she'd said, she hadn't thought Vanya would do this to me. And she'd tried to help. So, I held her tightly and pressed my head to hers.

"Did she force it on you too?" I asked.

"Yes. And she promised she'd never do it again. I should have known better. She's so *obsessed* with saving us. But these forced changes are wrong, and I told her if she ever did it again, I'd leave." She rubbed her thumb along my cheek. "I definitely have reason to now." But then her smile faded. "I can smell blood on you. Did you–"

I fought back angry tears and explained what had happened. I still expected Shae to be disgusted with me, but instead, she held me closer and tried to soothe my breaking heart. "I didn't know where else to go, what else to do. How do you deal with it? How do you handle being this thing and eating people?'

Shae stroked my hair. "I found a way around it that makes it possible for me to survive with the least amount of damage. And I can teach you. You don't have to go to her. You and I can be a pod now. Away from her. Away from the fighting and the nonsense that's going on between the other cryptids. Vanya's too power-hungry, and I want nothing of it."

I lifted my head and met her beautiful eyes. "You mean it? You'll help me?"

"I would have from the beginning if I'd known." She sighed in relief and pressed our foreheads together. "I'm so glad I don't have to keep this from you anymore. It got hard to resist you. You smelled so good."

My eyes widened. "Hang on…did you say no to dating me because you were afraid you were going to *eat* me?"

Despite the situation, Shae laughed. "No, I could resist that. But I knew, somehow, you'd find out what I was. And I didn't want you to be burdened with that life."

"Kinda don't have a choice now, do I?" I said and forced a smile. "But, does this mean, now that we know about each other, we can be together?"

Shae chuckled and kissed my cheek. "Let's take it one day at a time, okay? But first, let's go clean up that mess, and I'll take you to stay at my apartment. I can give you the 101 on how to survive as a siren."

I hugged her tightly. Before she left my embrace, I pulled her into another kiss.

Four Months Later

I sat on the edge of the hotel bed, holding my phone in my hand. I swiped through Tinder, taking stock of the people who had matched with me and the messages I'd received. Most of them were typical crappy one-liners, random dick pics, or actual conversations. But a couple had really caught my attention, especially when I used Shae's hack to research their background history thanks to the aid of a retired cop friend. And boy, were some of them doozies. Rapists. Sexual predators. Spouse abusers. People who had gotten away with murder. The whole gambit.

I set my phone on the nightstand and leaned back, enjoying the feel of green silk lingerie against my skin.

Shae had been true to her word and taught me about the world of sirens. By now, I could mostly change at will, though I couldn't jump into a pool yet without it happening naturally. Our basement freezer was filled with "special" filets, saved from our hunts, so we didn't have to go out often. Best of all, now that I was actually eating the proper food, I could enjoy normal food along with it. Sure, I still felt guilty about the kills, but much less now that we'd gotten into a pattern. No one could ignore my song. Once they heard it, I had them in my claws.

I hummed to myself, my voice carrying through the hotel room and into the bathroom where my next meal waited. He walked out in all his nude glory and grinned lasciviously at me. I crooked my finger.

Samuel Jenkins: history of sexual assault and leaving women tied, beaten, and robbed.

He grasped my wrist and kissed my neck. As I laid back on the bed, I smiled, fangs gleaming and claws growing on my webbed hands.

ABOUT ERIN CASEY

Erin Casey is an urban fantasy writer and author of The Purple Door District series. She's a Founder of The Writers' Rooms, a literary non-profit corporation that focuses on providing a free, safe environment to all writers no matter their income, skillset, race, and gender. Within the organization, she leads a fantasy/sci-fi group called The Violet Realm which meets twice a month. An advocate for mental health, she openly talks about her struggles with depression/anxiety/ADHD on her social media platforms and supports the LGBTQIA+ community. She firmly believes in supporting fellow authors be it through offering writing lessons in the Violet Realm, literary tips in her blog and on social media, or providing encouragement to those seeking to find their creative voice.

To learn more about her and her organization, visit erincasey.org

tiktok.com/@authorerincasey
instagram.com/erincaseyauthor
facebook.com/erincaseyauthor
goodreads.com/erincaseyauthor

DATE WITH A DEMON
BY R.A. LEWIS

This wasn't going quite how I'd expected. I might be dead soon.

The book said that if I drew the protective circle and cast the right protection spells, the demon couldn't get to me. That I would be safe.

But it was very deliberately and slowly dragging a slender finger through the salt circle I'd drawn on the floor of my room.

"Kalgraxxen, I banish you back to the demon realms in the name of Lillith," my voice trembled as I spoke. The demon just grinned as it broke through my circle. I took a step back, the spell book clutched tight against my chest, my stomach twisting into knots. This was going horribly wrong.

"You've made a grave mistake, girl." Its voice was resonant, pulling at the deepest, darkest parts of me. I backed up until my shoulder blades hit the wall beside my small closet, and there I stayed, watching in horror as its body shifted and changed, morphing from a black amorphous mass into the most achingly handsome young man I'd ever laid eyes on.

He was wearing a dark, tailored, three-piece suit with a crisp white shirt beneath. He straightened his tie and tugged on his shirt sleeves before stepping neatly out of my circle.

His golden eyes lifted to survey me. He had dark short-cropped hair, smooth tanned skin, and a slight five o'clock shadow. Given his appearance, he wasn't much older than me, but I wasn't a very good judge of age. I swallowed, my heart pounding so hard in my chest it threatened to burst through my rib cage and fly away. This had been my last option, a mistake I'd made in desperation.

Now I needed to try to salvage the situation.

I pushed off the wall and extended only a slightly shaking hand.

"Since you're here, can I call you something shorter than Kalgraxxen?"

The demon eyed my hand, then looked into my eyes and smirked. I could tell he didn't know what to make of me. I swallowed hard.

"You can call me Kal."

He reached out his large hand and enveloped mine. The moment our skin touched, I was flooded with cold, every nerve in my body tingling as if snowflakes had just touched down on every inch of me. I shivered slightly but smiled. He terrified me, but it was thrilling.

"Are you going to kill me, Kal?" I inquired sweetly. I might as well milk it before I died. Perhaps if he decided he liked me, then he'd keep me breathing. Would that be a better fate?

His eyes narrowed. "I'm still debating. Why did you summon me?"

I shrugged, fear blooming in my chest. It was easier to tell a dark amorphous mass your problems than the most handsome man you'd ever seen. I searched for an answer.

"Originally?" I snorted. I'd wanted revenge. But now, in the face of this demon, it seemed… inconsequential. I had a better idea. A crazy idea. "I needed a date for my prom."

Most of the kids in this school had been distant at best, cruel at worst. No one wanted to befriend the weird foster kid during the last six months of senior year. So, I'd kept my head down and ignored the taunts and jeers. Many of these kids had called me a freak. A weirdo. A leftover.

But the boys? The boys had been the worst. One, in particular, Adam, had asked me out, pretending to like me before dropping me off in the freezing cold in the middle of nowhere, miles from home. I'd barely made it back. My foster parents hadn't even noticed I was gone.

I was a fool to believe him.

I wanted to show them I wouldn't step down, I wouldn't stay home, that their jeers and taunts meant nothing. They hadn't broken me. Nothing in this world could.

One of Kal's eyebrows rose, and he took a few steps forward until he was inches from me. I drew in a sharp breath as he reached out and took the Book of Shadows out of my hands, closed it, and set it on my bedside table. Then he looked down at me from his considerably taller height. I trembled beneath his gaze. This was a being who could skewer me, disembowel me, devour me, or snap his fingers and instantly end me. He was more powerful than I could ever comprehend.

But something about him drew me in. Perhaps I'd gone mad.

He reached out and gently lifted a strand of my dark brown hair, twisting it around a finger.

"You summoned a ten-thousand-year-old demon because you needed a date to a school dance?"

"Uh-huh." I nodded slowly, never once taking my eyes off his lovely golden ones. Saying it out loud made me feel childish. But I stuck to my guns.

"I see." He dropped my hair and took a step back, looking at my black knee-length dress, black tights, and black combat boots. "If we're going to a dance together, then you'll need a different dress, little witch," he observed. I sagged slightly in relief and surprise.

It seemed my mistake wasn't going to kill me. Yet.

"I was actually hoping you could help me with that part," I trailed off at the blazing look in his eyes.

"What do you mean? Isn't agreeing to this stupidity help enough?"

I gestured around my drab room, the old and well-used furnishings, the holes in my comforter. Everything I owned was more than a little crappy. I had moved from home to home enough to know the difference between opulence and poverty. Everything I owned that was of value could fit into a large black garbage bag.

"I can't exactly afford a dress. Either I go like this, or you help me out."

Kal looked carefully around my room, moving around it methodically, picking up a few things and inspecting them. When he got to the stuffed black cat on my bed, his hand gently caressed it. It was so worn that the fur had rubbed off in places, and one eye was missing. It was the only thing I still had from when I'd first ended up in foster care after my parents had died. It was my most precious possession. I couldn't count how many nights I cried myself to sleep into that little cat.

When he turned back to me, his face was a mixture of sadness and anger. His golden eyes flashed in the near dark of my room, the only light coming from my altar of lit candles and those around the pentacle I'd drawn in salt in the center of my bedroom floor.

"You know that all magic has a price," he said. I nodded slowly, my stomach knotting. But I couldn't make myself ask what he'd require in return. I didn't want to know. I'd pay it. I'd pay anything. "When is the dance?" he continued.

"In an hour," I said sheepishly. Then I raised my chin. I had nothing to be ashamed of. "It's the last dance of my high school career, and I've never been to one before. I want to show them I'm not a coward."

His eyes widened slightly, and then he knowingly smiled, sending a thrill up my spine and warmth pooling in the pit of my stomach.

"Close your eyes," he commanded.

I obeyed, trembling slightly in anticipation. A frigid wind blew over me, raising goosebumps along my arms. It felt as though cool fabric was rustling over my skin. I squeezed my eyes even tighter, excitement trilling through me. Even once the wind died a few moments later, I didn't dare open my eyes.

"What's your name, little witch?" His voice was close now, but I kept my eyes closed.

"Morrigan."

A small laugh left him, and now he was behind me, circling me. I shivered again, realizing that now was a perfect opportunity for him to slit my throat, to kill me without my fighting back.

"Well, Morrigan, open your eyes," Kal said silkily into my ear.

I cracked my eyes open and then gasped. Before me, a full-length mirror gilded in gold hung suspended in the air. My reflection took my breath away. My ample curves were dressed in the most stunning black dress I'd ever seen in my life. Long lace sleeves, a fitted silhouette in black lace and silk, spilling to the floor and pooling around my feet. My hair, usually hanging in long brown frizzy curls, was now up in an elaborate style, ringlets hanging down around my face. My makeup was also immaculately done, black liner-smudged eyes peering out of my pale, freckle-covered face. I looked beautiful for the first time in my life, instead of the weird pale girl who dressed in black and never stayed in one place for very long.

"I look beautiful," I said in utter disbelief. I lightly fingered my hair and touched the lace sleeves in reverence.

Kal stood behind me, and I could see his reflection in the mirror. His handsome face broke into a smile. I smiled back, my face lighting up with unexpected joy. His magic was coming in handy. Maybe, I'd actually have a good night. Before he exacted whatever price he required.

"You are gorgeous," Kal said, looking me up and down. "Now, how were you planning on getting to this dance?" He came around to take my hand in his.

"Well, the school is only a few miles away, so I was going to walk," I trailed off at the frown on his face. "I mean, I am still wearing my combat boots under this dress," I said lamely, lifting the hem.

"No, that won't do at all."

He snapped his fingers, and suddenly, we were standing on the sidewalk outside the foster home I was currently staying in. I wobbled a bit at the unsettling effect of the magic but quickly regained my composure. Kal snapped his fingers a second time, and before I could process what had happened, there was a shiny black limo parked before us on the curb. I looked around in bewilderment.

"What?" I began, but Kal cut me off by opening the back door of the limo and giving me a small bow, his golden eyes aglow in the evening sunset. Hesitantly I stepped inside, sliding onto the leather seats. Kal's tall body folded in beside me, his close proximity making my pulse jump.

"So, tell me about your life," he prompted as the limo pulled out into the street, although I couldn't see a driver beyond the privacy screen. Kal put one arm around behind me on the seat and shifted his body so that he faced me. Lies bubbled to the surface of my mind, but the moment my eyes met his, the lies popped and disappeared before ever making it across my tongue.

I told him the truth.

About how my parents had died in a car crash when I was two, and I'd spent a few blissful years with my grandmother until she got cancer and died when I was seven. And then how I'd bounced around from foster home to foster home ever since, never staying in one place for more than a year. How most of my foster parents were strictly religious and how my witchcraft and pagan beliefs often offended them. None of them said that was why they asked for me to be moved, but I knew.

I told him about my current placement and how the foster parents just lived off the money from the state and never really provided for us. How the girls at school taunted me and how the boys abused me. How I'd gotten an afterschool job working in the library where I'd found the Book of Shadows that I'd used to summon him. And then finally, about how I had just turned eighteen and if I wasn't careful, they would kick me out before I'd finished these last two months of high school.

"Do you have plans to go to college?" he asked. His eyes had never left my face while I'd spoken.

I blushed and looked out the window, utterly unused to so much attention. I'd tried my whole life to blend into the background, and here I was, the center of his focus.

"I don't know. Maybe. There's a community college here that's not bad. I might go there for a few years before transferring to a four-year college. I need to save up some money first."

I let out a long sigh. I rarely planned for the future. It had always been so uncertain.

A cool hand touched my arm, and I turned back to Kal. He brushed a stray curl from my face and smiled. "Don't forget, this all has a price."

To anyone else, that smile might have been cruel or terrifying, but to me, it was oddly comforting. And I couldn't have said why. I would pay whatever price he asked, even if it meant I'd never get to see that future.

Then he turned to open the door, and I realized with a slight shock that we were already there. Outside my current high school, the front entrance lit up with lights and a crowd of well-dressed teenagers milling out front.

Once I'd climbed out of the limo, I clutched Kal's arm, both for physical and moral support. These kids made my life a living hell.

I couldn't lie and say their taunting and mockery didn't bother me. It did. I just wanted to belong somewhere. Anywhere. Even if it was at a dance on the arm of a demon.

Kal patted my hand and bent down to whisper in my ear.

"Stand up straight, Mor. You are far better than every single one of these mortals. Don't let them get under your skin."

I straightened, shoulders back, courage filling my breast.

The school's gym had been decorated to look like the inside of a casino. Poker tables were set up around the edges of the dancefloor, with men and women dealing cards and chips to players. No real money was changing hands. There even was a bar where kids could order virgin versions of cocktails and slot machines that gave out small prizes. A live band played covers of popular songs on the stage, and the dancefloor was already packed with undulating bodies.

I swallowed hard against the nervous knot in my throat and let Kal led me to the premade backdrop for the photographer. I turned to Kal and watched his golden eyes as he positioned me for the photo. Then the camera flashed, and I let Kal lead me away into the crowd. I felt like I was in a waking dream.

Whispers spread like wildfire as people watched us approach, then pass them by. I could hear them questioning why such a hot guy was with a freak like me. But there were other whispers as well that made my cheeks burn.

"Who is that?" one boy asked, awe in his voice.

"That's the new girl, Morrigan. Can't you tell? She's still just as pale as ever."

That voice I knew. It was Jessie Montaigne, the most popular girl in school. She was one of my biggest tormentors.

"Woah. She's hot!" the guy responded.

I blushed harder as Kal smirked beside me, tucking my arm into his and leading me to the bar.

"What would you like, Morrigan?" he asked, his voice silky smooth like whipped honey butter. I shrugged and tried to regain some composure and the snarkiness I usually carried as my armor.

"Surprise me, Kal."

He turned to the bartender and said something I couldn't quite catch. Instead, I surveyed the watching crowd. All eyes were on us, and tension buzzed in the air. It tingled along my skin and made my heart race.

When I turned back to Kal, he only had eyes for me. I blushed again and tried to look away, but he snagged my chin with his cool fingers. Then, while everyone watched, he bent down and gently brushed his lips against mine. I froze, my entire body stiffening as cold flooded me, spreading out from my lips and racing like electricity until it hit my toes. My knees trembled slightly as he drew away and accepted our drinks from the bartender, who gave us a knowing smile.

"Shall we go grab a seat?"

Kal nodded toward a small, secluded table in the corner by the stage, and I nodded in agreement, words completely failing me. He offered me his elbow once again, and I clutched at it gratefully, unsure if my legs would hold me as we walked through the parting crowd to the table.

I sat, and Kal handed me my drink. I took a sip of the orange and pink swirled mixture. It was wonderful and fruity. I looked up at Kal in delight and took a second sip.

"It's delicious!" I exclaimed.

"It's called a Virgin Sunset. It's a mixture of fruit juices and grenadine, and I thought it might help to perk you up." He winked at me, his seriousness slowly ebbing away and revealing a playful and attentive demon beneath.

Demon.

I had to keep reminding myself of that fact. This was fun and a welcome distraction from the dreary Saturday night I was going to have otherwise, but that kiss, and this feeling of unexpected joy and kinship, couldn't last. There was a price to pay, blood to exact. You didn't summon a demon for free, especially when that demon broke your protection spells. I put my drink down and turned to survey my classmates, who were slowly losing interest in us.

"What are your plans for the future? Beyond college, I mean?" Kal asked, leaning forward on the small table, his sole focus on me.

It was hard to get used to so much pointed attention. My eyes strayed to his lips before I looked away. I'd never had a boyfriend before, nor even a best friend, at least not since I was seven. No one had asked me questions about myself in a long time.

I stammered as I told him about my aspirations to open up my own occult shop or to study oceanography and then live in remote Alaska and study whales. Or maybe do both. I didn't really know.

Kal continued to pepper me with questions about myself, my childhood, my school subjects, my favorite things, all while we finished our drinks and played a few rounds of blackjack at one of the nearby tables. Finally, he stopped pestering me and took my hand, giving me a small and rather embarrassing bow.

"May I have this dance, lovely Morrigan?" his velvet voice floated up to me. I rolled my eyes and pulled him up.

"Of course, you may, Kal."

By now, the dance floor had cleared out a bit, and only the truly dedicated swayed there. Kal led me to the exact center and then twirled me around before pulling me in close against him, my chest pressed tight against his, his arm encircling my waist. I sucked in a sharp breath at his closeness. I'd never been this close to another being in my life. Every inch of me burned ice cold where it touched him, and my heart beat faster.

I looked up into his golden eyes, and his mouth quirked as if he knew something I didn't. I scowled at him. He was grinning now. I wondered with wild fluttering fear if this was the moment he'd take his price. I shuddered and began to pull away, fear of embarrassing myself welling up within me.

But Kal pulled me tighter against him and released my hand, burying it in the hair at the nape of my neck. He pulled my face to his, his lips pressing against mine. This time, his tongue explored my mouth, deepening the kiss, sending wild desire rushing through me. I was too startled to protest. I wasn't sure I wanted to.

I was on fire.

A cold flame seemed to lick up my skin as we kissed, his magic flowing through me, overwhelming me, consuming me. I was both sharply aware of my body and also dragged down and away into a deep ocean of desire and darkness where my physical self lost all meaning.

When he finally released me, our lips parting and warmth returning to the frozen air around us, I sucked in a breath, the warmth searing my lungs. All I wanted was to be drowning in him again. Drowning in his cold magic, in his embrace, in his kiss. I gently touched my swollen lips and looked up at him in awe. He smiled down at me and then led me off the dance floor.

The hour was late. The dance floor was empty, the lingering guests slowly moving toward the door.

How had the night flown by so quickly?

Gloomily I walked beside Kal as we exited the school. I turned toward where the limo had dropped us off, expecting it to be waiting for us once again, but the curb was empty. I frowned and turned back to Kal, who stood a few feet away, a surprisingly kind smile on his achingly handsome face.

"How are we getting home?" I asked. I was tired. Happy and giddy, but tired. As much as I didn't want this night to end, I knew it had to. I knew what awaited me at the end. My heart felt heavy in my chest.

"I thought we'd go for a walk." He held out his hand for mine, and I took it, boldly intertwining my fingers with his.

"Can you get me something more comfortable to wear for the walk home?" I complained, trying to lift the dragging skirt of my dress. Kal obligingly snapped his fingers, and a moment later, I was wearing a pair of tight black jeans, a comfy black sweater, and a small, pointed hat. I took the hat off and inspected it. It was one of those trendy felt black witch's hats, something I'd been coveting for a while but could never afford. I smiled at him and jammed it back into my head, my hair falling free of its elaborate do.

"Thank you. It's perfect."

I took his hand again, and we continued walking down the street. The sidewalk was bordered by a handrail, a small cliff dropped off leading down to houses, and the city below in the distance. Lights lit up the night sky like strange stars. I'd always liked seeing the city from up here. It was one of the few places I enjoyed. There was a bench up ahead, and I led Kal to it, sitting to enjoy the view.

Kal snapped his fingers, and his own clothing changed before he sat down beside me. He now wore a pair of dark wash jeans, a layered black sweater over a plaid button-down, and black converse shoes. I smiled. He looked like the very kind of boy I'd have a crush on.

But this was no boy. Tonight was ours, but soon he'd leave, I was sure. And there would be a price for all this. I'd summoned a demon from the underworld, after all, and magic didn't come without a price. And who was I? Some insignificant little witch who happened to summon a powerful demon by accident. He had more important things to do than spend time with me.

He put an arm around me, and I nestled into his side, refusing to spoil the moment. His skin was cool, but the bulky, oversized sweater he'd given me kept me warm, even in the early spring night air. We stayed like that for a while, neither of us talking, just enjoying each other's company. Finally, I stirred and looked up at him.

"When should we go? I know you probably have things to do now that I've summoned you to this plane. And I owe you." The last words came out hesitantly, ghastly images of what kind of price he might exact playing through my mind as the moment approached.

"My only plan, is you, Morrigan," he said, leaning in and kissing me gently. I sat back, pressing a hand to his chest, and eyed him.

"What? Why? I summoned you for a prom date, not beyond that. I'm nothing. Why would I be your plan?" I was talking far too quickly, something I did when I was nervous. "I'm flattered you took the time to go to this dance with me, but I'm sure you have better things to do-"

He put a slim finger to my lips, stopping me mid-sentence. He smiled, and I swallowed hard.

"I have been alive for untold centuries. I have done many important things. I have met influential people. I have started and fought wars. I have been famous. I have crumbled empires and raised them. I have done and seen it all. But I have not done and seen one thing."

"What is it?" I managed to whisper.

He looked deep into my eyes. Here it was—the price I owed.

"Love. Love is the one thing I have not experienced. And tonight, when I saw you, I knew you were different." He took my trembling hand and kissed my palm. "I want to see what it would be like to love you, Morrigan."

"What?" I whispered in disbelief.

"I could make all your dreams come true. I could build us a perfect life. Do you want that?"

I stuttered and shook. Fear, anticipation, excitement, disbelief, and something else rising from my core overwhelmed me.

"Of course I do." I barely got the words out. "But who am I to deserve this?"

"You are everything, Morrigan."

Then he was kissing me, pulling me onto his lap, and tangling his hands in my hair. I heard a snap of his fingers, and coolness swirled around us. When I opened my eyes, we were someplace new, someplace unknown to me.

A cozy cabin and a crackling fire. A soft couch and warm blankets. Behind us, a small kitchen was nestled against the far wall, and a hallway led to unseen rooms beyond. And directly in front of us were floor-to-ceiling windows, moonlight streaming in, and the view beyond was of the crashing ocean.

"Where are we?" I whispered.

"The Alaskan coast. Somewhere outside Juneau."

"What?" I stammered, my chest threatening to rip open, a lump in my throat. "Is this ours?" I asked in awe as I stood and wandered the cabin. My fingertips trailed the edge of the kitchen island.

"Every inch," Kal said as he followed.

There were two other rooms, one a cozy bedroom with a large king-sized bed that looked so inviting. On the bed sat my black stuffed cat. But as I picked it up to hug it, it squirmed in my grasp. I gasped and looked down at the very real sleek black cat in my arms that peered up at me with one bright green eye.

"Puss?" I asked in disbelief. The cat meowed and purred as I stroked it, still in shock at the sudden change.

Kal kissed me gently on the cheek before taking Puss from my arms and setting him on the bed. He led me down the hall to the other room.

After thoroughly investigating the other room with a desk and shelves full of books, including all the witchy things my heart desired, and the small loft above the kitchen that was filled with comfy places to read, I paused by the enormous windows and stared out into the night. The ocean was lit by a huge round, full moon. Questions tumbled through my head.

"What about the last months of high school?"

"I'm a great and powerful demon. I've already taken care of all that."

I put my arms around myself and shivered. Was this real? Was my price to pay happiness?

"What about college?"

"There's a nice college here in Juneau. Classes start in August."

Suddenly, Kal was behind me with a blanket, which he wrapped around my shoulders before wrapping me in his arms. Puss wove between my feet, purring so loud I felt it in my chest.

This was perfect. This was everything I'd ever wanted, and if I let myself, it could all be mine.

Kal kissed my temple and hugged me tighter.

"Welcome home, little witch."

I smiled.

The End

ABOUT R.A. LEWIS

R.A. Lewis is a sci-fi and fantasy author. She lives in Oregon with her husband, two dogs, four cats, and 247 fish. R.A. Lewis has two degrees from the University of Oregon in Psychology and Sociology and loves to explore mental illness, trauma, and the depths of emotion and passion in the human experience within her writing.

Her favorite ways to recharge (so she doesn't pull her hair out from arguing with her characters) are reading, daydreaming, hiking, spending time with her human and fur family, watching zombie movies/shows, swimming, working out, and napping.

You can visit her on Facebook (R.A.LewisAuthor), Instagram (@author.r.a.lewis), Amazon (ralewis), her website (www.authorralewis.com), Goodreads (@RALewis), or Pinterest (authorralewis). You can also follow her on Bookbub for reviews.

Find out more at: authorralewis.com

KIDS WILL BE KIDS
BY DELIARIA DAVIS

CHAPTER ONE

The screams of children playing attracted the djinn. He knew they would be the easiest to convince to let him use his powers because they didn't question where the magic came from. Children never questioned how they got what they wanted.

They always asked for candy, pets, and toys. But kids nowadays had been taught to be wary of strangers. How could he get close to these kids without alerting them to something weird? Something out of the ordinary?

Of course! He could just become one of them. Why not? It had helped him in the past to transform into his quarry, so why not now? While sneaking carefully up to the group, he listened to their conversion and hid among the playground toys.

"I wish we could be friends forever!"

"No. I wish we would never stop being friends, no matter what happened! Haven't you learned anything about making wishes? You can't leave *any* loopholes."

These kids were smart.

The djinn smiled to himself as he transformed into a child and walked out from under the slide.

"She's right, you know. If you leave a loophole, a genie can just manipulate your wish however they want," he said, now in jeans and a t-shirt.

"Really? My mommy says magic isn't real, so it doesn't matter what I wish for. It will never come true," a little girl yelled in a sing-song voice as she ran by them with a hula hoop on her hand swinging from side to side.

"Has your mommy ever met anyone who's magical? Or is she stuck on the magic of Disney and wanting to meet her own Prince Charming?" another little boy, this one throwing a frisbee, scoffed at her.

The djinn was excited now. These kids were exactly what he needed to fuel his powers and teach them not to throw wishes around like they were nothing. They wanted to be friends, but they were doing nothing but harassing each other. He didn't understand how this was friendship. He wouldn't grant their wish to be friends forever unless they proved they were *truly* friends. However, he could use them to make *others* in town make wishes for him to grant.

The hopes of wishers were how he fueled his powers, and if they were acting like baboons, how could he trust they would fuel his magic enough to leave this town?

"How does she know magic isn't real if she's never been affected by it?" the djinn asked. "I thought it was rude to tell lies."

"My mom never lies! She always tells me the truth. I bet your mom always tells you lies like magic is real and you can be anything you wanna be when you grow up." Clarissa stomped her foot and stuck her lip out.

"Clarissa! You don't know him. Stop being rude." The boy's attention turns back to the djinn. "Sorry about her. She's a little stuck on every word her mom says. I'm Ben. What's your name?" As the boy stuck out his hand, the djinn realized he must be the leader of the little group.

"Ben, why are you talking to him when he doesn't even look like he belongs here?" Clarissa pulled at Ben, trying to make him move away.

The djinn could tell that she wasn't getting anywhere, which became especially obvious when the other kids came up to Ben to see what the commotion was all about.

"I'm …" he paused as he thought of a name. Going with something generic, he threw out the first name he could think of, "Jim."

"Wanna play tag? We're looking for a fourth to play with."

Jim looked the group over, noticing a smaller child with them.

"What about if we play 'I Wish' instead? It's a game I made up. All you must do is get people to tell us what their deepest wish is or what the one thing they wish they'd always had is. It's fun. Trust me." As he walked toward the park's edge, he hoped these kids would be easy to convince.

"Come on, guys. It'll be fun. Wouldn't you like to make someone's day just by listening to them?"

"I don't know. What do you think, Fred? Do you want to go play Jim's game?" Ben squatted by the younger child, waiting on his answer.

"Let's do it. Sounds like fun." Fred nodded his head and walked after Jim, forcing the others to follow or be left behind.

CHAPTER TWO

The kids left the park and headed downtown. Jim was amazed he'd pulled this off. They'd left so easily without needing to call or check with their parents first.

He watched as they ran ahead of him, trying to get adults to stop and talk to them, wondering what the kids would hear.

"I wish those kids would leave me alone; that's what I wish for," he heard one person mutter as the kids ran off after trying to talk to them. He grinned and snapped his fingers, catching the attention of his new friends.

Little did the person know that he'd granted their wish, but not in the way they wanted. His little clique would leave the person alone. Forever. *No matter* what happened to them, even if they needed help, just because they couldn't be bothered to stop and answer a question.

"I wish I had those kids' energy. I miss those days."

Done. Except now they were an adult in a kid's body.

"What happened to Mr. Jemson? Did he just shrink?" Ben asked as he looked at what used to be a grown man.

"I don't know, but that was weird. It's like there's magic at work here. I'm getting scared." Jim said and smiled as he watched his new friends puzzle through the clues.

"Maybe, but I still don't believe in magic. I have to see it. Mommy said it's not real." Clarissa looked unsure of herself as she glanced again at Mr. Jemson.

"Why do you have to be so skeptical about everything? Why can't you go with what's happening around you?" Fred sneered at Clarissa, clearly annoyed because she was being so petty about their adventure. "You can go home." He pointed in the direction they'd come from.

She shook her head and shuddered as though she were afraid of going back alone.

"Hey, I thought you guys wanted to be friends forever?" Jim chuckled.

"We do, but sometimes she gets on our nerves. She doesn't believe in anything imaginative." Ben rolled his eyes at the two bickering behind him.

"Hey, look! Ms. Lark is up ahead. She believes in magic. Let's ask her if she has a wish!" Fred ran ahead of them to an older woman sitting on a bench waiting for the bus.

"Mrs. Lark, I have a question for you."

"Oh, Freddie, my favorite kid. What can I help you with?" the older woman smiled at the group as they stopped in front of her.

"We were wondering if you have a wish, you regret never making. Something you wanted so badly but never knew how, or what, to ask for."

Jim leaned in, expecting her to tell them something frivolous as older women tended to do, but was surprised by the words that came from her mouth.

"I have everything I could ever want. I've lived my life as well as I could, and to change anything at this point would be to change everything I know. That wouldn't be fair to anyone in my life. I guess the only thing I could ask for is that when it's my time to go, I go peacefully, not scared." She paused as if remembering her audience. "But you kids wouldn't understand that. It's better that way."

I don't think I've ever met anyone as selfless as this woman. I agree to grant her request. Her time is nowhere near, but that is a fair wish. She shall go peacefully in her sleep, and I will ensure it is so.

"That's awesome, Mrs. Lark. I wanna be like you when I grow up." Clarissa exclaimed as she ran off to find someone else to pester.

The kids continued along, and Jim heard the mumblings here and there of random wishes.

"I wish I didn't have to go to work." A snap of Jim's fingers.

"I wish I was thin." A second snap.

"I wish those dogs would shut up."

"I wish I wasn't hungry."

"I wish those kids would stop."

Snap, snap, snap.

"Why do you keep snapping?" the kids asked Jim in unison.

"I am? Didn't notice. Just a nervous habit." Jim snapped again, so he didn't appear suspicious. If they knew why he was snapping, that he was granting wishes, it wouldn't be a game anymore.

"Hey guys, we need to start back to the park so we can head home. It's getting dark out." Ben pointed to the darkening sky and turned toward the park.

The rest of the group groaned because they were having so much fun but followed Ben back to the park so they could head home for the night.

"True. You wouldn't want your parents to come looking for you and not find you where you said you were going to be." Jim agreed, trying to perk the group up. "We can always meet back up tomorrow and do this again. It was loads of fun."

Jim listened carefully, but no other wishes were made within earshot and the not wish from Ms. Lark played heavily on his mind. He had to figure out the best way to cast it after he left the children at the park.

"Goodbye, Jim! That was so much fun. *Can* we do it again tomorrow?" Ben bounced on the balls of his feet excitedly.

"Seriously, Ben? And pretend to believe in magic? Can we do something else?"

"Like, wish your mom believed in magic for a day so you would too?" Fred chimed in before anyone could stop him, snickering at Clarissa.

"I did say we could do this again, as long as you meet me here in the morning." Jim laughed and snapped his fingers before promising to meet them back at the park the next day.

CHAPTER THREE

The next day Clarissa came running through the park in Jim's direction like a bat out of Hell. "Jim! Jim!"

He was sure he knew what was about to happen.

Last night, he'd gone out as an adult to grant more wishes, and now the town was in chaos. It was glorious.

"What's up, Clarissa?"

"My mom … she … she's a believer. I didn't tell her what we did yesterday, but now she believes in magic. Can you believe that? Did you do this?"

Before Jim could answer Clarissa's question, the rest of the group showed up. Fred dragging Ben behind him, and Ben appeared distressed.

Jim laughed at his own observation. Of course, something was wrong. Everything would seem wrong to these kids. "Hey, guys. I told you I would meet you here. What's up? You look like something is wrong."

"The whole town has gone crazy. It's like yesterday's game has come to life, and everyone's wishes came true! What happened? I know we said we believe in magic, but we never meant for *this* to happen." Ben spoke up before Fred could say anything.

"Nothing is wrong. Everything is perfect. Every wish has been granted; everyone has what they asked for. No one wants for anything now. How is that a problem?" Jim asked them, confused at how he had done anything wrong. Wasn't the point of fixing problems granting wishes?

"What are you talking about?" Clarissa asked Jim as confusion covered her tiny face.

"Ah, you children don't understand yet. When you make a wish, you must be specific. You must know exactly what you want and how you want it. Adults forget these things and make wishes willy-nilly, causing chaos all around them. Teens and young adults get it the most because they are still exploring and witnessing the magic around them." Laughing, Jim opened his arms and spun.

"This isn't good, Jim. How do we fix it? What can we do?" Ben begged his new friend.

"There's nothing you can do. We can only make things even perfecter. Make a wish, sing a song, dance in the rain!" Jim snapped his fingers, and the clouds started to rain Skittles. "Today, nothing makes sense. Have a candy." He held out his hand to the children. He let his palm fill with the colored drops falling from the clouds before throwing them back toward the sky.

CHAPTER FOUR

"We need to fix this, Jim. We liked things the way they were before," Fred said as he plopped down onto the slide.

"I thought this would be funner for you. You get to be friends, your parents had their wishes granted, the whole town has, and we can play.

What better day than today is there?" Jim looked at the children, still confused as to why they were complaining about the wishes.

"But what about the old people who made wishes? What happened to them?" Clarissa threw her hands to her mouth as she thought about what could have happened to them. "What if there's no one to take care of them anymore?"

"I didn't think about that, but they should be fine. They're already grown and used to taking care of themselves," Jim replied.

"What about the doctors and nurses who take care of people? Are they okay?"

These kids ask too many important questions. I wonder if I should have worked with a different group who wouldn't have cared so much.

Jim rubbed his brow. "I'm sure they're all okay."

"We want to find out what's going on and fix it. Please help us. Please?" the children begged Jim as he stood there. He hadn't counted on them wanting things turned back to how they had been. This had never happened to him before.

"Do you know the tale of Pandora and her box?" he asked them as they stared at him, waiting.

"She opened a box of evil into the world. Chaos, monsters, lies, all things the gods told her to keep locked away in the box they'd given her. But because she couldn't keep her curiosity at bay and had to see inside, they escaped. This is like that. The adults unleashed their own version of Pandora's Box because they couldn't help but wish for frivolous things."

The kids looked at him in wonder.

"That's not true. There's no way one person could do that much harm to the world." Fred glared at Jim, expecting him to come clean about the story and tell them it was all a lie.

Jim shook his head. "That's not what I meant, Fred. I meant that when people wish for things, look into things they have no business with, then things go wrong. That's what happened here. People wished for things, and things went wrong."

"Oh. But can you fix it?" Fred's eyes started to fill with tears, and

Jim wondered why he would start crying over the adults being stuck in this mess when the kids in town were fine.

"I don't know if I can. You would have to believe that I was a genie or something, and I didn't think that those existed. At least that is what *one* of you told me yesterday." He looked at Clarissa and raised his eyebrow.

"But now my mommy believes in magic. I told you that," she shouted at him. "You have to help us."

"Ah, I don't have to do anything." Jim smiled as he transformed into his normal form. "That's better. Do you know how hard it is not to do something stupid when you look like a kid all the time?"

With skin of wispy blue and long flowing black hair, Jim now floated around the kids as they stared at him in amazement and Clarissa with downright terror.

Finally, a shrill shriek filled the air as Clarissa attempted to run away, only to be dragged back by Jim. He gathered the group together so he could continue talking to them without them running from him.

Shocked gasps trailed from the other two boys as they stood there, staring at him in shock.

"Wh-What are you going to do to us?" she squeaked as she tried to back away, but her feet wouldn't move, frozen to the spot by the mist surrounding them.

"Nothing. You want something from me, and I want something from you. I want you to learn a lesson about doubting everything you see and hear. You want me to fix all the chaos. One cannot be done without the other."

"Is that all this will take?" Ben stepped forward, placing himself between Jim and his friends.

"Djinns don't lie, boy. Humans, on the other hand, have been known to cause quite a bit of chaos on their own. Pandora's Box is true. I came from that box. It was I who convinced her to open the lid. All you humans are the same. Easy to convince to do my deeds if I whisper the right words."

"Why would you want that released on the world?"

"I didn't. I only wanted her to open it enough to let me free. The dumb twit dropped the box, and everything came spilling out. I was going to help her until the Gods showed up and got in my way. I was stuck in a bottle until I was freed, and now here I am. I enjoy mischief. It's who and what I am."

"Teach us how to help you so that we can reverse what you created. Take back the wishes. We want our town back to how it was before you heard us talking about magic." Ben laid out his demands to Jim.

"Ben, I know what you want already. No need to try and un-loop-hole me. I already told you my terms." Jim said as he slipped back into the form of the child he had taken before.

CHAPTER FIVE

The group left the park in search of their first *victim* to help. It wasn't long before they came across a police officer acting like a duck.

"Did you really make him act like a duck?" Clarissa glared at Jim.

"No. His actual wish was to be whatever animal his mind was set on whenever he woke up. I guess today is a duck. I thought it was an odd wish but to each their own."

"Can you fix it?" Ben looked at Jim hopefully.

"Of course, I can, but what's the lesson here?"

"Don't wish for stupid things out loud?" Fred chimed in before anyone else could.

"No. He's a cop. Think deeper."

"Be extremely specific in what you say, or you could let someone off on a technicality. At least that's what my dad always says. He's a lawyer." Clarissa said from behind them, trying to hide her giggles.

"Close enough." He snapped his fingers, and the man stopped acting like a duck and looked around, confused.

"What the hell am I doing out here? I don't even remember waking up this morning."

"Hey, Officer Coolidge. You might want to make sure everything is okay at the station. The whole town has gone crazy," Ben let him know before they continued on their way.

"Thanks, kid."

CHAPTER SIX

Jim took the kids around to fix wishes until he found another one he thought could teach them something. The woman was dancing through her yard, singing, and jumping joyfully, though she looked as though it was causing her great pain to keep going.

"Okay, what lesson would you have from this one?"

"Don't dance if you can't take the pain?" Fred chimed in again.

"Think outside the box a little more."

The children watched on, each giving several answers that were met with resistance until Ben smiled and stepped forward.

"I think I know," Ben spoke clearly and with confidence. "Life's a dance, and even if you're smiling, it might be killing you inside?"

"Very good. How did you come to that?"

"It's something my mom used to tell us. She used to teach dance until she broke her ankle and couldn't do it anymore. That just because the ballerinas were smiling while they danced didn't mean they weren't dying on the inside."

"Your mother is a highly intelligent woman. Do any of you know who this is?"

"She's my teacher, Ms. Hailey," Fred whispered, staring in awe at the way she was dancing.

Jim nodded as he gently snapped his fingers, bringing her back to Earth so she wouldn't fall to the ground below her.

Exhausted, she slumped to the grass, crying. The group ran to her and wrapped their arms around the teacher, thankful to have her in one piece.

"I didn't know wishing I could dance would turn out so bad," she muttered.

The kids turned and stared at Jim, who just shrugged. "She wasn't clear when she made her wish. I told all of you that you must be clear when you wish, or I can interpret it however I please."

When he walked away, leaving the kids with the teacher, he didn't wait to see if they followed. He knew they were learning from the mistakes of the adults, from the mistakes they watched get corrected.

Ben grabbed his arm, stopping him. "How many more wishes do we have to undo?"

"A lot. Everyone in this town had wishes, and I granted most of them last night. Very few wishes went ungranted, and very few were wished for properly. What do you want me to do? Not grant them all?"

"You have to. It's not like you can remember who the good wishes were with and who the bad were with, right?" Clarissa asked.

"Clarissa, is this what you really want? You really want your mom to not believe in what you see for yourself?"

She stopped what she was doing to look at Jim, the look of confusion on her face making it clear she had no idea what he meant.

So many wishes were made that I don't think I could get them all undone one at a time, at least not soon, and I'm sure I'd miss some. I can undo them all at once if I want to, but I can't tell them that yet. At least not until they ask if I can.

"Let's continue along. We have many more wishes to undo, and the day s moving fast. Not every wish has a lesson. Not every lesson has a wish. If you want everything back to normal before you have to go home, then we need to move." Jim hustled the children along.

"Clarissa, you never did answer my question. Do you want your mom to forget that she believes in magic?"

"No, I guess I don't. If she can believe in magic for one day, then I can take that. Isn't there an easier way to un-grant all these wishes for everyone, though? A faster way?"

Finally.

"I thought you would never ask. I can do a mass un-granting of all the wishes, but you must be careful using magic like this. Weird things can happen. Wishes I didn't grant can come undone. Love can be lost, and things can go missing. Is that really what you want me to do?"

He looked at each face as they thought, and he could tell that they really were thinking about what he'd just told them. Did they really want to risk losing their favorite toy or something unknown to them going missing because he had to do something drastic to fix this?

"Well? What will it be, guys? I may have an eternity to wait, but your town doesn't."

"Just do it. We can risk losing something small in return for our town going back to normal. Small as in a toy or two. Nothing living. I don't want to lose my family. None of us want to lose our friends or family. Our pets either." Ben looked Jim square in the eye and challenged him to take anything important.

"Got it. Nothing living. Now, if you'll pardon me, I need to concentrate so I can break these spells." Jim walked away from the group and clapped his hands together.

Let's see if I remember how to do this. It's a snap to grant the wishes. So, it must be a double snap and a clap to reverse them all at once. If that doesn't do it, then I don't know what will at this point in the game.

Jim closed his eyes and snapped both his hands, then clapped and took a deep breath as he waited to see what would happen. He cracked his eye slightly to see if anything had changed and was surprised to find the town sparkling just as his magic flew back at him.

The reversed spells gave no clue as to what had changed, but all manner of colors flew in his direction: greens, blues, purples, and even some black and yellow. He stood his ground as the first wave slammed into him, making him stumble.

CHAPTER SEVEN

"Are you okay?" Fred ran up to Jim as another wave of magic slammed into him, bringing him to one knee.

"I've never taken back so many wishes before. They're all smashing into me in waves as they come back. This is new." He gasped as more waves hit him harder and faster.

"Is there anything we can do for you?" Clarissa asked, wringing her hands as she watched him writhe in pain.

"Not unless you can make this stop, and I don't know how you could do that."

"I think I do," Ben smiled. "I wish the returning magic would disappear and Jim's pain would go away."

As soon as Jim heard the words, he had no choice but to snap his fingers, and his pain was gone. The magic stopped ramming into him, and he watched it fade away.

He couldn't believe that the kids had figured out how to help him. They really were good friends. Even if they did fight and bicker with each other, something fierce, they'd taught him that much.

"Thanks, guys. I wasn't sure what to do there. Not with everything attacking me the way it was. Ben, you really are a good friend. Thank you for helping me." Jim stuck his hand out for Ben to shake once again, and he took it, pulling Jim into a hug.

"You did the right thing, you know, reversing all the wishes. Even if some of them were good wishes and done for the right reasons, not all wishes, even good ones, are supposed to be granted. We learned that watching this, haven't we guys?" Ben looked at his friends as they smiled at Jim.

"Yeah. I don't think I'm going to wish for anything anytime soon, especially knowing what I know about magic now." Clarissa nodded her head as she looked at her feet.

"I don't know. I like magic and the thought of having wishes granted." Fred laughed as he ran up to Ben and tugged on his arm. "In fact, I think I want us to get our wish to stay friends forever no matter what happens or tries to get in our way. Then we can always be there for each other and help each other through everything that gets in our way as we get older."

Jim just shook his head at Fred, knowing that the youngster had learned nothing in the last twenty-four hours and even less in the last two. "Fred, why don't you just work really hard on our friendship, and that will make us stay friends forever, okay?"

"But making it a wish would make it easier."

"Nothing easy was ever worth doing twice, bud. That's my word of advice for you. As for everyone else, there was one wish we heard that I never granted: Ms. Lark's. I've been thinking about it, and her wish was the most selfless wish I heard, and I would like to grant it. It serves her no purpose in life. Since I agree with her wish and because she'll never know that it's been granted, she'll receive it, no strings attached. Do you lot understand me?"

Looking up at him, all three nodded their heads collectively, then let their gaze drop to their feet.

Jim looked beyond the park, knowing it was time for him to be on his way, even though he'd grown quite fond of the small group. "I know our time has been short, and I know that you want me to stay because I can see it in your expressions, but my time has come. I have other places to go on my journey and more lessons to teach. I hope that you take what you learned with me and apply it to your life. Remember, kids, be careful what you wish for.

ABOUT DELIARIA DAVIS

USA Today Bestselling Author, Deliaria Davis, grew up in the cold winters and mild summers of Anchorage, Alaska, where her heart remains to this day. She met her husband there and would return in a heartbeat.

She has five amazing kids, and when she isn't writing she is helping her youngest son with therapy for his disabilities.

Currently, Del resides in Spokane, WA, where she is hoping to someday be able to afford a house big enough for each of her kids to have their own door to slam.

Until then, she will continue to write whatever pops into her head, edit in her spare time, and loves to interact with her fans.

tiktok.com/@deliariadavisauthor
facebook.com/deliariadavis
twitter.com/deliariadavis
goodreads.com/deliariadavis

THE WISHING WELL
BY MELISSA E. BECKWITH

Now, this is a dark tale of caution—or perhaps maybe even a horror story—in any case, I can tell you, this isn't some kind of fairytale princess love story. Some wishes are made on a falling star. Some wishes are made over candles on a cake. Still, others are sent into the ethos over broken bones. And some should never have been sent into the ether at all...

CLAIRE

It was an unremarkable day, just like all the others before. Like an endless string of fake pearls, one creamy bead following the next, indistinguishable from those on either side.

She stuck her hand into her purse, which sat on her lap, and felt the cold steel of her gun. Feeling reassured, she quickly pulled her hand out, barely noticing the frigid air on her fingers.

It was cold, and she could feel the bite of it through the thin fabric of her pants as she sat on a hard metal park bench. She watched as the bright red and yellow leaves of the trees shimmered in the bitter breeze.

People strolled by walking their dogs, most talking into their phones. They looked cold and impatient as if they wished they could just will their dogs to do their business so they could get back to the warmth of their luxury loft apartments across the street. She didn't care enough to notice the people's faces, but she had started recognizing familiar dogs.

She had been coming to this park during the day for a couple of weeks now. Yesterday it had rained all day, but the morning had been gray, so she was prepared and had brought an umbrella. She sat on the damp bench, watching water drip from the thin aluminum fingers of her bright red umbrella, a color much too cheerful for the gray afternoon. She had been the only one in the park all day. A cop had driven slowly by, and she thought he was going to stop and tell her to leave—mistaking her for a homeless person. But he finally drove away, perhaps deciding either her umbrella was too happy a color for a homeless person or she wasn't worth getting out and getting soaked in the rain just to remove her from the park.

Today was a different story, though. The day was still gray—as almost every day would be until spring—but at least it wasn't raining.

She wished she could say she hadn't always been like this, but that would be a lie. Her childhood had been dull like a raggedy, old beige carpet, sprinkled with disappointment and boredom. Her parents had been busy and wholly uninterested in their children, so they raised three kids equally uninterested in them or even each other. Her sister, Clementine, had gone to college and married well. She received an exquisite, professionally designed Christmas card from her every year, but other than that, she never heard from her. Her sister was too important to bother herself with such pedestrian things as social media.

Her brother, Christopher, had disappeared years ago. She hadn't heard from him in over fifteen years. She wondered if he was even still alive. She guessed he got that personality trait from their father, who had left when she was a teenager and was never seen again. She heard years later that he had remarried and started another family. If he really did, she had never cared enough to confirm. Their mother had died seven years ago, and their brother hadn't even bothered to show up to her service.

Claire had married right after high school to the first boy that ever showed her any interest. She wasn't exactly popular with her chubby body, straight brown hair, and gray eyes. It was the 80s, and everything was supposed to be flamboyant. She was not.

Her husband, Bart, wasn't either, but he was a hard worker. Before their first anniversary, they had their daughter, and life went on much as it had done with her parents. Bart worked long hours as a commercial plumber, and she worked a boring job at a bank. Their daughter, Polly, grew up with a front door key hanging on her backpack to let herself in after school, just as she herself had grown up. And then Polly went off to college, got a good job, married, and only called on birthdays and Christmas. Claire had raised her daughter just as she had been raised, and she had no one to blame but herself.

Her hand glided back down into her purse, and she ran her fingers down the length of her gun again. It was cold and woke her from her tedious, hazy recollections reminding her that today was the day. It was time.

She wouldn't do it here, where people find her. She didn't want to scar anyone for a decision that was her own. Her legs were still and sure when she stood up. Her feet were heavy as she walked the feeling back into them. She followed a path along the trees that lined the winding border of the manicured grass and the wild forest beyond, now spattered with fall colors.

After a while, she came to a small opening in the woods. She looked around and made sure she wasn't being watched. Of course, she wasn't —she was invisible as a plump, middle-aged woman. No one cared what she was doing or where she was going, so she slipped into the tree line and disappeared from the world.

The trees were close and thorny bushes made it hard to make her way toward the center of the woods. After several minutes she became tired and looked up. The opening she had crawled through wasn't visible any longer. She didn't think she had gotten far enough away for it to have been totally hidden from her view, but the thick woods made it easy to get turned around. She looked up into the riotously colored leaves and took a deep breath. They were so beautiful, and she had a brief moment of uncertainty. But then she took another breath and pushed on toward a destination. She figured she'd know when she got there.

After a while, the brush all but disappeared, and the trees didn't seem so thick. She brushed off stray dead leaves clinking to her sweater when a deep caw made her jump. She looked up to see a shiny black raven perched on a low tree branch. It was the first raven she had ever seen outside of a picture in a book. They weren't common in the Indiana town where she had lived her whole life. It cocked its head, turning a beady eye down to look at her. Suddenly, she felt exposed and looked around to make sure she and the bird were alone—they were. With a cry and a heavy swoop, the raven took flight, gliding deeper into the woods. Not exactly knowing why, she followed.

Out of breath, she got to an open space and eased herself down on the leaf litter, not caring about the dirt. Looking around, she was overcome with the feeling that this would be a good place to sleep forever. Again, she looked up to the red, yellow, and orange leaves shivering in a breeze that didn't seem so harsh any longer. They looked like thousands of tiny hands waving down at her. She felt unease and that perhaps she was making the wrong decision. But she had thought about this for decades and planned it for months. She would not back out now.

She plunged her hand into her purse and brought out her gun in a moment of pretend bravery. It was so cold and heavy in her hands. She had only shot it a few times at a gun range during a safety class for women. She didn't even know why she had taken the class. It certainly wasn't required for new gun owners in Indiana. Maybe she thought it would give her a connection to another human or perhaps a second thought to what she had already decided?

It had not. There were three other women in the class. One was blatantly flirting with the instructor, one was completing the class to ease her parent's misgivings, and the other woman was deadly quiet as if someone was going to pay for crossing her.

Suddenly, she seemed to feel every single moment of her life that had brought her to this culmination. Every sorrow, every discontent, every moment of loneliness, every missed opportunity for someone to have shown her love.

But she also thought about the wonderful moments. Her teenaged wedding to Bart, as sad as it was. The birth of their daughter. Polly's high school graduation, her college graduation, and then a few years after, her wedding. She thought about the text she had gotten a few weeks ago informing Claire that she would finally be a grandma. Polly and her husband had been trying to have a baby for many years. And now they would have one.

She knew then that she couldn't go through with it. As if on cue, the forgotten raven gave a screech that echoed through the small clearing, and she looked up at the bird now sitting on a branch across from her. A large hole she had not noticed earlier gaped open in the middle of the clearing. A shaft of light broke through the trees and shone directly down onto the hole, illumining hundreds of tiny shining objects scattered inside.

She looked down at the gun in her hand, shook her head, and stuffed the thing back into her purse—mind made up. With a bit of effort, she stood back up and walked over to the hole. Small coins littered the ground inside. Some were American, but a lot were not. She recognized some from Canada and Mexico, the others she couldn't identify, but they looked ancient. They were crusted and worn, looking old and tarnished even in the bright shaft of sunlight.

For reasons she would never be able to understand, she decided that these coins were wishes and this yawning hole was some kind of wishing well. She knew it as certain as she knew she was a human. So, she fished an old dirty dime from her purse and held it up into the shaft of light. The dime had old, flaky, green paint splattered across its face like a scar.

"I wish I was someone else!" she said as she tossed the coin into the well…and waited. She leaned in to try and hear the dime hit bottom, but it was as if there was no bottom because she heard no splash or a thud as if the well had gone dry. She took a second to wonder at that but then decided to head home and get warm.

Chalking it up to her bad luck, she turned to leave. After taking a few steps in the direction she thought was home, she heard the soft whistle of something slicing through the air. She looked up just in time to see her dime sail over her head and land with a tiny thump on the ground right in front of her. Stunned, she looked down at it, wondering who had thrown that coin back out of the well, when she heard something crashing through the brush. She turned just in time to see a hideous monster heading straight for her. His mangey brown fur grew in tufts all over a body well over eight feet tall. He ran on four muscular legs with long, knobby toes and enormous curved claws.

Without sparing a thought of what that creature might be or what it was doing in Indiana, she spun around and started running. Still, almost immediately, she was bowled over by the monster that had sprinted into the clearing, sending her flying. Her purse fell from her shoulder and flew over her head, sending her gun skidding to a stop in the dead fall leaves.

Sprawling on the ground, she looked over her shoulder at the monster that appeared to be considering whether to eat her or not. It took huge whiffs of her through its black, wet nose and opened its maw, which was full of long, pointed teeth. Sour-smelling drool hung from its chin and dripped onto the ground.

Just as the beast reared its ugly head, ready to strike, an arrow arced across the opening and pierced its neck. It looked surprised as a tiny figure entered the clearing, dropping her bow. The monster screamed and lunged at the small woman, but she expertly maneuvered away from its gaping jaws, making a somersault landing next to the spilled gun. The monster gave another cry and went in to bite her, but several shots rang out, stunning the monster. It looked confused and then fell over. She looked over to the woman pointing the lost gun at the now vanquished monster.

In shock, she rose to her feet slowly and looked at the woman, who calmly gathered the purse's spilled contents and handed it back to her as if nothing had happened. Mechanically, she took her purse and hung it over her shoulder. What sort of questions could one ask in this kind of situation?

"Hi. I'm Nimm." The woman stuck out her petite hand.

She shook her hand because she didn't know what else to do. "Hello. I'm Claire."

"Well, Claire, it looks like you're the latest recruit. So, follow me." She turned and walked away, picking up her bow and quiver of arrows on the way.

"What? Wait a minute!" Claire called after her.

Nimm turned around and took a deep breath. "I know you're new, but you knew," she said and pointed to the dark hole.

"What? I didn't know. I don't know anything! What are you talking about?"

"The coin you tossed. It was a wish, right?"

Claire tried to recall the wish she had made. "…I guess."

"Well, then, that's your wish."

"But it came back. It was thrown out!"

Nimm pinned her with a direct look under hazel eyes that suddenly turned a glowing green. "Of course it did. Your wish was accepted. Otherwise, we would not be having this conversation. Now, follow me." She spun around and marched out of the clearing.

"But wait, I'm not ready."

"Wishes don't wait until you're ready, my dear." She called over her shoulder. "Follow me!" She motioned, and Claire couldn't help but follow her. They walked deeper into the woods. The bushes and trees seemed to part as Claire and Nimm walked past. At some point, they had walked so far that Claire was sure they should have reached the end of that tract of woods and come upon a subdivision she knew had to be there somewhere. Nevertheless, the woods stretched on.

Finally, they stopped at the base of a huge tree that looked very similar to the pictures of redwoods that Claire had seen in books. Its ruddy bark was rough, and the tree was so tall its crown was out of sight above in the canopy somewhere. The trunk's circumference was so wide that a truck could have easily driven through it. Nimm walked over and touched the tree and a large door silently opened.

Claire followed Nimm into the tree onto a wooden platform. A glowing ball of green light hovered above them, giving them a bit of light. The top of the inside of the tree (if that's what it really was) was lost in darkness, though. The air was cool and smelled earthy and damp. There was a small, black panel on one side of the platform, and Nimm pushed in a six-digit code. The unmistakable sound of a single bell rang, and the platform descended, the orb of light following them down.

As shock from the proceeding events wore off, Claire finally took notice of what Nimm looked like. She was stunned to see that Nimm had wings folded down her back, her bow and quiver of arrows still slung over her shoulder. Claire was of average height for a woman, but Nimm only came to her shoulder. She was built like a bird, but clearly, she was far from fragile. Nimm had killed that monster with ease, saving them both from being eaten. She had shoulder-length straight brown hair and looked to be in her early twenties.

As if she felt Claire's scrutiny, Nimm looked up at her. "Questions?"

"Well…um, what are you?"

"I am of the Fae." She turned her face forward just as the platform came to a stop. "And you'll soon need to choose what you want to be." A door quickly opened, and Claire was immediately hit with a wave of noise and movement. They stepped out of the elevator into a cavernous room filled with all kinds of creatures busy at work or talking and laughing with others. There were dozens of desks with stacks of papers lining the walls and rows down the middle of what she could only describe as a giant office space.

After the quietness of the woods, the noise and bustle of this space assaulted Claire. She didn't want to leave the platform, but Nimm reached over and grabbed her arm, giving her little choice.

"The Unit Commander will be expecting us, so we must hurry."

Claire followed Nimm out of the elevator, and they made their way through the crowded room. Not one person looked human. Everyone seemed to be some kind of fairytale creature. Some beautiful and delicate, some scary and huge. Claire gaped at them all as they hurried by. No one seemed to even notice her.

Nimm stopped and turned around with an annoyed look on her face, so Claire hurried to catch up. They quickly made their way through the bustling office and down one of the many hallways that led off the main room. They passed several doors before Nimm turned and entered a good-sized reception area.

A man who looked more like a huge frog sat behind a tidy desk. He looked up when they entered and smiled at Nimm. "The day is still too early to deal with Fae!" he croaked in a friendly voice, his double chin quivering with mirth. His skin was the most amazing shade of greenish-blue and was covered in what looked like small warts.

"Don't you have a hot date with a plate full of dead flies, Hubert?" Nimm joked, flashing him a charming smile.

Hubert gave Nimm a sheepish grin, then looked over at Claire with his bulbous eyes. "This is the new recruit?"

"Aye, she is. Is Commander North in her office?"

"She's waiting for you." Hubert lifted his pudgy arm, motioning toward an office door on the other side of the reception area. Claire couldn't keep herself from staring at his long, webbed fingers tipped with tiny claws. Hubert seemed like a jovial fellow, but she still hurried past him and through the door that Nimm had opened for her.

The Unit Commander's large office was tastefully decorated with antiques, relics, and decorations that looked like they were right out of a home decor magazine from the Victorian era, right down to the elaborate art that hung on the papered walls. Was that the original painting of The Lady of Shalott?

Claire was so taken aback by the décor, she wasn't immediately aware that she was being studied. Finally, her attention fell to a woman standing behind an overly ornate mahogany desk. The woman was wearing some kind of navy-blue uniform blazer and matching skirt.

There were bars on her shoulders and several pins hanging on the right breast of the jacket. Ropes of shiny black hair were meticulously pinned to her head in an elaborate design. Her hands rested on the top of the desk. She had perfectly manicured nails polished a bright red that matched her crimson lipstick. She looked to be in her early forties, but it was impossible to tell. Her piercing blue eyes had only a hint of laugh lines.

"I am Unit Commander North. Approach."

Claire slowly walked up to the desk. Nimm had already taken a seat in one of the overstuffed leather chairs in front of the desk. The commander pointed to the other chair, "Please, sit." Claire sat as Unit Commander North took her seat also. It was then she noticed the woman's pointed ears and her skin that seemed to sparkle.

"I'm sure you have a lot of questions."

"A few," Claire said flatly. The woman gave Claire a smile that didn't reach her eyes. That would explain her lack of laugh lines.

The commander took a deep breath, then pinned Claire with those sapphire-blue eyes again. "Claire Smith. Fifty-two, wife, mother, soon-to-be grandmother, and ex-bank teller." Claire wanted to look away under her stare, but she forced herself to glare right back at the woman —elf? How did she have all this information?

"You are an acute underachiever that has taken the easy road your whole life, and now you are depressed that you never had the bravery to make something of your life. You are chronically bored and lonely." The woman sat back and crossed her arms. Claire couldn't tell if she was smirking at her or if that was just an elven facial trait. Now she spared a moment to look over at Nimm, who was casually watching as if she had seen this insult-a-thon many times before. Maybe she had.

"How do you have all this information? And what the hell is this place?" Claire asked, looking back over at the elf commander.

The commander started nonchalantly inspecting her perfect nails. "An extensive file was made the moment you threw that coin in the well and was delivered to me. And as far as what this place is, well, we are protectors. We are the Bureau of Inter-Species Investigation and Enforcement. I am the BISIE North American Unit Commander."

"Oooookay. Well, I need to be on my way home now." Claire stood up, but the look the commander nailed her with made her sit back down.

"You want to go back to your petty, boring life when I am offering you a position here at the BISIE?"

"You're offering me a job?"

"Yes. It's part of the Wishing Well Agreement."

Claire looked over to Nimm again, who nodded her head in acknowledgment. "What if I don't want the job?" she asked, looking back at the commander.

"I'm afraid the time to refuse has passed. It passed the moment you threw that coin in the well, and your request was accepted, as demonstrated by the coin being tossed back." Claire took a deep breath. This was all too weird. She was going to have to find out more before she could escape.

The elf must have seen acquiescence in Claire's eyes because she flashed a broad smile, her brightly painted lips parting to show perfect teeth. "Special Agent Nimm Veckel, please show Probie Smith to the Reassignment Department."

Nimm led her through a confusing maze of hallways until they reached two giant-sized doors with a plaque that read *Reassignment Department*. Nimm punched a code into a keypad, and the doors quickly swung open. They walked into another reception area where a woman stood near a cabinet filing a stack of papers. The woman had tall, pointy ears and a long nose with whiskers. A lengthy braid of red and white hair fell to the small of her back, ending where a bushy red tail twitched over the same navy uniform skirt that the commander wore.

"Another new recruit, I see," she said cheerfully as she walked over to her desk, picked up a paper, and quickly scanned it. "Claire Smith from Indiana," she stated. "I see here she's a four twenty-five."

"That's right," Nimm answered.

"All right, treatment room six is open. When she's finished, please see her to reassignment bay twelve."

"Okie-Dokie." Claire jumped when two more doors on a far wall slid open with a whoosh. "Follow me," Nimm said and disappeared into a dimly lit hallway. They stopped at room six, and Nimm opened the door. An automatic light flashed on, revealing an oversized metal chair with a mechanical arm reaching up over the back, ending in a shiny helmet with several lights that suddenly came to life.

"Oh, hell no."

"It's a requirement for all new recruits with a four-two-five alert before reassignment can proceed."

"You're insane if you think I'm getting into that chair." Claire folded her arms over her chest.

Nimm drew her brows together, and Claire got the distinct impression she was losing her patience. "Look, Probie, I don't make the rules, but you need treatment before reassignment."

"Treatment for what?"

"Did you forget what you were about to do to yourself this afternoon?" Claire unfolded her arms and let her eyes drop to the floor. When she heard Nimm let out a long sigh, she looked back up at the Fae. "The chair will realign your malfunctioning brainwaves and chemical imbalances. You need this to be strong enough to endure the reassignment."

Claire took a step back. "Endure?"

Nimm gave a growl and, with more strength than a tiny creature should have possessed, shoved her into the room and shut the door with a slam. "I'll be back when you're done," she called, and Claire could hear her footsteps going back down the hall.

The situation was getting ridiculous, but she didn't see a way to avoid this, and, who knows, maybe it would work. After the commander had read off the list of Claire's woes, she realized she had been deeply depressed for a long time. Maybe this contraption would actually work.

With a sigh, Claire quickly sat in the chair before she could lose her courage. Her heart pounded in her chest. She was just about to jump out of the chair when straps appeared out of the armrests and clamped over her wrists. She let out an alarmed squeak, and then the helmet came down over her head.

———

She had no way of knowing how long the process lasted. All she could remember was walking down the sugar-white sands of a sunny beach, the emerald waters of an ocean gently lapping at the shore. She was the only one on the beach, yet she didn't feel the dull ache of loneliness, just peace and contentment.

She just realized that the helmet had receded back up to its resting place, and the clamps on her wrists were gone as Nimm poked her head in the door. "Feeling better?"

"Actually, I feel great!"

Nimm smiled. "Okay, now pick who you want to be, and let's start your new life!"

———

Now, let me tell you the story of Eunice Love. You might want to cheer for her, but do you know for sure that she is the heroine of this story? I guess you'll have to keep reading to find out for sure. I know I said this wasn't a love story, but rather, this is Love's story...

———

EUNICE

With a mighty push, Eunice entered the giant revolving door, setting the glass wheel spinning with an unsettling suction sound. She hurried outside—always terrified in that split second between inside and outside—that she'd be trapped, somehow captured, in an invisible prison that she lacked the ability to escape from. Ironically, that seemed a metaphor for her life.

Once safely outside the building, she started her slow walk to the town square and the quiet park bench where she sat every afternoon ruminating over the day's happenings. The fall equinox had passed a couple of weeks before, and the days were growing colder, so she pulled her coat tighter and turned her face up to the gray sky. Even though she had made this same walk repeatedly for the past nine years, she let herself appreciate the colonial-era and Greek Revival style buildings with their ornate facades and interesting color combinations that lined Main Street. She rounded the corner and made her way down Market Street and into Town Square Park. The mammoth gazebo was so heavily decorated for fall with pumpkins, bales of hay, and such that it brought a smile to Eunice's face, despite the monotonous tone her life had taken on.

After she got her undergraduate degree, she decided to stay in college because she didn't really have anything else she wanted to do, so she earned her master's degree in Classical Literature and suddenly found that she needed to decide. Either she would become an academic, or she had to finally leave college.

She had wanted to get away from the party life, and she didn't really fit in with the college lifers. However, she definitely did not want to go back to her hometown, so on a whim, she just started driving and ended up in a small town that she had found too charming to leave. For the past nine years, she had worked as the program director at the historical society of the picturesque town of Fairy Trail, Vermont. It was only a part-time position, so she picked up a few shifts as a delivery driver—one of three in the whole town—and she could pay her bills, but lately, she had been feeling listless. She pictured herself as a boulder setting forgotten under one of the stone bridges in town, watching the world pass as fingers of green moss grew around her as a testament to her stagnation.

She walked up to a park bench and sat looking up at the sky again. It was gray, but it didn't look as if rain was imminent. It would be dark soon, so parents were hurrying their kids out of the park, probably bribing them with promises of dinner. The park quickly emptied, and Eunice found herself alone.

As she looked across the park, her mind wandered to a conversation that she had had earlier with an old man who came into the historical society. He mentioned that her name, Eunice, had seemed so old-fashioned for such a young woman. She had given him a stiff chuckle at the time, but it still vexed her. She had been teased mercilessly as a child because of that name. When she'd complain to her parents about it, her dad would say she should be proud to have her grandma's name. She wasn't.

As her gaze swept across the park, her eyes fell on a dark shape in the middle of one of the grassy areas. She knew every stone and blade of grass in this park, and that hole had not been there yesterday. She looked around to see if there were any city workers she hadn't noticed before, but she was still all alone in the park.

Curious, she got up and walked over to the inky pit. Musty, ice-cold air drifted up and touched her face. She was surprised that the city had just left it open and unmarked, as any distracted person walking by could easily have fallen in. She noticed dozens of coins littering the grass all around the hole. Again, she looked around the park to see if there was anyone nearby that might have dropped their purse full of change. Still alone. Story of her life.

As she leaned forward to look into the dark abyss, she was instantly overcome with the notion that this was a wishing well. She looked around at all the different coins lying forgotten on the grass and just knew that they had all been wishes. At the absurdity of the thought, laughter bubbled up and echoed across the deserted park ask dusk settled in.

"Oh, what the hell," Eunice said as she dug into her change purse and pulled out a dime. She held it up into the dying light and said, "I wish I could be someone else." With a silly smile on her face, she threw the dime into the pit, expecting to hear it splash into a pool of unseen water.

When she heard nothing, she shrugged, turned, and stared, walking away. She didn't want to admit it to herself, but she felt disappointed. Ha! Did she think she would suddenly be an interesting person with an interesting life on her way to do something…interesting?

She let out a gasp as something plopped at her feet. Startled, she looked down to see the coin that she had just dropped into the hole! She spun around, expecting to see someone climbing out of the gloomy well…probably deathly pale with long fingers of algae clinging to their hair and clothes, looking at her with dead eyes… but there was no one.

Putting a hand on her racing heart, she tried to calm herself. No well-zombies were coming after her. She turned around and quickly started walking out of the park. There was a frozen dinner waiting for her in her freezer, and she just wanted to get home.

An ear-splitting screech stopped her in her tracks. She looked up just in time to see a black, winged man-like creature swoop out of the sky. It picked Eunice up and flew into the quickly approaching night. She screamed and looked at the park just as the town's streetlamps winked on. She fought against the urge to fight with the creature because she was now too far above the ground to survive a fall. Instead, she hung on. The creature looked at her with glowing yellow eyes as it cradled her in its arms, holding her tight to its chest. It had a wicked grin on its warty face. When it hissed at her, she smelled rotten meat and gaged. Its skin was black, bumpy, and rough. Its enormous membrane-covered wings pumped hard, lifting them higher with every stroke.

As Eunice was trying to wrap her brain around how she was being carried off into the sky by a monster, a man riding a huge winged horse brandishing a long sword flew up to the creature and slashed down at one of its wings. It darted at the last minute, almost dropping her. She screamed and clung tighter to the creature's thick, lumpy skin. It screeched at the man and squirted some kind of substance from its open mouth, which the horse deftly avoided.

The man yelled something in a language she didn't understand, then swooped in again, but this time when he brought his sword down, it connected, cleaving the monster's right wing from its body. It gave a blood-curdling scream, and Eunice plummeted through the night sky.

She couldn't see the ground below her in the dark, but she knew it was rushing up to meet her. She closed her eyes, expecting to hit the hard surface at any second when she was plucked from the sky by the man riding the winged horse. He was wearing a chain-mail tunic, which she gripped onto with all her strength. He pulled her up to sit on the horse in front of him, the long white feathers of the horse's wings tickling her legs as they carried them through the night.

They flew down into a wooded area and landed in a small clearing. The man slid from the horse without a word, then helped her from its broad back. He whispered a few words she didn't know, and small balls of light sparked and floated above them, lighting up the clearing. He then walked up to his winged horse and tenderly rubbed its nose. He said a few more words, soothing the magnificent steed. Then he stood back, sang a few words to a poetic-sounding song, and the horse disappeared in a flash of light.

Eunice gasped and took a few steps back, her eyes wide. She tried to get her brain to work enough to make her run away, but all she could do was stare at the man. His thick, shoulder-length hair was black, and he had a neatly trimmed beard and dark eyes.

"Come," he said with an accent that sounded Mediterranean. "Unit Commander North is expecting you." He turned and started walking away, the mysterious globes of light showing a path. She wanted to run away but found all she could do was silently follow him. She figured she was just in shock and probably just having a strange dream. Maybe she had fainted in the park? If so, she needed to wake herself up quickly.

However, she meekly followed the tall, chain-mailed man to the far side of the clearing and into the trunk of the most massive tree she had ever seen. She didn't voice any objections as a lift lowered them deep down into some kind of subterranean hub of fairytale creatures. She had barely spoken when she was taken into a terribly outdated office and sat in front of an elf with bright red lipstick who proclaimed herself the commander of something with a bunch of letters and then gave her a job. She was then led down a long hall into a place they called the Reassignment Department.

She now stood before a very tall, very wide man with green skin. Despite his warty appearance, he had a shock of shiny black hair and perfectly straight, sparkling white teeth. "All right, ginger, what will it be?" He looked her up and down frankly and rubbed his broad chin. "Let's see. You strike me as maybe Fae or even a princess?" When she didn't reply, he narrowed his eyes. "You couldn't pull off an ogre," he said, putting his green, spatulate hand on his barrel chest. "Maybe you'd prefer an animal-type? You look like you'd fit nicely as a fox."

Eunice felt numb. Her brain was fuzzy. It was like everything was at the same time going in slow motion but also very quickly. She couldn't make sense of it. She looked over to the man who had saved her life, who was now standing quietly by her side. He was looking at her with expectation, and when she didn't say anything, his brows rose in encouragement.

Eunice swallowed and looked back over at the ogre. "Um, maybe a mermaid?" she answered in a quivering voice. He took a deep breath, cocked his head, and looked up toward the ceiling as if contemplating her choice. "Well, we do have several positions in waterways and a Pacific sector that do need filling...."

"I think Unit Commander North already has a case in mind for her, and it requires legs," the man standing beside her said.

Eunice tried to make her mind work, but she just couldn't form coherent thoughts. Finally, she took a deep breath and let it out with a sigh. "Hecate. I want to be Hecate," she stated with confidence.

The man beside her sucked in his breath. "A goddess? Such hubris!"

The ogre laughed. "You should talk, Supervisory Special Agent Bellerophon. You're a demigod!"

Bellerophon crossed his arms, his chain mail making a loud clinking sound. "I suppose you do have a point," he conceded.

The ogre made some notations on a file on his desk, then pointed down another long hallway. "Take her to reassignment bay eleven next to the other Probie."

CLAIRE

When Claire woke up, she felt even better than she had when she left the treatment chair. She felt strong and light and could feel power radiating throughout her body. Nimm smiled and threw her some clothes. "An elven warrior princess. Good choice, milady." She made a ridiculously exaggerated bow and then led Claire over to a full-length mirror.

After dressing, Claire looked at herself in the mirror and was overcome with delight. She was tall, trim, and strong and would never be seen as dumpy and old, let alone average, ever again! Her hair was pale blonde and fell in thick ribbons down to her tiny waist. Her breasts were the perfect size and no longer sagged, and her legs were long and lean. Her eyes were the same white color as her hair and were quite exotic.

She scanned her body with sheer giddiness. She was wearing a golden circlet across her brow with an emerald in the center, golden hoop earrings in her pert, pointed ears, a deep green tunic with short sleeves that showed off the pale skin of her strong arms, and tight, black leggings with sturdy leather boots. She twirled around and laughed as she was overcome with happiness.

When she got ahold of herself, she looked over at Nimm, who was smiling. "It's orgasmic, isn't it?" All Claire could do was nod her head and giggle. "Okay, let's get going. You can pick a new name later. Senior Special Agent Bellerophon—who evidently has a new Probie of his own—has gotten a special assignment handed down to him from the Special Agent in charge. It seems one of our agents has gone missing."

When Nimm and Claire walked into a large conference room, a

man stood in the corner with thick arms folded across a broad chest. He had olive-toned skin and shiny black hair and was breathtakingly handsome. Her eyes must have been wide because Nimm snickered as she walked by and took her seat at the table. Embarrassed, Claire closed her mouth and quietly sat next to Nimm.

It was then she noticed there was a woman in the room as well. She walked over and took a seat across from Claire. She was tall and strong and flawlessly beautiful, but the sheer power that radiated from her was what caught Claire's attention. Her sleek black hair was braided into an intricate design, and she wore a circlet on her brow as well, but it was made of silver and moonstones and labradorite. Her eyes were as blue as ice, and she wore a black sleeveless tunic and leggings that hugged her body tightly. To say she was striking was a severe understatement.

The man took a seat next to the woman and cleared his throat. "Since we are all here now, let's get started," he said with an accent. "My name is Supervisory Special Agent Bellerophon, and this is Probationary Special Agent…." He took a deep breath and signed it out loudly. "Hecate…"

Bellerophon then motioned across the table. "Probie, this is Special Agent Nimm Veckel and her Probie, Special Agent Eunice Smith." Mr. Hottie was all business.

"Approximately seven days ago, Senior Special Agent Whynn went missing. We've had people on it over the past week, but no one has come up with any clues to his disappearance. Special Agent in-charge seems to think our Probies will have some luck. We'll visit his apartment first to see if you ladies can pick up on any clues."

"And remember to use your intuition. You aren't as you were—sense dead in your human state. You might pick up on clues that others have missed because of…connections," Nimm interjected, and a look that Claire didn't understand passed between her and Bellerophon.

"Also, mundane humans will no longer be able to see you as your old selves, and they will only be able to see a human version of your new bodies. They couldn't handle seeing us as we really are." He motioned to everyone at the table. He stood up. "Let's head to the transport."

The transport was actually back at that elevator that brought them to the facilities. However, when the doors opened up, they were in a parking garage in Santa Monica, California. Curiously, there was an unlocked car with keys in the ignition. They drove a short distance to a small cottage on the beach. The air was warm, and Claire could smell the salt in the breeze. Seagulls called to each other over a sandy beach. She had always wanted to visit Southern California. How odd that it would be as an elf!

After Bellerophon disarmed some kind of invisible warding system, the group walked into the cottage through a large sliding glass door. Claire was immediately struck by a familiar odor. It reminded her of her childhood, for some reason. She pushed it out of her mind because she had never been to California or even a beach. But her mind kept nagging at her. It was almost like a smokey or earthy scent. She wanted to say it might have been from a pipe. Her father, Benjamin, had smoked a pipe. He had left her family when she was only fourteen, so she couldn't be certain what she was smelling was the same tobacco. She chuckled to herself, knowing there weren't many modern people who smoked tobacco from a pipe like an old grandpa.

Hecate plopped down on the floor and crossed her long legs, resting her open palms on her knees with her forefingers and thumbs touching, and closed her eyes. As she meditated, Claire could see a bright white light emanating from her aura out into the room. A deep indigo color pulsed and glowed between her brows. It was almost the weirdest thing she had seen since she threw the dime into that hole.

Claire slowly looked around the house. Everything was very tidy, even if the houseplants had started to droop. There were no family photos at all, but there was an old painting that looked similar to one that had hung in her family's living room when she was growing up.

Claire shook her head, dismissing it as having had to be one of many copies, especially if a copy had made its way all the way out here to California, so far away from her childhood living room in Indiana.

She drifted into the only bedroom in the cottage and sat on the twin bed. Wanting to do her part in this investigation and taking a cue from Hecate, she closed her eyes and breathed in deeply. She remembered Nimm's advice to use her intuition and was struck by such a familiar feeling, though she could not identify its source. It was as if a presence in this cottage was well known to her, but she couldn't explain it.

After a while, she walked back into the small living room as Hecate gracefully stood up. "Someone known to me has been here," she announced. It was the first words she had heard the woman speak. It was as if she was trying to be confident but hadn't yet gotten up her nerve. Suddenly, she was reminded of her daughter, Polly, and wondered how she was feeling, if she had morning sickness, or if she had felt her baby move yet. A sadness passed over her at the thought she wouldn't be able to see her daughter and grandchild.

"Do you know who it might be?" Bellerophon asked.

"No. I'm sorry. Just that the energy here is familiar, and it's from more than just one person who I have known."

"Do you know anyone in California?" asked Nimm. Hecate just shook her head.

Bellerophon sighed. "Well, there is a person of interest that frequents a nearby establishment. No one has got eyes on him yet, but we can leave you two to stake the place out while Special Agent Nimm and I check on another lead."

A little while later, Hecate and Claire were sitting in the car parked across the street from a rundown music store. Old vinyl records hung on clear lines in the windows, and posters of Janice Joplin and Jimi Hendrix hung on the wall. They weren't in a very busy part of town, so they'd be easy to spot if anyone came out or went into the store.

Bellerophon had explained to them that they were looking for a person with a *mark* on them that he said the person of interest had picked up by sneaking into the beach cottage days ago. As far as he knew, the person of interest didn't know they carried the mark, and no other agent had spotted him yet. With little more than zero information to go on, Claire wasn't hopeful they'd find this person of interest.

"So, where did you get the name Hecate?"

The woman looked over at her and smiled. "Hecate was the Greek goddess of witchcraft and magic. I thought that if I could be anyone, I might as well be her." She shrugged, then continued to survey the music store.

"I guess I'll have to pick out a name when we get back. What was your old name? If I'm allowed to ask."

"They didn't say anything about secrecy, so I guess I can tell you. It was Eunice."

Claire smiled. "My grandma's name was Eunice."

"So was mine! Fortunately for you, your parents didn't decide to name you after your grandmother."

"Yeah," Claire chuckled. "Did you…throw a coin into a hole?"

Hecate/Eunice looked back over at her. "I did," she said quietly.

"How bizarre all this was here, and we never knew."

"True, but now I can do magic." She laughed. It seemed the woman was loosening up. "Look! There he is!" She pointed and sat forward in her seat.

An elderly man wearing shorts and a t-shirt meandered down the street and into the music store. The *mark* he was carrying was a huge glowing bullseye. She couldn't believe he didn't see it! The two women slowly exited the car and nonchalantly walked across the street and into the music store. The man's bright gray hair and bullseye stood out as he perused the records in the country-western section.

"Ugh! My dad listened to country music. Gross," Hecate whispered. Claire frowned. So did her father. And she also hated country music because of it.

They were casually making their way over to the man—not really sure what they'd do when they got there—when Bellerophon burst through the door. "Stop right where you are!"

Without even looking up, the man turned and started to run to the back of the store. Claire guessed he knew there was an exit back there.

Hecate threw up her arms, and a purple light shot out from her fingers and grabbed the old man. He stopped in his tracks, obviously unable to move. Claire jumped high in the air over an aisle of records doing a summersault in the air and landing gracefully on her feet. Hecate joined her, and then they strolled over to the man, stopping in front of him.

"Dad?" they both asked in unison.

EUNICE

Eunice looked at Claire; sure her eyes were as wide as the other woman's. "What?" they both said at the same time. Just then, Nimm and Bellerophon ran up to them. Bellerophon conjured a pair of handcuffs and shackled the old man—her father.

Eunice let her holding spell dissipate and turned to Claire. She wanted to say something, but she didn't know what. Claire opened her mouth as if she were going to speak, then shut it again.

"They finally realize they are sisters." Bellerophon's voice was light, almost mocking, and it took everything Eunice had not to use her magic on him.

Nimm had the good sense to look sheepish. "Unit Commander North ordered us not to mention it to you two for fear you wouldn't work together."

"Why wouldn't we want to work together?" Eunice asked.

Claire let out a loud sigh and walked out of the store, the clerk looking completely baffled at what had just happened in his store.

Back at Head Quarters, Eunice's (and apparently Claire's) father sat in an interrogation room across a table from Bellerophon and Nimm.

She and Claire stood outside the room, watching from behind a double-sided mirror.

"He looks so old," Claire whispered, peering into the glass.

"He is old," Eunice countered. Claire looked over at Eunice with those striking white eyes.

She turned to look back at their father. "I haven't seen him in thirty-eight years. He's never even met my daughter."

"You have a daughter?"

"Yes. And I'll soon be a grandma. That was…until I became…an elf."

Eunice stared at her sister in wonder. "I am an aunt?"

Claire looked over at her again and smiled. "I guess so."

"He told me he had had another family before I was born."

"Did he tell you he left my mother with three teenagers?"

"No, but I guessed it. He didn't get along with my mother, either, if that makes you feel better."

"It doesn't."

Eunice's attention was drawn to the interrogation, which they could hear through the glass. "How do you know Whynn?" Nimm asked.

"We met at a little bar on Venice Beach a few years ago. I went to listen to the live music they have on Fridays. He struck up a conversation. We hit it off, so we'd meet up for dinners or a drink and just talk, ya know? He was a nice guy. We'd talk about music. He said he played a little guitar. I'm alone, gone through two wives, so it was nice to have someone to talk to occasionally."

Eunice felt her chest tighten. He and her mother fought a lot, and Eunice didn't see him much after leaving for college. He attended her first college graduation and told her how proud he was of her…but she hadn't seen him since then. She hadn't even spoken on the phone with him for five of six years…maybe longer.

"Why would Whynn develop a friendship with a random old man?" Nimm asked.

"He claimed to be my son, but I didn't believe him." The old man's handcuffs raddled as he scratched his nose. "He doesn't look anything like I remember my son. And a father never forgets the face of their children," he stated with confidence and sat back in his squeaky chair. Claire snorted, and Eunice could tell she was barely restraining her anger.

"Senior Special Agent Whynn told you he was your son?" Bellerophon's voice was skeptical, and he shared a pointed look with Nimm.

"He did, sir. Of course, I thought he was lying, but then he started telling me things from his childhood that only my son would know. He described his sisters Clementine and Claire just as they were as kids. He knew things only my son would know. So, after a while, I started to believe him." He shrugged and dragged a hand over his stubbly chin.

"Do you know the whereabouts of Senior Special Agent Whynn?" Bellerophon's voice was even tighter than usual—he was losing patience. He pushed around a file that was on the desk. What information it held, Eunice didn't know.

"His name is Christopher!" her father yelled. "He's not just a name in your file, he's my son, and I love him!" he said in a dramatic huff.

Claire let out a breath that sounded like she had been holding for a while and flew into the room, stopping right next to their father. "You hypocritical old man! You left us when we were just kids. You didn't care then, and you certainly don't care now." She put her hands on her hips and stared down at him as if she wanted to do him in.

"Probie, wait outside," Bellerophon ordered.

Completely ignoring him, Claire bent down and twisted the chair so she was face to face with their father. "Come on, old man. Admit it. You never cared for the family you walked away from. The children you left behind. For what? Freedom? Another woman? What was it?"

"You must be Claire. Only my sweet little middle child would ever talk to her father like that." He was sneering at her! Eunice clenched her fists, feeling her nails bite into her palms, but she stayed outside the room, watching through the double-sided mirror.

"It was tough raising you kids, especially with your nagging mother. So yeah, I left. And I was free. Until I made the mistake of getting married again to that cold shrew back east, she made your mother look like a lamb. But I knocked her up, so I had to stay."

"Uh-oh," Nimm said, and both she and Bellerophon stood up.

***

CLAIRE

Claire heard a blood-curdling scream and turned just in time to see Eunice/Hecate run into the room. "You disgusting toad of a man!" she screamed and hit him with a blue light that wrapped around his neck. Their father started choking, and Claire backed away in shock.

"You better tell us where our brother is, or I won't hesitate to end you!"

The blue light disappeared, and their father grabbed his throat with his shackled hands. Then he had the audacity to smile up at her. "Let me guess, Eunice?" I knew you were a firecracker under all that fake timidness.

"I wouldn't provoke her, old man. She's a goddess now." Claire pointed at Eunice with her thumb and then crossed her arms across her chest.

"Meh, women are all the same. You girls have to love your father. It's the natural order of things. You all need the firm hand of a man. You'll come around and see everything I did was because I love you."

Eunice roared and threw out her hand. A purple light burst out of her fingers and pinned their father up against the stone wall of the interrogation room.

"Probie, put that man down! He's our suspect, and we need information out of him," Bellerophon yelled, but if Eunice heard him, Claire couldn't tell.

Eunice walked up to their father, plastered against the wall with a comically frightened look on his face. Claire walked up to stand beside her sister. Calmly, Eunice/Hecate said, "Tell me where our brother is...now."

"I don't know for sure. But when he didn't show up for dinner last week, I went over to his place, but he wasn't there. I had introduced him to an acquaintance of mine a few weeks before. I thought it was strange this acquaintance kept asking me so many questions about Christopher. I kind of let it slip that he was my son and was in some kind of super-secret government agency. And then I didn't see either of them again."

"Ugh!" Nimm let out an exasperated breath. "Where does this acquaintance live?" Nimm asked as she approached.

"I don't know." Eunice/Hecate squeezed her hand tighter, and their father left out a gasp. "Okay, okay. I've seen him leave a warehouse down by the harbor. You can't miss it. It's painted pink!"

"I know of this place," Bellerophon said quietly. "It's been on our radar for a while now."

Eunice/Hecate turned to look at him. "So, we don't need this weasel anymore?"

"No, Mr. Benjamin Love can rot in our dungeons for a while."

Eunice/Hecate scribbled something in the air, and their father disappeared in a puff of purple smoke, leaving a fat, warty toad sitting on the floor. "I hope the dungeons are in a smelly swamp somewhere. See, ya, Dad," she said, turned, and then walked out of the interrogation room.

EUNICE

As the sun was finally setting on what seemed to be the longest day of Eunice's life, they pulled up to the pink warehouse in Long Beach. "According to Senior Special Agent Whynn's file, he had been working deep undercover for quite some time. Were you aware of this investigation?" Nimm asked Bellerophon.

"I was not aware until Unit Commander North briefed me a few days ago."

"I had heard through the grapevine that a few agents had gone missing, but I didn't know there were undercover units on it."

"Apparently, the working theory is that there is some assassination ring targeting BISIE agents." Eunice wanted to ask them why anyone would want to assassinate agents, but then she realized she didn't even know what it was they did at the BISIE exactly. Probably something like making sure the magical types followed the rules and such.

"How long has our brother been an agent, exactly? If that information isn't classified," Claire asked.

"According to his file, fifteen years. That was before I joined. I think I may have seen him around a few times."

"I remember him from when he was a Probie," Bellerophon laughed. "I thought it was so strange that he smoked a pipe, but I guess it fit his chosen persona."

"I thought I smelled pipe smoke in his cottage. It must be the same tobacco blend our father smoked…." Claire's voice trailed off.

"You two stay here and watch that door. Special Agent Nimm and I will do some recon around back." Bellerophon and Nimm exited the car and snuck around the building as night fell.

As the women sat in the car watching for anyone coming or going from the building, Eunice wondered how long she had been in this… world. Could she call it that? She had no idea how long the re-assignment had taken, but it was nighttime when she was taken from Fairy Trail. It could have been a day or a week…or longer. She had no idea and hadn't really had the time to think about it until now. In Southern California, you couldn't even tell if it was still fall. She wondered how Emily and Watson were doing at the Historical Society and if they were looking for her.

"Hecate, you were pretty impressive in the interrogation." Claire was sitting next to her in the back seat of the Toyota.

"You can call me Eunice." She smiled at her sister. "I don't know how impressive I looked, but it felt pretty good to finally get that off my chest."

Claire ran her fingers over the feathers of a quiver full of arrows that were sitting next to her. A bow that Nimm had given her earlier sat on her lap. Claire had told them that she had no idea how to use a bow, but both Bellerophon and Nimm assured her that her new persona would know just how to use it. I guess that explained how Eunice had been so adept at using magic so suddenly.

"Was he a good father to you?"

"He was…absent. Even when he was there, he wasn't, you know," Eunice said.

"Yeah, it was the same with us. To be honest, it was sort of a relief when he left. At least he and Mom weren't fighting anymore."

"Yeah, it was a relief when I went off to college."

"What did you study?" Claire asked.

"I got my undergrad in creative writing and my graduate degree in Classical Lit."

"Oh, are you a writer?"

Eunice laughed. "I wanted to be, but I just couldn't find my muse. So, I'm the Director of the Historical Society of Fairy Trail, Vermont."

"Well…that sounds like fun."

"It's not, really."

Claire patted her on the knee. "You're young still. You've still got time to write many books."

"What about you? What do you do?"

"I worked at a bank for forever. I started as a teller and worked my way up to a loan officer—boring-ass stuff. I was fired a few weeks ago. Well, I guess it was a few weeks ago. I've lost track of time now. I just couldn't bear to go into the bank and do the same stinkin' work I had been doing for years and years." Claire shrugged and looked out the window.

"Are you married?"

"Yeah."

"Just, yeah? What does he do? Is he handsome?"

Claire turned back to look at her and laughed. "Bart, hot?" She laughed again. "He's okay, I guess. And he's a plumber."

"Well, tell me about your daughter. What's her name?"

"Polly. After college, she opened her own art studio. She's good, too. Now she's preparing for a baby, of course." Claire's voice trailed off, and her face crumbled. A tear rolled down her cheek, which she quickly swiped away.

"Are you sorry you made your wish?"

Claire sighed. "I am. Are you?"

"I might have been a bit hasty at deciding to leave my life so completely and abruptly."

"You sound like a professor," Claire teased.

Just then, Bellerophon boomed through her head. "Okay, Probies, meet us around the back of the warehouse. We have movement." From the look on Claire's face, she must have received the telepathic message as well.

"I guess it's go time. Let's go find our brother." Claire grabbed her bow and quiver and jumped out of the car, and Eunice followed. They made their way around to the back of the warehouse, where Bellerophon and Nimm were waiting for them. A tiny green light illuminated their forms in the dark alleyway.

"Special Agent Nimm and I have observed at least thirteen people in the warehouse. We've identified three of them as the missing BISIE agents, and they are being held captive. One of them is Senior Special Agent Whynn."

Claire had a concerned look on her face. Eunice had never met Christopher before, and she'd only seen a few pictures of him from when he was younger. But she guessed she wouldn't recognize him anyway with his new persona.

"Follow Agent Nimm, Probies, and remember, we don't want anyone dead. We need to question these jokers and find out who their leader is." Bellerophon pulled back a loose piece of siding, which made a loud creaking sound. Eunice held her breath, waiting to hear yells of alarm coming from inside, but everything was quiet, so they entered the building.

They crept along the inside wall until they heard voices, then they ducked behind some wooden crates. The air was cool, damp, and salty.

Eunice peeked around the corner and could see several magical creatures milling about under shafts of weak, yellow light. She guessed these were the bad guys. Claire sucked in her breath, and Eunice followed her gaze up to three cages suspended high above the ground. There were two Fae and a halfling sitting dejectedly in their cages which swung slightly in the air. Since both the Fae were female, Eunice deduced the halfling was her long-lost brother, Christopher, or Whynn as he was known in the BISIE.

Bellerophon pointed to a dark elf sitting just outside the lighted area working on a computer. "We need to get that guy first," he whispered. "Claire, you and I will aim for him. Eunice, just start zapping people. Hold them on the ground as long as you can. If we can take the dark elf out, the others will be thrown into confusion." Bellerophon pulled out a bow and quiver that must have been magically hidden since Eunice hadn't seen him carrying it. "Our arrows will just stun, so don't be afraid to aim at soft spots," he told her sister.

"While you guys keep them distracted, I'll fly up and release the Fae and try to get your brother safely down." Nimm didn't look confident the plan would work, but she snuck off into the shadows nearer to the captives with no hesitation.

"Ready?" Bellerophon's voice was barely a whisper. Eunice nodded and looked over to her sister, who did the same. Bellerophon and Claire stood, took aim at the dark elf, and let their arrows fly. Eunice stood up and called her magic. Her palms heated up as a purple glow gathered around her fingers. The arrows cut through the air with a hiss, but before anyone could react to the sound, they harmlessly struck an invisible barrier and clattered to the ground.

"Uh-oh," Claire said as a dark elf wizard ran out from the shadows, green light circling her hands. She shot out a ball of energy that sent them all springing away. Claire tumbled and nimbly came back to her feet. Quick as lightning, she shot three arrows into the group of creatures, who were now looking in their direction. All three arrows hit their targets. They fell to the ground, stunned.

Bellerophon shot his own arrows that took out another three, their still bodies lying on the floor. Eunice sent a shot of energy toward the wizard, but she was expecting it and had put up a barrier that sent her ball of energy ricocheting through the warehouse. She spared a second to look up in time to see Nimm let the second Fae free.

Bellerophon had pulled a sword and was advancing toward the male dark elf, who pulled his own sword and was ready for a battle. Claire was busy hitting more targets with her stun arrows as reinforcements ran in from the shadows.

Eunice sent long fingers of energy to wrap around the wrists and ankles of several of the newcomers, but she had to jump out of the way again from another green ball of energy sent by the wizard. A wooden crate beside her burst into flames. She was definitely not using her magic to stun.

Now Eunice was angry. She threw her hands up into the air, calling for a colony of bats that she had sensed earlier. They flew in through a broken window and attacked the wizard. The woman screamed and flailed her arms in the air. Eunice flung a heavy ball of energy that struck her in the chest—she went down hard. Eunice put her palms to the ground and called up strong roots that broke through the cement floor of the warehouse and wrapped the wizard up like a mummy, and then she sealed them with powerful magic.

Nimm had grabbed Christopher and slowly lowered him down to the ground. Eunice took a deep breath and carefully approached the fight. Most of the creatures were lying stunned on the ground. Bellerophon and the dark elf were still fighting, their sword clashing. Claire shot the last of the enemies, who fell to the floor with a thud.

Suddenly, a massive troll lumbered into the light and grabbed up Eunice. Its colossal hand fit all the way around her torso. She screamed as it squeezed, her insides protesting, her bones popping. She couldn't concentrate enough through the pain to use her magic.

Just then, Christopher jumped up onto the shoulders of the great troll with an agility that she did not know halflings possessed. He held up a small short sword that glowed brightly with a shocking yellow color and stuck it deep between the troll's shoulder blades. The troll screamed out, released Eunice, and dropped to the floor, making the whole building shake. He didn't look stunned.

The halfling leaped from his back and ran over to Eunice. "Are you okay?" he asked breathlessly.

"Yes. I'm okay." He helped her to her feet as Claire sent a stun arrow into the dark elf's back, and he collapsed. She ran over to Eunice and Christopher, her ice-blue eyes wide with concern, and took her sister into her arms, hugging her tightly.

When they parted, the halfling embraced Claire, tears coming down his chubby cheeks. He only came up to her waist, and Eunice had to stifle a laugh. "Claire, I've missed you." He looked up at her. "So many times I wanted to visit and talk with you, but I couldn't." Claire didn't reply as tears streamed from her haunted eyes. Clearly, she had forgiven him for disappearing so many years before.

CLAIRE

The next morning, after they had all gone back to HQ, got patched up for cuts and bruises, and had a restful sleep, Claire, Eunice, and Christopher sat in a meeting room. They had all been debriefed last night before they were allowed to retire to their rooms to sleep. Claire thought she wouldn't be able to sleep after everything that had happened, but she was out as soon as she laid down. Now they were waiting for Unit Commander North.

"I was at Mom's funeral, you know. Of course, you didn't recognize me, but I was there."

Claire gave him a sad smile. "Now, I kind of figured you had been there."

"How is Polly? I hear you're going to be a grandmother."

"She's okay, I guess. She doesn't tell me much. I guess I raised her like our parents raised us." She shrugged. "I don't know why I thought she'd turn out differently." Neither Christopher nor Eunice replied.

There was nothing to say. It wasn't like she could go back to her old life and fix her mistakes. She had thrown that away with that old, paint-stained dime. Her chest and throat grew tight, and she fought back the tears of regret. How could she have so easily thrown away what she had?

Claire's eyes slipped to Christopher, who was lost in his own thoughts. She wondered if he was saddened by never marrying and having his own children. And then she looked over to her youngest sister. She, too, was deep in thought. She was still young. She wondered if Eunice felt remorse for her decision to become someone else.

Just then, the door to the room was thrown open, and Unit Commander North strolled in with Bellerophon and Nimm behind her. She wore that navy uniform again, her dark hair pinned up in a complicated Victorian style. "Well, if this was a party, I'd be sorely disappointed." She stood at the desk in front of them and crossed her arms. "Such long faces for those who have been given so much."

"We've given up so much as well," Christopher said, clearly not intimidated by the tall, commanding elf.

"That is true," she said, pretending to inspect her perfectly painted nails. "But look at you three now! A warrior halfling, an elven princess, and a Greek goddess, for goodness's sake. You couldn't ask for more."

"I could ask for my old life back." That was from Eunice.

"You could. But you made a wish…and it was granted."

"There was no small print to read, giving us the option to opt-out," her sister retorted.

Unit Commander North snorted. "So it seems." Her eyes narrowed, and she pinned them each with a withering stare. "It has come to the attention of the director that you three are bringing in so much negative energy with your sadness that you will be given a choice that no one else has ever been granted." Again, her eyes slid to each of them to emphasize her displeasure.

"Do tell," Christopher said.

Unit Commander North fished something out of one of her tiny pockets. She placed a coin in front of Christopher, one in front of Eunice, and one in front of Claire.

Claire looked down and sucked in her breath when she saw that very same green paint-smeared dime she had tossed into that blasted hole. She quickly looked back up at the commander. "Does this mean we can go home?" She fought against letting hope bloom.

Unit Commander North crossed her arms again and looked down her straight nose at them. "It does." All three of the siblings let out a sigh and looked at each other with smiles of relief. "However, there is a caveat." Claire held her breath. "You three will almost certainly not remember any of this. You will go back just as you came: sad, hopeless, and wishing you were someone else."

Fear crept through Claire's bones as she remembered what she had been about to do to herself that day that she had disappeared from her world. But then she remembered that she had changed her mind. She had made the right choice. She was strong enough to survive and make the changes needed for her to be happy and repair her relationships. She looked to her brother and sister too, who wore an expression of strength and determination. They all faced the commander and waited. "Very well, then." Unit Commander North held up her hand and snapped her fingers. Claire heard a deafening crack, and then everything went dark.

Claire woke up in her bed. She rolled over and stared at her clock. Eight in the morning, Bart must have already left for work. She sat up and rubbed her aching head. She'd had the most fantastical dream. It was so weird, and none of it made sense.

She sighed a long mournful breath and then pulled herself from her bed. She went to the bathroom and took some aspirin, then slowly dressed. She caught herself going through the motions of getting ready to sit at the park all day, just as she had for weeks. But then she looked outside her window and saw the sun was shining and noticed how beautiful the fall trees looked. And then she realized she didn't want to sit at the park all day moping and feeling sorry for herself.

She poured herself some coffee and sat down with a sigh, mindlessly started rubbing her head until she realized her headache was gone. She thought about that weird dream that she had had and how real it had seemed. Then, abruptly, she knew exactly where she wanted to go.

Quickly, she packed a bag, went downstairs, and left a note for Bart.

Dear Bart,

I need some time to reconnect with my family. I'll be gone for a few days or maybe a week. I'll call you later. I love you.

P.S. I lost my job.

Getting in her car, she asked Google for directions to a place she only had a vague memory of and was surprised when she found out that Fairy Trail, Vermont, was, in fact, an actual place!

The sun was just setting when Claire walked into Town Square Park, located in the middle of Fairy Trail, two days later. She spotted the stunning red-head sitting on a park bench and knew beyond a shadow of a doubt this was who she was looking for. She sat next to the young woman, who looked at her and immediately started crying and took her into a tight embrace.

"You never told me where you lived! I was afraid I'd never find you," she spoke between sobs, obviously realizing Claire was her sister.

After a few moments, they ended their hug, and Claire looked at her little sister. "You should have known I'd find you."

I said this wasn't a love story, and perhaps it wasn't the type most people would think of, but on second thought, this was most definitely a love story.

Claire and Eunice flew to California and found their brother Christopher, who was more than a little disoriented since he had spent a decade and a half in that magical world of fae, fairy, and foe.

The three developed strong bonds that eventually included their older sister, Clementine, and her family. Claire became a grandmother several times over, Eunice got married and had two children of her own, and even Christopher found love, bringing a stepfamily into their tight bunch. No one ever mentioned the BISIE, and it still isn't clear if they even remembered it. But what is clear is that love always finds a way.

The End

ABOUT MELISSA E. BECKWITH

Melissa E. Beckwith is a science fiction and fantasy author living in southern Indiana with her husband, Shih Tzu, and two kitties. Her hobbies include spending time with her grandsons, painting, reading, yoga, camping, gardening, and making YouTube videos. She is a practicing pagan and an aspiring homesteader.

Find out more at: melissaebeckwith.com

tiktok.com/@melissaebeckwith
instagram.com/author_melissa_e_beckwith
facebook.com/AuthorMelissaEBeckwith
goodreads.com/melissaebeckwithfantasyauthor

SOUL TEA
BY L.R. BRADEN

Qadira cradled the warm metal cup between her age-spotted hands. She blew a ribbon of steam off the dull-brown drink, then pressed the rim to her lips and downed the contents. She grimaced, sucking a long hiss of breath between her teeth. The brew was stale and bitter, the last dregs of an old batch. She waited for the feeling of refreshment the tea should have brought but felt only the aches in her aging joints that meant a storm was on its way.

Perhaps my long journey is finally coming to an end.

Sighing, she tucked a wayward lock of gray hair behind her ear and set the hammered gold cup on the tray beside its counterpart—a golden teapot with a dark ruby set in its lid. She pushed to her feet with a groan, struggling to free herself from the deep cushions of her faded blue couch. The service rattled slightly as she lifted it in her shaky grip and carried it down the narrow wooden stairs that connected the upper apartment to the shop where she made her living. She placed the tray back in its glass display case between a diamond necklace and a set of antique, jewel-encrusted daggers. Then she flipped the sign in the window. *Jinn's Jewels* was open for business.

Tristan Mallory stroked the lapels of his gray pinstripe suit as he strolled down the shady sidewalk, relishing the smooth, soft fabric.

This is how a man should dress.

He glanced at the scuffed boots, baggy slacks, and worn jackets of the men he passed—outfits he might have worn a year ago before he found a more lucrative way of life.

Dumb shmucks, wasting away at a nine-to-five when there's an easier way. But it had only been his fall and subsequent desperation that had allowed him to make the final leap to his new life. It hadn't been an easy transition.

Tristan lifted his chin and quickened his pace as though he could outrun the memory of those times. He would never again be a have-not—not if he had any say in the matter.

Families with strollers and blankets dotted the wide grass lawn of Central Park. Stone tables with chessboard tops nestled under shading trellises bordering a cobblestone patio. Society's rejects stretched out on rough wooden benches, enjoying their time in the sun before the park's patrol came to shuffle them off. Vendors stood beside their carts. The smell of roasted hazelnuts, boiled hotdogs, and oversalted pretzels wafted on the breeze in a bracing combination. The scent tickled Tristan's nose. He coughed softly into his fist, noting a scratchy rawness at the back of his throat and a catch in his chest—lingering symptoms of a week-old cold.

He passed a group of people stretching on yoga mats under the shade of an old oak. Joggers bounced along the dirt trail that bordered the more dignified cinder path Tristan followed as he headed toward the distant sounds of midday traffic. He skirted a reflecting pool with a fountain circled by three dancing girls, their moment of whimsical play frozen in bronze, passed under a wrought iron arch, and stepped onto Fifth Avenue. Retracing his steps from the day before, he headed east for a few blocks, then turned left on Lexington.

If memory serves...

He spotted the shop he was looking for two blocks up—a rundown storefront sandwiched between a Chinese restaurant and a corner deli, with three stories of apartments stacked on top. The red awning above the door advertised *Jinn's Jewels: Old World Treasures* in bold white letters. The window display was filled with the type of dime-store junk designed to pull in tourists—blown glass vases, jewelry boxes, trays of old coins, glass-eyed dolls, and hand-painted china sets pawned off by unenthusiastic heirs. He'd passed the place yesterday and wouldn't have given it a second look except for the gilt and enamel clock on the bottom shelf with the ugly golden cherubs. That little beauty was worth five thousand, easy. And where there was one treasure, there might be more.

As he crossed the street, the scent of hot oil and fresh bread from the shop's neighbors grew stronger. He pushed through the front door, and a small brass bell clanged to life. He stepped onto a faded blue rug that covered the weathered wood directly in front of the cash register and looked around. The shop was a hoarder's paradise. Shelves piled with knickknacks three layers deep, and towering overhead pressed in around him. Blind corners, an outdated security system, an inventory nightmare... exactly the kind of place he loved to find. He rubbed his gloved hands together, wincing slightly at the chronic twinge in his wrist from years at a computer.

"Welcome, welcome." An elderly woman with wrinkled brown skin and graying hair shuffled out of the back of the store. "Can I help you find anything in particular?"

Tristan gave the shopkeeper a polite smile. "Just looking."

The woman looked him up and down and mirrored his smile. "There are many hidden treasures here. Let me know if anything catches your eye."

He watched the old woman take her post behind the cash register, then wandered down the center aisle. As he'd hoped, the timepiece wasn't the only "hidden treasure" in the shop. An etched sterling humidor, an enameled cigarette case, a framed limited-edition baseball card, and a collection of golden signet rings all showed promise.

Despite the libelous slurs of the tabloids following his misguided dabble with insider trading, Tristan had quite a nose for value. A few months of honing that skill and a strong desire to rise above his circumstances were all he'd needed, not only to get back on his feet after his world imploded but to outgrow the man he'd been. What would his bitch of an ex-wife say if she could see him now? Or the snot-nosed little prick who'd sacked him when his deal went south, and the lawsuits started rolling in?

He shook his head and straightened his shoulders. *To hell with them. I'm beyond all that now and much better off.*

Circling back to the front of the store, Tristan picked up a cheap silver ring and a small wooden puzzle box—both worthless—and headed for the register. He made a point of looking around. "Don't you have any help here, granny?"

Her smile showed a slight gap between her top front teeth. "I manage all right on my own."

As he passed the display case to the left of the register, his attention snagged on a hammered gold teapot with a ruby set in the lid. The shop seemed to vanish as an intense urge to hold the pot surged over him. He swayed on his feet. His fingers itched with the need to reach out.

"Are you all right, son?"

The shop snapped back into focus. Tristan jerked his attention to the woman behind the register. She was staring at him. Her brow was pinched with concern, but the way she leaned toward him seemed almost… eager.

He shook his head and took the last few steps to set his purchases on the counter. "Just a little dizzy. I missed lunch."

"Do you need something?" She pointed to the door at the back of the shop through which she'd emerged. "I have—"

"I'm fine."

The words came out too fast to be convincing, and the woman's frown grew.

To ease the sting of his response, he added, "Thanks for offering."

The woman pursed her lips but proceeded to ring up his purchases. *My days of groveling for handouts are over. I take what I want.*

He looked back at the display case. The teapot and its matching cup were nestled between an Asscher-cut diamond tennis necklace and a set of daggers with jewels set in their hilts that he hadn't even noticed before, focused as he'd been on the teapot. He wasn't sure where the overwhelming impulse to hold that teapot had come from, but the contents of the case would definitely be worth a few extra seconds to pop the lock when he came back.

"That's an interesting teapot." He hadn't meant to say the words out loud.

The woman followed his gaze. A secretive smile curved her lips. "Yes, it is." She went back to ringing up his items. "But I'm afraid that one's not for sale."

"Oh?" He frowned. "Why not?"

"I've grown quite attached to it, I'm afraid. It would take a special sort of person to claim it."

He placed a hand over his heart in mock injury. "Are you saying I'm not special?"

She looked him up and down like a stray dog eyeing a steak. "We'll see."

Tristan shifted his weight, disconcerted by the way the woman continued to examine him. *Creepy old bat.*

She ran his credit card and handed it back with his purchases. "Please, come again."

He took his bag and forced a smile. "I will."

After a few hours of research to familiarize himself with the old lady's security system, a leisurely dinner, and a quick stop to pick up his gear, Tristan hunkered down in a doorway across the street from *Jinn's Jewels*. He watched as the sign in the door was flipped to "closed," and the windows went dark. Worn boots, a tattered wool cap, and the stained overcoat that covered his fine silk suit and hid the black leather bag tucked against his abdomen effectively hid him from view. Experience had taught him that being homeless made him invisible. People didn't just not notice him, they actively avoided looking at him. Now that his state of dress was a costume and not his true existence, he found that fact extremely useful, but the ruse made his skin crawl. Even though the garments were clean and lacked the pungent stench of lived-in clothes, he couldn't wait to discard them, along with the memories that clung to them.

Once the Chinese restaurant closed for the night, foot traffic on the street all but vanished. The lights above the antique shop winked out one by one as the residents of the rooms above turned in for the night.

Tristan blew a cloud of breath into his wool mittens, tucked his hands under his armpits, and huddled lower in the meager shelter of the tanning salon he'd staked out, just as he had on dozens of nights before he'd found his true calling. Spring had come to the city late, and while the daytime temperatures were climbing, the nights were still cold enough to make him yearn for the silk sheets and down comforter of his penthouse apartment on the other side of town.

When the number of cars on the street dwindled, Tristan stood, shuffled to the other side of the road, and settled into the doorway of the shop he intended to rob. There he pulled his coat close around him and tucked his chin to his chest in a posture of sleep. The smells of oil and exhaust faded as the night claimed the street, and even the light traffic of the graveyard workers vanished. The air became so still that it was almost possible to imagine there weren't over a million people sharing the island with him.

When the sky was at its blackest, Tristan pushed the ragged cuff of his disguise up enough to check the time on his watch. Then he pulled two thin strips of metal from his pocket. The handful of stars bright enough to pierce the ambient glow of the sleeping city twinkled like diamonds above, watching in silent witness as he picked the lock with a skill born from long hours of practice.

There was a muffled *snick* of tumblers falling into place. He smiled.

With one last look at the deserted street, he turned the handle and slipped into the dark store.

Tristan paused for a moment on the worn rug in front of the cash register to gain his bearings. The warm glow of a distant streetlight filtered through the front window, outlining the shelves and their contents as dim silhouettes. Red lights flashed on the alarm box he'd spotted next to the door on his earlier visit, and he circled the checkout counter to reach it. The unit was as much of an antique as the trinkets sold in the shop. He had the system off in seconds.

Pulling out the black bag tucked between his costume coat and the silk suit hidden beneath, he headed for the display case at the end of the counter. There were enough treasures in the shop to make this one of his most lucrative heists yet, and that teapot he'd been drawn to earlier would be the pièce de résistance.

The back of the display cabinet was locked, but a few twists with his picks swung the small door wide. He grabbed the jeweled daggers first, sliding them one at a time into the bag. Next went the diamond necklace. Then his wool-gloved fingers wrapped around the handle of the golden teapot.

An electric jolt shot through his body. He flinched at the sensation and started to pull away, then tightened his grip as his earlier, inexplicable need to claim the teapot returned. He pulled it out and turned it over in his hands, inspecting it from every angle.

Hello, baby. What makes you so special?

He rubbed one thumb over a smudge that marred the reflective golden surface.

White light flared around him. He dropped his sack with a clatter and took a stumbling step back, but he kept his grip on the teapot. He reached for the counter to steady himself.

His hand met only empty space.

The light that had blinded him faded to a dim glow that came from everywhere and nowhere. Bluish-gray clouds swirled around him, above him. He looked down. The floor was gone.

His gut clenched. His heart pounded in his ears as adrenaline surged through him. Clutching the golden teapot to his chest like a talisman against the insanity surrounding him, Tristan scrunched his eyes closed and shook his head.

Nope. Not happening. It's some kind of trick. Or maybe I'm having a mental breakdown, but I am one hundred percent definitely not floating above a big, swirling—

"Tristan Mallory."

He jumped and snapped his eyes open.

The billowing smoke before him coalesced into a woman with mahogany skin, amber eyes, and charcoal black hair that fell to her waist. Strips of translucent fabric draped her body, gathered at her waist under a belt of shimmering gold scales dotted with blood-red gemstones. She wore no shoes, but fine golden chains circled her ankles. Matching chains decorated her wrists and were woven through her dark hair. She was the most beautiful woman Tristan had ever laid eyes on.

"I offer you that which you desire." The woman's voice filled the ethereal space like a church choir—a harmony of too many notes to have come from a single person.

Tristan opened and closed his mouth a few times, searching for words as his thoughts skittered just out of reach. Eventually, he came up with, "Who are you?"

The woman placed her fingertips against her chest. "I am a jinn."

He frowned. "A what?"

"You may be more familiar with the term genie."

His eyes widened. He looked down at the teapot clutched against his chest as his brain finally clicked into gear. "So... you grant wishes?"

She held up one hand with her thumb and index finger folded down. "Three wishes to remake the world however you choose." She lowered her hand. "But I warn you to think carefully before making your choice. Once asked, a wish cannot be undone."

"Can I wish for more wishes?"

"No."

"Why not?"

She arched one dark eyebrow. "Because you can't."

Tristan took a deep breath and paced across the smoky expanse, but the space around him remained disturbingly constant, giving the illusion he was walking in place. The jinn also remained in the same relative position, though she didn't seem to move. He turned and walked in the opposite direction, which had the same effect. He chewed the inside of his lower lip and looked down at the teapot cradled in his hands.

The power to remake the world however I want. To never again have my life dictated by the whims of others. To never have to go without. A giddy laugh bubbled up in his throat.

"I want unlimited wealth."

"That is your first wish?"

He nodded.

"Are you certain?" An odd expression crossed her face as though she wanted to say something more but held herself in check.

Tristan frowned. *Why is she hesitating? Is there something wrong with my wish?*

He turned his request over in his mind, looking for flaws.

The woman waited with the patience of a statue.

He cleared his throat. "I wish to have unlimited, instantly accessible wealth, regardless of changes in currency, location, or any other factors, for as long as I live."

She closed her eyes and nodded.

When she looked at him again, her eyes glowed with an opalescent sheen. "Granted."

"I also wish to live forever at the peak of physical health."

Again, she nodded. "Granted."

He stretched one hand out in front of him and flexed his fingers. The chronic carpal tunnel he'd developed from years at a keyboard ached in his wrist. He took a deep breath and felt a phlegmy catch in his chest.

"I said 'peak physical health.' As in young, in shape, and never sick. I feel exactly the same as I did a second ago, and that sure as shit isn't peak physical health."

"The effects of your wishes will only be felt once all three are granted, thereby defining the parameters of the world you will reenter."

"Reenter? Wait, you mean I'm stuck here in this"—he waved a hand—"whatever this is until I make my final wish?"

She nodded.

"What if I want to save my last wish for later?"

"You may take as long as you like to consider—there is no time in this place—but you cannot leave until all three wishes are made."

"Well, there's some fine print for you. Why didn't you mention that earlier?"

"You didn't ask."

"Anything else I should know about?"

She shrugged. "That's up to you."

Tristan gritted his teeth. *All the power in the universe, and I still get tripped up by a stupid oversight... just like with that damned investment that sank my career even though I thought I had all my t's crossed and i's dotted. One missing piece of information, and it all turns to shit.*

His breath caught, and his eyebrows lifted as a thought struck him. A smile curved his lips. "Okay then, final wish. I wish to know *everything.*"

A shadow passed over the jinn's features, casting them in sorrow, but when she opened her mouth, the multi-layered song of her voice said only, "Granted."

The strange in-between place dissolved around them. Tristan's feet rested not on gray smoke or the worn wooden floorboards of the antique shop but on glossy white tiles. The walls were painted pale blue. The ceiling was a grid of yellowed office panels. A hospital bed with plastic rails and padded restraints was the only furniture in the room.

Tristan backed away from the bed, twisting to glare at the ethereal woman who seemed entirely out of place in that setting. "Where are we?"

The answer popped into his head before the question left his lips. He was in a psychiatric hospital. The best money could buy.

Panicked confusion flooded him for a moment, but his location wasn't the only thing he learned. A mathematical formula that would redefine how humans understood physics; the atomic weight of an element that wouldn't be discovered for hundreds of years; the capital city of the third planet in the Xirchonari Alliance in the Andromeda galaxy, and schematics for an engine that could reach it in seven years all flooded his mind, followed by a stream of memories from a past that never happened —a past in which he'd patented inventions that changed civilization and became the single most brilliant, and wealthy, man in the world.

Three wishes to remake the world. He took a deep breath and stretched his arms wide without a single twinge of discomfort. The rattle in his chest was gone. *A new past, a new life, with unlimited wealth, health, and knowledge.*

He grinned. This was it... his golden ticket. He was finally getting everything he wanted, everything he deserved. With the information rushing into his head, he could corner the market in every industry, answer every philosophical debate, dictate the course of human history. Governments would bow to his whims in exchange for what he could give them. He had all the power. And thanks to his first two wishes, he'd have all of eternity to enjoy his success in perfect health and happiness.

But why bring me to a hospital?

He glanced again at the hospital bed, then back to the woman who'd rewritten reality. She watched, impassive and impartial, as visions of his newly minted past marched toward his present. He tried to filter his thoughts, to focus on events that would explain his current surroundings, but the flood of information was growing stronger, pulling him along in its current.

He knew the amount of rain that fell on the plains of Mongolia in

1832; the population of a nameless village on the western border of Ghana that was wiped out by polio, except for a little girl named Lahari who walked three days to find help and thus spread the disease; all 7,462 possible hands in five-card poker and the odds of getting each one…

A throbbing ache built behind Tristan's eyes. He clutched his temples.

A little boy in France was crying over a skinned knee after denting the front rim of his bike on a rock he hadn't seen. A middle-aged woman in Uruguay hung laundry on her balcony railing while chatting with her neighbor in Spanish—a language Tristan had never bothered to study but now seemed to know fluently. A fly buzzing around the lid of an outhouse toilet at a trailhead in Colorado flapped its wings two hundred times in the second before Tristan's focus shifted away….

He dropped to his knees, fingers digging into the sides of his skull. He looked up. The opalescent sheen faded from the jinn's eyes. She met his gaze with rich amber.

"What… did you…" His voice trailed off as his jaw locked shut in pain, but he needn't have bothered asking. The answer was there, in his mind.

A human brain—his brain—couldn't hold all the knowledge in the universe without being overloaded. Even if it could, there was an infinite amount of new information to be processed every second. Every thought, every sound, every action, every birth, death, choice, and every possible consequence of every choice not made. He had it all, and it was ripping his mind apart.

This isn't right. He tore at his hair and tried to speak the words out loud, but he couldn't seem to remember how to make the right sounds. *I asked for perfect health.*

This isn't an illness, his thoughts supplied. *There is no disease. No infection. No damage. You simply cannot function while your brain is being kept so busy with the flow of information running through it.*

A strangled cry tore from his throat, and he fell forward onto the cold tiles. His muscles went slack as control of his motor functions was buried under layer after layer of facts.

The door behind the jinn opened. Two men in white scrubs stepped through.

"Hello, how'd you get down there?" asked a wide, bald man with a friendly smile. Neither man seemed to notice the jinn, and when the orderly moved toward Tristan, he stepped right through her.

Tristan tried to speak, but an airy grunt was all he could manage.

The second man remained near the door. His blue eyes darted back and forth behind thick glasses as he read over Tristan's file on the tablet he held. And, of course, Tristan knew exactly what was on that screen.

Sudden collapse… full mental breakdown… catatonic state…

Every test had been run. Every specialist consulted. Money was no object, but no one had been able to explain his symptoms. His brain seemed to be working properly. In fact, it was extremely active. He just wouldn't respond to outside stimuli.

The large orderly rolled Tristan onto his back and lifted him to the bed.

Tristan tried to thrash, but his limbs didn't respond. He tried to scream, but his words had been stolen. He watched the scene unfolding around him as though it was playing out on one of a thousand monitors he couldn't look away from.

The bedsprings creaked under his weight.

The man by the door reached the end of Tristan's file and whistled softly. "Other than being a vegetable, this guy is in perfect health. Like, textbook perfect."

"Lucky guy." The orderly tightened the bed restraints around Tristan's wrists, patted him on the cheek, and turned away. "How 'bout Ramon's for lunch?"

"Eh. I was thinking Mexican."

The door to Tristan's prison swung closed. The voices of his captors faded as they weighed the pros and cons of pasta versus burritos.

Tristan's heart pounded a steady rhythm, his chest rose and fell, but none of his other muscles would respond. He felt as though he could run forever and not get winded if he could just get out of the damned bed.

Maybe I can find a way to sort the thoughts, to access only what I need. If I can regain even minimal speech functions, I can turn this around, build a repository to partition my consciousness. I can fix myself. The knowledge is all in my head.

But even as the first seeds of his plan began to germinate, they were squashed by the sheer weight of other ideas pressing in on him from all sides. His focus scattered. The solution to his problem was blown to the far corners of his mind and blocked off by the new information pouring in. If this kept up, he'd lose any concept of what was happening, who he was. He'd be adrift in an ocean of disconnected information, impotent against its currents. And because of his first two wishes... that tetherless existence would have no end.

His gaze locked on the beautiful woman no one else had been able to see. He glared for all he was worth. *You tricked me.*

She shook her head. "I merely granted the wish. The choice was yours." Then she evaporated like steam blown off a mug of hot tea.

As her words pierced the chaos of his mind, another piece of information clicked into place—the truth of what had happened to him. The jinn hadn't altered reality to his wishes. She'd removed him from reality altogether, ripping his soul from his body to become the sustenance on which she survived. His fate had been sealed with the first wish he made. That's why she'd made him ask three times—to give him a chance to back out—but the greed that had drawn him to the pot in the first place had won, as it usually did. In all the times she'd performed this ritual, only once had a person chosen not to make a wish.

The faces of the jinn's other victims flashed through his mind, stretching back centuries—souls held in limbo for the length of their stolen lives. But the others had been content in their prisons, believing they were living out their wishes in the real world. Tristan knew better. The "wishes" the jinn granted were just window dressing to hide the truth. Even if he could find a way to free his mind from the bombardment of thoughts he now suffered, he'd still be trapped in an endless dream; his consciousness held separate from the passage of time for what would feel like eternity. He was helpless in both the real world and his fantasy, and because of his final wish, he was fully aware of both.

With that, the last shreds of coherent thought slipped free of his grasp. There was only the endless parade of silent knowledge as he railed in the background of his mind.

Settling back into her physical body, Qadira knelt beside the would-be-burglar and peeled his fingers away from the golden teapot. The man's eyes stared skyward, unblinking. His skin took on a grayish tint. What she knelt beside now was no more than an empty shell, its precious contents transferred and kept safe in a more practical container. Her joints ached as she straightened, and she sighed, remembering the ease with which she had moved in that other, incorporeal place. Circling the fallen man, she wrapped the pot in a black cloth and tucked it away beneath the checkout counter. Then she pulled out her cell phone, called the police, and settled on a tall metal stool to wait. Five minutes later, red and blue lights flashed through the store's front window. Quadira went out to meet them.

The uniformed young woman who followed her back into the shop stared down at the dead man. She stood with her hands on her hips and pursed her lips. "You say you called because you heard the bell on the front door?"

Qadira nodded and wrung her hands in feigned agitation. "I assumed it was a burglar, but do you suppose it was just some homeless man looking to get warm?"

"Vagrants don't usually know how to pick locks or disarm security alarms." The officer tilted her head and frowned. She knelt beside the corpse and used a pen to lift the cuff of his grimy coat enough to reveal a shiny gold watch. "Or wear Jaeger-LeCoultre watches." Snapping on a pair of white gloves, she reached into each of his coat pockets and came up empty. Then she opened the coat to reveal a well-tailored suit. A quick search of *those* pockets revealed a wallet with ID.

"Tristan Mallory. He lives on the Upper West Side." She glanced at Qadira. "Ring any bells?"

Qadira shook her head. "But now that I see him in a clean suit, he does resemble a young man who visited the shop earlier today."

"Might've been casing the place." The officer sighed and straightened. "We'll need the M.E. to confirm cause of death, but since there are no obvious wounds and you say you found him on the floor like this, I'm guessing heart attack." She shook her head. "Talk about instant karma."

Qadira frowned at the dead man. "He must've made some pretty bad choices to end up like this."

It took three hours for the crime scene investigators to confirm myocardial infarction as the cause of death and clear the scene. Since nothing was missing, they assumed the man had been working alone and had died shortly after disabling the alarm. "Open and shut."

Qadira settled on her faded blue couch and tucked a woolly red blanket around her legs. Golden light poured through the window as the rosy dawn turned the mirrored glass of the city into pillars of fire. Leaning forward, she lifted the handle of the golden teapot and tipped its contents into the matching cup. Bright opalescence swirled in the bowl. She wrapped both hands around the hammered metal and blew steam off the pearly surface. She inhaled, savoring the sweet aroma of vitality and untapped potential.

She lifted the cup in salute. "To your very long life."

When the liquid touched her tongue, it sent a zing of energy cascading through her body. The slight tremor in her hands stilled. When she opened her eyes, the milky patches in her vision were gone. She breathed deep and exhaled slowly without a hitch or cough. The aches in her joints eased, and her wrinkled skin pulled tight.

The tea left a slightly sour aftertaste at the back of her throat. Not as pleasant as the mellow flavor brewed from contented ignorance, but unavoidable given the circumstances—and it still carried the sweet tang of greed on which she thrived. She tucked a strand of glossy black hair behind her ear and set the empty cup beside the teapot. She would spend the day packing up the shop. She had most of a life left to live before the call of her curse drew another greedy soul to her door. She intended to make the most of it.

L.R. Braden is the bestselling author of the Magicsmith urban fantasy series, the standalone novel Demon Riding Shotgun, and several works of short fiction. Her writing has won the Eric Hoffer Book Award for Sci-fi/Fantasy, the First Horizon Award for debut authors, and the Imadjinn Award for Best Urban Fantasy Novel. She was also honored to be a finalist for the Rocky Mountain Fiction Writers 2021 Writer of the Year award. She and her family live in the foothills of the Colorado Rockies, where she spends her time writing, playing, enjoying the outdoors, and weaving metal into intricate chainmail jewelry that she sells in her Etsy shop, WimsiDesign.

Find out more at: lrbraden.com

instagram.com/laurenrbraden
facebook.com/LRBraden
twitter.com/LaurenRBraden
goodreads.com/lrbraden

ESCAPE: A METAFICTION FANTASY ADVENTURE

BY S. R. BREAKER

Reading is an excellent escape from reality.
But what if... you couldn't escape from your escape?

CHAPTER ONE - ONE WISH

"Do you want to hear the story or not?"

Breathless, Cash turned, giving the arguably tacky, medieval barmaid outfit I had on a wary look up and down through narrowed eyes. "Does it explain the wench look?"

Running along the sandy shore of a tropical island was probably the last place I looked to belong right then. I waved impatiently, pulling the damn neckline up as much as I could while trying to keep up. "Of course."

Cash rolled his eyes, mostly in resignation, possibly also in incredulity.

Not that I could blame him. I had accidentally dragged him into this world.

I had only met Cash yesterday, or technically, three stories ago. He didn't really know me.

He wouldn't have known that my standard outfits for the day were sweatpants and the ratty, too-large college sweater I could never be bothered to replace, that I preferred the company of fictional characters to real people and that most of my time outside classes was spent binge-reading at the library.

Incidentally, that's where I'd met him.

Everyone knew libraries were supposed to transport you to the plethora of wild and vast imaginative worlds—you know, in your mind.

But how was I supposed to know the quietest area in the back of the University library, by the dusty, rare, and old books section that nobody ever wandered to, had the powers to actually take you there?

"You made a wish?" Cash repeated as I relayed my tale of woe.

I nodded, picking up the hem of my skirt as I splashed over a puddle in the sand. "I think I finally figured it out from the last place. I told you I'm a literary major, right?" I began. "I was really getting into this fantastic book about medieval Scotland," I gushed, eyes wide, no longer caring that I was splashing salt water everywhere. "And...all I said was 'I wish these stories are real'—"

I paused to take a deep breath, and the rest of my words rushed out of my mouth. "Which was obviously a *huge* mistake because *everyone knows* you should *never* make wishes. It's way too easy to blur the line between wishes and curses. You should never mess with either! You'd know this if you read Aladdin or definitely 'The Three Wishes.' I mean, come on, the written word is a powerful thing, let alone the spoken word. Really, poems are like spells. Literature is magic in itself."

Cash shook his head, not turning back. "Okay. Wow."

I smiled, somewhat proud of my analysis. "Amazing, huh?"

But he blew out a breath. "You *are* a nutcase. How could I not have seen it sooner?"

I gave him a suffering look. *Nice.* The guy had probably never cracked a book open in his entire life. I had seen him around campus before, but all I knew about Cash was that he played lacrosse, and he wore plaid shirts—a lot.

He glanced behind us and finally slowed down. "I think that monster is gone." He shook his shaggy, wet blond hair out of his face and frowned in distaste at his drenched clothes.

"So, I just escaped a bloodthirsty kelpie from a tavern in 1743 Scotland." I gestured up and down him. "I don't know what the hell happened to you."

He glared at me. "I woke up almost getting swallowed by the ocean before you, and that thing appeared."

"Ooh." I curled my lips in the semblance of an apology. I surveyed our surroundings and motioned inland toward the treeline. "Maybe there's shelter this way."

But Cash's expression soured as he towered over me. "So, this *is* all your fault. You got me into this mess. You almost drowned me just now on the beach—"

"Hey, man," I argued, putting my hands up. "Nobody else was supposed to be in the rare books section. I didn't even know you were there. Let alone that the library was magic. No wonder those librarians always knew so much. I guess that's what the 'Restricted Area' sign was for."

"The sign *you* also ignored?"

I rolled my eyes in exasperation and waded my way through the long grass. The sky had darkened, and the moon was blocked with what few clouds there were. The crashing of waves against the shore was muted now. "Look, the point is at least I'll know what to expect now, right? So, as long as you're with me, you'll be safe," I reassured.

"Would have been more helpful if you'd figured that out before that grimy, angry mob chased us from before," he put in.

I rolled my eyes again.

He caught my elbow. "Hey, wish us back right the hell now!"

I shot him an irritated grimace and shrugged him off. "I've tried already. It didn't work." I spun around to forge ahead.

"Uh...Astrid?"

"Look, if you're going to—" I broke off my groan of complaint as I followed his gaze up to the sky and squinted. "What's...that?"

"I thought you were supposed to know," Cash said, backing away.

"Well, I know it's not Superman," I quipped, my mouth dropping open in dread.

A bright thing in the sky sped toward the beach, accompanied by a low rumbling that became louder as it got closer, and closer, and closer…

"It's uh…it's…" I blinked, backing up myself.

"Uh, I think we'd better—," Cash started, getting ready to run again. "Yeah."

We took off once more, heading deeper into the forest.

I glanced back to see if we had run far enough in time to see the big, red thing slam into what must have been the neighboring shore-line, and it exploded with a roar. I winced and paused from running to watch the giant tidal wave of sand, earth, and trees.

"Oh, my god, what the hell was that?"

Cash looked past my shoulder, and his eyes widened. "I don't know, but here comes another one!"

I saw it, yelped, and bolted again, snagging my arm as I ran past a tree branch, "Ow!" but I ignored it and kept running. The loud rumbling grew and grew. My legs were lead, and my lungs burned.

Searing heat almost burned the frizzy hairs sticking up the top of my head as the fireball zoomed past us, and Cash and I dropped to the ground.

Cash shot me a look. "What the hell were you reading? Armageddon?" he mocked before we covered our heads with our arms, and just in time, since the ball of fire exploded in the forest up ahead, the shockwave reverberated through the trees around us.

Branches and debris rained down.

After a few minutes, it was all quiet again.

I opened my eyes.

Cash looked up. "Is it over?"

Panting, I surveyed the sky as I sat up myself. "Yeah, I think there were just two of them."

He let out an aggravated cry, collapsing back on the ground. "For god's sake, and I thought lacrosse practice was exhausting."

Two meteors... An inkling of thought occurred to me, and I dropped my gaze. But no. It couldn't possibly be.

"*Grribit...*"

"What?" I asked.

"What—I didn't say anything," Cash replied.

"*Ribbit...*"

I frowned, looked around, and all of a sudden, about a thousand frogs leaped out from the bushes.

I let out a laugh as they all hippity-hopped about.

"Gross!" Cash cringed, trying to avoid touching them. "What is this from? 'The Ten Commandments?'"

"Those were locusts," I pointed out.

"Whatever."

An angry, loud croak made Cash jump.

I laughed again. "Don't sit on them." I pushed to stand and held out my hand to help Cash up. "Look, let's just keep moving." I beckoned for him to follow me, glancing up to try to get some bearings, but I could no longer see through the trees.

I picked my way through the weeds and vines on the ground. "Which book do you suppose we're in now?" I asked, still trying to focus on my footing.

He didn't reply.

"Cash?" I turned to look.

He was gone.

CHAPTER TWO - MAGICAL

"Oh—what?" I groaned aloud and tried to peer back through the woods to see if he had lagged behind. I didn't know whether I should go back and look for him or not. It wasn't like he was my responsibility.

Or okay. Maybe he was.

I groaned again and started to head back anyway. "Cash!" I called out. "Caaaash! Where are you? Cash, you'd better not be trying to scare me like this."

The shadowy forest was giving me The Blair Witch Project vibes. "Cash!" I pushed through some vines and branches again. "This is so not good for—whoops—" I almost fell off balance.

I straightened up and checked to see what had caused my almost fall.

The large hole in the ground, like an animal trap, must have been previously camouflaged by the leaves on the ground.

I peeked into it. "Cash!"

My voice echoed several times. *Whoa, that is one deep hole.*

"Cash! Tell me you're not in that hole," I called again, starting to pace back and forth on the damp ground. What was I supposed to do now? I moaned in frustration.

"Oh, for—" I threw up my hands before unceremoniously jumping in.

"Aaaaahhh—!"

The hole was super deep and super dark. I lost track because I was screaming for so long. *This is ridiculous.* I stopped screaming, sighed, and crossed my arms over my chest. "Jeez, when does this end?" I mused aloud, all the while the wind rushed past me, blowing my hair around. "What is this, Alice's rabbit hole? I wasn't reading Lewis Carroll."

I kept falling.

And falling.

When my legs finally gave way, I landed on my rump on the ground. "Oof—ow!"

I squinted from the light and shielded my eyes from the sun before spotting Cash unconscious on the ground a few feet away. I crept up beside him and shook his shoulder to wake him up. "Hey, hey, Cash."

A clump of grass by his arm caught my eye. In fact, all the grass and leaves on the trees and plants were—

"Blue," I whispered, straightening up.

To the right, a castle stood with flags and banners getting whipped in the wind while two suns lit up the sky. To the left, in complete contrast, was a blackened sky with no moon or even any stars.

"Hey, hey, you," a voice called from behind us.

At that moment, Cash woke up with a groan. He blinked, saw the sky, blinked again—twice—then sat up with a start.

I followed his gaze. The sky was cut jagged down the middle. I smiled in wonder.

"Where are we?" Cash asked, looking mystified.

I turned to face the girl who had spoken behind us.

"This is 'The Great Divide'," she and I both replied at the same time.

The girl with mysterious blue eyes smiled back. "Hello, Astrid."

<hr>

"Oh my god, this is amazing," I couldn't help but breathe.

"Ow!" Cash hissed.

Freya shot him a steady look. "Sorry," she spoke flatly as she checked the bruise on his head. "The Serendipity said you'd be coming." Her statement was directed at me.

My chuckle was wry. "Yeah, she knows everything, doesn't she?"

Lightning flashed, and thunder rumbled once—pointedly.

I bit my lip, muffling my laughter. "Sorry!" I called out loud.

Freya looked up at the sky. "That old willow." She rolled her eyes as she tended to Cash's head.

Cash was studying my expression. He could already smell something fishy. "What exactly is going on here now?"

"Uh…well." I cracked a sly grin. "See, when I was at the library yesterday, aside from medieval Scottish literature, I had also brought along my old writing journal. It's for ideas," I relayed with a sheepish nod. "I write poetry sometimes, short stories. And somehow…" I gestured around us. "I think we're in one of my unfinished uh…scribblings."

Cash's jaw dropped.

I put my hands up again. "Hey, I wouldn't believe me either, but this is literally the Harry Potter fanfic I wrote when I was thirteen." I stopped again and smacked my hand on my forehead. "Apocalyptica."

"What?" He looked up.

"Apocalyptica," I repeated. "Those things before. In that story, I'd invented a natural disaster called 'twin meteorites'," I explained before pausing. "But they were never supposed to hit the ground."

"Oh my god," Cash groaned. "What else kind of catastrophes did you make up?"

"Nothing!" I exclaimed in my defense. "That was the only one."

"What about the frogs?"

I snapped my fingers. "Oh, those were probably from 'Romancing the Frog.'"

"Romancing the what?" Cash sputtered out.

I sighed heavily. "Yes, yes, I write romance too. It's hilarious."

He choked down his laughter. "Sorry." He pursed his lips. "Sorry," he said and burst out laughing again.

"Whatever," I taunted as Freya finished up with him and walked over to me. "You'd better hope we don't run into my fire-breathing dragon. I'd totally sick her on you."

We were camped under a blue tree, right smack in the middle of the Neutral—what I'd called the middle part of 'The Great Divide.'

I had created a world that was literally split down the middle, where the good creatures lived on the light side, the bad creatures lived on the dark side, and the ever-shifting borderland between the two sides was where a human girl had been stranded.

Freya.

I sat up before she could examine me. "I'm fine."

She gave me such a sharp look I thought it could actually cut.

"Oh, all right." I gave in and showed her my arm. It was bleeding from when I snagged it on a tree a while ago.

Freya cleaned the wound. "You need stitches."

I bit my lip, wincing at the pain, but shut up about it. "Are Luna and Draco still here?"

"Of course." She gave me an even look. "You never finished the story, remember?"

I gave her another sheepish grin. "Yeah, sorry about that."

She finished with my arm quite quickly. "I should have a look at your head too."

"My what?"

"Your head," she repeated. "You hurt it running from the mob in the English hamlet a few stories back. It was temporarily camouflaged, but the injury is back now."

Self-satisfied, I shot her authoritative tone a look. "I always knew you would be a compelling character."

Freya shot me another mysterious look but said nothing. Her hand hovered over the back of my head. I hissed at the momentary little sting of pain.

Cash was watching the two of us, another incredulous expression on his face. "Well, you two seem awfully at home here," he huffed. "Meanwhile, can we at least find some new clothes? I'm still all wet, and you're..." His gaze darted down to my chest like he couldn't help it.

Eyes wide, I flushed deep red and spun away. "It's not like I chose this outfit. It was the lady barkeep from—"

"A-hem." Freya cleared her throat. "Worry about that later. The Serendipity should be ready to see you now."

"What's that? Some kind of doctor?" Cash brushed his jeans off as he stood.

Freya shot him a dull look and looked over at me. "Why don't you update your friend," she suggested. "I've already given the grand tour once. It's your turn."

"If you say so." I shrugged as the two of us followed Freya to walk through the woods.

Cash fell into step beside me, but he was watching warily as Freya would pause every so often as if to get her bearings, as though she was sniffing her way through the forest. "Okay," he whispered to me. "She's freaking me out."

"She's supposed to," I told him. "She's been here too long."

"She's a bossy know-it-all," he remarked under his breath.

"Problem, Cash?" Freya asked loudly, not turning back to us.

"Oh, I forgot," I added. "She hears everything too."

Cash made a face at me before asking, "So, who *is* this Serendipity character?"

"She's a big willow tree that used to be the kingdom's adviser," I relayed. "Now she's still a great seer and the voice of knowledge in this world, but she's sort of...rooted."

"I didn't know that." Freya glanced back just then. "She used to be the adviser?"

"Oh...yeah, I hadn't written that down yet," I recalled.

We arrived at a crossroads with a tall signpost. Several wooden arrows were nailed onto it, giving different directions.

"Hey, check it out." I approached the signpost with a grin and pointed to one wooden arrow where my name 'Astrid' was carved right on it, and wherever I moved, its pointer arrow swung around, moving to follow me. "Cool, huh?"

Cash gave me a look of disbelief. "Are you actually enjoying this?"

"What?" I threw up my hands. He just didn't understand. To be able to see and touch things that I'd only imagined in my head? It was brilliant!

I stuck my tongue out at him. "You're such a stick in the mud. I don't even know why you had to come along on my wish anyway."

"Hey, we should get a move on," Freya beckoned us, her eyes warily surveilling the sky.

The arched doorway in the clearing up ahead was made of big, mossy stone and not connected to anything. It stood in the middle of the path as though it simply took one straight through to the other side. I studied the textures of the doorway in delight, running my fingers past the slippery blue moss.

Freya held the gadget in her hand toward the door and waited for two beeps. "All clear." She motioned us in first.

I pulled Cash over to walk through the doorway.

He resisted. "Hey, where does that go exactly?"

"Would you just trust me, please?" I coaxed, tugging him forward.

CHAPTER THREE - SERENDIPITY

We passed through the doorway and were instantly transported to a completely different part of the forest. The mist from a lagoon of calm purple water warmed the air. We were surrounded by giant cedar and willow trees whose low-hanging vines swayed in the light breeze.

I looked back as Freya seemed to appear out of nowhere.

"You'll have to excuse the Serendipity today," Freya began as we approached the biggest willow tree. "She's…kind of grumpy."

"Are we on the Nightlands?" I asked, slightly wide-eyed.

Freya pointed up to the sky.

New moon. It meant The Serendipity was fully on the dark side of 'The Great Divide.' That was as ominous as things went around here.

"So where is this great serendipitous thing, or person, or whatever it is anyway?" Cash drawled, stepping back in ridicule.

The ground directly beneath us shook violently. I held my arms out to maintain my balance.

"Whoa." Cash bent his knees to keep steady. "Is that an earthquake?"

"Oh great, here we go," Freya muttered.

A large root from the base of the big willow tree lifted and wound around Cash's leg to pick him up right off the ground.

"Whoa!" he cried as the tree lifted him up off the ground, upside-down, and shook him a little.

A gnarled face appeared at the center of the trunk of the willow tree.

Cash yelped. "What the—?"

"Your friend has a problem, Astrid," the Serendipity said in the voice of a creaky old woman before it unceremoniously dropped Cash back down on the ground.

"Ow!" Cash landed in a heap.

I stifled my laughter.

"*I* am the Serendipity," the willow tree then started. "So sorry to have kept you waiting."

Cash shifted awkwardly to sit up, groaning before he muttered, "De nada."

"Are you okay?" I asked, biting my lip to keep from laughing again as I came over to help him up.

Cash shot me a dark look.

"Astrid," the Serendipity boomed.

"Whoa—what?" I snapped to attention, whirling around.

"Why have you not finished the story?" the tree demanded. "Your heroes are stuck in the kingdom being trained by a moron, and The Great Divide continues its collapse until you finish writing this story."

"I know, I know!" I wrinkled my nose at its reproach. "It's just—I'm busy with school and stuff."

The Serendipity raised a worn, wooden, knowing eyebrow at me. "And yet, you have time for this, what is it called—Face…book?"

I colored. "What?" I gave it an innocent look. "I can do what I want with my time," I replied defensively. "Look, would you just please tell me how we can get out of here?"

The tree shot me a scrutinizing look, pausing before it spoke again. "The story has to run its course," it said. "You cannot skip pages. You, of all people, should know that, Astrid."

I frowned, looking around at a loss. "So…how long does the story run?"

Cash was listening intently. Freya was filing her nails.

"You tell me, Astrid." The Serendipity shrugged with all of its branches, and the ground tremored again.

"Willow!" Freya scolded. "Stop moving the ground."

My jaw dropped in skepticism of the tree's reply. "Me? I don't know!"

"Then how am *I* to know?" The Serendipity countered.

Cash looked more frustrated. "Wait. I thought you were supposed to know everything?"

"I know many things," the tree answered. "But it is the creator who knows everything." The tree face looked straight at me and, in a vague, ominous sort of tone, said, "Only you can get yourself out, Astrid."

After a moment, the face on the tree began to fade and disappear until it eventually receded back beneath the wrinkled bark of the thick tree trunk.

"Great, now what the hell was that supposed to mean?" I threw up my hands, turning to Cash and Freya.

Freya's shoulders lifted briefly.

"Well, this was a stupid waste of time," Cash said with an annoyed sigh.

The ground trembled again, and Cash jumped. "Okay, all right, I'm sorry!" he yelled, raising his hands in defeat. "Jeez, I can't believe I'm apologizing to a tree!" He stalked off.

Freya met my gaze, and we both rolled our eyes.

I walked around the little lagoon. "This world is just incredible...." I looked up as a flock of silver birds flew by, interrupting the quiet with the flapping of their wings. A silver feather floated down to the ground, and I picked it up. "Awesome," I breathed, studying it. It glowed in my hand.

Freya watched all this, amused. "You want to stay here," she spoke in wonder as if she had read my mind. "Your wish. It was to leave the real world and come here. Why?"

"Oh, come on, real life is so boring," I explained. "Can you even imagine? There's no adventure there. No mystery. No excitement." I approached the tree trunk to examine its rough texture. "Plus, this place has everything!"

"Then why did you ask the Serendipity how to leave?" Freya's eyebrows rose in question.

I gave her a look. "For Cash! *He* desperately wants to leave here."

"But you both don't belong here. You know that," she pointed out.

"I know that," I replied with a slight annoyance.

"And it's not like you're immortal in this world," she rationalized, pointing to my arm. "At some point, you might actually come into some real danger. I mean, if I had a choice, do you think I would choose to be stuck here?"

I made a face, guilt gnawing in the back of my head. Freya's words felt heavy. She was totally killing my buzz.

But this was my greatest dream come true. How often was one able to actually live through adventures in her books? I was planning to even go back to medieval Scotland next. Especially since I wouldn't be caught off-guard by kelpies and events again because I already knew what would happen.

I shook off Freya's warnings and glanced around. Cash was nowhere in sight again. "Where did Cash go now?" I sighed tiredly.

Just then, a figure came out from the shadows.

Freya reacted quickly, pulling out her gadget as four green warthog trolls came out. One of them had Cash in a chokehold. Two other trolls were holding big, spiky batons and swinging them around.

Then the largest one of the trolls stepped forward.

I gasped. *Kreed.*

I had almost forgotten about the villain. I had modeled him after Mario Brothers' King Koopa, with a mix of the features of a warthog and green lizard-like scales all over.

I swallowed hard, making a face, my heart pounding in my chest in full dread. Seeing him now, he looked even more disgusting and feral than I would have imagined. Not to mention the acrid smell. Everything about him was so vivid.

"I think you'll want to put that away, Miss Freya." Kreed's grin was sly.

Freya shot him a distasteful look even as she had no choice but to lower her weapon. "What do you want now, Kreed?"

Kreed held up his index finger and slowly pointed it directly at me. "Just her—"

"No—" I stepped back as one of the warthog trolls approached me.

"—or the boy dies," Kreed finished with the most casual of tones.

Cash's eyes widened, and he struggled against the troll that was holding him, his protests muffled as he choked.

"Kreed, let them go," Freya ordered. "You don't need them. They're not important."

"Are you offering something else in exchange then?" Kreed asked with a catch in his voice.

Freya opened her mouth to reply.

"No, Freya," I cut in, then looked up at Kreed. "I'll go," I said with a short nod.

"I knew we should have left the Nightlands way faster," Freya muttered with a shake of her head.

One of the warthog trolls yanked on my arm. "Ow," I said loudly, pointedly, but not before I looked up and shot Freya a steady look, catching her nod in understanding before Cash and I were dragged out of view.

CHAPTER FOUR - BAD PROMPT

Kreed's lair was a swamp. Like, it was literally a swamp in the middle of the blue forest that somehow had rudimentary ruins and wall-like structures built around certain areas, like someone's sloppy Warcraft game.

Cash and I were thrown into the smelly, dirty, gross dungeon, which despite the crudeness of the rest of the complex, was at the top of a heavily-fortified stone tower.

"Ow!" I yelped again. "Do they have to take the phrase 'throwing in the dungeon' so literally?" I complained, pushing to straighten up before walking over to Cash. "Don't worry, Cash," I told him. "Freya will have a plan to rescue us soon."

"I'm not worrying!" he snapped, pushing away from me. "Do I look worried?"

I winced, taken aback. "Well, thank you for saving your neck —*again!*" I made a face then groaned. "I should have known stuff like this would happen with unfinished stories."

"Stuff like what?"

"Stuff I don't know to expect." I rubbed my forehead in frustration.

"Do all humans make this much noise?" Kreed came down to the dungeons right after his trolls had locked us in. He sounded amused as he made his observation.

I looked up at him dully, past the dungeon bars. "No, you're lucky. Usually, we're a lot noisier."

Kreed paused from walking away and turned back to me. "You're pretty chatty for a prisoner," he growled. "Let's see how brave you'll be later when I—" He stopped short to grin again. "Well, let's not talk business just yet," he bid before heading for the exit, his words echoing against the walls. "Maybe later."

"Oh yeah? Let's see what I write about you next time, huh, you overgrown reptile!" I yelled out after him.

"Astrid!" Cash hissed. His eyebrows snapped together.

"What?"

"Would you quit upsetting the antagonists?" He shook his head in grave annoyance as he sank to the floor. "Just give it up."

I blew out a huge breath before sinking beside him. "Also, next time I write a dungeon, I'm putting in a couch," I declared. "And maybe a carpet, and a fridge—and one of those air freshener thingies."

Despite our situation, Cash chuckled, collapsing against my shoulder.

I slumped back against him. "Sorry, I got you into this—again."

"Hey, look, you saved my neck. Again." He elbowed me. "That was very brave, by the way."

"Forget it," I dismissed. "Besides, the best-case scenario is that we fall asleep and wake up in another story altogether."

"Yeah, something upbeat, please?" he suggested wryly. "What else were you reading?"

I grimaced. "Shakespeare and some Scottish historical fiction —sorry."

That made him laugh. "Oh boy, I'm guessing there's no Disney version." He shook his head in ridicule.

"What?" I elbowed him back defensively. "These stories are haunting and beautiful. And I just wanted to feel that…epicness, you know? I wanted to feel a part of something…bigger than myself. Big worlds. Big adventure. Big love."

His forehead creased as he studied my faraway expression. "I'm sure you can have all that in the real world too."

I pursed my lips in skepticism at his rationale. Sure, because the real world was chock full of possibilities. I was tempted to dare him to come up with anything parallel to a Lord of the Rings adventure or a quest for Camelot in real life.

He brushed off his pants distractedly as he went on. "You can't just keep your head buried in your books, you know, hiding them behind finance textbooks, reading in class," he pointed out.

I shot him a surprised look. "What—how—?"

He gave me a matter-of-fact look. "I sit behind you."

But I just stared blankly at him.

"We have Financial Management class together twice a week."

"We do?"

Cash turned his head away. "Oh my god, you didn't even notice me." He bit his bottom lip, giving me an almost hesitant, diffident sideways look. "See what you miss when you're not paying attention?"

There was a soft light in his eyes as I looked into them. I furrowed my eyebrows in curious astonishment, but before I could respond—

"Hey you, the girl," someone called.

I jumped, startled as I looked up. I'd almost forgotten when and where we were.

One of the warthog trolls was motioning me toward the door, and my stomach churned in dread.

Oh, here we go. I stood up, brushing my skirt off.

Cash had also stood up to follow me, but after I'd gone through, the troll shut the cage door with a loud clank. "Hey! Where are you taking her?" he demanded with a surprisingly courageous tone of voice as he shook the bars in protest.

"No, let him watch," a voice undoubtedly Kreed's boomed out, and the troll opened the door again to let Cash out as well.

The warthogs escorted us out to a dank chamber adjacent to the dungeons. I was hoping the room wouldn't look like a torture chamber, but despite the fact that the room was completely bare, save for a small log table in one corner, that's what it looked like to me: a torture chamber.

Kreed stood in the middle of the room.

One troll nudged me forward while another held Cash back to stand off to one side.

A toadstool chair materialized out of thin air in front of the log table.

"Please have a seat," Kreed instructed me.

"No, thank you, I'm—"

"SIT!" he boomed.

I fell into the seat with a startle. "What do you want, Kreed?" I glanced worriedly back at Cash.

Just then, an entire stack of paper scrolls and several old-fashioned feather quills materialized on the log table in front of me in the same manner as the chair.

"Write," Kreed ordered.

"What?" I made a face, not understanding.

"Finish it." His tone was ominous, and his words were punctuated by thunder and lightning.

I winced and picked up a quill. "You mean...the story?"

Kreed didn't reply. He knew I had understood.

"Um…" I paused and tried to remember where I had left off five years ago.

I vaguely remembered that the main protagonist was supposed to be formulating some type of plan to conquer the Nightlands. I blinked a few times and tried to think of what might happen in the next scene.

I dipped the quill in the inkpot and started to write.

All of a sudden, an electric shock shot right through me, trapping my scream in my throat altogether. I seized in my seat for a few seconds before it stopped, and I collapsed against the log table, heaving as every inch of me was now aching, spots dancing before my eyes. *What the—?*

It was lightning coming out of Kreed's fingers.

Shit. It *was* a torture chamber.

"No!" Cash tried to rush to me, but the warthog troll held him back.

My head bent, I clenched my teeth as I willed the pain to subside.

"I want you to write that I become the ruler of this world." Kreed lowered his hand a few inches.

"What, no way—!" I had started to protest as another electric shock blasted at me from Kreed's hand. "Holy shhh—!" I cried out. It was as though my skin was being peeled off, my internal organs set on fire. After a few more moments, I slumped against the desk again.

"ASTRID—!" Cash was thrashing against his captors, but his struggle was futile.

"Write it…or die," Kreed commanded.

My hands were shaking so badly I could barely grip the quill, but I tried to do what he said. I was trying to think of a way to outsmart him, perhaps to disguise the story as an ending he would have wanted. But every wrong notion I wrote down swiftly rewarded me with a fresh jolt of agony. My forehead slammed on the table as I fell over, incredibly weakened, my brain fried.

"Stop it!" Cash cried out in indignation. "How do you expect her to think, much less write, when you're doing that?"

I tried to mumble, "He has a point," but I was sure I was incoherent.

Kreed lifted his hand, aimed it at Cash, and unceremoniously gave him a dose of the same electroshock.

Cash crumpled to the ground.

"No!" I exclaimed with a short, sudden burst of energy before I flopped again. "Ohhh shit. You're such a jerk."

Kreed turned his lightning hands back to me, and I seized in my chair again, in complete and absolute, red-hot pain, this time so much so that I couldn't keep my balance on the chair.

I tumbled to the floor in a heap, taking a pile of papers to scatter in a mess down with me, and I only had enough energy left for a small groan.

"Now, write!" Kreed boomed out.

My eyelids felt heavy. I tried to move my arm, but it was no use. My head throbbed. There was stabbing pain in my chest. Every inch of me prickled like a thousand fire ants feasting on my flesh. I was jelly. My eyes shut in exhaustion.

Kreed walked up to me to kick me in the side with his boot, but when I still didn't move, he let out a loud grunt. "You're useless." Then he snarled loudly, stopping to glare. "You will write tomorrow," he stated. "And you *will* finish it."

I tried to shake my head, but nothing in my body was cooperating right then.

"Tomorrow!" Kreed boomed, then somehow, he disappeared into thin air with a *poof* of smoke.

The warthog trolls hauled Cash and me back to the dungeons and threw us back in. I hit the wall again. "Ow!" I crumpled to the ground. I didn't have enough strength to get up. I strained to turn my head to see Cash, also slumped on the ground.

He gave me a weary smile. "That was a good plan."

"Thank you," I was able to get out before I lost consciousness.

CHAPTER FIVE - NOVEL

I woke up with something heavy on my back, and I sat up with a start before pain shot all through me again. "Ow—dammit!" I groaned, squeezing my fists to get a hold of myself.

It was still dark—then again, of course, it was always dark in the Nightlands.

A hard thump made me whirl around to see an upside-down tortoise shell spinning around on the floor. I squinted at it as I had never seen a big tortoise up close before.

Then the tortoise's head popped out, and I jumped again. "Whoa!"

But the tortoise smiled up at me.

"Noble!" I blinked in recognition. Noble was one of Freya's animal friends from the Neutral. "How did you get in here?" I rasped. My throat still felt like sandpaper.

"Uh, would you mind terribly turning me over first? I'm getting a frightful headache," the tortoise asked.

I grunted to pick up the shell to turn it right side up. "Sorry." I glanced back over at Cash, but he was still asleep.

"Ah, that's much better," Noble said with a sigh before shooting me a stern look. "Well, Miss Astrid, what have you gotten yourself into now?"

I sat back and frowned. "Oh, please." Still feeling weak, I collapsed against the wall. "I get the message already. I'll finish the story as soon as I get back."

Noble looked self-satisfied. "It's a good thing those silly guards don't take notice of small animals."

"Yeah, that's great," I agreed. "But how exactly were you planning on helping us get out of here? We're not travel-sized like you."

"Oh, of course, silly me. Freya said to give this to you." Noble produced a skeleton key out from under his shell.

"Does it open the dungeon cell? How did Freya get this?"

"Well," Noble relayed, scratching the top of his head. "Let's just say she went to collect on a rather large debt."

"Okay..." I turned the key over in my hand. "So, what if this key does get us out of the dungeon? What about the guards outside?"

Noble snorted as he retrieved something else inexplicably large from inside his shell. "That's where this should come in handy."

I stared at the rough, baton-like wooden stick similar to the warthogs' ones. "You're kidding." I took the stick, marveling at its weight. "Wow, this is heavy."

Noble padded over toward Cash, who was still asleep, and nudged him in his side with his nose. "So, this is the other human Freya said you were saving."

I tilted my head. "Saving? I guess so."

Cash stirred then and woke up staring straight into Noble's giant green nose. He froze, looking like he had instantly gone into shock.

Noble tilted his head and met Cash's gaze. "Hello, human."

"Aaahh!" Cash shot up to his feet and backed up against the wall, heaving.

Noble shot Cash a weird look, then glanced at me. "Your friend has a problem, Astrid."

I managed a short laugh. "That's what the Serendipity said."

Cash darted a stunned look over to me, even as he clutched his aching head. "The t-turtle," he stammered. "It talked... You're talking to the turtle...."

"I am a tortoise," Noble corrected, sounding slightly offended. "Calm down, boy. Be a man."

Cash's forehead creased in incredulity. "The turtle—is telling *me* to be a man."

I rolled my eyes. "Shut up a minute. I'm trying to come up with an escape plan."

Cash spotted the big stick in my hands. "What are you gonna do with that?"

"Me? Nothing," I replied, taking a deep breath and grunting to straighten up before handing the stick to him. "You whack all the trolls that we pass by."

"What?"

"Batter up." I gave him a pointed gesture, then moved to the door and bent down to start fiddling with the lock on the dungeon cell before looking back at Noble. "Are you sure this is gonna work?"

Noble shrugged in as much as a tortoise could shrug. "Freya said it will," he reassured. "Besides, Kreed never checks on prisoners. He thinks everyone always follows what he says."

"Can't say I blame him," I agreed, frowning in concentration at the lock. "He lives in a 2D world."

The lock gave a soft click.

"Open sesame," I murmured as I swung the cell door open. I took a cautious few steps out of the cage to scout around for warthog trolls. Then I stepped back in to report. "One bogey three o'clock," I relayed before chuckling. "I've always wanted to say that."

Cash rolled his eyes.

"I should go," Noble said. "The river is right below this tower. I'll swim back to the Neutral."

I shot Noble a surprised look. "Are you sure? I didn't know tortoises could swim."

Noble gave me a wink. "There are still a few surprises in this world, Miss Astrid." Then it motioned. "Get me up on the window."

I was standing by the cell door to keep a lookout, so I gestured for Cash to help Noble.

Cash stared at me in disbelief. "Oh, you have got to be kidding me." After a moment and a resigned groan, he made a face in distaste before moving to daintily pick up the tortoise to perch it onto the windowsill.

"Hey, I'm not the one who hasn't taken a real bath in days, human," Noble reminded him before looking back at me with a smile. "It was nice to see you, Astrid."

"Thanks, Noble." I gave him a mock salute. "Careful on the landing."

"Of course," Noble said, nodding somewhat regally before pushing himself off the window.

"Ooh." Cash curled his lips. "Hope he didn't end up turtle soup."

I grinned. "He's one tough tortoise."

"Hey." Cash approached me, already looking me up and down in grave concern. "A-Are you okay? That thing—before… I tried to stop them—I thought—" He closed his eyes for a moment as if reliving my torture before forcibly shaking it off.

Despite everything, I couldn't help an appreciative smile. I mean, this was all my fault. I had brought him to this dangerous place and put his life in mortal danger at every turn, but he was still worried about me. "I'm fine, Cash." I took a deep breath. "I'm also a tough tortoise."

Cash broke a small smile back as he held my gaze. "I'm glad."

I willed my pulse not to race, clearing my throat after a moment and looking away before gesturing for us to head out. "Ready for this?"

"No, but okay." He practiced swinging the big stick a few times.

We left the dungeon and headed down the hall. The first warthog troll was easy to strike down. Then we continued down the tower, heading for the exit out of the lair. Cash whacked another two warthogs in the way, and soon we were outside.

"It's just like whack-a-mole." Cash looked pleased with himself.

I didn't want to stop to think about it, but there was a suspicious nagging in the back of my mind, wondering why it seemed so easy for us to escape. Surely, there should have been more guards.

But we kept going as I seriously just wanted to get out of the Nightlands.

We'd made it to the bottom of a hill and paused where a trail forked, and I stopped to catch my breath, but Cash gasped, his eyes trained above us.

I almost didn't want to look but lined up in a formation at the top of the ridge were a couple dozen of Kreed's warthog trolls with Kreed himself standing front and center of his army.

"Going somewhere?" Kreed drawled as he shot more of his lightning fingers down the hill at us.

Cash and I ducked behind the bushes.

"Oh, shit."

"Astrid, what the hell is wrong with your story?" Cash whined. "It doesn't want to let us escape!"

"Dammit," I cursed again and tried to think.

"What do we do now?" Cash asked. "Those weird monsters have the whole way blocked."

My eyes widened when the rumbling started again. I peeked over the bushes to see that half of Kreed's army had begun their charge, rampaging down the hill, headed straight for us.

"Ohhh, shit!"

"Astrid, do something!" Cash urged, his voice shaking.

"Do what?" I was at a loss.

"Wish us back." He turned to brace his hands on my shoulders.

"We've tried that before, remember?"

"But you didn't mean it before, did you?" he guessed. "Wish us back to the real world right now!"

I dropped my gaze, hesitating. He wasn't wrong. I definitely didn't wish to go back that strongly before. But if I wished us back right now, there was no telling if I would be able to wish myself away into books again. This might be a once-in-a-lifetime opportunity.

There must surely be a way for me to stay and not be under attack by Kreed's army. I racked my brain, trying to rationalize. "This isn't really real. Maybe nothing will happen."

"Oh, yeah, so you didn't almost just die before? You weren't in absolute pain when you were being tortured?" Cash mocked, plastering himself against the shrubs even lower. "I for damn sure as hell was!"

I grimaced, looking over the bushes as Kreed's trolls were getting closer. Their feral growls and the sound of their weapons clashing made my heart pound in my chest, in my throat, in my ears. I could barely hear anything else.

Was I really going to die here? In this fictional world I created? All because of my stupid wish?

"There is no escape!" Kreed laughed out loud, and the ground trembled more ferociously.

I gritted my teeth, still heaving. My head spun.

"Real or not, do you want to risk it?" Cash prompted meaningfully. "This only stops when you let go, Astrid. I *promise* you there is nothing in these fake worlds that you can't get in reality and better. I mean, the world is only as exciting as you make it, but you'll never find that out unless you join in!"

I screwed up my face in aggravation, mostly because he was making so much sense, and I didn't want to be wrong. "Oh, go away, Cash! You're not even supposed to be here in the first place!"

And Cash winced as though I'd struck him. "Oh my god." He stopped and blinked. "Astrid, I think I've figured it out! Why I came along with you on your wish."

"What?" I shot him a strange look.

He turned to me with a grin, his eyes wide, breathing heavily. "This whole time, we thought you had to bring me back. But it was the other way around! I've been sent here to bring *you* back. To reality. To remind you of what's real."

Kreed's roar of laughter mingled with the warthog army's growls in the night air, but I couldn't look away from Cash's imploring eyes.

He took my hand in his and gave it a soft squeeze. "I'm real, Astrid. Come back to the real world with me. Please."

My breathing was coming in short gasps.

This was it. End of the line. It was time to return to reality before I got completely trapped in Wonderland.

Just like Freya.

She hadn't been left with a choice. But I was.

"Trust me," Cash assured, his eyes bright. "It's all about to get better."

I stared into his eyes, my chest tightening, and a huge, deep breath of concession released from me. I swallowed hard, bent my head, squeezing my eyes shut before whispering fervently in my mind.

I wish...

I opened my eyes again as a strong gale rose up like it was coming from the ground. It swirled around me, around us, rustling leaves to dance in a large spiral, twirling and whirling everything in sight, the leaves, the trees, the trolls.

I turned to meet Cash's gaze—still wide-eyed, amazed, grateful.

He cracked a smile that barely hung around his mouth and shrugged.

I smiled back at him before my vision blurred and the world began to tumble away.

Everyone in the Great Divide shielded their eyes from the sudden burst of blinding light. The people in the kingdom all stopped what they were doing to watch the unidentified beam shooting up into the sky. The Neutrals all looked up in curiosity.

"Hey, what's going on yonder?" a forest squirrel asked the girl sitting on a toadstool.

Freya spotted Noble at the edge of the clearing and caught him wink before she turned her gaze toward the Nightlands too.

After a moment, the bright light blinked off, followed by a rumble of thunder and lightning, like someone's outcry of frustration echoing across the land.

Freya chuckled. "Novel exit."

The End

ABOUT S. R. BREAKER

S. R. Breaker lives in New Zealand with her husband and two kids. She writes offbeat, easy reading young adult science fiction and fantasy books.

Suburban mum by day and author by night, she loves to live vicariously through her characters. They don't have to vacuum all day long and are almost always guaranteed to survive any fantastical or thrilling incidents, no matter how treacherous she writes them.

She likes binge-watching TV shows and reading books that take her to far enough unknown worlds—but then still have enough time to wash the dishes after.

Find out more at: breakerworlds.com

tiktok.com/@sbreakerauthor
instagram.com/sbreakerauthor
facebook.com/SBreakerWrites
goodreads.com/sbreaker

PROWTIED
BY BAREND NIEUWSTRATEN III

Gargling abrasive foam, Dirro screamed at the sea. Not out of the fear he had in abundance but to aid in the expulsion of seawater from his mouth as the higher waves smacked against him. Especially when the prow, to which he was tied, dipped forward into the great blue drink. Wooden breasts of a carved mermaid held his head in place as he faced the sea ahead of the ship that wore him as a second figurehead. The storm had stirred the sea into a frenzy of bow-tossing madness, and Dirro was experiencing it with the entirety of the ship's protective hull behind him.

It had been harrowing enough when the sea was calm and the sun was out. Even though his olive Sond Islander skin had undermined part of the torture's design, taking to the sun far better than the pale Umber skin that reddened and blistered when so exposed. Umbers, who devised this punishment, typically for their own kind. Umbers, who made up the bulk of the crew who put him there. This was a punishment that left most men dry and raw, but with the storm, it had become a voyage into a blue hell of swelling moving mountains made of brine, crashing against his bound and naked body.

He had been accused of breaking into the stores and taking bread and wine in a banquet for one. He assumed he was accused by the one who actually did it but didn't want to rule out the possibility they simply cast blame on the one with the darkest skin. Being sentenced to three days prowtied, he spent every waking moment cultivating hatred in his heart for all the souls who still stood safely on the ship behind him. Three days and three nights with only two mercies. One being that they wrapped him in a blanket at night, and the other being that they fed him water at dusk and dawn. It wasn't much water, and he was forced to sup it from the lowered hand of one of his so-called shipmates. Like the nocturnal wrappings, it was just enough to keep him alive to see him through his punishment.

"When you sentence an innocent man to punishment by the sea itself," he had said, as they stripped him on the deck the day before last, "you insult the gods who dwell in it. Erequean the sea queen, Aqueos the leviathan, and R'tuleas the sea colossus. Make certain," he warned, as they began to tie his wrists and ankles. "For at least one amongst you knows I'm innocent. I will call for his doom, and you will know I was innocent when it comes for him."

Now he stared at the sea, uttering those names of the children of Oceal, who ruled the seas and oceans. "Erequean, Aqueous, R'tuleas," he called upon them as the waves smashed against his cold bare body. "Hear my prayer," he yelled, closing his mouth so as not to choke on the brine when it crashed into his face. "Unworthy men make for you to claim my life for crimes they themselves committed. I ask of you to claim us all." He repeated the spiteful prayer over and over. Louder, until his voice roared into the blue madness about him, raw and growling like a bear.

It began to rain. Not that that made much difference to Dirro, whose black curly hair was already soaked straight from his violent salty bath. But the hard rain was loud as it showered the deck and assaulted the flapping sails. Distracted by the storm, the crew saw not what Dirro's eyes caught. Elsewise the words they yelled back and forth behind him would pertain to the distant object. Only revealing itself in fleeting glimpses, when one swell would briefly elevate it higher than the ones between them. Dirro smiled, knowing that even if he made to warn them, they would not hear his words. "Another ship," Dirro mumbled to himself, sarcastically, cautionary. He saw numerous opportunities unfolding before him. Pirates, marauders from the southern continent, or even a friendly ship bound to crash into them. He even welcomed the notion of Stormrider, the fabled burnt ghost ship legend said appeared in storms, harvesting ships' crews to replace its own long-dead men. But sadly, he was certain he spotted sails, which were told to be absent on the winter tree masts of Stormrider.

Dirro watched, praying if the vessel were hostile or bound for an ill-fated collision, no one would see it until too late. High waves crashed past the prow and onto the deck, forcing Dirro to catch what breath he may in opportune moments between submersions. By the time he saw the other ship clearly, it was practically upon them. He recognized the deep interweaving patterns carved into the wood, the wide sails, and the vertically erect prow that usually depicted a stylized and symbolic pattern of some animal. However, this ship had lost its original long-necked figurehead, replacing it with the mounted skull of a frostdrake. Its muzzle pointed downward, making its eye sockets seem angry, and its backward curving horns pointed to the sky. The men and women aboard gripped the railing in one hand with either an axe or a large iron grappling hook in the other. They bore long thick beards and hair, mostly white and blond, wearing thick furs soaked by the rain, with grim faces to match. A few spared an eye or two to glance briefly at the naked man strapped to the prow as they passed him. Dirro laughed, raising their menacing brows, and making some of them even smile.

There was a battle, but unable to turn his head, Dirro only heard it. He recognized many of the voices of the dying and injured. Not that he needed to know the source of the screams to determine who was winning. The frostdrake skull was large. If these marauders from the frozen lands had killed one at sea, the treacherous sea dogs behind him stood no reasonable chance. As the last cries of the dying reduced to groans and whimpering, the dominant voices upon deck, yelling orders, were not in a tongue Dirro understood.

It was not until both ships sailed out of the storm and into calmer waters that heavy footsteps fell upon the prow. They had finally come to cut him free and either drop him into the sea or use him for some sport that Dirro could only imagine would be needlessly violent in nature. He found he cared little. He'd outlived the rest. That was all that mattered.

The wet ropes binding him had been sawing into his skin, rubbing it raw where he was bound. At this point, he was just happy to be rid of it. If they meant to show him his own lungs before ending his suffering, so be it.

They brought him back on deck, holding him up before a man, presumably left in charge of the conquered ship. Dirro was only a couple inches shy of six feet, but the man before him stood half a foot taller, broader shouldered with far bulkier muscle. He looked the naked Sond Islander up and down and began speaking a tongue of which Dirro knew no word. It sounded like he was asking him if he spoke their language. Dirro gave an apologetic shrug and shook his head, "Sorry, I don't understand you."

The man said something that made several of his tall companions laugh—a joke lost on Dirro. "Trondl," the man in charge said, pointing to himself.

"Trondl," Dirro repeated, pointing to the man, who smiled with mild satisfaction before pointing to Dirro.

"Dirro," the naked captive said, pointing to himself.

"Dirro?" Trondl said contemplatively. "Dirro," he repeated. "Fra Sonde Ay-nyah?" he asked.

Dirro recognized what sounded like his homeland. "Am I from the Sond Islands? Sond Islands?" he tried to clarify, pointing to himself and nodding.

"Ah," Trondl said before asking a question to the others that contained their tongue's version of the Sond Islands again. He got only shrugs and shaking heads in return.

Certain that he was asking his crew about the language, Dirro turned to the rest and said, "Kestrian?" with a shrug. "Anyone speak Kestrian?" The tongue of his dead shipmates.

Trondl shook his head, saying what sounded like "nigh."

Though one of the others stepped forward, leaning on his two-handed axe. "Kestrian?" he asked. "Hello..." he said, rolling his eyes back in thought. "Go to hells..." he added, racking his brain for more. "I like your breasts."

Dirro laughed, and the man leaning on his large axe smiled proudly as he translated his three Kestrian phrases to the others in their own language, making them laugh as well. At least he knew what he was saying.

There was a quick exchange in which it seemed Trondl was seeing if the other man knew any more, but the multi-lingual greeting, cursing, breast admirer had seemingly exhausted his knowledge of the Kestrian tongue, presumably believing they were the only phrases he'd ever really need.

They seemed quite friendly, despite slaughtering the entire crew. Of three things, Dirro seemed certain; they weren't going to kill him, the language barrier was going to be tedious enough to make him wish they had, and that amongst the words being thrown about, what sounded like "slah-vah" was most likely their word for 'slave' in the cold-southern tongue they spoke.

***

Many days passed—weeks' worth, if not months. Dirro lost count. He learned more of their tongue than they did of his, but barely enough to exchange basic commands like one might issue a dog. "Scrub," or possibly "clean," would be uttered while pointing to the deck to have him scrub the deck. Their word for "eat" or "food" was said when a filled bowl was passed to him. Most of the words he learned were merely their names so he could fetch them when commanded to. He felt like little more than a beast, though none raised a hand to him or even angered when he struggled to understand something. What made it hard to pick up their language was the fact that many of them would refrain from speaking around him purely because they knew he didn't understand. Instead, they would resort to nods, facial expressions, and hand gestures.

As far as being a slave went, the conditions were surprisingly lacking in cruelty, at least from what he had always imagined or, indeed, how history described it when anyone from his own continent had enslaved others. Aside from the implication of violence at the first sign of disobedience, the arrangement was almost civilized.

One of the women, Hleeni, who typically, amongst her kind, stood a few inches taller than him, would fetch him late at night. A rare occurrence at first, but, over time, she eventually began coming for him almost nightly. She would lead him somewhere quiet on the ship and make him pleasure her. Not so much forcefully, but compliance was implied to be compulsory as a slave to her people. It was rarely in ways that rendered mutual pleasure, and of the large, strong women aboard, she was far from the comeliest, but Dirro was simply thankful it was her, and not one of the men, that used him in such ways.

On one such night, they were disturbed by a nearby noise. The sound of a short struggle, flesh being cut by blade, and a collapsing body hitting the deck beyond some bulkhead, before being dragged away. Hleeni grabbed her axe and took Dirro to investigate. They inspected the surrounding corridors and rooms and found blood on the wood. There had been plenty spilled when the current crew replaced the former, but this was fresh. Dirro wanted to speculate, but there was little point. All he could do was look to Hleeni and tilt his head with concern, wondering if he had permanently cursed the ship in calling upon the wrath of three gods in his rage.

Hleeni led Dirro to Trondl's quarters. Concerned words were exchanged, with only the odd word sounding familiar. Then there was yelling as Trondl left his cabin and made for the deck. He made an order to one of his men, and soon there was bell ringing and scrambling below. All were summoned to the deck. As the bell echoed across the sea, the strong men and women who had claimed the ship while Dirro was prowtied, assembled. Trondl, and those directly under him, waited for some time. But the number on the deck ceased growing when more should have been present. Without adequate explanation, their number had dwindled. There was little where else to look for blame than Dirro. As words were exchanged and the assembly looked around for an answer, they eventually landed there too. All Dirro could do was shrug and shake his head as they began to debate the notion of a vengeful slave. Now, more than ever, he regretted the failure to learn their tongue. Though the best he could hope to do was express the notion that he had cursed the ship to the gods of the sea. Trondl and his crew would unlikely welcome that news. For though he had welcomed death when they first came, he'd had much time to let his anger subside. While he had no love for his current life, he had lost his hatred for it.

As the untranslated accusatory speculation began, Hleeni reluctantly stepped forward. Hopefully, explaining that they had heard the reported noises together. While this began to draw curiosity, forcing her to explain why they were together at so late an hour, a thought occurred to Dirro.

"Umbers," he said as soon as the possibility struck him. Survivors, hiding somewhere below

Trondl's eyes widened. "Umbers?"

Dirro pointed downward to the deck and beyond. "Umbers," he quietly cautioned, suspecting some to be still hiding. Survivors of the assault skulking about below deck somewhere. The thought angered him. He had been prowtied, falsely accused of a crime that one of them had committed, and punished by all. Now they were down there incriminating him again, and, worse yet, they would have to be stealing supplies to survive, hidden for so long. The very crime for which he had been unjustly punished resulting in his slavery by those who had delivered the vengeance he had demanded from the sea. It was the only reason he had accepted his current fate. If any of his former shipmates still lived, the gods of the sea had failed him.

Trondl looked down as if looking through the wood of the deck, searching. He screwed his brow tightly in fury and grimaced with disgust. A string of foreign curses slipped through his teeth, with "Umbers" buried somewhere in the middle.

The marauding crew of southern reavers split into small groups and began searching the ship, deck by deck, section by section. Dirro was no exception, taken by Trondl to accompany his small search party. There seemed little organization to their method, giving plenty of opportunity for any quiet Umbers hiding to shift about. Still, Dirro was glad to be with the leader of his enslavers. At least if they found anyone, it would quickly clear his name. Though, if this search found nothing, they'd likely fall back to assuming Dirro was getting revenge. He had to make sure they improved their technique before their number dwindled further. The problem was communicating the detail to which they seemed uncustomed observing.

One of the others held his arm across Trondl's chest to halt him in the cargo deck. Pointing with his other hand to small puddles on the floor, he stepped forward and knelt, rubbing his fingers in the liquid and bringing them to his tongue. He tasted it and said their word for "seawater."

Dirro understood at least enough of the ensuing conversation to glean that they believed men to have climbed aboard.

As the man who tasted the brine stood, amidst the speculation that was clearing Dirro's name, something moved in the shadows behind him. The tip of a blade sprouted from his chest as a sword impaled him from behind. Dirro stepped back in shock as the killer pushed the impaled man to his knees.

The assailant seemed an obese man at first, but as he stepped into the torchlight, Dirro partially recognized him. His clothes and hair were wet, and his face turned a light blue-green where one might expect the pale pink of an Umber. Dirro knew that long mustache, the eyebrow ring, the upturned nose. Rike was his name. A crewman who had served with Dirro until the current inhabitants took the ship. Only now, he was bloated and blue like those of men whose bodies washed ashore several days after drowning. His throat had been cut on one side, and the wound was dark. His eyes were milky and frosted.

One of Trondl's men pushed Dirro aside to avenge his dying friend, either not realizing that a dead man was standing before him or not caring. These men and women who took the ship and enslaved Dirro seemed to know little fear. But as he engaged and Trondl made to follow, more bloated corpses emerged from behind crates and barrels, dripping brine from their soaked hair and clothing. All faces Dirro vaguely recalled, distorted by swelling that puffed cheeks and chins and ironed out wrinkles.

Unarmed, all Dirro could do was back away from the fight of two marauders against four drowned men. They fought for their fallen crewmate and for their own lives as these wet corpses had returned to reclaim their vessel from those who had tossed them into the sea. Dirro made to run, but a fifth walking corpse knocked him down to get past and join the fight. His blade buried deep into Trondl's back before Dirro could regain his footing.

Soon the three men who'd come to hunt vengeful stowaways were laying on the wooden decking, bleeding out as the five drowned and bloated Umbers turned to Dirro. They spoke in unison with a deep whisper that bubbled like an old pipe smoker about to cough up a pound of phlegm. "Go then," they said, pointing their swords at him. "Send us more souls."

"What's happening?" Dirro asked.

"Your prayer was heard," they said, speaking not in their usual coarse and common Umber accents with regional inflections that betrayed their low illiterate upbringing, but instead, sounding almost scholarly with noble precision. "The deep currents delivered us to fulfill your will. This ship is cursed, as you demanded. All will fall who remain or attempt to claim it."

Dirro's eyes widened in fear, as much at their words as at the haunting hissing chorus in which they were delivered. "And what of me?"

"Flee or stay, live or die."

"But the water is freezing in these parts," he found himself bargaining when he knew he should be running. "I'll never make it to any-"

"Flee or stay, live or die," they repeated.

Dirro fled, skidding on the wet floor as he scurried in terror. Behind him he could hear the grunting of the three he'd been grouped with, being hewn where they lay by the swords of the drowned. He charged upstairs to the next deck, trying to find another group. He hoped they'd find Trondl and the other two still being killed instead of finding them dead and again assuming he was responsible.

He ran into another group of four and yelled "Trondl" at them as he pointed to the stairs. With barely enough words in common to get through his day-to-day duties, he was hardly equipped to express the complexity of the situation beyond the panic in his voice as he yelled their captain's name. It seemed to be sufficiently effective to propel them urgently past him.

As he climbed the decks, fearful that his enslavers might still turn on him, he heard the clashing of blades. More of his former crew were onboard, assaulting the small hunting parties searching for stowaway Umbers. Instead, they were finding the ones they had already tossed into the sea. Not back for vengeance for their own lives, but as part of the very same curse Dirro had called down upon them in anger and fury. He had doomed two crews merely by yelling at the sea.

When Dirro reached the top deck, he was almost relieved to find the southerners fighting on the quarterdeck as the bloated wet corpses of his former crewmates climbed the stern. A harrowing sight, but one that meant he could make for a rowboat without being stopped by his enslavers.

As he untied the ropes securing the small boat, he became certain he had escalated the situation by engaging with those who had killed Trondl. They might have continued to act in the shadows, subtly picking away at the numbers. Now, there was a battle in every part of the ship.

As other southerners upon the deck noticed Dirro's escape, they ran toward him and to other boats. Hleeni, spattered with blood, found him and helped him release the boat with three men. They soon had the small vessel in the water and began climbing the scramble net down into it. As Dirro climbed in, he steadied it for the others, holding onto the net as they followed him down. Hleeni and one of the men made it aboard before hearing the last man yell in pain. Looking up, they saw him slain by one of the dead Umbers, falling lifelessly into the sea. As the other man dropped into the boat, Hleeni began rowing as he and Dirro pushed away from the ship.

Two other boats seemed to make it away as the ship sailed on. One of the others had managed to distance itself while another passing close by the stern of the ship, began to rock as more of the drowned men climbed out of the sea. Those aboard the boat fought but were soon capsized and dragged down into the water. Some jumped from the ship to escape, risking the cold over fighting dead men, but they were either followed by the drowned men or attacked by those already in the water, still making for the ship.

The two boats rowed for all they were worth. With no food and no water, they exerted themselves, moving as fast as they could hope to in the cold sea. They headed south toward the even colder lands of the continent from which they came—the icy bottom of the world.

Two days passed unfed and unquenched with only the boat cover as a blanket. Made to keep the idle boats from filling with rain, they huddled beneath the stiff treated canvas during the cold nights, when even rowing for warmth became too much to endure. All three of Dirro's companions seemed to weather the cold better than he. They were large, strong, and from these very parts. But even they were used to braving it on higher land or deck. They periodically rubbed their arms and legs while Dirro openly shivered to near convulsion. Hleeni held him close when they slept when he would dream of fire and food.

Dirro was shaken awake by Hleeni as the boat dragged and scraped along the shallows of a cold beach, all but washed ashore on a cold white morning. She quickly woke the other two as Dirro looked upon the cliffs rising before them out of the mist that hovered over the cold land. The four dragged the boat ashore across the frosty gray sand. They stowed it upside-down in the recess of a low rocky outcropping at the base of the cliff so they could take the craft's cover with them without leaving it to be filled with ice when they returned.

They moved back toward the shoreline to get a better view up and down the coast, looking for signs of civilization, or whatever passed for it in these parts, Dirro pondered. He was now walking on the very continent from which southern raiders came. Whatever hell or watery grave they had escaped from, manifest by Dirro's angered words, this was far from salvation. He had gone from treachery from his crew-mates, to slavery by his liberators, to retribution by walking horrors he had called upon the world in a fit of mad rage. Now, upon the shores of Craguhr, he was left to guess his next fate, if it indeed extended beyond freezing to death upon this beach.

There were five possible kingdoms in which he could be standing. Some were almost hospitable, or so he'd been told, while others were little better than the frozen wastes that lay south beyond them, where direorcs and frost elves were known to dwell. He was fairly confident they had to be in the western half, unless he was lucky enough to have instead landed upon Ohtylos, a kingdom just to the north of Craguhr.

Dirro looked to the skies as he suddenly remembered frostdrakes and white dragons were known to inhabit the skies of these parts. There he saw a faint flickering orange light, high above the cliff. He furrowed his brows and squinted as he tried to see clearly through the mist. One of the others stood beside him to see what he was looking at.

Words were exchanged amongst the other three, and after a few vague gestures, it seemed they were climbing up to get closer to the warm light. Uncertain if he was still officially a slave to what remained of the marauders' number, Dirro gladly took the duty of carrying the boat cover without question, partially unraveling it to wrap around his shivering body.

They found a winding rocky path that led to the higher ground. A narrow passage that looked naturally formed, though Dirro was certain it had merely been carved out so long ago that the elements concealed the evidence by smoothing out the ancient masonry. A rising channel carved into the rock shielded them from much of the cold winds.

The path led for hours, exhausting them. Mostly Dirro, who had been born in a place that had a far more intimate relationship with the sun. He dreamt of its golden shores and crystal blue sea as each blink grew longer and more indulgent. He remembered the sun glistening off the olive skin and curly black hair of the beautiful young women who would bathe naked in it. It was half the reason he fell in love with the sea, though becoming a sailor took him away from all that.

He felt a hand lightly slap his cheeks repeatedly, bringing him back to the cold, harsh reality of his true surroundings. Hleeni shook him awake, making him realize he was somehow drifting off while walking. Dazed, he wasn't sure if she was waking him to save him from passing out and collapsing or if she was somehow aware of his daydream involving other women and acting out of some kind of impossibly intuitive jealousy. She spoke words of warning either way. As always, he failed to understand them. Though, he was confident drifting off in the cold while walking presented some detriment to his health. He nodded and soldiered on.

The higher they climbed, the less cover the path provided. Emerging from it, they found a rise leading to the narrow cliff under which they had stowed their craft. There they saw a mighty structure of old stonework surrounded by a gathering of smaller ruined, blackened structures cradled within what looked like the palm of a tremendous stony hand. Great rocky spires rose around it like pointy fingers, covered in frost. Light flickered within several windows as they approached it, all exhausted from the long climb.

Dirro recognized the architecture on approach. It was the work of the Order of Light. A cathedral. He'd seen their like in his travels. Paliodor Cathedral upon the high coast of Cliffguard in the southern

Umberlands, Stormbreach Cathedral on the north coast of Westmeer, Oud Dom Cathedral on the north shore of Nordmeer, Khalub Ja Cathedral on the island of the same name, south of the Heruusian capital of Perahn, and on a clear day, the sunken spires of Bhurz'Gol Cathedral beneath the waves, far north of Rhuel. It had stayed remarkably intact, though beyond use, as it followed the northern half of the Dwarven continent into the sea during the Great Sink two centuries ago. If this were indeed one of them, it would make the sixth of all twelve that had been built that Dirro had seen with his own eyes. Though clearly, the locals had mixed feelings about its erection, seeing as it appeared to have been put to the torch. Faceted amber glass sat in the windows where stained glass typically displayed brilliant colors and patterns in all the others he had seen.

As the others knocked upon the great wooden doors, they too appeared less extravagant in design than those upon the great religious structures Dirro had previously observed. Much like the windows, the doors had to be recreations built quickly for functionality over the elaborate artistic expression contained within their predecessors. Stripped of much of its splendor, seeing the building like this was like seeing a king dressed in peasant clothing. Carved large upon its stone façade, above the doors, the great twelve-pointed star of the order still proudly brandished itself to visitors as a reminder of its former glory.

A small viewing door opened within one revealing the top half of a gray-haired man's wrinkled face. Looking to the three southern marauders with reserved trepidation, he spoke their tongue in an inquisitive tone, and there was a short exchange that seemed to be bringing them no closer to entering the building and leaving the cold behind them.

"Is that an Umber accent I hear?" Dirro asked in the Kestrian tongue, noticing familiar inflections and tone. The query stopped the conversation dead in its tracks as the old man's eyes looked him up and down.

"It is," he replied in his native language, sounding more like a question than an answer.

"I thought so," Dirro said with a smile. "Been sailing with Umbers long enough to recognize that accent in any language."

"There's more than one Umber accent," the old man said with a cocked brow. "There's seven kingdoms in the Umberlands last time I checked."

"And yours is from the kingdom of Orbreath," Dirro said, watching the old man's eyes widen and then crease as he smiled out of view.

"Very good," he said, impressed.

Dirro took a step forward. "Perhaps we can talk more of such things on the other side of this door," he suggested. "We're quite cold, and we've been through a great ordeal."

"If they can be persuaded to abandon their weapons, and you can vouch for their behavior," the old man inside said. "But generally, we do not allow their kind entry, being precisely the kind of folk who put this place to the torch in the first place."

"I do not speak their language," Dirro said, "and as their slave, I do not command them. But I am certain they'd be grateful enough for the warmth of your hearths to the point they would not think to disrupt-"

"Slavers?" the old man said disapprovingly. "Bloody savages. They must enter here unarmed, with you a free man."

"Well, please tell them as much, for I cannot," Dirro pleaded, shaking. "After all I've survived, it would be a shame to die upon your steps."

The old man spoke again in the language of the other three, scornfully and with loud authority. They looked to each other, with Hleeni being the first to toss her axe on the ground behind them. She growled at the other two, who reluctantly complied, saying something else with a hand on Dirro's shoulder.

The old man grunted approvingly and shut the small hatch as the other door opened, pulled by a pair of wardens of the Order of Light to whom the rule of no weapons clearly did not apply. They watched them enter with their hands on the hilts of their sheathed swords, then ran to fetch the discarded weapons, donned in chainmail armor.

The cathedral was grand by design, though the ceiling was lower than its outside walls. Built later, it was much like the windows and doors, humble and practical. When the doors shut, one of the wardens handed the weapons to one of several nearby monks, gathered by corners of the partitioned foyer to see who had arrived.

"Well, I suppose that means you're a free man now," the old monk said, patting Dirro on the back. "I am brother Tenbry. Welcome to what's left of Icecrown Cathedral."

"I'm Dirro, that's Hleeni, and..." Dirro paused as he looked to his other two companions, "I don't think I ever learned their names."

"Hjor," one of them said, discerning the introduction. "Tunbr," he added, pointing to the other.

"Come," the old monk said, "I'm sure there's a story behind your arrival here, as I don't think you were sent by the order, and I'm sure you'd prefer to tell it over some hot porridge."

"It's a dark tale, I'm afraid," Dirro warned, wondering just how much he should tell their new hosts. "Dark and wild."

"More of a dinner tale, eh?" the old monk joked, leading them through the humble carpentry of restoration work that supplemented the surviving masonry.

The twelve pillars that framed the central isle remained intact, depicting in statues the twelve Avantheonian gods exclusively worshiped by the Order of Light. Dirro looked at them in wonder, dreading explaining to those who shun worship of younger gods that he wrought their wrath.

<hr>

Dirro told his tale in a quiet, long-hall full of long tables where all who dwelled in the cathedral had already eaten earlier. Brother Tenbry heard the tale with a furrowed brow and shook his head at almost every part. "It says much of your character that you brought your enslaving captors with you to this shelter," he said.

Dirro shrugged, idly scraping the wooden spoon around the wooden bowl to capture what little remnants he might have missed when he wolfed down its contents. "I simply made to escape, and they just came with me. It didn't occur to me to tell them to fetch their own boat. They brought me here as much I brought them. We came together."

Brother Tenbry signaled one of the monks in the kitchen, and one soon emerged with a bucket and ladle to refill the four bowls. "That was indeed a dark tale, as you promised," he said. "And there are many lessons to be learned from it. But you came here for shelter, not to be shamed and lectured. One way or another, the Twelve brought you here to us."

Dirro was too busy enjoying a second bowl of hot nourishment to argue the theological interpretation. "I've seen five of the great cathedrals. The ones you keep by the sea. But I did not know they was here, in these parts. Though, to be honest, I'm not sure exactly which parts I'm in."

"No," the monk said. "This place is rarely spoken of outside these walls. We're in the western kingdom of Angvajaald. A few days travel to anywhere, halfway between the coastal cities of Valkenheim, the capital to the west, and Iceburn to the east. The city of Frostfall is directly south and far closer than either of those. Though, not a pleasant journey and hardly worth the peril."

"What's the story behind this place?" Dirro asked in the small space between mouthfuls of hot nourishment.

The monk puffed his cheeks and blew out air as if about to undertake an exhaustive task. "Where to begin?" he asked himself. "Depends how much you want to know. If you want a thorough explanation, I'd speak to Brother Beryn in the library."

"There' s a library in here?"

"Oh yes, even when the cathedral was at its best, there was more built beneath the entry level than above. The basements and crypts run deep. I'll give you a tour when you've rested. But this is one of the four lost cathedrals and the only of which we've managed to reclaim. I fear we'll never be allowed by the locals to restore it to its former glory, lest they put it to the torch again. But it serves its own purpose within the restrictions set by the authority of the kingdom."

"Restrictions?"

"Well, you see, our order is not traditionally welcomed here. This place only exists because the faith had the Kestrian empire behind it when it was built. Burning this place was part of the rally cry of those who sailed north to bring down that empire. Again, if you want a proper history lesson, I recommend you speak with Brother Beryn."

"But what are these restrictions?"

"We may never truly run this place as the cathedral it once was, as we would any of the other remaining eight. No divinions, no priests, not even deacons may dwell here. All who are sent here, whatever they may have been before, must take the mantle of 'brother' and run this place as more of a monastery. The once illustriously grand design of those components that burned or broke seven centuries ago has been rebuilt and recast in humility and humbleness, as have those who have been sent here."

"Sent here?" Dirro asked.

"Oh yes, I'm afraid few volunteers walked these walls over the years," Brother Tenbry said, with eyes that betrayed an old remorse. "This is a place of redemption. Cold, isolated, redemption. All who have come to reside here, I confess, have earned the privilege through some folly of judgment or waywardness."

"A punishment," Dirro said.

"A second chance," Brother Tenbry corrected.

Dirro lowered his spoon in contemplation and looked to his three companions. Former masters who were now merely fellow survivors, devouring down their second bowls of boiled oats. He had gone from situation to situation, always surrounded by agents of adversary; Umbers who mistreated him, enslaving marauders, sea-risen corpses, the very cold and whatever dwelled in the sea below, and now some sort of prison for disgraced ranks of the Order of Light, sent away for some crime to the bottom of the world.

"I suppose you're wondering right now what transgression I committed that saw me sent to this place," Brother Tenbry guessed.

"After everything I've been through, I'm wondering what transgression sent everyone here," Dirro said.

The old monk smiled with an amused huff. "I would condemn such curiosity as judgmental in any newly arrived addition to our family, but as you've been seemingly punished several times for a single crime, I find it a little understandable. It is not my place to open old wounds, so I will not confess indiscretions on behalf of others, especially as few would be crimes that you should fear here and now. Though crime is crime, only a few were truly severe. This is not a haven for those who've escaped a king's justice. Though, I won't lie, there are those here who escaped the noose. Good men whose good deeds were acknowledged by a Master of Justice when an advocate of the order spoke on their behalf."

"So, it's mostly just... vow breakers?" Dirro asked. "With the odd lucky criminal thrown in."

"I suppose you could say that," Brother Tenbry said, nodding. "But remember, if they are here, it is because they submitted themselves to the judgment of the order. They are not wild criminals who were chased down and dragged here in chains. Remorse brought many here. These are not prisoners."

Though there is nowhere for them to go, if they choose to leave, Dirro thought, assessing that the inhospitable cold and race of marauders beyond the walls of the cathedral were as good as iron bars.

"I'll at least tell you that I was once a priest," Brother Tenbry said. "Soon to become a divinion, until my own insatiable hunger got the better of me."

As Dirro took in another spoon of porridge, he realized the monk was comparing his story to Dirro's own. He had failed to impress upon this former priest that he was innocent of the crime for which he was punished and plunged into turmoil. Furthermore, it dawned on him that it was the second time Brother Tenbry had essentially neglected to acknowledge his innocence.

"Having not lost my eye for the young ladies," the monk continued, "I'm afraid my confessional chamber had become a house of sin and exploitation. The redemption for which they had come was, instead, twisted into nothing more than gratification of the flesh for my own selfish desires." He looked across the room to an empty corner in contemplation. "When I had seduced too many who were bonded in the light of the Twelve to husbands, to whom several confessed the unconventional method of administered atonement, I employed...."

"You soon found yourself sent here," Dirro concluded.

The monk nodded before Dirro's eyes wandered to Hleeni.

"I had an appetite for young Umber ladies," the monk reassured him with a dismissive smile. "While debate may be had at the effectiveness of my redemption, being less a path of self-improvement and merely the result of the removal of temptation, I can assure you that tall muscly Crag women present no moral dilemma to *me*. Otherwise, I'd have long ago fled this place in their pursuit, were I still so weak of flesh." He looked to the large, strong women. "And while there may have been theological leverage in my abuse of trust, there was no breach of consent. I cannot say the same for every last soul dwelling within these walls. I will arrange for you to share a room... if you wish. Though, I imagine, there is little protection you could offer her that she couldn't provide herself, but at least you'd be able to keep an eye on her for your own piece of mind."

Dirro contemplated the complexity of how to respond to the offer. Between Hleeni and himself, the balance of power in leveraging pleasures of the flesh was in exact reverse order to Tenbry's past and the crimes of anyone else in this place. As a slave of her people, it was *he* who was used for *her* gratification. Now that he was technically free of those bonds, this was his chance to escape that arrangement. Uncertain how to proceed, he found his head nodding and his hand shoveling another spoonful of breakfast into his mouth as if his body was rebelling and made to silence him before protesting the arrangement.

"Very good," Brother Tenbry said. "I shall make the arrangements. It seems you've chosen your own path of redemption in protecting your former captor's virtue."

A third time, this disgraced priest had alluded to Dirro's crime as a fact. "Redemption?" he asked in reserved protest. "I told you, I did not steal any food on that ship. I was innocent. Falsely accused and nearly killed for the crime of another."

"Of innocence of that crime, I *do* take your word," the monk said, with a raised palm of reassurance that turned into a pointed finger of accusation. "But in the eyes of the order, who now shelter you from the elements and dangers outside, you have committed other offenses."

"What?" Dirro asked, offended.

"You have communed with lesser gods, for a start," he said. "But as an outsider, I can forgive your ill choice of devotion. Being plunged repeatedly into a storming sea must have seemed a baptism of sorts, as that punishment drove you temporarily mad with fear and anger. It is not my place to judge the heathen beliefs of sailors as a tradition of ignorance. But there is still that matter of calling down such fierce retribution upon your shipmates. An entire crew killed by your words for the crime of only one. Then another crew. Abominations of flesh brought into existence by your dark pact. Necromancy by proxy. There have been none who lived and died within these walls who could claim so great a crime. If every soul sent here in the last seven-hundred years anteed their sins together, they'd struggle to match the number of lives struck down by their hands or misdeeds against those slain by your tongue."

Dirro reflected on his words, as he knew what he had done and had done it willingly. Despite the consequences, he had felt no remorse for his actions before this moment, when his sins had been laid bare before his feet. The enormity of his vengeance could put many a wartime soldier to shame. Part of him even agreed, perhaps, he belonged in this place, while another part of him was starting to realize he was a prisoner.

———

Growing tired after the four had quickly remedied days of starvation and thirst with an act that was hard to define as gluttony with bellies full of little more than oats and water, they were shown to rooms. Somewhere deep beneath the cathedral floor, in a hall that had been partitioned into sleeping quarters. They were guided by another monk to their rooms. Hjor and Tunbr were given the first available room. Three wooden walls and a stone one, with two beds separated by a very simple wooden dresser. Two deep drawers, one for each monk expected to inhabit the room. Atop it, a wooden pail with water and two large, folded washcloths on either side for humble bathing. A small lantern, fixed to the wall by an iron bracket, was lit by the monk who explained everything to them in their Crag tongue. Next, Dirro and Hleeni were shown to their room a few doors down. It was identical in every way, but the explanation was delivered a second time in the Kestrian tongue. Then they were left to rest.

Dirro chose the bed on the left and sat upon it with a sigh. It was a firm monastic bed made for functionality over comfort, but it was still softer than stone or wood and far better than sleeping on a boat in open water. Hleeni walked in between the beds and looked down at the pail of water. Picking up the cloth on her side and rubbing her thumb over it, she nodded with approval.

She sat across from him, and they both began removing their footwear. As soon as his feet were free, Dirro made to lie down while Hleeni stood and continued to disrobe. Soon she stood naked before him, surprised to see him stretching out as she plunged the cloth into the water. She looked at him, clearly confused that he wouldn't want to clean himself before sleeping, but her gaze almost felt like judgment as she rang out her cloth. Sighing again, he sat back up and stood. She wiped her face with her wet cloth as he began to discard the clothes that had belonged to one of his dead shipmates. Together they bathed, standing close in the confined space between the beds, rubbing themselves down, cleansing themselves of a layer of sea salt and days of sweat. It was the first time he'd been naked with her in such a functional capacity. Despite the nature of the intimacy they had shared, not being one of mutual attraction but duty of thraldom, standing close before her in this quiet place, he found himself actually wanting something to happen. Maybe it was familiarity or habit. He didn't care. He stepped forward, pressing his body against hers. She smiled, relieved more than anything, it seemed. She put her hands on either side of his face and kissed him.

The pair shifted to one side, crawling together into her bed. They joined, not as master and slave, but as two who wanted to be together with no shared language to communicate that fact. Brother Tenbry's assurance that she was not the sort of woman he preyed upon in his confessional, not being a soft gullible Umber lady, only brought into sharp focus the fact that Dirro enjoyed strong women. As his hands slid over every inch of her body beneath the blanket they shared, touching her for his own pleasure rather than by her physical instruction, he wondered if being stuck in this place was going to be so bad a fate after all.

When they were done, they held each other and faded into sleep. As he drifted, Dirro wondered if the nature of this new version of their relationship would be something they would have to keep hidden from the others who dwelled in this place or if they would be allowed to continue in this cathedral-turned-monastery. Either way, it seemed safest not to draw attention to it. He would need to find a safe way to communicate that to her.

When they woke, it was hard to tell what time of day it was. Though it was very quiet. There was a pattern of holes high above the door to allow lantern light from the corridor in, so they were never truly in pitch blackness. But it shed no light on whether it was day or night. Not this far down.

Dirro gently slid out of Hleeni's unconscious embrace. Collecting his clothes off the floor, he was deterred by their smell. He remembered the monk saying something about garments in the drawers when they were first shown to the room. From the top one, he found the brown robes, waste cord, and footwraps of a monk's uniform. He smirked, defeated, feeling he'd been unwittingly inducted into this outcast brotherhood. He dressed himself and felt a hand caress his back when he sat to wrap his feet. He looked back, and the pair shared a smile. Turning back to the drawers, he opened the bottom one to find another set of monk's garments.

"I'm going to have a look around," he told her in the Kestrian tongue, pointing to his eyes and then twirling an upward finger about to try and clarify. "Did you want to come?" he asked, offering her the other robes.

She quickly clothed herself as a monk. It was an odd look for her. A southern warmaiden in brown sackcloth over her strong but unmistakably feminine frame. He smiled at the absurdity of it, and she smiled back, seemingly amused at the outfit herself. He gave her one last kiss before leaving the room and hoped that made it clear that their physical affections belonged only on that side of the door.

Together they wandered the quiet halls and made their way upward to the cathedral, where no light came from outside. Snoring came from one of the pews where an old monk had fallen asleep. No doubt there to keep an eye on the two lanterns lit to provide minimal light in the large room.

Climbing down the stairs on the other side of the cathedral to where they had been previously led, Dirro found the library. An impressive collection of old tomes and bindings were dimly lit by far too few candles and lanterns, though it still seemed the brightest section at such a dark hour. Amongst the shelves, a skinny hooded monk stood upon a ladder. Reaching for a book, he partially turned his head at the pair's entry, not looking to them, simply reacting to them.

"Ah, company," he said, curious. "A rarity during daylight, an obscurity during the evening, and an anomaly at this late hour." His accent was unusual. Not too dissimilar to that of sailors Dirro had met from Nordmeer, or Hjaanmar, and not so foreign-sounding in these parts, but just a little sharper and more ridged somehow.

"Well, we fell asleep early and found ourselves awake," Dirro said.

The old monk straightened. "You sound Sondish."

Dirro smiled. "I am," he said, impressed.

"That should please Brother Vandrez," the skinny monk said, grabbing the book he was after. "At least when he wakes in a few hours."

"You must be Brother Beryn," Dirro guessed.

"I suppose I must be," Brother Beryn said, slowly descending the ladder. "Excuse the rate of my dismount. At my age, you have to move slowly to avoid tearing anything important."

"Something to look forward to," Dirro said.

The monk hummed, mildly amused. "How old are you?"

"Thirty-four."

"Ooh, a good age," the skinny monk said nostalgically. "Where was I at thirty-four? Not all that far from here, come to think of it. How intriguing. I appear to have come full circle," he mumbled. "Tell me, young man, do you have a name?"

"Dirro," he said. "And this is Hleeni."

"Well, Dirro, let me give you some advice," he said as his feet finally touched the ground. "Find somewhere nice and dry. Hard for the hells of it. Nothing jagged, mind you. Somewhere, flat, dry, and hard." He turned around, his face obscured mostly by his hood, just revealing an old chin, nose, and mouth surrounded by loose, wrinkled skin. "Then fall over. Trip. Hit that ground, hard as you can."

Dirro looked to Hleeni, but not understanding a word, she could offer no explanation. "Excuse me?" he asked, wondering if he should feel insulted.

"I don't mean that as a recommendation to injure yourself," he said, dismissively waving his free hand. "It's not some hostile expression. I just mean that you should fall over while you're still young enough to enjoy doing so without it causing you permanent damage that'll end up haunting you every winter to follow. In ten years, you won't even be able to watch someone else fall over without it sending a cold rush of panic down your legs and up your back, even though it might still be safe enough for you to do so. Ten years later, you'll want to avoid it. Ten years after *that,* you'll live in fear of it, with your life flashing before your eyes if you even lose your balance for a moment in another ten years on top of that. So, fall while you can, before you find yourself counting and assessing every step to make sure it isn't your last."

Dirro smiled and began to nod. "I'll try to take less care with my every step for the next few years."

"Don't worry. It'll come sooner than you think if you don't master tying your footwraps properly," Brother Beryn said, pointing to Dirro's feet.

Dirro looked down and saw his left footwrap half unraveled. He looked about and made for a nearby stool upon which he intended to fix it.

"The other thing to look forward to," Brother Beryn said, approaching a reading desk, "is losing interest in being concise and direct when you wish to communicate a point. Especially to someone far younger than you, who can afford the lost time."

Dirro laughed as he rewrapped his foot and ankle.

The monk exchanged a brief greeting in Hleeni's tongue before sitting by the desk. "So, you must be the group everyone's been talking about. Your story's causing quite a stir, you know. Just in the time, you were sleeping off your escape. When the excitement of it wears off, I'm quite sure it'll be the basis for some interesting discourse and theological debate."

"Oh?"

"Well, at first glance, it serves as a cautionary tale, warning us against praying to what the order typically refers to as lesser gods. But upon reflection, it also boasts of their responsiveness and effectiveness. Something overlooked by Brother Tenbry in his rush to dispense wisdom, struggling to shake off his priestly instincts."

Dirro did not expect to hear such a frank assessment of one monk from another. "Though everyone who comes here must come with a story of how they ended up here," he said. "Many of which must serve to create debate or provide some lesson."

"Oh, yes," Brother Beryn said, gently turning to place his book on the desk behind him. "But you can't possibly imagine that anyone else here has a story as gripping as yours. Many will have questions, and many will want you to tell them the story, expecting Brother Tenbry will have omitted any enjoyable details. I myself have questions, but perhaps I'll wait till you're sick of answering them. Even though I think they'll be questions others won't think to ask."

"And what is *your* story?" Dirro asked. "For I suppose that should be the price I ask in exchange for queries and retellings."

"Far from a bargain here, I fear. I'm the one person here who came by choice."

"Choice? Brother Tenbry said there were few volunteers from time to time, but why would you choose to come to this place?"

"The answer surrounds you, bound and shelved," the old monk said, pointing with open palms to the walls of books about them. "I'm on a personal quest for knowledge. Specific knowledge, but I'm picking up far more than I expected to. Filling my head with all sorts of things. Slowly becoming an expert in everything."

"Oh? And what knowledge do you hope to gain from that red tome behind you?" Dirro asked.

"Red, is it?" Brother Beryn looked back and hummed, curious. "I'm afraid I'm color blind. For some reason, I was imagining it was green."

Dirro smiled inquisitively. "You imagine colors you've never seen?"

"I wasn't born this way," he said with a half-smile. "Just one of the prices I've paid for being around so long."

Dirro had heard of people going blind or seeing everything blurred as they grew old, but he had never heard of people losing color. "Something else to look forward to," he mumbled. "Brother Tenbry said you were the person to ask about the history of this place. He said something about four lost cathedrals."

"Oh, yes?" Brother Beryn said. "Alasiar, Bhurz'Gol, Northlook, and good old Icecrown, here. The first was taken, the next sank, and the other two burned."

"I have seen the spires of Bhurz'Gol Cathedral in the sea north of Rhuel," Dirro said as Hleeni began to wander, looking at the shelves about her. He couldn't imagine her being able to enjoy any of the books beyond some of the decorative stitching in their spines. Not an entirely uncharitable thought, as he was no better. The written word was nothing more than a secret silent language of scholars and nobles to him.

"Yes, they certainly built *that* at the wrong end of the continent. Now, I imagine, covered in coral, housing sharks, blue dragons, seadrakes, and Aquari. As bad an investment of effort as building upon the frozen shores of a continent to mark territory at the furthest overreach of reckless and unwelcomed expansion. Twice, no less." He tilted his head in contemplation. "Then again, Alasair Cathedral was built in the heart of greater Kestrus, now Hjaanmar. An elaborate hall for the Halforn line of Jarls."

"So, Northlook is like this place?"

"They built an entire city around that one, making for a prize too valuable to destroy completely." He pointed westward. "When they torched the cathedral there, they made a much better effort, stacking the pews and wooden fixtures, building the flames so high it collapsed the great roof. Then, as the monks did here, the locals built their own roof, and now it serves as a granary and store for the city that now belongs to the kingdom of Ferrensyl. This place was not so effectively destroyed beyond damaging its roof to the point that much of it had to be torn down and replaced. Yet no one from Angvjaald really wanted to live here, I suppose. The surrounding abbey and devotional support buildings were all destroyed, leaving this structure alone, surrounded by a pile of ash and black ruin within a high rocky cage. In the years that followed the fall of the empire, the remaining faith petitioned the king of Angvjaald to use this place as it is today. He agreed, as long they swore never to run it as a cathedral again, forbidding them from rebuilding the supporting structures or restoring it to its former glory. With no one serving as priest nor divinion. Merely a place to serve as a monastery for those disgraced within the order."

"And the odd volunteer," Dirro said, gesturing to the old man.

"A rare breed within these walls. Far too infrequent to balance the number of men who *should* probably be sent here yet haven't been."

"It sounds like you have little faith in the men of your order," Dirro said. "Your brothers."

"Broth...?" the old monk stopped himself. The sharpness and bitterness of the single slipped syllable echoed throughout the library, catching even Hleeni's attention, turning her around. It was not the reaction Dirro was expecting. Nor the reaction the old monk clearly wished to covey. He raised an apologetic hand and smiled, almost amused by his own reaction. "Some latent bitterness there, I suppose. Another great benefit of old age. More time behind you in which to pile resentful memories, even long after you've outlived those who've wronged you."

Dirro leaned forward, furrowing his brow. "You were wronged by some within the order?"

"Amongst others."

"Is that why you came here willingly?" Dirro asked, intrigued. "Did you hope to find someone you knew here?"

Brother Beryn huffed, tickled by the notion. "Coming to this remote place just to gloat at someone? That would take a level of spite even I would have to admire and aspire to. No, no. It was long before I put on these brown robes that I did clash with men in white tabards, surcoats, and cloaks that bore the tilted golden star. It was a very different time. Had I done a tenth of the things I did before donning this sackcloth *after* I fastened them to my frame, I'd have been sent here far sooner than I chose to come." He smiled, almost proudly, from under his hood. "I was once a very different man to the one who stands before you now. Had you known me in my youth, you would not recognize me now."

"But you somehow found your way to the light of the Twelve?"

"If you like. Amongst the men you'll find within these walls, there's probably more variety in the tales of how each man came to wear the cloth over the ones that explain how they came to dwell in *this* place. But you'll have plenty of time to collect those stories during your stay. Learnt in exchange for your own dark tale that you'll repeat until you've refined the telling of it. But Brother Tenbry will no doubt want to talk with you first to ensure you cleanse your account to suit certain sensibilities before repeating it. So, before the sun rises and someone wakes him, why don't you tell me your tale and spare no detail?"

With the dawn came the sound of footwraps on stone. Movement echoed within the once great cathedral as the daily routines began. After sharing his tale with the librarian monk, Dirro had returned to his room with Hleeni. There they waited to be visited upon to be told where to go. After all he had been through, he was in no rush to be assigned duty, but while sleeping in this great shelter, he didn't feel right turning up to breakfast without first being told what might be expected of him in return.

As predicted by Brother Beryn, a young monk had been sent to fetch the pair, as well as the other two companions who had arrived with them. Dirro was escorted with his trio of former slave masters, now equals in the eyes of their hosts. It was weird to see these men who had carved through his former crew in brown sackcloth robes of the order.

Gathered across a desk from Brother Tenbry in some sort of formalized vestry, they were given the rules of conduct in two languages. Mostly simple rules that differed little from those of any civilized place, they were supplemented with more religious observations with limitations to wandering the nearby grounds.

"Now, Dirro," Brother Tenbry said, after speaking to the other three for a while, "I wish to address your experiences at sea. I think it would be most practical if you all left the telling of that tale to me. To avoid repetition and exhaustion, perhaps it's best that I relay the events during mass in a manner that will most benefit the ears of all present."

"That seems the wisest course," Dirro said, coached by Brother Beryn in the library to placate the acting abbot. A gesture that immediately seemed to pay off as the monk leaned back in his chair, looking pleased. "I have barely had time to tell top from bottom of it. A man of your learning seems better equipped to make such decisions."

Flattered into gleaming, Brother Tenbry nodded. "Good, good, it's settled then," he said. "Now, onto other matters. As you've been stranded in a boat together without food nor water, I think it would be unreasonable to put you to tasks so soon. Rest, eat, walk around, and build up your strength for a few days, and when you feel up to it, if you wish to contribute, there are many daily duties with which you could help."

Dirro nodded, wondering what many of those duties could possibly be. "Rushing to escape the cold, I did not take a good look around the surrounding grounds, but I saw no farm to grow wheat and oats, nor vegetables and fruit. Of what I have heard of monks and monasteries, that is typically the...."

"...primary source of labor, yes," Brother Tenbry said. "There is a small patch on which we grow things, though it cannot be relied upon as local beast and man alike tend to prune it prematurely. But we continue to keep at it, seemingly as an act of both penance and a charity that makes our presence more tolerable to those who pass through this way."

"So, you rely on what others don't steal to survive?"

Brother Tenbry shook his head. "We'd starve if *that* were the case. A ship of the order brings us supplies on rotation from the Umber kingdom of Cliffguard. In addition to crates of other supplies, they send us barrels of oil, grain, potatoes, and sometimes fruit. There are trees planted long ago by monks who once lived here in the woodlands nearby where fruit grows: apples, tangerines, pears, and the like. But again, the local population tends to get to it. Though they have no love of lemons, so there's that. A sour way to stop your teeth falling out."

"There's a ship that ferries between here and the Umberlands?" Dirro asked.

The monk slowly exhaled through his nose, less than enthusiastic about Dirro's interest in a vessel that could take him away. "The

Torenus, yes. It sails between the southern Umberlands, Ohtylos, and here."

"It's very compassionate of them to send you supples," Dirro said, attempting to shift focus and downplay his otherwise obvious interest in escaping the cold outpost for outcasts. "Especially paying for such cargo to be delivered so."

"The Torenus is one of six ships belonging to the order. So, there is no fee nor expense in shipping us the supplies they do. In addition to the food and those supplies, we are also sent materials that we use to make goods used by the rest of the order. Tabards, robes, sashes, and the sort."

"Ah," Dirro said, exaggerating his interest, "so, that would be these other duties then." He refrained from asking when the Torenus was next due, preferring to keep his captor or host more relaxed. It seemed a question wiser to reserve for Brother Beryn next time he visited the library.

"Well, yes," Brother Tenbry said, interlocking his fingers as he leaned forward. Before he could continue, a bell began ringing and echoed down the halls. "Oh, sounds like breakfast is ready."

———

Dirro followed a line of monks into the dining hall. He was too hungry to notice last time when he felt he'd eaten his own weight in porridge, just how low the ceiling was. Especially coming straight from a ship where he'd been getting about the lower decks, half bent over for months. He at least didn't have to duck here, though his tall companions were cutting it close, tilting their heads as they passed wooden beams.

After accepting a bowl from the serving bench that separated the kitchen, he and his companions sat at one of the long tables as other monks slowly began to fill the seats on either side of them. Dirro looked about the sea of brown sackcloth where monks were devouring boiled oats, hoping to spot Brother Beryn to ask about the ship that Brother Tenbry had mentioned.

"Ah, you must be Brother Dirro," one of the nearby monks said. "I'm Brother Lonny."

"Well, just Dirro," he said. "But, nice to meet you."

"Sorry, of course," the young monk smiled, shaking his head. "Force of habit. When you call everyone you see, every day, Brother this or Brother that, you can't help it."

"Except the wardens," Dirro guessed.

"No, even them. They might still wear the armor and be the only amongst us to carry swords, but we're all just brothers in Icecrown."

"But Brother Tenbry is the senior brother."

"He is the abbot, even though we bear no titles in this place. But so far, everyone just remembers who's in charge. A system that seems to work." He shrugged.

"But there must be some sort of... ranks," Dirro speculated as he pointed to the kitchen. "There are a handful of men in the kitchen, but one of them must be in charge of it?"

"Oh well, yes. Brother Nembil's in charge of the kitchen. But again, he doesn't really need a title for that. Everyone under him just remembers that."

"And Brother Beryn is in charge of the library."

"Yes. Though, as he came here of his own accord, there's a sort of implied seniority with him. As there is with age, so he's got it two-fold. Typically, a volunteer would assume the role of abbot if not the title, but he took to the library."

"Is that why he isn't here?" Dirro asked, sweeping the room with his eyes again. "Does he follow his own routine?"

The young monk shrugged, eating his porridge, holding up his wooden spoon to declare his intention to speak once his mouth was clear. "I've never really kept an eye out for him, but I don't ever recall seeing him in here now that you mention it. But I know he often stays up quite late down there, keeping odd hours as a result. I think someone might even take his food to him as they do with the wardens on duty. At his age, the stairs are probably a bit much."

"Are you talking about Brother Beryn?" another nearby monk queried as he emptied his bowl.

Brother Lonny nodded.

"I don't think he even leaves the library," the other monk said, grabbing his bowl and spoon in one hand and his cup in the other. He looked to Dirro. "He speaks little to the rest of us, preferring the company of books and the silent conversation of the written word. The inked scrawlings of scholars long since departed from this world. He spends more time amongst the dead than the living." The monk took a final sip from his cup and stood. "Welcome to Icecrown, by the way," he said before leaving.

"And that was Brother Theold," Brother Lonny said, flicking a gesturing hand between Dirro and the departed monk as if introducing them. "Bit of a grim fellow, but nice enough in his own way."

Dirro smirked before looking to his companions, talking amongst themselves in their own tongue. He couldn't imagine that they'd want to stay much longer than a couple of days to recover, nor would they be pressured to. They were in their homeland or at least their home continent. Though it was a vast land, being a broad row of cold kingdoms that lined the foot of every map of Middseya, their journey home could be had on foot, while Dirro's salvation would have to be had by sea.

As more monks departed, leaving space around them, Brother Lonny looked about before leaning forward. "Say, do you enjoy a bit of a *drink*?" he asked in a quiet tone.

"You mean like wine and ale?" Dirro asked, earning a nod from the monk. "I do. But I didn't think monks partook."

"Don't know where you got that notion," Brother Lonny said, almost defensively. "White Order monks make some of the best ales and wines in all of Middseya. We even have a small vineyard outside, but their lot keep pinching the grapes," he said, tilting his head toward Dirro's companions. "But, uh, a couple of my friends make a bit of a...

guess you'd call it a cider of sorts, from what bits of fruit and bread they can squirrel away."

Dirro winced at the sound of this ill-defined drink his new friend seemed to be describing. "I see."

"Look, I'm not promising some delicious Westmeerian draft or Ortalean wine here. Your tongue won't thank you, but if you miss the feeling that comes with drinks of the fermented variety, this should do the trick," he whispered. "This is an invitation for you alone, of course. A rare honor, as the batch is always small, and there's not enough to go around. So, best you speak of it to no one."

"Especially Brother Tenbry?" Dirro guessed.

"He'd be far happier not knowing about it."

"Very well," Dirro agreed. "Though even the water here tastes strange."

"That's the lemons. We squeeze them into the water we have at breakfast. It's supposed to be good for us, and no one wants to eat them straight. If the order sent us honey, we could at least make tarts. But then, if they thought we deserved such treats, they'd send us wine and ale."

Dirro smiled and nodded. "Makes sense."

"I'll come find you when it's time. Late." Brother Lonny gathered his empty woodware and left the table with a nod to all four and a wink to Dirro.

While he bore them no resentment, Dirro tired of Hjor and Tunbr's company. As both his liberators and enslavers, he had no idea what kind of relationship they thought they had with him. Were they sticking with him as all four were outsiders? Were they guarding what they considered to be their property, expecting Dirro to leave with them as their slave when the time came? Brother Beryn seemed the best person to help clarify—if he was even awake.

Dirro led the other three to the library by virtue of him going there and the others typically following. Sure enough, the old skinny monk was sat at a desk, thumbing through some thick tome. "You're back," he stirred, still hunched over his great book. "The few brothers who come down here are mercifully slow readers, so I don't see them too often. Amongst the few who *can* read, many don't believe they deserve the luxury, so many don't bother. At least until a random conversation that requires research to determine the truth of conflicting speculation drives them down here for an answer. Yet, here you are, already on your second visit." He smiled from under his hood. "And you've brought more friends."

"Sorry to disturb you, Brother Beryn," Dirro said, approaching him. "I'm afraid I have more questions."

"Sorry? Disturb? Afraid?" he repeated Dirro's words as he shuffled around to face him. "Did I not tell you that you were welcomed to visit me any time? Or did I imagine that? It's so hard to tell at my age."

"No, you did, you did," Dirro said.

"Then let us dispense with the formality of apologetic declarations of intrusion," the old monk said. "A habit I'd suggest you picked up from being around Umbers too long, but it seems unlikely a habit one might find amongst sailors. Unless your ship transported nobility."

Dirro huffed, amused. "No, the Scaled Maiden was a cargo ship and its crew rougher than the hide of a tiger shark. Her captain and mates were navel men, expected to lead the ship into battle if ever the… actually, I'm not sure precisely which kingdom of the Umberlands they owed their allegiance to. It never really came up, and they were never called upon while I was aboard."

"Well, either way, you say you have questions?"

"Ah yes. Speaking of ships, Brother Tenbry mentioned the Torenus. Perhaps by accident, but I did not think he would wish me to express too much interest in her comings and goings."

"No, as I guessed, he likely sees you as one of his flock now. Part of his redemption. Why? What did you want to know about the Torenus?"

"Its comings and goings," Dirro shrugged. "When is it next due?"

Brother Beryn thought about it a moment. "I do think it's due in a few weeks, actually. It seems to have a bit of a seasonal rotation, from what I've observed—or been told at some point. Hard to say. I've put so much information in my head since I got here." He gestured to the surrounding forest of books about him. "Did Brother Tenrby generously offer to commandeer your story?"

"Just as you predicted."

The old monk smiled again.

"The other thing is, I have these three with me most of the time, but I don't speak their language. Even though I've been with their kind for longer than I'd care to admit while picking up only a few words."

"Is there something you wish me to say to them?"

"I don't really know where to begin. I'm yet to be convinced I want to stay in this place, but I have no desire to resume my life as a slave. I don't yet know what my next step should be or what they intend to do. I don't know how to ask why they keep following me around or what they want without causing some offense."

"They don't look like the kind you'd want to offend, no." He looked at the other three a moment. "If I had to guess, I'd say the woman's following you around, and they're following her around. They're more outsiders here than you are, so they've no one else to talk to. Few here speak any Crag, and few here would be all that comfortable around them. They've probably picked up on that." He spoke to the other three in their tongue, and a conversation quickly ensued. It was Dirro's turn to wordlessly wander about the library.

As the hour passed, the old monk explained what he could to Dirro. Though the crew of the ship they had originally been on had men and women from several of the southern kingdoms, the three marauders were from the neighboring kingdom of Ferrensyl. Their captain had ordered Trondl to take the Scaled Maiden to an isolated cove in their homeland, where their ship often docked. Ultimately, it was the desire of Hjor and Tunbr to make their way back there and wait for their captain and tell him of the fate that Trondl and the rest had suffered.

"Did you explain to them why those dead men came back?" Dirro asked.

"I do not think they would still be seated so calmly if I had," Brother Beryn assured him. "But once Brother Tenbry delivers his sermon on the perils of calling upon lesser gods for aid, all the brothers will know. Then the secrecy of your dark pact will rely upon the discretion of everyone else here. At least the ones who speak the Crag tongue."

"Gods, he's going to get me killed," Dirro realized, standing up. "I should not have revealed so much. I'd better talk to him."

The old monk gestured for Dirro to sit, calmly shaking his head. "It's far too late for that. This is precisely the sort of thing on which priests of the order thrive. The condemnation of heathenism is half their reason for living. You'd be better off convincing these three that Brother Tenbry sent the dead men to slay their crewmates so that they kill him before he can deliver his next sermon. Though the ensuing chaos would probably still end up claiming your life." Brother Beryn smiled, shaking his hand at Dirro, who looked utterly stunned by the old monk's words. "That was a joke. I thought you'd laugh."

"Oh gods," DIrro said, burying his face in his hands.

"Well, I'll take that as a sour assessment of my humor," the old monk said before Hleeni asked him something. "The woman wants to know what *you* plan to do?"

"About this?" Dirro asked, raising his confused and panicked face.

"No, about this place. The other two want to get back to their marauder's hideaway and await their captain, but she wants to know what you intend to do. Stay, leave, what?"

"Get murdered by these three in the following days or take my chances out in the cold, running for someplace where I'd likely be enslaved again, I guess."

"For all the failings that saw the men who dwell here sent here, they are at least a compassionate lot. They feed and house these three because it is the sort of thing they were brought up to believe in. Or at least because they believe it will buy their way back into the good graces of the Twelve. But there would be no love for Crag marauders amongst this exiled brotherhood. Most of them are Umbers and would resent that they prey upon the seas their countrymen sail. I dare say all of them would pride themselves as being civilized men and view these three as nothing more than savages. I don't imagine any here would feel they have anything to gain in engaging them in conversation. As far as most would be concerned, these are practically the same people who steal what they plant, prevent them from restoring this place, and who put it to the torch, to begin with."

Dirro slowly nodded, wanting to be reassured by the notion.

"So, assuming you live, what do you intend to do?" Brother Beryn asked. "Because I think she wants to go wherever you go if she can."

Dirro looked to Hleeni, who looked back at him with inquisitive eyes. Tall, broad, and strong, with a hard but feminine face. Her eyes revealed a vulnerability as she awaited his answer. "I suppose some-where we can both go, where neither of us would be considered an enemy or a slave."

Though Dirro was merely thinking aloud, the monk translated his words. She took Dirro's hand and smiled, speaking back in her language.

"She seems keen on that notion," the old librarian relayed.

After smiling back at her, Dirro looked to Brother Beryn. "I don't suppose you'd be interested in teaching me that language?"

"I'm not entirely convinced either of us will be around long enough for you to master it, but I could teach you a few words here and there while our paths are crossed."

"I would appreciate that."

Dirro struggled to sleep. Clinging naked to Hleeni in one of their beds, he watched her fade away, blissfully unaware that the death of her crew was the result of his words to the sea. He imagined her strangling him to death with the same vigor with which she had made love to him if Brother Beryn had indeed been wrong about the other monks talking to his companions.

He was startled by a light knocking on his door. He quickly slipped out of bed and into his brown robe, quietly shuffling barefoot to the door as he tied his cord. "Who is it?" he whispered.

"Brother Lonny," a familiar voice whispered back from the other side of the door.

Dirro opened the door just a crack to find the friendly young monk tilting his hand toward his mouth as if an invisible cup was in his grasp. Dirro sighed with relief. He looked back to Hleeni, fast asleep, and nodded back to Brother Lonny.

He was led down deep beneath the cathedral into a quiet corner of some storage room. Dark and filled with barrels and crates organized into unintentional partitions between a network of stonework columns that each arched four ways. A couple of candles were lit within small iron plates, sitting atop a pair of crates to keep the light lower than the surrounding barrels.

"I hope this isn't where the oil is stored," Dirro whispered to Brother Lonny's amusement.

There were three monks sitting on the floor where one was ladling liquid from a small open barrel into wooden cups from the dining hall. Dirro recognized him from the kitchen.

"All right, brothers, this is Dirro," Brother Lonny introduced to a whispered chorus of greetings. "These are Brothers Nedrick, Erwyn, and Padwick."

Dirro raised a friendly hand and found a space to sit. If there had ever been a time he felt he needed a drink, it was now. All politely waited till each of them was holding a filled cup.

Brother Nedrick held up his drink. "Blessings to all," he said. "Especially those who drink fast." He took a quick swig and shuddered while Dirro was still only sniffing his cup. "Ooh, ooh oh, that's a tangy one."

The others all drank, and Dirro joined them. It tasted of sour bruised apple and had a light fizz to it. An earthy aftertaste made him wince.

"Tasty, yes?" Brother Nedrick asked, looking to Dirro with hopeful eyes.

"Ah," Dirro stalled. Soon all eyes were upon him in anticipation. "Yes, delightful," he lied.

The monks looked to each other and burst out laughing. Their voices echoed in the low crypt.

"Delightful, like the sweat off an old goat's sack," Brother Erwyn laughed.

Dirro smiled as Brother Lonny slapped him on the shoulder. "Kind words, kind words."

"Aye," Brother Nedrick said, still chuckling as he reached for Dirro's cup to refill it. "You've earned a second."

"How often do you do this?" Dirro asked.

"I only risk keeping one batch going at a time, so if I ever get caught, I can claim it was a one-time experiment," Brother Nedrick told him, ladling more of the mixed crypt cider into Dirro's cup. "Then, when it's ready, we try to stretch it out over a few nights. Can't afford to get pass-out drunk and be found sleeping on the stairs or something."

"Just enough to take the edge off being stranded so close to the frozen arse of the world and forgotten," Brother Lonny added. "And it certainly does the trick."

"Though if they did catch you, where would they send you?" Dirro asked, earning a round of chuckles and shrugs. He leaned forward and looked down at the small barrel.

"Yes, I'm afraid you got here a bit late," Brother Nedrick said. "We're already on night three. But if you'd got here a little later, you'd have missed out altogether."

"I suppose the Twelve work in mysterious ways," Dirro said, holding up his cup.

"That they do," Brother Lonny said, clinking his cup with Dirro's. "Especially for the only man to ever sleep under this roof sharing a room with a woman."

Dirro smiled nervously.

"Ah," Brother Lonny said, with a smile creeping across his face. "So, there's more to this."

"Brother Tenbry thought it best she neither share with a monk, her shipmates, nor be given a room alone," Dirro explained. "I'm watching over her."

"She's a Crag pirate," Brother Nedrick said. "No brother, no matter how tempted, would be fool enough to try anything there. A big lass as she is and all. I don't think she needs your protection."

"It's been a while since I've seen a woman," Brother Lonny said, "but I'm pretty sure I recognize the look she gives you when we're eating."

"What sort of look is that?" Dirro asked innocently.

Brother Lonny wiggled his eyebrows. "The look of a woman who's being protected well beyond satisfaction," he said to an eruption of laughter.

Dirro couldn't help but laugh along while confessing nothing.

Brother Nedrick soon remembered to hush them. "Not one of the details I reckon we'll hear in Brother Tenbry's sermon on Solday mass," he suggested.

"I look forward to hearing his version of my tale," Dirro said sarcastically. "I should warn you that I gave my word that I would leave that to him, though. If you were expecting me to tell you of my travels this night."

"I didn't invite you down here to squeeze a story out of you, if that's what you think," Brother Lonny said. " I just figured you could use some friends in here, and as a sailor, I figured you'd want to make friends with the few here who enjoy a bit of a drink."

"Well, I can, and I do, so thanks for that."

Dirro had to be shaken awake by Hleeni as the breakfast bell rang. Still feeling the touch of fermentation, he pulled her in and kissed her. She smiled as he reached for her thighs, but she shook her head. "Breakfast," she said.

It sobered him to hear her say the word in the Kestrian tongue. Before he could react, she pulled him to his feet and helped him dress.

It gave him time to realize she had at least been sufficiently exposed to the word in the short time they'd been there.

Brothers Lonny, Erwyn, and Padwick all sat to one side of Dirro while his usual companions sat on the other, with Hleeni across from him. With darkened eye bags, his new friends shared a smile of deviously shared glee, peppered with remorse. DIrro spared a thought for poor Brother Nedrick, who would have had to rise earlier than all of them to get the food prepared.

"Morning, brothers, Dirro," Brother Tenbry said, passing his table. He then offered a greeting in the Crag tongue to the other three. But the conversation seemed to exceed a customary greeting, and soon they were all nodding in agreement.

"What's happening?" Dirro asked, masking his nervousness.

"Oh, I do beg your pardon," the abbot said. "I was just asking your friends here if they'd care to stretch their legs and let us use their bountiful frames to help carry up some barrels from the garden."

"Garden?"

"Where we grow what vegetables and fruit we can," the senior monk clarified. "Down the mountain. I told you about that, didn't I?"

"Oh yes," Dirro recalled, his mind fogged by a turned juice that had been emptied from a small barrel many yards beneath him. "Of course."

"The brothers who usually do the task will no doubt be glad of the assistance," Brother Tenbry said. "Then, perhaps, we'll soon find you something that might sufficiently interest you to occupy your days. I've been told you've been spending time in the library."

"Yes," Dirro said, feeling he should be less surprised at how quickly word travels in such a place.

"I didn't think most sailors read."

"It's rare," the illiterate sailor said.

The abbot raised his brow and gave an impressed frown before moving along.

"Oh, I didn't know you could read," Brother Lonny said, impressed.

"Neither did I," Dirro said, with a half-concerned smirk that amused his new friends.

When breakfast was done and the three southern marauders joined the harvesting group of monks and accompanying wardens, Dirro found his way to Brother Tenbry again.

"I think we need to talk about this sermon of yours and how it might affect my safety with the three who came with me," Dirro said, addressing the abbot in his vestry.

"You fear reprisal, should loose tongues communicate the cause of their loss," Brother Tenbry guessed.

"Well, yes."

"Did you think that wouldn't occur to me?" he asked. "There are still a few days before I speak to the congregation. For that is why I have had the extra sets of arms bring what may be harvested from the grounds below. I intend to pack them a few days' worth of food to sustain them so that they can find their way to a nearby town or city that'll take them in. These parts have come a long way, but there's a lot of land between civilized places here. Either they'll find their own kind or at least bluff their way across the lands until they do. Either way, they do not belong here."

"So, you mean to send them away before you speak of what happened?" DIrro asked, relieved.

"Of course. Hope that puts your heart at ease."

Dirro nodded, though he wondered how to proceed next. For he didn't wish Hleeni to be sent away, nor did he want to draw attention to the nature of their relationship. He played out as many verbal exchanges as he could in his head of every possible way he could think to probe for the answer he needed, and they all ended terribly. "Ah..." he stalled as he thought, "when do you mean to send them away?"

"In the next day or so."

Dirro nodded and asked nothing more.

"In the next day or so," Dirro repeated the abbot's words to Brother Beryn.

"Well, that should save us from the language lessons then," the old monk said, putting a book away from a pile he had in his hands. "And it solves your little dilemma. Yet here you are pacing like a soldier on picket duty on a cold night."

"Hleeni wants to go wherever I go, and I wish the same."

"Ah, of course, that." Brother Beryn looked to Dirro. "Sit down before you wear a hole in the stonework."

Dirro complied. "Sorry."

"So, you're looking for options," the skinny monk said, checking the spine of a book before shuffling others on the shelf to shift open a gap where he felt it belonged. "First option: stay here and embrace the monastic life, learning one trade or another to fill your days in exchange for food and shelter. The men within these walls, despite their transgressions, are far from the worst within the order that I have met. Hleeni would return to her kind and continue marauding and reaving with her old companions."

Dirro shook his head.

"Second option: You leave with the three of them, re-join their original crew on the ship that attacked yours, and resume your life as a slave. You'd still get to be with Hleeni, but you'd be a slave."

Dirro squinted and shook his head again.

"Third option: pretend to take the first option but get Hleeni to wait for you in the city of Valkenheim while the other two press on along the coast. Then you sneak out one night on your own and hope you survive the journey in a land where you don't speak the language and where you're just as likely to run into the hospitable as the inhospitable."

"These options don't appear to be getting any better," Dirro said. "Isn't there an option where Hleeni and I just leave and take the boat along the coast to some dock where we can trade it for fare on a ship?"

"The boat you arrived in?" Brother Beryn asked incredulously. "If you think that's still down there, you've gone mad."

"What do you mean?"

"You don't think Brother Tenbry would want that temptation laying about for any brothers thinking of bailing themselves out of this prison? It was probably smashed for firewood the day you arrived as you slept."

"What?" Dirro stood. In the back of his mind, that boat always represented an option.

"Why? Were you hoping to row your way back to Sondaal?"

Dirro sat back down with an awkward grimace. The boat was, in most scenarios, useless if he was realistic about it. He sighed, exhausted, turning on the small bench so he could lay the top half of his body upon it. "And those are my three options."

"Of course, you could always join me," the monk offered.

"Here in the library? I did give Brother Tenbry the impression that that was my intention."

"No, I think I've gained all the knowledge I can from this place. I was planning on moving on soon anyway. You and your woman could come with me for as long as it suits you. I could use the company."

Dirro lifted his head and looked at the old monk in disbelief. The frail-looking, skinny, old monk as dusty as the books he was shelving. "Ah, you have an adventure or two still planned ahead then, aye?" he cynically asked.

The old monk chuckled to himself. "You think I'll crumble into a pile of bones four steps out the door, don't you?"

Dirro sat up just so he could shrug. "I don't know what the polite thing is to say here. No? I think you could make eight?"

The old monk laughed. "That's very kind of you." He shook his head as he put the last book of his bundle away. "Well, the offer's there if you change your mind. I would have thought following an old man around with your woman would be more appealing than the three options you scorned. But what do I know?"

"If we could get work on a ship," Dirro said as the thought occurred to him.

"Keen to get back on the open seas again, even after what happened to you?" Brother Beryn reminded him. "I suppose you at least know the gods of the sea listen when you talk, but I'm sure you've used up all your favors there. Of course, the real trick would be finding a ship that wants a couple of deckhands and means to treat them to their own private cabin, as if they were a pair of paying passengers. Know you of such a generous posting?"

"Not so far, but then I haven't looked for work for a while, so I'm hoping such postings are common now," Dirro said, throwing his hands out in feigned optimism to the old monk's amusement.

Dirro was touring the upper halls just below the main cathedral floor with Hleeni, Hjor, and Tunbr when an unfamiliar bell rang. At least an hour too soon to be dinner, they saw several monks pop their heads through doorways, curious.

"What's going on?" he asked a nearby monk.

"I don't know," he said. "It's the same bell they rang when *you* arrived."

Curious, Dirro made for the stairs. He wondered if the other rowboat that had escaped the Scaled Maiden had finally made it. At the very least, he thought it would mean more companions for Hjor and Tunbr to travel with.

"What's happening?" Dirro asked another monk on the Cathedral floor as others gathered about.

"Brother Hendel said he saw someone wash up on the beach when he was cleaning the windows," the monk Dirro hadn't met said of another he didn't know. "A couple of the wardens went to fetch him."

"It was bad enough getting here by boat," Dirro said to his companions, who understood none of it. "The poor bastard will be half-frozen."

When the door opened, wardens walked in a man who could barely move, so piled in blankets Dirro couldn't see him, especially with all the other monks gathering. Another warden carried the visitor's sword in its scabbard, having disarmed the man who would be lucky enough to live, let alone swing a sword again.

"Quick, get him to a hearth," Brother Tenbry ordered, his voice echoing through the main section of the cathedral as they led him away.

All nearby were curious but dispersed when Brother Tenbry gave them a look that reminded them, they all had duties elsewhere. He soon disappeared down the stairs, following those that were tending to the survivor of the sea.

The dining hall was awash with low chatter as rumors spread like wildfire over dinner.

"I heard he's in a pretty bad way," Brother Lonny said. "Heard they had trouble even getting him into a seat, he was so frozen. Brother Belistair said he was practically blue."

Brother Erwyn shook his head. "He'll be lucky to make it through the night."

"No luck about it," Brother Padwick said. "He'll likely lose half his fingers and toes."

"You talking about the feller they found on the beach?" another monk, sitting past Brother Lonny's little drinking group, asked.

"Aye," Brother Lonny said.

"I heard they reckon he's got half a chance on account of him being such a fat feller," the other monk said. "All that blubber should've kept him warm as a walrus."

"Fat?" Dirro asked, dropping his spoon into his vegetable soup. "Fat… like bloated?'

"So, they say."

"Bloated, blue, and crawled out of the sea?" Dirro stood up, "Hells," he yelled, beckoning Hleeni to follow as he dashed to the head table where Brother Tenbry usually sat. "Where's Brother Tenbry?" he demanded of the senior monks.

"With the rescued man, I think," one of them said.

Several of the monks stood or made to move as Dirro charged urgently out of the room and down the hall. As he made it to the stairs that led to the cathedral, he realized he was leading the three souls he'd saved from the wrath of the sea gods to what he believed to be one of their agents. "Back to the library," he quietly said.

As he ran back, he passed those who slowly followed him out of the dining hall. His drinking companions watched, confused, as he charged back in the other direction.

"What's going on?" Brother Lonny asked, but Dirro didn't have time to explain and took the stairs down into the library.

Brother Beryn watched the four visitors run into the library. "For someone who can't read, you certainly can't seem to stay away from-"

"I think one of the dead sailors is here," Dirro said urgently. "They say the rescue's a blue, bloated man who came out of the sea. I think the invitation to flee was only meant for me."

"And what did you hope an old man and a room of books would do?" Brother Beryn asked.

"I hoped you would explain to them, " Dirro said, pointing to his Crag companions, "and keep them here while I go and make sure. I didn't want to lead them right to him if it is."

"Go then," the skinny old monk agreed. He began speaking to the other three in their tongue as Dirro ran back up the stairs alone.

Still in the corridor as Dirro passed them, Brother Lonny and his little group followed their new friend to where he'd seen the rescued man taken. Several other curious monks seemed to follow behind them.

A warden standing in the doorway of the room where they were thawing the rescued man turned around upon hearing the approaching footsteps. "What's all this?" he asked.

"I need to see the man you found," Dirro said. He looked past the warden to see the man in a chair by the fire, with his back to the door, still covered in blankets.

"We have it under control," the warden assured him.

Brother Tenbry was crouched by the man's side when he looked up to see the small throng gathered outside. "Oh dear," he sighed before standing up. "I see discipline has slipped. I'm sure our new visitor appreciates your concern, but right now-"

"Brother Tenbry, I need to see his face," Dirro interrupted.

"It's in no great state," the abbot whispered to be tactful. "But we're doing what we can to save him."

"I don't think he's a survivor," Dirro warned, refusing to take his eyes off the man by the fire. "I think he might be one of my former crewmates."

"Oh, well," the senior monk started, almost excited before he realized what Dirro was saying and turned his head back slowly. "By the Twelve," he exclaimed.

The man by the fire was twitching under his blankets, shifting his elbows and knees, trying to regain mobility. Dirro imagined a lone risen crewman sent to reclaim the three souls that had escaped, frozen stiff by the deeps as it neared the icy continent—now thawing its dead, waterlogged flesh to regain movement.

The man in blankets slowly leaned toward the fire, trying to stand, only scraping his feet on the floor. Dirro slipped through the warden and abbot as another warden and monk on either side of the half-frozen man looked to Dirro's cautious approach.

Dirro kept as far as he could, staying near the wall as he side-stepped his way around to glimpse the man's face. There was a puddle of water growing at his feet.

"If you are what I think you are, I take back my words," Dirro said as he fearfully inched closer. "The ship is taken, the guilty punished. There is no need for further retribution."

The monk beside the man stepped back as he seemed to connect what Dirro was saying with whatever he had managed to hear of Dirro's tale. The warden stepped back and rested his hand on the hilt of his own sheathed sword.

The struggling blanketed man managed to stand. The blankets slid onto the floor, revealing the wet clothes of an Umber crewman. The skin of his hands was hued blue and puffed. Seaweed was stuck in his hair and about his now tight clothing as his body ballooned out from above and below his belt. Wounds inflicted by Crag marauders were clear to see as the holes in his clothing were stretched open by his brine-bloated frame.

"Everyone, get out," Dirro warned.

A waterlogged gargling issued from the cold man's throat like a flooded pipe being blown clear. "Flee or stay, live or die," he said in a fearsome whisper.

"Out," Dirro shouted.

Before the warden holding the dead man's sheathed sword could react, the bloated Umber turned and drew it, stiff at the elbows. "Flee or stay, live or die," he repeated.

"Brother Holmwick," the abbot called to the warden, who instinctively drew his own sword in response.

"Don't fight him," Dirro warned.

"Surrender your weapon," the warden warned the dead man, not entirely understanding the situation.

The dead man ignored him, looking up and around. Either testing his own thawed mobility or somehow looking for his three souls to claim, guided by some sight beyond vision, or at least some vision that was unimpaired by layers of stone and wood, he made to take a step but still struggled to move. He patiently waited, close to the fire.

"Brother Holmwick, is it?" Dirro called to the warden. "You cannot slay this foe. Please step away. I would not have your death on my hands as well."

"Come, we must barricade the room," brother Tenbry declared.

"Go then, get what you need," the warden said. "I'll hold him here if he tries to move."

"*We* will," Brother Belistair said, drawing his sword.

Brother Tenbry ordered the gathered monks to drag nearby benches toward the doorway. Many of the monks had gathered nearby, mumbling in panic and confusion as they watched a handful of their fellow monks scrambling at the abbot's orders.

Dirro helped move the benches before he heard the all too familiar sound of iron clashing against iron. Swords had met in combat. When he looked up, one of the wardens stumbled out of the room, clutching at his throat, blood pouring between his fingers. More clashes came from the room as almost everyone froze, shocked by what they saw. Brother Theold rushed to the injured man's side, pulling him away from the doorway and attempting to hold the man's wound shut as the warden dropped to one knee.

The sound of a sword rung as it hit the stone floor in the room with the hearth, followed by the heavy thud of a body, snared by the rustling of chainmail. The drowned man emerged alone, impaled by a sword in his belly that seemed to bring him no distress.

"In the light of the Twelve, I command you to leave this place," Brother Tenbry yelled at the creature reborn of the sea. A bloated corpse that looked around at the robed men about him. "I banish you, abomination," Brother Tenbry continued. "You may not walk this holy ground."

"Flee or stay, live or die," the unwelcomed creature spoke before heading across the main cathedral toward the stairs that led toward the library.

Dirro rushed into the room and picked up the other warden's sword from the floor. Faster than the stilted wet corpse, Dirro ran for the north stairs to race the avenging dead sailor to his Crag companions. He heard others follow behind him but didn't look back, ignoring those vocally deterring him.

He could hear the echo of more sword fighting as another warden engaged Dirro's former crewmate. He tightened his face in remorse as he ran but reminded himself that he had warned them. It brought him little consolation as he heard a sword ring off the stairs in the distance.

He ran down the dark corridor, the path less traveled to access the library, and he heard more fighting. There was yelling in the Crag tongue. Tunbr's voice echoed down the south stairs as Hjor ran up with Hleeni close behind. Dirro managed to grab her arm. "No," he yelled, pulling her away. "Hjor," he called, but the marauder was up the stairs, between Dirro and the sea-raised sailor. He could not contribute to the fight in such confines, only lead Hleeni back into the library. He took her to the far end and stood before her, holding the sword toward the entrance. He knew the blade would be more effective in her hand, but if he could buy her a few moments more of life, he would do it.

As he stood, poised for a fight he couldn't win, he felt his heart throwing itself against his breastbone in fear. Brother Tenbry's voice grew, following the man-shaped creature from a safe distance, yelling at it, attempting to command it with the authority of the priest he once was.

"I command you, abomination, I command you," the abbot yelled. "By the power of the Twelve, I compel you to flee." But his words were like waves crashing upon a cliff. If they were having any effect, it would take centuries to show. His voice weakened, presumably at the sight of whatever became of Hjor and Tunbr and of sheer exhaustion as whatever authority he thought his faith had given him was shown to be impotent. The work of the gods he called 'lesser' was clearly more powerful than whatever he believed the Twelve had bestowed upon him.

The dead man, blue and bloated, came through the door first. The sword in his belly, torn from him by one of the two men who now lay dying, if not already dead, on the stairs. Water leaked from his wound instead of the dark blood jellied about the tear. The sound of it dribbling onto the stone floor of the library pattered as an exhausted Brother Tenbry crawled in, far too unfit for the pursuit the man of near seventy gallantly gave.

"You can't take her," Dirro yelled as it ambled toward him. "I won't allow it."

It opened its mouth once more, "Stay or flee-"

"Silence," Brother Beryn's voice filled the library with a commanding tone from an unlit corner. "I command you halt, dead thing." He stepped out from the shadows with his hand held out. "This is not the domain of your masters, and you *will* recognize my authority here."

The dead man's feet stopped, seemingly to the creature's own surprise, who looked down then, back to the skinny old monk.

"Lower your weapon," he said, and the arm holding the sword

returned to the dead man's hip, scraping the point of the blade against the stone floor.

Brother Tenbry looked up from the floor by the doorway in wonder, clutching at his overworked heart, as Brother Beryn walked up to the walking corpse and placed his hand upon its face.

"Rest, dead thing," he said and guided Dirro's former crewmate to the floor in an almost caring manner. It was as if aiding a person who had fainted. The sight of such a skinny and frail old man supporting such a large and bloated one displayed a remarkable strength for someone his age.

Dirro lowered the warden's sword as the librarian looked to the abbot.

"How?" the old monk on the floor asked the even older one crouching by the wet corpse. He slowly shook his head in confusion as he puffed.

"Perhaps it's from reading all these books," the skinny monk said to the plump one on the floor. "Several do cover this sort of thing. Perhaps it is because I have not fallen from grace and your redemption is not yet complete in the eyes of the Twelve. Perhaps it is because I have dealt with similar things before in my many years."

The abbot looked to the floor as he caught his breath. Wounded by Brother Beryn's words, he seemed lost in reflection. Several monks stood at the door, and a couple helped their abbot up to put him on a bench. A pair approached the librarian, but he raised his hand and shook his hooded head.

"Only I know what must be done here," the librarian said. "I shall take this body back out into the cold and deal with it accordingly. I must do this alone." As the other monks nodded and backed away, the old skinny monk turned to Dirro and Hleeni. "Unless you've changed your mind about coming with me," he said quietly.

Dirro just stared at him, uncertain of how to respond. He was still taking in what he had just witnessed.

"I do not think more than one was sent to dispatch your southern friends, but should you encounter another thing like this again, I could protect you from it," Brother Beryn offered.

The hairs on the back of Dirro's neck stood. There was, at that moment, a strange energy about the old monk he found unsettling. Something dark. He watched the other monks lead the abbot out of the library as Hleeni went to check on her companions. When it was just the two men standing before each other and over a bloated corpse, he spoke. "Why do I somehow get the feeling that I would see more horrors like this if I came with you than if I didn't."

"You have already seen more horrors than most ever would," the old monk reminded him. "And it was you who wrought this horror, not I. I merely dealt with it."

"There was nothing 'merely' about what you did," Dirro said, pointing to the corpse. "And there were no holy words in the ones you spoke to dismiss this thing. I fear something darker at play."

Brother Beryn smiled. "A couple of days in those monk robes, and you're already beginning to sound like one of them."

Noticing that the volunteer librarian had said 'them' instead of 'us' when referring to the brotherhood, Dirro was confident the man was no true monk. His soured words when speaking of the order made so much more sense now, as did the things he'd said of a time before he wore the robes. Whatever purpose he had come here for, it was nothing holy. Fearing to press the matter, he just smiled. "Perhaps."

"It was interesting meeting you, DIrro. I wish you well in whichever path you choose. Go to your woman."

Dirro nodded. "Thank you for everything."

Though neither of them said the words, he could tell it was a goodbye.

Hjor had been killed on the stairs by the dead man who crawled out of the sea. Tunbr weathered his wounds, whereas only one of the three wardens who faced it, survived.

Brother Beryn dragged the blue corpse out into the cold and made it clear that he was not returning. Many were surprised at the frail old monk's strength, dragging the corpse alone on a wooden sled by rope over his skinny shoulders. He passed well beyond view as he made his way south. The monks speculated that he meant to sacrifice himself to the elements while performing whatever rites he knew to cleanse the body of its unholy contamination. Some even speculated that he had once been a paladin, while Dirro silently suspected he was the exact opposite.

Brother Tenbry delivered his sermon to the brothers' great interest, having witnessed some of what Dirro had faced first-hand. Though the cautionary tale that hinged on Dirro's choices did feature in the speech, it became more about the former priest's own redemption—humbled by the experience while at the same time making Dirro's story about himself. DIrro was amused but also moved by the abbot's gift for words and the faults he laid bare. Whatever manner of unholy shadow Brother Beryn truly walked in, he had managed to fill the abbot's heart with a brighter light and strengthen his faith.

More effective than his words from the pulpit, Brother Tenbry's bedside words to Tunbr seemed to take root. Another story of redemption took place to fill the following week's sermon as the abbot somehow convinced the wounded marauder that his path had been guided by the hands of the Twelve. Turning him from a life of murder and theft to one of devotion and protection, the senior monk convinced him to serve as a warden to protect the cathedral. Brother Tunbr became the face of redemption and a welcomed addition to the cathedral-turned-monastery.

Hleeni and DIrro stayed for weeks, though the nature of their relationship became harder to hide. Once he realized, Brother Tenbry only allowed them to continue sharing a room if they agreed to be married under him, in the light of the Twelve. They agreed. But a monastery was no place for a wedded couple to dwell, and so when the Torenus came to deliver supplies and collect the works of the monks for the order, Dirro and Hleeni bordered it.

On the ship, they were issued a cabin to share as passengers, and during their journey, Dirro negotiated for two positions as crewmen. It meant a reduced pay to keep their small cabin, placating the existing crew who slept in closely hung and stacked hammocks.

And so Dirro and Hleeni worked and lived aboard the Torenus, traveling between the Umber kingdom of Cliffguard, Vekriarecht Cathedral in Ohtylos, and the ruins of Icecrown in Angvjaald. Each time Dirro made sure he was part of the crew who delivered the supplies up the mountain so he could see those he had met during his stay there.

And to smuggle a little wine or ale, when he could manage it, for Brother Lonny's secret little drinking group to occasionally save them from Brother Nedrick's earthy mystery cider.

ABOUT BAREND NIEUWSTRATEN III

Barend Nieuwstraten III grew up and lives in Sydney, Australia, where he was born to Dutch and Indian immigrants. He has worked in film, short film, television, music, and online comics. He is now primarily working on a collection of stories set within a high fantasy world, a science fiction alternate future, as well as a steampunk storyverse, often dipping his toes in horror in the process. With over twenty stories published in anthologies, he continues to work on short stories, stand-alone novels, and an epic series.

A discovery writer not knowing what will happen when he begins typing, he endeavours to drag his readers on the same unknown journey through the fog of his subconscious.

Find out more at: barend3.blogspot.com

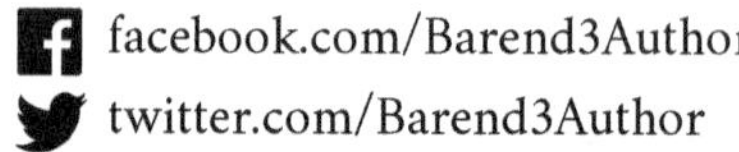

ELLA'S WISH
BY JOELLE NICHOLE

CHAPTER ONE

There are a lot of benefits to being a witch. Love spells are not one of them, unfortunately.

Which brings me to my current predicament. There's this girl on campus that's been begging me for a love spell.

Please, Ella, please, just one teensy weensy little love potion. We all know you're a witch. Drew was insistent after our world religions class last night. Both she and Ana have been trying to manipulate me all term.

I sigh. Humans. They definitely don't understand what a witch truly is. They never have, given their history of hangings and burnings, drownings… I could go on, but you get the point.

I peek up from where I'm cleaning the tables at the student center's main coffee house, sparing a glance at my intended target. Charmant Blake is surrounded by half the ice hockey team, and his smile is dazzling. Of freaking course.

If I didn't know any better, I'd say there was Fae blood in his lineage, but there are no Fae here. This I know for sure.

"Hey, can we get some of them chocolate chip cookies, Ella?" he calls.

My heart, treacherous thing that she is, thumps harder in my chest. And Ana wants me to make him fall for *her*.

I wouldn't. Even if I could. Because love can't be spelled. Lust, sure, infatuation, of course. But not love.

"Sure thing," I tell him, and I head behind the counter to grab some more.

I know I shouldn't wait on them. Truthfully, I don't really know why I even bother working here, except that it keeps me dialed in to the campus gossip, and I love me some gossip. Besides, it keeps the boredom at bay. I can't party it up twenty-four-seven at the clubs. And there are only so many times you can ace advanced women's studies. The course hasn't changed *that* much in fifteen years. I have matriculated college a lot. High school too.

A text from my sister distracts me as I plate the cookies.

Gran wants to know if we'll be back for break or not.

I smile. Ruby can't stand being at the Ignis Coven Manor, and who could blame her, really? But I love going home. I don't feel settled when we're not there.

Of course, I reply. We always go home for breaks, no matter which city or college town we've set up shop in. At least when we start in college instead of high school, we don't have to find some way to have "adults" with us. But it limits the time we can stay in one place.

I can feel Ruby's groan through our telepathic connection, but I ignore her. I'm not going to let her dampen my enthusiasm. I can't wait to get home. I need some distance from this place. Truthfully, I could just use some distance, period. From everyone. But I won't admit that aloud. Or let Ruby hear it in my thoughts.

Whatever you want, Ellie-cakes, she texts back. I'm not even sure why we bother to text. We've been able to communicate through magic since we were kids. It's not a gift all witches have, but being an Elderbrand has its advantages.

"Ms. Ella?" Charmant asks, "You need a hand with those cookies?"

From anyone else, it would be grousing. But from him, it's a genuine offer. "Uh, sure." I can't help the small blush that raises to my cheeks. I've definitely had the hots for this guy since I spotted him on campus last year when I started posing as a freshman.

Charmant heads closer, and I smile at him. He smiles back, and for a moment, I sink into those bright green eyes. I want him, and I let him know it. Except, I can't have him. I blink rapidly and let my gaze fall to the plate of cookies. I will *not* be labeled the campus slut. Been there, done that.

I shiver.

Nope, this time, college is all about not making things complicated.

It's not that I give a crap what people think of me. It's just that Rubes and I have to stay on the DL. Too much attention means picking up and moving again sooner rather than later. And I like it here. We're closer to home than we normally are, and I need that. Even though Ruby needs to be out in the world, I don't.

"Thanks, love," Charmant says. "You're sweet, you know that, El?"

I smile at him sweetly but keep myself in check. Keep at least a few inches between us at all times. That way, I can't be too tempted by him. There's no screwing my way through the college population. We're going elsewhere for my needs. "Thanks, Char, you, too. Better get back over there with that plate before your boys expire."

He nods once, acknowledging our boundaries again. The ones I have firmly kept in place for months. I know he's interested. He's not subtle about it, which I find endearing as hell. *Sigh.*

I turn back to pretending he doesn't exist and casually wind my way through the café to catch up on the gossip. People are always so caught up on the same things. Who's doing whom, who might be the next disaster, who's got the best party. Thank Goddess, I grew up with Ruby and Gran and the rest of the coven at the manor. I might be half-human, but it's exhausting pretending to care about this crap all the time. I need… something else. Something *more*. There has to be more to our lives than waiting for Ruby to find her mate so she can take Gran's place and bring the Ignis Coven into the twenty-first century.

Hours later, when I'm taking out the trash and trying to pretend I'm not bored out of my mind, I can't help but think what it would be like if I could just walk away from all this. Just hop in the car and drive until I find somewhere else, somewhere away from all this mundanity. All this waiting for the other shoe to drop. I mean, it's not like I'm the one who has to take over for Gran. The coven doesn't really need me. But Ruby does.

I just wish…

What, dear Ella, what do you wish? The voice behind me makes me shiver. I can feel the kiss of power against my skin before I even turn. Whoever said that is *not* human. And I'm not stupid enough to fight something I don't know.

When I've faced the ethereal shape that spoke, my breath catches. The scene of beauty behind the creature is staggering. I stare at it, at the lush green and blue grass, at the foliage that seems to go on endlessly, at the beautiful fuchsia sky, at the animals I've definitely never seen before. For a moment, I'm captivated, enthralled by the look of this place, by its feel, by the pull of *home*. If I didn't know any better, I'd say that was Azure. Where I come from. Or at least, where the Ignis witches come from. I've never seen it because it doesn't exist anymore.

I shake myself. Whatever I'm seeing isn't real. The blue figure before me becomes more solid as if it's becoming more real the longer I stare at it. I throw up every shield I have, locking myself down, determined to keep out any magical parries from this being.

I know better. I can't finish the sentence. Not aloud. Not even in my head. I bite my lip and close my eyes, keeping my mind blank. I pull on all the reserves I have, every part of patience I've ever needed. I don't know how it's possible, but this must be a Djinn. There are legends that some crossed over into the human realm thousands of years ago when the covens came here from Azure. But I've never seen one, and neither has anyone in the coven, as far as I know.

"I do not wish anything." I make my voice firm as I say it, and then I turn my back to this creature and go about my business, ensuring I am wishing for nothing. Djinn are tricksters. Even if I wanted something I couldn't get myself, I would never use a Djinn to do it. I have to tell Ruby about this. And the coven.

If there's a Djinn loose in Seattle, we better be on the lookout for the consequences and figure out how to save the humans from its power. I feel the breeze of energy around me as I finish cleaning up and get ready to head back to the apartment Ruby and I share.

Except, I don't want to lead it home with me. I know it's following me, hoping for a weakness, waiting for me to make the wrong move. One single utterance, even an errant thought, is all this being needs to wreak havoc. A college campus is rife with people desperate enough to make wishes every five seconds. Someone summoned it here.

I reach out to my sister through our mind-link. We don't use it all that often, each preferring to keep our thoughts to ourselves, not to intrude too much. But this requires immediate discussion.

Ruby, we have a big *problem. Meet me at Q in ten.*

A nightclub might not be the best place to bring a Djinn either, but if it's focused on us, it won't be focused on the desperate humans around us.

I head to the club, knowing I'm not dressed for it but uncaring. Ruby always gets us in anyway.

"I could help with the outfit change?" the voice whispers in my ear.

I ignore it, and it doesn't speak again, but I can feel the damned thing following me the entire ride there. I will have to be mindful of every thought, every utterance until it's gone. There are legends on how to outwit a Djinn and how to get rid of one. I just have to find the right way to outsmart it before the third wish from the summoner is cast. Otherwise, it'll be set free to terrorize the world with its magic.

CHAPTER TWO

When I get to Q, Ruby is already waiting at the door for me. I can feel how on edge she is, see it in her body language. Crap. Maybe bringing her in on this is a mistake, but I'm not stupid enough to try to figure this out on my own. I know she gets emotional when I'm in trouble. I haven't exactly been the easiest sister to be around. She has reason to feel like she constantly has to watch out for me. I'm working on that.

"Hey." She glances around like she can feel it too. I'm sure she can.

"Djinn."

"Damn." She nods once and then grabs my hand and pulls me toward her.

The bouncer opens the door for us without a word, and we slide inside, where the music is thumping despite it being almost dead in here.

"I didn't want to bring it home."

"We got this, sis. Let's grab a drink."

We head to the bar, and Ruby orders us two gin and juices. We're regulars, so the bartender knows that means ginger ale and cranberry juice. Much as we'd love to, witches can't get drunk. And really, a drunk Ruby is *not* something I want to see.

"Just showed up on campus, promising me the world, of course." No need for much preamble here. We head toward a corner with a few tables and decently comfortable chairs.

"Well, what do you say I introduce myself and blast it back to whatever lamp it crawled out of?" Ruby's anger is apparent in her words.

I hate knowing that she might lose control over this. I hate that I can't handle it on my own. Ruby has more raw power than anyone in our coven, including Gran, and we all know it.

I hear a chuckle, and a shiver runs through me again. Ruby shows no sign that she's heard it. Well, isn't that just ducky? My own personal little magical trickster. Just what this semester really needed.

"You could just wish me away," it says in my ear.

"You know they don't actually live in lamps."

Ruby shrugs. "As if I care."

She's going to go in all half-cocked and hot-headed and cause a natural disaster. A forest fire. A volcanic eruption. *Something* horrible that will end with casualties. I should never have told her.

"And before you speak, I know you can't change the past," I tell my unwelcome passenger.

Ruby cocks her head, and her high ponytail swings to one side.

"You're looking cute," I say instead, not bothering to explain.

"Thanks, sis."

"I better stay on campus a few days. Keep my distance."

I try to ignore the hurt in Ruby's dark eyes, but it stings. We work through a few more options, half mentally, half aloud in our own shorthand, trying to ensure we aren't understood by anything other than one another. The plan boils down to this: I keep my mind and my mouth shut while Ruby investigates where the Djinn came from and what it's doing here, and how we can send it back to whatever hole it crawled out of.

We head out of Q, and as soon as we're outside, my blood sizzles with the fire of magic. I flick my gaze to Ruby, but she's calm beside me, her gaze searching the dark sky above us. "What the hell?" she demands.

I follow her gaze up, up, up. A dragon is barreling down on us. Screams erupt from every direction as people catch sight of the stuff of their nightmares. It flaps its wings, and somebody shoves past us, knocking me into the street.

"Ella!" Ruby screams as the giant creature aims its claws right at me.

Then she spins, hands up, and flames shoot toward the dragon. "Get away from my sister!"

More screams from around us. I shove myself upright and grab for her. This is not good. Public displays of magic are messy. Dragons? How in the world are we going to get out of this one?

"I'm fine," I tell her.

The dragon darts out of the line of fire, but the building next to it isn't so lucky. Flames engulf it quickly, spurred by Ruby's magic.

"Sis, come on, stop!" I holler. But she doesn't hear me.

She's lost in her own rage now. The dragon comes at us again, and Ruby flings more fire. People are shrieking in earnest now, dark clouds of smoke billowing out around us. I get in Ruby's face. Someone is going to get hurt. And the bright gold scales of the dragon are fading behind the black clouds above us. I can't tell if it's still there or not, but honestly, Ruby poses a much bigger threat now.

I get in her face, making sure she can see me, and scream at her, verbally and through our mind link, "Rubes, enough. We're safe. I'm safe."

Soon, the people around us won't be. I hear sirens in the distance. I have to get us out of here. She lowers her hands, her red eyes slowly morphing into the normal brown color. She blinks, and her wild gaze darts around us at the fires. She swears, and I take her shaking hands in mine.

"Breathe, Rubes. Get it under control. Now." I don't normally order her around like this. But I need her to hear me. The fires around us are intense. I can't control the flames she's started. It's her magic, not mine, and she has to get a handle on it.

She takes a few deep breaths, and the fire around us begins to recede, leaving ash and soot in its wake. Several people around are still running, screaming, but others have stopped, helping anyone who's coughing or injured. I look up, and there's no dragon.

It's as if it was never there.

The firetrucks have arrived, and I pull Ruby past the chaos of people around us so she can focus on bringing the fire under control.

The firefighters are running into the building, either not recognizing or not caring that the flames were not behaving properly. Ruby takes a few deep breaths, and I can feel the magic being pulled back into her, see the flames slowly lower then disappear altogether. Then several people are being pulled from inside the building.

"Is anyone... Did I?" Ruby's horrified voice snaps my attention back to her.

I shake my head. I don't know if she's hurt anyone. And it's all my fault. There's no doubt that dragon was coming for me. I have no idea why, but if Ruby had just left it alone… "Damn it, Ruby, just stop trying to protect me." Just once, I wish I didn't have to worry about my sister and her temper.

"Oh, Ella." Ruby's face falls.

But it's too late. How could I have been so stupid? I didn't say it aloud, but Ruby heard it loud and clear, and that means…

"Done," the Djinn says. And then, before my eyes, Ruby begins to disappear.

Oh, Goddess, no. I lunge for her, grasping again for her hands, but all I catch is air. She smiles at me as her body shimmers before me.

I'll be okay. Love and light. Ruby's voice whispers through my mind.

And then she's gone.

CHAPTER THREE

Twelve hours. I have twelve hours to undo this, and then the magic is permanent. The magic of these creatures is intense, but it's volatile, and it has rules. Much like our fire magic does. That's my only saving grace.

My phone rings, and I know without pulling it from my pocket that it's Gran.

"What happened?" she demands as soon as I hit *answer*.

"It's a Djinn. Ruby's… I don't know. Gone. I made a wish. I didn't mean to. But you know those creatures…."

"Find who summoned it," Gran says without admonishing me or asking any further details. "Get the Djinn to break the contract before the human makes their final wish and sets it free upon the rest of the world. Until then, it's bound to them. It can still wreak havoc, but only to a point, and only when close by its human tether."

"I'm sorry," I feel compelled to say.

"Tosh, dear. Shall I send in some help?"

"Not yet. I don't want to risk anyone else getting hurt." I should

have handled this on my own from the start. Then Ruby wouldn't be…
I shake the thought away. I can't think of her as gone. Not yet. There's
time to save her. I just have to figure out how. I'm all-in on the campus
gossip. I gotta figure out who wants what they can't have and is willing
to go to any lengths to get it—someone like Ana.

"Okay, my darling. Call me if you need us. We'll be there in a flash."

So much for keeping things low-key. A dragon. That Djinn
conjured a literal freaking dragon to come after me so I would make a
wish. I'm gonna find this effer and make it pay. A lick of rage unfurls
inside me. It's… unnatural for me, but I can't say I hate it.

"Thanks, Gran. Love and light."

"Love and light," she says, and then she ends the call. Not one for
wasting words, my Gran.

A small smile spreads at the love I feel for her, despite my rather
dire circumstances. She could have yelled at me. She should have, by all
rights. I know better than to make such a stupid mistake, it's just that
sometimes, I feel like my sister's keeper, and I hate it. I just want her to
find her flipping mate already so that she can get control of her powers
and I can figure out who I am outside of my role as the baby sister of
the hot-headed future leader. The one who's so like our mother it
terrifies everyone.

I hover around the edge of the scene of the fire that disappeared
without any water for a few, trying to see if anyone was hurt because
of our foolishness. I'm fairly certain there aren't any major injuries.
Goddess knows what the heck the news reports will be. I'm sure
someone captured the dragon on a phone. But I got much bigger
issues.

Even if Ana isn't the one responsible for the magic, she might know
something I don't. It's as good a place as any to start. I have eleven and
a half hours left. I head toward the Beta Phi sorority, intent to find Ana
as quickly as possible and get her to talk to me. I can no longer feel the
Djinn's presence, but that doesn't mean it isn't hovering.

I knock but don't wait for someone to answer before I check the
door and then push my way inside.

After a moment, one of the new pledges is coming down the stairs. How do I know she's a pledge? Well, she's wearing a potato sack for a dress, and her face is covered in applesauce. I fight the urge to sneer. This whole concept of humiliating your *sisters* is lost on me. If these people knew anything about true sisterhood, they'd never treat each other like this.

I give her a small smile. "I'm looking for Ana. It's urgent."

The young woman looks around like I'm making a mistake. "Me?" she squeaks. She's beautiful. Even in a potato sack. Even with applesauce on her face. I want to tell her she's far too good for this nonsense. Even though I barely know her. I'm pretty sure her name is Cindy.

"Do you know where she is?"

"I'm not supposed to talk," Cindy says.

Okay, that's enough of this crap. "Why don't you get out of here?"

"I… can't," she whispers.

"Of course, you can, Cindy. Just come the rest of the way down the stairs and walk right out the front door. No one's going to stop you. I'll make sure of it." I let her see the truth in my face. I'm going to help her leave if that's what she wants. Ruby's faded into nothingness, and I have precious few hours to save her, but this person needs my help. Ruby will understand if I'm delayed a little. I take a few steps toward her, and the instant terror on Cindy's face makes me pause.

"Pledge four, where the hell– " Ana's voice cuts off as she sees me in the foyer. "Ella?"

"I have that, um, thing we talked about last night after class," I lie.

Just her reaction will probably tell me whether or not she's made a wish with the Djinn. Her eyes sparkle, and she grins. So, she probably still wants the love spell. I try not to be discouraged.

"Out, four!" she yells Cindy.

Cindy gives another squeak, and then she disappears back up the stairs before I can say a word.

I hear a door open, then loud screams, and then *slam*. I can't let myself get derailed. If Ana isn't the summoner, I'll have my work cut out for me finding who is, but I'll be back for Cindy. And anyone else who wants out of this hellhole, I promise myself.

"Great, come on up." Ana turns with a practiced flourish, convinced I'll follow her every order. I'll play along as long as it suits me.

I sprint up the stairs and down the hall to her room. No doubt it's the biggest one in this Italianate house. I'd call it old, but given where I grew up, that's a silly comparison. Ignis Manor is centuries older than this house.

"So, what do you have for me?" she says like she's the kingpin in a mob movie. She sits on the bench at the foot of her four-poster bed, and I fight the urge to gag. I've had plenty of interaction with people like Ana before. Entitled, bored, convinced that they're the best thing since sliced bread. Which is also not that old and was obviously the best thing since the birth of Betty White, and that's it.

I'm getting sidetracked. I feel the Djinn's presence stronger here.

"What is it about Charmant that makes you want him so much?"

A little practiced pout of her pink lips. She'd be pretty, ya know, if she weren't such a witch with a B. Her ugliness stems from within, just like most of the other sorority sisters here. There's a knock on the door, but Ana yells, "Not now," and turns her attention back to me. "He's the most wanted guy in school. So, he must be mine. It's that's simple."

Gag.

"Right. Okay, so you haven't already gotten some magical help elsewhere?"

She stares at me like I'm an idiot. "Would I have come to you if I already had help?"

Right because in her mind of the social hierarchy, I don't even rate an honorable mention. I roll my eyes. "Fine."

She glares. She's not used to anyone not fawning at her feet.

"Don't screw around with magic, Ana. It won't end well for you," I warn.

This time she rolls her eyes. "Whatever. Do you have a spell for me or not, *witch?*"

It's the witch that does me in. I stalk toward her, pinning her with a killer stare. The one reserved for men who touch when they're not invited. She holds her glare on me. Not so easily intimidated, huh? Well, we'll see about that.

"Do not screw with me, little girl." The four candles on her dresser light, their flames a foot high. "And stay away from Charmant." He doesn't need this viper in his life. Just because I can't have him doesn't mean I'll let her sink her fangs into him. The flames shoot higher, and I step back from her, just enough so I can catch a little ball of fire in my hands. "Understand?"

I proffer her the ball of flame. She stares at it, wide-eyed for a moment, and then the shouting from down the hall steals our attention.

I extinguish the flames and rush to the door.

"Cindy! Cindy, over here!"

"No, this way!"

The shouting is getting louder as I near the end of the hall.

When I get to the door, Ana is beside me, and the fear is still in her eyes. *Good.* So much for being the good girl on this campus. I can't worry about that now. I push the door open before Ana can grab the handle, and inside is utter bedlam.

There are overturned tables and chairs everywhere, wine and beer pouring out of open bottles, cups, and cans, applesauce everywhere. And Cindy is standing on a table in the corner of the room. I can see the glimmer of glamour around her. Why didn't I notice it before? Maybe it wasn't there, or maybe I was too distracted by the sad horror in her eyes. Now, she's fending off all the women in the room with a beer funnel, swinging it wide as she shrieks.

"No, this isn't it. This wasn't what I wanted. It wasn't a wish!"

Wish summoner found.

Now I just have to get her out of here and figure out how to save her from the Djinn's trickery.

And, ya know, bring my sister back from the ether. Can't forget about that. I push my way through the throng of co-eds, bashing this way and that. The floor is slick, so they slip and slide out of my way easily enough. I don't want to hurt anyone, but I'm not exactly being gentle. They're trying to get to Cindy with a fervor that means only one thing, magic.

"Cindy!" I yell to her.

She looks down at me, eyes wide, terror etched on her every feature.

"Help me. You said you would help me."

"And I will. But I need you to stop talking. And as much as you can, stop thinking!"

"Little witch!" The Djinn's voice is like thunder in my ears, but I ignore it.

"You bitch!" Ana screams, and then she's running toward me, just as I reach up to grab Cindy's hand to help her down.

Ana slams into the side of me, and then we're falling into a mess of limbs and sticky substances. Cindy careens to the floor with us as the table gives way under the press of people.

Ugh!

Enough of this crap.

I light one of the curtains on fire, and the sudden rush of heat and smoke distracts the spelled women, providing just enough commotion. I scramble to my feet and grab Cindy's arm. I help yank her to her feet and then pull her against me and run for the door, half supporting her body weight. She's sagging against me. I power through the hoard and then extinguish the flames before slamming the door closed. I push a table from the hallway in front of the door, knowing it won't hold them for long.

"Are you okay?"

She nods. Clearly, she understands the dangers of speaking. I can only pray that she's schooling her thoughts enough not to give the Djinn another opening. That had to have been wish number two. Which means that one more, and she's going to set it free. Whatever I do, I have to stop her from making another wish.

We get to the bottom of the stairs, and just as I'm about to pull the front door open, it flings inward, and we jump back. Cindy lets out a scream, and then we're being swarmed by people. Every one of them yelling for Cindy.

Wish fulfillment at its worst. To be popular or well-liked, even loved, maybe? This kind of psychotic devotion and demand for her attention is the closest the Djinn can get to creating real feelings inside people. It's only because of my half-witch side that I'm mostly immune to it. Though I have to say, even to me, there's a sparkle in Cindy now that I didn't quite notice before the wish.

How in the world am I going to get us out of this?

There's an open window behind us. "Out there. Hide. I'll find you. And whatever you do, don't make a wish. No matter what happens. Whatever comes next will be way worse, I promise."

She heads for the window, and I shove as many people back from us as I can. I suck in a deep breath and concentrate, pulling in as much energy as I can. There's power in wishes. And I can use it if I can harness enough of it. Fire is my specialty, and that's where the Djinn's magic stems from as well.

I surround myself in a ring of fire, flames dancing ten or twelve feet in the air all around me. I have perfect control over my fire, unlike some people.

I push the fire closer to everyone in front of me and a few step back, but others do not. Crap. Crap!

I pull the flames back before I hurt someone. If I go out the window with Cindy, they'll just follow me. I can't kill them. They don't know what they're doing. They're pawns in a magical game they know nothing about. What would Ruby do?

If I let any of these crazed zealots near Cindy, they'll love her to death. Or until she's desperate enough to make her third wish.

Screw what Ruby would do. I have to figure this out on my own. What would *Ella* do? I'm always trying to figure out who I am, separate from Ruby, from our mom and the disaster she left in her wake. I'm not Ruby. I'm not my mom. Or my Gran.

I'm me. Ella Elderbrand, half-human, half-fire-witch. The one who's always laughing and carefree on the outside. I've been the party girl, the campus slut, the bookworm, the class clown. But none of them is *me*.

I've wanted to figure that person out for a very long time. And now, because of an awful wish, I'm going to have to find the answers. Okay, plan. I need a distraction, like upstairs, but bigger and one that isn't going to hurt anyone. I don't have any supplies with me. I'm sure there's something in the kitchen I could use. If I can get to it. I lower the level of fire so I can see better.

Charmant pushes his way toward me. I hadn't even noticed him in the crowd.

"You okay?" he shouts over the noise.

He's not spelled.

How is he not spelled?

I reach for him, and when our fingers touch, I gasp. He startles, and something inside me shifts. I... oh Goddess. I pull him toward me, and he walks through the ring of fire like it's nothing.

"You're..."

"Not human." He shakes his head.

Right, yeah, noticed that. But he's also not getting burned by my fire, which means only one thing. Charmant Clement is my mate.

I cannot deal with this right now. "We have to get to Cindy. She's in trouble with a capital T. But every time I try to get out of here, I burn someone. They're not in control of themselves. I don't want to kill anyone."

He nods. "I can help with that." The fire around us morphs into brambles, woven around and around so thick I can't see through it. The hoard bashes against it, pulling, scraping. I hear cries of pain, but they don't stop. At least no one will kill themselves on the sticks. Charmant opens a small section, creating an archway for us to scramble through the branches. We climb out the window, and I look around for Cindy.

I don't see or hear her. Which, hopefully, means she's well enough hidden from all her admirers as well. I must have provided enough distraction with the fire that they didn't notice her slip away.

Charmant glances up, and his gaze lands on a small, white bird. It chirrups at him and then flies away.

"Come on." He grabs my hand, and that zing sizzles through me again, and my heart stutters. I'm trying to think back over every interaction we've had over the past several months. Have I seriously *never* touched him? Not once? The mating bond only starts upon the first touch of skin, magic, or blood.

When we reach a dark corner of campus, full of trees and bushes, the bird lands atop a branch, and Charmant nods at me once. Who needs a locator spell when you can talk to birds?

He hasn't let go of my hand, and I can feel the pulse of magic arcing between us. My fire and his deep earthiness.

"Cindy, it's me. It's safe to come out."

She slowly emerges from beneath the branches of the hazel tree, and the potato sack has turned into a stunning gold gown. "Cindy, you didn't!"

She shakes her head. "I didn't. I swear!"

"Sorry, that one's on me," Charmant says. He grins wickedly at Cindy, and she blushes furiously. "Not that you couldn't pull off that whole potato sack look. Better than Marilyn, in fact, but I thought you might like something clean."

She glances at our clasped hands and then smooths her fingers down the silken folds of the dress. She looks back up at him. "It's beautiful. Thank you."

"Of course. Though I suppose it's probably impractical, given how conspicuous it is." Charmant smiles at her.

I think my mate is likely to stay a bit of a flirt, mating bond or not. I suppose it's good. I've never been the jealous type.

I can feel the tug of our bond, but I do my best to ignore it. I won't be able to for long, but I have to save Ruby first. Lust can wait.

"We have to go back to where you summoned the Djinn," I tell Cindy. "And get rid of it."

Char lets out a small whistle. "That will not be easy, love."

"I know, but we don't have a choice. I…" I swallow hard. I hate admitting it aloud. Especially now, especially before Charmant, who Fate has chosen for me. I want him to want me for me. I want him to like me for me. Not because of some stupid mating bond neither of us has control over.

"What is it, El?" he asks. "Whatever it is, we can fix it. We can figure it out, together."

"Did you know?" I ask him, suddenly desperate to figure him out. To discover why he's here. "Did my gran send you?"

He laughs, shaking his head. "I don't know your Gran, love. But did I know you would be mine one day?" He lifts my hand to his and kisses the back of it like he's Mr. Darcy. "Yes, that I knew for sure."

And then he shifts a glamor I didn't even know had been there, and I see him in truth. Bright silver hair trailing down his back, long, elegant ears that end at the top in a lovely point, swirling purple and blue eyes. But that smile. That smile is the same. Dazzling. Making my stomach flip and my heart pound. His skin shimmers with the sparkle of diamonds in the brightest sunlight, and for a moment, I'm utterly captivated. I lean toward him and touch his lips with mine. Power blasts through us, knocking me back with its force. I land on my ass a few feet away.

"Ella!" he shouts, but he's just as flat on his rear.

Ella, hurry.

Ruby's strained voice in my head pushes me back into action.

"We have to go. Right now. Cindy, show us where it started." Ruby needs me. Really needs me this time. Not to save her from herself or her magic. But to save her from my stupidity.

I won't let her down.

CHAPTER FOUR

I stare at the window to the basement of the off-campus house. "In there?"

Cindy nods. "I was just sitting down there feeling sorry for myself when...."

I hold up a hand to stop her from saying anything else. I can feel the Djinn is close. He's not going to go down without a fight. I can't communicate with Char or Cindy without risking the Djinn hearing us. I can't clue it in.

"I'm going in. Alone." I stare at Charmant, trying to communicate with him that I am not serious and hoping the mating bond will make him stupid enough to disobey me. It usually does. "I don't care what you hear or see or feel. You don't come in after me. Got it?"

"El..." he starts.

"I can take care of myself. Which you would know if you paid any real attention."

He quirks a brow. Just one. And my insides quiver. *No, damn it, Ella, get control of yourself.*

"I need you to stay out here with Cindy. If I mess up in there, she needs some kind of protection."

Before we left the darkened hill where Cindy was hiding, Charmant created something less flashy for her than a bright gold dress and gold slippers! I knew this boy had a flare for the dramatic, but sheesh, I didn't realize how much.

"Okay, I get it." He winks at me. "You don't need some knight in shining armor or even your big sister to fight the dragon for you."

Guess he saw that then.

How embarrassing. Ugh. Has he been following me? "You're sure you don't know my gran?"

He shakes his head, and I get caught up in watching his hair move around him like it's caught in a breeze. He truly is a beauty. Fae. I've been mated to a Fae. I didn't know any of them survived the collapse of Azure.

I shake myself and turn toward the window of the basement. I pry it open and shove myself inside before I can throw myself at Charmant. Those hormones are riding me hard, and I cannot do anything about it right now.

I clear my throat.

"Djinn, I'm ready to make a deal. Show yourself."

"Is that a wish, dear Ella?" he asks as he materializes before me. Purple and blue hues sparkle around him in brilliant kaleidoscopes.

"Not yet. Let's get some things clear first. I'm going to let Cindy make her last wish to free you from your prison."

I can see the spark in his eyes as I say this. But I know he won't just believe me. I have to show him that I'm serious. That there are things I want, things I need and will do anything to get.

"I want my coven. I want my sister back. I want some more power. I want things I'm sure you can't give me, but…." I let my voice trail off.

He narrows his eyes at me. "We shall see. Once you make an official wish, of course."

Ah, so he isn't going to fall that easily into the trap, is he?

"And I want out of my mating bond. No power in existence can do that. I want the bond itself to disintegrate. I don't want anything to happen to that doofus out there. I just want us to be free of one another." Goddess, I hope Charmant won't take that to heart. I'm sure he can hear me. Fae hearing is at least as good as werewolf hearing. Thank the universe that Fate didn't match me with one of *those* things.

I refocus my attention. Charmant will either understand what I'm doing, or he won't, but I need all my wits about me to face off against this Djinn.

"But mating bonds are set by powers far beyond mine or yours. And you know it. There's no way for you to give me what I want."

"I could just kill him."

I sigh dramatically, pulling on all my years of blending in with normal humans. "Stupid mating bonds. If you kill him before we've sealed our Fate, I'll go insane. If you do it after, I'll always feel as if part of me is missing." I pout, sticking out my bottom lip as far as it will go.

He grins at me. "I know."

"Is there anything you *don't* know?" If I play into this creature's ego enough, I'll convince him that I need the help, that my situation has changed enough to want this more than I want my sister back, even. "If anyone knows how to get out of a mating bond with my sanity and soul intact, it's a Djinn. Hey, what's your name, by the way? I hate just calling you the Djinn in my head. It feels so impersonal." I risk a small smile like I'm not sure he'll accept my olive branch.

I know names have power. I can't control it if I know the name, but it helps. It creates a rapport of sorts, at least.

"You may call me Kala." Kala gives a slight dip of his head. Djinn don't really have gender.

"Thank you, Kala." I sigh. "Any thoughts on how you might get me out of this bond? Some way I can… you know, do the special asking thing for it?" I'm careful not to say the w-word.

"I might. But you're asking an awful lot of me." He cocks his head to the side. "How do I know you'll keep up your end of the deal?"

Djinn love a good deal.

"If you don't give me what I want, I'll kill Cindy."

He laughs, and I can tell he doesn't believe me. "Of course, you wouldn't. You witches are all the same. Virtuous. Meddlesome."

Kala clearly has a long memory. I've heard the stories of when the covens bound the Djinn to objects that could contain their powers and the prison cells they were trapped in when they still tried to wreak havoc in Azure. If I kill Cindy before she's wished her final wish, it will send Kala back into whatever object he was contained in here. Kala's smile is devious. "Unless, of course, you're different."

I cross my arms. "I might not be that different. But I am *highly* motivated to get out of my bond. I never would consider this otherwise. You're my only option." I try to sound as desperate as I am, even if the reasons are not the ones I'm giving Kala. I need my sister back. The hours are ticking by. I don't have that many left. It's almost daybreak already. "I'll do whatever I have to do." And I mean that, mostly. My sister is too important to me. If it means giving up Charmant, letting myself go insane, I don't care. As long as Ruby comes back in one piece. I don't think she'd ever forgive me if I killed an innocent woman to save her, though. That's the line I can't cross. But I have to make Kala believe I will do just that.

"So, let me get this right, if I give you your sister, break your mating bond without you going insane or missing part of your soul, you'll give me that human and make her wish for something so I can be free?"

"Yes."

"And if I don't do those things...."

"Mr. Wrapped Around my Pinkie out there will kill your human tether, and you'll go back to whatever hellhole you crawled out of for another thousand years until someone summons you again. What do you think I brought her here for?"

I'm running out of time. "Tick tock, Kala. This deal expires when the sun rises. Because this itch of needing to seal my mating bond is already irritating the crap out of me. I want it gone. Now. So, either do it, or I'll tell him to kill the human."

"Won't that be like cutting off your nose to spite your face?"

I shrug.

"I don't trust you."

"I don't care. Now, stop stalling. Either you're powerful enough to give me what I want, or you're not, and this is a complete waste of my time."

He presses his lips into a line. Kala apparently doesn't appreciate my calling his powers into question. Good. I'm trying to goad him into giving me what I want.

"Bring my sister back first. As a show of good faith."

"I can't undo a wish, and you know it."

"Wow, you really are as useless as the others say. Okay, clearly, this isn't going to work." I turn and raise my voice. "Do it, darling! She's of no use to us any longer."

I don't wait for a response but turn back to watch Kala's face contort in anger. He lunges for me, morphing into a small dragon as he moves. I crouch and roll to the side, and even pint-sized, a dragon is a dangerous creature. I shoot fire at Kala, and he darts my blast.

Fire soars past me, scorching the edges of my hair. I'm not used to that. I'm immune to most types of fire. But not dragon's breath. I cough at the sudden burning smell. Ew. A moment later, Charmant and Cindy are in the room.

"You idiot!" I scream at him. "You were supposed to kill her."

I know Charmant has *no* idea what the hell is going on, but he has to know I couldn't possibly mean that. I lunge for Cindy at the same time as I shoot another mass of fire at Kala, aimed right for his throat. The dragon dodges, but the magic connects with the wing, and it screams.

"Cindy," I whisper, praying I won't be heard.

"I wish for a full-sized, usable, silver sword to materialize on the floor before me, touching nothing else in the room except for the floor," Charmant, clever little Fae that he is, has made a wish in an infallible manner. Fae are almost as tricky as Djinn.

A sword clatters to the floor before him as I tell Cindy, "Wish for the sword to kill you."

"What?" she demands.

"You'll be okay. Trust me. Do it. Hurry."

She stares at me, wide-eyed, like I'm absolutely insane. I'm sure I sound like I am.

Charmant picks up the sword and charges Kala. "I'll take you down, beast." Bless him. He may not know exactly what I'm up to, but he knows I need the Djinn distracted. And he's giving me time to get us all out of this mess alive, trusting that I'm going to succeed. That I don't need him to fight my battles for me. But, hey, we all could use a little help from time to time, right?

Charmant and Kala circle each other, and he advances on the dragon, then backs off when flames threaten to turn him to cinders.

"Cindy, now. Say exactly that. 'I, you know what, for the sword to kill me. It's not going to be fun, but you will be okay. I swear."

She'll die, but only for a second.

A Djinn is forbidden to kill who summoned them. Or they would simply kill the summoner and be free from their prisons forever. And who the hell would use a wish to kill themselves? No one. It's a loophole in the rules. If Cindy wishes for death, and uses her *last* wish to do it, the last wish can't set him free because a dead summoner means a voided contract. And the magics Kala brought down upon us all will cease to have ever existed.

Ruby will come back. Cindy's wish to be popular will disappear, and no one will remember their actions. The evidence of a dragon terrorizing downtown Seattle will disappear, and the memories will seem like a fuzzy bad dream.

"I wish for the sword to kill me," Cindy whispers, her voice warbling.

The sword shoots from Charmant's hand and straight toward Cindy. She shrieks.

"No!" Kala shouts just as the sword pierces through Cindy's heart.

"I'm so sorry." I grab her body as it falls. And then the sword disappears. She gasps. "You're okay, you're okay, Cindy. It's okay."

"It is *not* okay. You killed me! I was dead."

"Yeah, but only for like a second, right?" Ruby asks.

I risk a glance around the room. No Kala. And no Charmant either. Just Ruby.

What. The. Hell.

CHAPTER FIVE

"Seriously, El? Like you can't just stay in with your big sister tonight?"

I'm going out of my mind with need. I absolutely cannot. I have to find Charmant. Right this second. Or I'm going to lose my mind. I can feel him. He's close. He's been close for hours. But he won't show himself.

Poor Cindy will probably never speak to me again, no matter how many times I tell her that this was the only way to, well, save the world.

Okay, maybe that's a touch dramatic, a little bit of a stretch. But not by much.

"Just for a little bit. I promise I'll be back soon."

One way or another. Either I'm going to put a high heel up Charmant's rear, or I'm going to finish this mating ritual. Perhaps both. Both is good.

I like both.

I adjust said high heel, securing the shoe around my ankle, and then clear my throat. I know I should tell Ruby where I'm going. Not because I need her protection, but because finding my mate is *huge*, but I just can't.

I deserve something to myself. My whole life has revolved around my family. My place in the coven, my place as the youngest Elderbrand, my place as the future leader's little sister. Right now, here, this isn't me as any of those things. This is me as Ella. Just Ella.

Ruby shakes her head, throws a piece of popcorn at me, and then blows me a kiss. "Love and light, sis."

"Love and light." I chuck the piece of popcorn back at her and head out. It'll be a while before memories are fuzzy enough for us to be back out in the world around here. So, we'll keep to ourselves. I'll take the rest of the term off for medical reasons, and next semester, when the rumor mill has moved far past the weird fires, appearing bramble walls, and that girl who saved Cindy's life, Ruby and I will reemerge. Like we always do.

As soon as I'm a few feet from the front door of our apartment, Charmant comes out of the shadows.

"Okay, so I kind of lied. Well, sort of. I really don't know your gran, but I do know who she is and who you are and who your sister is," he says without any more context. "And by the grace of all things holy, can I please, please touch you? I feel like I'm dying."

The urge to kiss him overwhelms the urge to kick him. "You lied to me."

"I know. I suck."

"You could have knocked on the door."

"Your sister scares the shit out of me."

I glare.

"But you scare me way, way more, I swear. Did I mention I suck? And please, kiss me. Please, love, we'll figure out the rest once my blood stops boiling."

"You only want me because of the mating bond."

He shakes his head. "Not true. I told you I knew you'd be mine. Long before we touched. I made sure that didn't happen until it couldn't be avoided."

He's rambling. Damn. He's so cute when he's rambling. Wait… "Just how long have you been hovering at the edges of my life? Just how did you know we'd been mated?"

His glamour no longer works on me, so when his eyes darken from silver and purple to the deepest midnight blue, I see every detail. He tilts his head as if debating just how much to tell me. "Honesty, Charmant, total honesty, or I will walk away from this. I will lock myself in a dungeon and let the time expire, come what may. I won't be mated to someone who lies to me." I never thought I'd have to have this conversation.

"Since before you were born." He stops breathing. I can see the sudden preternatural stillness that only Fae and vampires have.

"How old are you?"

We're starting to get odd glances from passersby. He threads his fingers through mine, and electrical magic shoots through my entire body. I *want* him with such fire that it is earth-shattering. I let him tug me into the alley beside my building. But I yank my hand back.

"Three hundred or so human years."

Witches age differently than humans, so I'm no stranger to being a lot older than I look, but I'm not anywhere near *that* old. He's vibrating now with the magic, with the need, with the desire I can see pooling in his eyes. He crowds me against the wall. "Ella, please," he begs.

"Tell me all of it. Right now, Charmant." I know I'm torturing him. I'm torturing us both. But I want the truth. I deserve the truth.

"Fae have been here since the gateway between Azure and this world was opened. We managed to save centuries of prophecies from our world before it was destroyed. You're in them. So is your sister. And others. I haven't been near you until recently. But I always knew where you were. I was always waiting for the right time. For the right push."

I can feel the sincerity in his voice. I can see it in his eyes. Fate. It plays with all of us, doesn't it?

"I was supposed to wait longer. But when I saw you in that mob of people, surrounded by fire, alight with power and magic and strength... I couldn't wait anymore." His body is inches from mine, his head lowering toward me.

Listening to the way he describes me when I felt at my weakest... it makes my heart squeeze and my belly flip. I want him. We both know it. I've wanted him a long time. Was that Fate? Was it the bond waiting to be ignited?

"Please, Ella, please forgive me. Please have me. Let me be yours. For all eternity." His lips are almost touching mine.

I ache for him. I yearn for him. Does it matter if it's Fate? Do prophecies have to come true? Or do we simply *make* them come true because we know them ahead of time?

Screw it.

I don't care. All that matters is that Charmant is here, that the boy, the man I've wanted to be closer to for months, the one that saw me at my weakest, at my most indecisive, and who saw not weakness, but strength, is here. Mine for the taking. He trusted me to defeat the Djinn without interfering, without trying to play the hero.

I thread my fingers through his silvery hair and seal my lips against his. He surges forward, his body pinning mine against the wall and kissing me with such emotion that my legs wobble. I kiss him senseless, until my lungs are burning for air. We have a lot left to discuss. We have hours of conversations ahead of us. But right now, right now, I need him. And we need somewhere a lot less public. Sex magic is powerful.

"Bring me home with you," I whisper when we come up for air.

He picks me up, and then we're in a meadow. We could be anywhere, but I see the same hazel tree Cindy was hiding behind at the edge of the clearing. "You mean to tell me there's a Sidhe mound in the middle of campus?"

He shrugs sheepishly. "Uh, yeah."

I stop resisting the urge to kick him, and he feigns injury to the hip my heel connected with, stumbling and almost "dropping" me. When he gets to one knee, he gently sets me on the grass before him and lowers his head. "No more half-truths or lies or secrets. I swear it. You will only ever have truth from me from this moment forward. This is my solemn vow."

A solemn vow from a Fae is an unbreakable bond. Charmant has just made it impossible to lie to me. Forever. He looks up at me then.

"So, if I asked you if I looked fat in this dress, you'd have to tell me?"

"You say fat like it's a bad word."

A smile curves my lips. Sometimes I forget that I've probably been just as influenced by being around human culture as any whole human has. I haven't been intimate with anyone magical before.

"But to answer your question, I do not think you are anything less than stunning. Now. Always."

"That's always the right answer," I tell him with a smile.

"Outstanding. Now, sweet, dear, wonderful Ella, will you please put me out of my misery?" That begging edge in his voice does me in.

I reach for him then and pull him against my body. "Yes, please."

He lifts me again and kisses me over and over again as he walks us across the meadow and toward the village. I take no notice of where we are until he's laid me on his bed, and I can instruct him on exactly how to make him mine. Forever.

✳

When I stumble back into the apartment at dawn, Ruby's waiting at the kitchen bar for me.

"Did you seriously hook up with some rando while I was disappearing?" Ruby shakes her head. "Sis. I can't even with you." Her smile is wide, but I can see the touch of worry in her eyes. She knows something else is up. But I can't tell her Char's Fae and my mate without telling her the rest. Prophecies, big baddies coming our way, the fate of the world in the balance… Nuh-uh. Ruby's already made it her mission to fight the need to have a mate because of Fate. If I put this on her, she'll just fight harder. She's too stubborn for her own good. And I'm not going to put that kind of pressure on her. I won't. It's not fair.

"Look, girl, I can't help it. You know how I am." I wink at her. Let her think I'm still the party girl. Still the carefree silly sister she's always known. Maybe someday soon, I'll tell her that I'm dating Charmant, and then, down the line, I can tell her the rest. I know she'll be pissed at me, but I can't be worried about that right now.

I only wish… nope. No way. Nuh-uh.

Never doing that again.

Ruby will have to find her mate on her own. I ain't gonna wish her one. I learned that lesson.

ABOUT JOELLE NICHOLE

Joelle Nichole is the supernatural penname of bestselling contemporary author Rachell Nichole. As Jo, she writes about sassy witches, scorching shifters, and spellbinding stories of fairytales and romance. She lives in Pennsylvania with a mountain of books, an ongoing caffeine addiction, and her family.

Find out more at: joellenichole.com

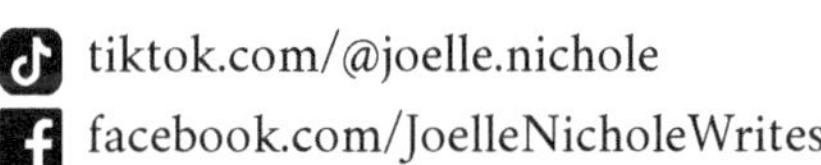

tiktok.com/@joelle.nichole

facebook.com/JoelleNicholeWrites

IN THE DYING LIGHT
BY JO HOLLOWAY

"Real wishes, the ones made by a witch when she comes into her power, always come at a cost."

CHAPTER 1

My brother is lucky I'm so careful because sometimes I want to wish him out of existence. If I made a wish like that, it would come true, so he should be a little less of a jerk to me and a little more afraid of what I could do.

"I know it wasn't real, Jacks, but I swear, I can describe him perfectly. We were at the edge of the forest. The man had shaggy, blond hair and this wild look in his eyes. I saw you kill him."

Jacks leans against the counter and fans himself as if he might faint. "Oh, my shimmering sunbeams. She had a *vision*. She must be a *witch* or something." My brother gasps dramatically, eyes twinkling with mirth as he puts a mocking hand to his mouth. He drops it when I pin him with a glare.

I'm still feeling the rush of adrenaline after waking up screaming from the vivid dream—sweat chills on my skin. "Obviously, it wasn't a vision, you halfwit. You don't have to tease."

"Well, at least you hate me now, so I know I've done my job. Every brother must be hated at least once a day. I'm fairly sure that's a rule."

"You're exceeding your quota," I tell him, but that only makes him smile.

"That's because I excel at everything I do." Finally, he sees the disquiet in my face and lifts his hands in a gesture of peace. "Relax, Amber. Why would I kill anyone?"

"I don't know. It was just a dream."

It didn't feel like a dream. Watching my older brother murder that man has left me feeling cold and shaky all over. In the doorway to the bedroom behind me, my blankets are still on the floor where I kicked them off. It was my brother's voice calling out to ask what was wrong that brought the room around me into focus and pulled me from the hazy forest of my dream.

I look around again and remind myself I'm safe in my home. The same low log walls and thatched roof surround me with familiar comfort. Nothing is out of place, and there's absolutely no reason for Jacks or anyone else to slaughter anybody. Plus, we never go to the forest. I make sure of that.

Jacks stands by the kitchen, looking the same as always. No blood covers him. No cold, calculating gaze rests in his eyes. No sword dangles from his hand. He gives me his classic easy grin. "You're probably just hungry. That always gives me nightmares. Dad should be back from his fishing trip tomorrow. I bet we'll have a full table by dinner."

"I hope so." It's been a long time since we had a full table. It's been a long time since anyone around here did. "I should check on the garden. The fielder berries are coming in, and I'll need to be quick to beat the birds to them."

He reaches over to ruffle my hair, shoving a curtain of black across my eyes. "That's our little Amber. Always with dirt under your nails. Always living up to the Goldenroot family name."

I'm hardly little. I came of age last season, not that we did anything to celebrate. How could we when there's nothing with which to celebrate? I give Jacks a shove. "At least I'm willing to get dirty for honest work. What have you been up to while I slept?"

"Oh, you know. A bit of this. A bit of that."

"Sunny skies, Jacks. What scheme are you plotting this time?"

"Who, me?"

I plant my hands on my hips and glare in steely silence. His eyes are the same shade of murky green as mine, and I'm perfectly aware of how cold that gaze can be when its full intensity is turned on you. Our mother used to use her stare the same way.

"Fine...you nosy little pest. If you must know, I'm meeting Locke later. He's bringing me some good stuff. I'll head straight to the market after and turn it around for a tidy profit. When Dad brings home fish, we'll have it with a full feast, spirits included," he says with a wink.

"Jacks, just...No. So much no. For starters, Locke is a smuggler, not a charity. How are you paying him for whatever he's bringing you?"

"Hey, don't sound so disgusted. That smuggler brings all sorts of useful things, plus he's a nice guy."

"I'm sure you think so." I scowl at my idiot brother. He would trust a cockatrice if it promised him an easy path to riches or fun.

"He is. And he's fair. He won't cheat me, and you'll like what he's bringing this time. I'll save some for you."

My eyes narrow, but I have to admit, I'm curious. "What?"

"Seeds." Jacks grins, knowing he's hit my weakness. "New plants. Things he swears will grow here in low light, without the full sun."

"Edible things?"

Jacks waggles his eyebrows at me while he backs toward the front door. "Trust me, baby sister. Your big brother will provide."

With that, he ducks out the door to make one of his dramatic exits, but I'm not done with him. I chase after him to the front gate.

"No spirits, Jacks! If you waste money, I swear...."

He wafts a hand through the air, batting my words away without acknowledgment as he disappears down the lane, his figure fading in the ever-present haze until I can no longer see him. I'll be the one murdering someone if Jacks comes home with drink instead of food, although I wouldn't say no to some cream if he can manage it. How long has it been since we had a creamy stew instead of the watery soups made from the failing vegetables in our garden? My stomach rumbles in response. "Yeah, that sounds about right," I say to my empty belly as I stride back inside.

The realization strikes me that Jacks never did tell me how he's going to pay for the goods he receives from the smuggler. I know the type of smuggler Locke is, and no matter whether he sets fair prices, items brought from another world are never cheap.

"Oh no. Please say you didn't, Jacks." I hurry to the shelf above the sink and pick up the tin at the far left. The little boy in his red shirt dances across the golden field embossed on the lacquered side, smiling as always, but there's no rattle to accompany his romp.

I can't stifle my groan. For the love of sunshine! Jacks took our last three coins.

My basket is woefully empty. I've checked every bed in the garden, and all I have to show for it are a single pea pod, two underdeveloped tubers, and a small collection of greens. If I'm lucky, I'll have a few berries to sweeten what will be a very paltry salad for tonight.

I make my way down the steep path beyond the bottom of the garden, where the rocks appear darker than they used to. It's like they never completely dry now without the sun's light shining fully on them. Remembering the days in my childhood when these rocks gleamed pale and bright and dry is like imagining another world. It seems so far removed from the way we live now.

Back then, the Mist was something we heard about, not something we lived with. It used to be contained to Aglonbriar forest, and as long as we steered clear of the woods and the beastly sounds that came from it, we could go about our lives without thinking of the Mist. Now, it's everywhere. It's a constant haze that blocks the sunshine. It's a fog that obscures our view of the town from the top of the hill. It's the lingering presence of something not right that dims the world into half-light and heaviness.

Before she got sick, my mother took me to Aglonbriar forest to warn me of the dangers of the Mist. I can still picture it…still feel the enchantment of watching its tendrils curl around the trunks of the trees lining the woods. My mother must have known something even then.

"It's not right," she said to me. "Can you feel it?"

I looked up at her with my twin braids bobbing at the sides of my head and my little eyes shining. "What is it, Mama?"

"Nothing good, Amber, darling. Nothing good. Promise you'll keep your brother away from it. You and I, we can watch over it, but the others aren't safe here so close to it. No one else is safe from the touch of the Mist."

For some reason, I didn't think to ask why she and I could be close to it, nor what it would do to everyone else. I was scared enough that all I thought about was getting away and never returning.

Now that I know enough to ask the right questions, Mama's not around to answer. While I may not have sensed the wrongness of the Mist quite as my mother did that day, I've kept an eye on it the way she said. Even after my mother explained why I was safe from it, it never felt any less dangerous. Since then, I've seen it spread, and I've seen the devastation that spreads with it. I'm not safe from that. No one is.

At the bottom of the path, I step off the last rock. Turning the corner around the hedge, I let out a shriek.

"No. Shoo. Away." My hands wave above my head as I rush the fielder berry bushes like a madwoman. Birds lift from the branches, squawking and flapping, sending me ducking. My fingers graze the feathers of a Dusted greenwing, and I'm tempted to grab hold of it and wring its pretty iridescent neck, but it's too fast for me.

With the last of the birds scared off, I examine the damage with a pit in my stomach. All the green berries I'd nurtured this far along… gone—every last one. Even the birds are so desperate for something to eat that they'll take the belly ache from underripe fruit over going hungry.

The farther the Mist extends from the forest, the more we lose the light from the sky. It already blocked the sun enough that our light is a dim orange glow these days. Crops died out. Gardens are failing. Herds had to be moved to lands closer to the sea where grass still grows enough to feed them.

People left, too. Those with the resources to pick up and leave—to start over somewhere else—have done so, which leaves the rest of us here, fighting to survive alongside the wild creatures.

I sink to the damp dirt and let the stinging in my eyes condense into tears. I don't know what we're going to do. Not everyone who stayed in this dying place is willing to accept the changes. There are those who ventured into the Mist, hoping to find out what causes it and stop it. Not a single one ever returned.

There are others who look to me with resentful shadows in their gazes as if I'm the one responsible. Or as if I should have fixed this. Their eyes weigh heavy on me because I constantly wonder if they're right.

One wish.

That's all it would take.

I could wish for anything. Any wish will activate my powers and determine my magic's affinity.

"Listen carefully, Amber," my mother said after we went to see the Mist that day. "You're a witch, like me." I already knew that much, so I held my tongue and waited for her to say more. I used to hang on every word my mother said to me. "That means a great many things. For one thing, you are safe from the Mist, and that means you have a responsibility to keep others safe from it too.

"Being a witch means you will have enormous power, but that power can do as much harm as good. Guard your one wish. You only get one chance to define the rest of your life and commit your magic to its full form. Use it wrong, and you'll be as likely to lose everything and everyone you ever loved as you are to get what you truly want. Wishes are tricky that way. Real wishes, the ones made by a witch when she comes into her power, always come at a cost."

"How will I know what to wish for?" Even at that age, the pressure felt immense.

"You'll know. When the time is right, you'll know. But before then, you must be vigilant. Never wish on anything. Never utter the phrase *I wish* or form the complete thought. You must not wish for anything at all. Not until you are certain."

I never have.

How can I ever be certain? And what could I even wish for that might fix our broken world?

After our mother died from her illness, I told Jacks about the wish and how it would activate my powers. He immediately wanted me to use it to wish our mother back to life. We fought about it for days. He called me selfish and every bad word he could remember, plus some he made up. I hollered that I couldn't. I had no idea what such a wish would do. Would everyone who ever died come back to life? Would our mother come back the same or as some tortured version? Would I spend my life dealing in death? She warned me there would be a cost, and a wish dealing in life and death was likely to have too high a cost to be worth any reward.

Our mother wouldn't have wanted that for me, but it started me down a path of doubt I still wander on today. There are simply too many ways for a wish to go wrong or a power to be corrupted. It's safer not to try.

Looking up at the barren bushes, though, I'm tempted to wish for something rash. An end to hunger. Limitless food. All the coin we could ever need. I'm tempted to wish for the Mist to go away so things could go back to how they were, and this region could be lush and prosperous again. We could stop being cut off from the rest of Anterra by the barrier of the Mist cutting our world in two. There's another side to Anterra that no one here has seen in their lifetime except Mrs. Blackiron, and she's so old no one knows if her stories are true. Even the settlements on the other side of the Yellow Plain are lost to all of us but the bravest willing to make the crossing in the pale light where the Mist is thinnest. Not all of them make it there. Or back.

Tears roll down my cheeks. One drops over my top lip, and I savor the salty taste. It's more flavor than I've tasted in days, and it's enough to give me the fortitude to rise again. I have to find a way to go on.

"Right, then, wicked birds. I hope you enjoyed your little feast, you greedy feathered vermin. Don't think you've beat me, though." I shake a fist in the air to the amusement of a pair of steelhawks perched on the withered dusk pear tree. "I bet there are wild mushrooms near the forest edge, and you, feathery fowls, will not dare to go so far into the Mist, will you? No? Didn't think so."

I may be a witch without powers, but I'm still a witch, and I have one advantage. The Mist doesn't affect me.

It's too bad I can't say the same for the beasts that dwell within it.

My basket has a pleasant weight to it as I make the long walk back to town. My trip to the edge of Aglonbriar forest was quick, the walk there and back far exceeding any time spent in the proximity of those woods. I wasn't about to linger when I felt the same wrongness my mother spoke about all those years ago. I skirted the edge of the trees, feeling the creepy sensation of eyes prickling the back of my neck, coming from somewhere deep in the shadows. I jumped at every small sound, but the damp vegetation made my quarry plentiful, and as soon as I had a good collection of mushrooms, I hurried away, heart racing.

The Mist thins the farther I go across the Yellow Plain toward home, and I start to breathe easier. Soon the disturbing feeling fades, and I'm rather pleased with myself. None of these will taste particularly good, but at least we'll have full bellies tonight. There are enough to last us until tomorrow when our father should return, hopefully bringing an abundant catch with him, and I can use some of the mushrooms with fish bones to make a good soup stock.

Ahead, a bright spot in the gloom catches my eye. A single blossom of blue herdsbloom flowers amid the scrub grass, growing defiantly despite the lack of light. Smiling, I head over. Many would call it a weed, but I've always found these spiky blossoms beautiful. This plant is resilient and stubborn. It's just what all of us who have stayed here need to be, and I admire it for its ability to flower in these conditions, to bring beauty to the bleakness.

Kneeling, I dig around the base to lift the entire plant by the root and place it in my basket. The moment I reach my own garden, I kneel again at the bed along the back of the house and replace the flower into soil. Patting it down, I hope its resilience will allow it to continue to bloom here. Sunshine only knows I could use a little beauty in my life.

I've barely finished packing the dirt tight around it and stood to brush off my hands when Jacks comes whistling up the walk. Rounding the corner of the house, I come face to face with my brother. He looks pleased, but I've learned never to trust that grin. It's the look he gets when he comes up with another scheme.

"Jacks, what did you do?" No matter how much I search him, I can see no evidence of his efforts for the day. He's empty-handed, something he proves when he holds his palms up to me.

"Well," he starts. Never a good sign.

My eyes narrow.

"Locke didn't show…."

Relief passes through me. "Oh, good. Then you still have our coins. Give them back to me right now, and I'm putting them somewhere you can't find them this time. I can't believe you took them without discussing it with me. When you said you were going to meet Locke, I thought you meant some sort of trade."

"Not so fast. I don't have the coins," Jacks says.

"What do you mean you don't have them? You're empty-handed, Jacks. You must have them."

"Well…I was going to use them to buy some faerie dog teeth or hyda stones to trade with Locke, something rare enough to be of interest but not too expensive. But there was none of that to be had today, and then Locke didn't show anyway, so I returned to the market to see what else I could find."

My foot taps the dusty path. This story had better get good and fast.

"Well, crabby old Mr. Direblood finally decided to kill another of his phasia birds—"

"He did?" My hands drop to my sides. It's been a month since there was fresh meat at the market. My mouth actually starts to salivate before I remember that Jacks is standing here holding nothing.

"Yes, and I saw him first. I got half the bird for the three coins, and then traded the pieces. The drumstick went to Mrs. Kindborn for a ruby ring and the rest to Kasia for three woolen blankets."

I blink in disbelief. What use could we have for any of those items? We have blankets, and we have enough dying plants to fuel our fire each night. Jacks feels the force of my ire and hurries on.

"Some of the big drafty houses in town are getting cold with the Mist spreading, and they don't have land to provide fuel, so I figured I could trade the blankets to them for silver and items worth far more at market, but for which they have no use anymore."

"For which *no one* has use anymore. Including us!" Fury stains my cheeks hot.

"*And*," Jacks continues pointedly, "which I could then trade to someone who could take them far away, like someone headed to the far shores. I had already spotted her, see?"

"You know I don't."

"Patience, dear sister. I'm getting there."

"Please get there faster."

"Enjoy this journey. Appreciate my brilliance for a moment, won't you? See, I spotted her, and I just knew. She had an air about her."

"Jacks, if this is about a woman—"

"No. Blue skies, no. She must have been a hundred years old." Jacks shudders and then returns to his proud stance. "No, little sister, I made this final trade for you. See, the woman is a witch."

"What? How do you know?" I'm certain no traveling trader was a hundred years old, and I have my doubts about the rest. Dread snakes through my belly at what Jacks hasn't told me yet.

"I know because she told me."

"She just came out and told you? Did you not find that odd?" My voice rises in pitch, reaching a screechy note by the end.

"No. Why would I? Mom was a witch. You are."

"Exactly. And do you hear me announcing it to everyone I meet? This town only tolerates me staying here after they found out about Mother because I have no powers. Half of them are scared of my magic awakening, and the other half blame me for not using it to save us all yet. But don't think that would stop them casting me out the moment I did, especially if anything went wrong. There's no winning as a witch. Most people don't take kindly to us, so most witches are exceedingly quiet about it."

"Well, this one was perfectly happy to chat about it."

"Oh? Then what was her stone?"

Jacks tilts his head in obvious confusion.

"Her stone, Jacks. It's every gemstone witch's namesake. Surely my brilliant brother remembered that small fact and thought to ask what it was as confirmation."

He pauses, and my heart sinks. "It doesn't matter. You'll love what I got from her. It's exactly what we need."

I look him up and down, still trying to figure out what he's hiding. Where is this horde of riches he must have acquired to look so pleased with himself? At this point, I'd be happy if all he managed was to get a couple coins back by the end.

"This better be good, Jacks."

"Hold out your hands and close your eyes." His grin doubles in size.

"I'm not a little girl."

"Amber."

"You can't be serious."

"*Am*-ber..."

"Oh, for the love of sunshine. Fine." I thrust my hands out and close my eyes as he roots in his pocket. Despite my reservations, my breath shakes in anticipation.

Fingertips brush my palm. One at a time, the small weights of three objects drop into my hand. I don't wait. My eyes fly open immediately to inspect them.

"Hey," he protests.

I barely hear him over the sound of the pit in my stomach opening up. I'm gawking at three purplish beans. That's it.

That's his big treasure.

"Surprise," he says, beaming.

"What is this? We have beans. They're dead. Or dying. Everything is." My pulse turns frantic. Our last coins are gone. The garden is failing. There's nothing left.

"We don't have *these* beans. She was a witch, remember? These beans are magic."

CHAPTER 2

It's a solid hour before my voice gives out from screaming at my brother. Of all the idiotic things Jacks has done, this one tops them all. I don't know how he has remained so cheerful all these days as we come closer and closer to losing everything, but look where that happiness has got him now. Always thinking he's coming out on top. Always thinking he has the answer. He may believe he's a master schemer—that he has the next best trade—but he's nothing more than a gullible fool.

I stare down at the almost-empty table. This is what believing in people and trusting strangers gets you—three sun-forsaken beans from a fraud witch.

I can't speak to him for the rest of the night, and not just because of my voice failing. I can barely look at him as I shove a plate of mushrooms and tubers at him. To his credit, he rides out the storm in silence without trying to apologize or make amends, and he doesn't comment on the bland and paltry dish. It's times like these I have to be extra cautious with my thoughts, so I don't accidentally wish my brother into oblivion. With all the frustration boiling inside me, I'd probably send the whole town with him.

Despite the looming disaster at our doorstep, the sun rises again the next morning. At least, I assume it does, since the sky lightens from black to muted yellow, and I can see across the garden in the orange light. At a loss, I go for a short walk down the lane and find I'm not the only one reaching the point of desperation. A couple stand in their mostly dead garden, talking quietly about moving to Winterset. It's down the road at the far corner of the Yellow Plain, where the Mist is still thin and hasn't covered the village yet. Plus, it's closer to the sea, so there would be less distance to travel for fishermen and those going to the ports to trade.

We've talked with our father about moving there, too. But it's not as though we could take our land with us, such as it is, and no one will buy our house here. We would leave here with nothing. No means to buy shelter, let alone food, so how is that any better than what we have here?

Closer to town, there's a faint buzz of energy in the air. The fishing parties are due back today, and it's all the hope we have to cling to. Feeling slightly better from the fresh air, I return home and find myself in front of the table where I left the three purple beans the night before. My finger traces the smooth surface of one. We have several bean plants, none of them thriving, but I don't recognize this one. It must be a variety that comes from somewhere far from here.

"Magic," I scoff under my breath. The beans are clearly not magic, but it's worth planting one to see if they do any better here than the others. If it grows, maybe I can sell the other two beans and salvage something from this mess. Everyone around here wants food plants that will grow in this light.

Without much hope, I select one at random—they all look the same —and take it to the sink. "Okay. Let's see what you want. Do you want to soak first or be planted directly?" Turning the bean over in my fingers, I'm not expecting any response, so I jump at Jacks's voice behind me.

"I knew you'd come around. They'll grow. You'll see," he says.

His confidence is aggravating, but I don't have the voice or energy for more yelling. Besides, I'm trying to hold on to the hopeful vibe today. Our father should be back by late afternoon. He'll have food. He'll know what to do next.

In the end, I decide to plant the bean as it is. I clear a patch of dirt in the middle of the garden where the fountain squash used to be before it withered, and I till the dirt with some ash from our hearth until it is as inviting a plot as I can make it.

"Look here, bean. I'm counting on you. Got it?"

Two steelhawks watch me curiously from the barren branches of the dusk pear tree. They should be used to me talking to my garden by now. I pat down the freshly planted bean, and then I stand and watch over it for several minutes. Finally, I shake my head and head back into the cottage to wash up. It's not as if I actually expected it to magically sprout immediately.

"Do you see him?" I ask Jacks, who is tall enough to see over the heads of the crowd.

"Not yet," he answers.

The whole town seems to have turned out to greet the return of the fishing party. I only care to find our father. The knot of worry in my stomach hasn't left since Jacks took our last coins, and only my father's calm reassurance (plus some fish on the table) will be able to soothe me now. Every time he's gone, I feel it's my responsibility to get us through. It certainly won't be Jacks who does.

My brother disappeared again this morning while I was planting the bean, probably off to find some fun or spend some time with one of the many willing and available young women of our town (the less I know about that, the better), but he returned in time to be by my side for this. There's a certain comfort in his presence, which I'm definitely not telling him about. I'm still mad, after all.

The first delighted cries of recognition ring out, and families push forward. Women and men run to find their partners, children race to greet their parents, and Jacks cranes his neck to spot our father. The shouts die down into excited babble all around us, but still, Jacks doesn't pull me forward. Did our father fall behind on the journey back? Did he catch so much fish that he stayed a day to sell some?

When Jacks stills beside me, I look to him expectantly. There's no grin of recognition, though. He's not smiling, only staring ahead at something I can't see. It becomes apparent that it was Cassil Stonecrop when the man comes to a stop in front of us, his eyes still locked on Jacks.

No one speaks. My throat closes over at the weight in the silence.

Cassil drops his gaze and shuffles his feet. When he looks up, his eyes meet mine, and the ground falls away beneath me.

No. "N-o." The word comes out broken.

"Where?" Jacks says. I've never heard his voice so flat.

Cassil focuses on him again. "We hit a storm off the Basking Reef. Bad one. He went down trying to reach Daysline Cove. Whole fleet searched the area all night and the next day as soon as we could get back out, but we never found him. Never found any of 'em."

The words come to me through a veil, but as it hits me, I pick out the other sounds I missed before. Not all the conversations around us are joyful reunions and crows of success. Several families huddle together, and soft sobs carry to me from a mother and daughter holding each other nearby. Our town, already teetering on the brink of destruction, has just been dealt a terrible blow.

The next few days are a blur. For once, Jacks and I have plenty of food as members of the community stop by to offer their condolences and bring dishes of food with them. The irony is I don't feel the slightest bit hungry and only eat a few bites, to be polite. I feel like I drowned along with my father, and now I'm watching the world pass me by from deep in the dark waters. After years of fading light, everything is dull.

The food is generous and offered out of pure kindness, but it only makes me feel worse. No one has any to spare. Jacks stays home during the days, greeting the people and charming them as always, while I wait for them to leave so I can crawl back under my blankets.

But at night, Jacks disappears. I suppose I'm glad at least one of us is finding a warm bed to sleep in. I can't sleep at all in the cold cottage, so I spend my nights wandering our garden by the barest glow of moonlight, too numb to feel the biting cold. I don't feel the warmth of the fire either when I finally sink into the chair in front of our hearth to wait for daylight and welcome Jacks home with a silent hug.

All that time, my mind is on one thing—My wish.

In the light of day, I search the garden for anything that might be growing. I check on the bean, but nothing has changed. Imagine my surprise.

I'm flooded with memories of both our parents and of better days while I go through the motions of gathering whatever I can find before the birds get it, but the weight of my wish crushes all the rest.

We lost six people in the storm. My father's entire crew of five, plus one other who fell overboard from Cassil's boat. No wonder he looked so grim. The whole town is grim. We have six fewer people to sustain us. Six people who used to supply food and coin to this region…Gone. Even if I knew what to wish for, would magic be enough to save us? What if I wish for something that only makes the situation worse? I would be responsible for the lives of all those remaining here.

By the fifth day, the neighbors' visits slow to a trickle, and Jacks slips away at midday. Not wanting to be in the cottage if someone comes to the door, I wander the familiar worn paths of the garden again.

The blue herdsbloom has wilted and sagged where I transplanted it.

The bright blue blossom shriveled and died almost immediately, but that could be from the trauma of being uprooted. It might still recover. I absolutely will not shed a tear over it. That's not what this thickness in my throat is. I can't be so invested in a weed.

The food plants are far more important. With that thought firmly held in my mind, joining the solid wall I've constructed against the ache of indecision over my magic, I make my way to the bed with our so-called magic bean.

I'm not expecting much. Maybe a bump in the earth where a sprout will break through in the next day or two. I'm not expecting it to have burst out of the ground and wound up the pole I stuck there one day when I was feeling whimsical. I can't let myself hope for things like that.

What I am not expecting at all is the sight that greets me.

The plot of earth is completely turned up. Dirt has been tossed every which way.

"No!" I shriek, dropping to my knees to dig through the loose soil. "No, no. Come on."

My fingers find nothing.

A sharp cry of a steelhawk has my head snapping over to the dusk pear where only one of the mated pair watches me. I want to scream. I want to rage, catch every bird and cook them all in a pie. Instead, my face drops to the cradle of my hands. I hadn't realized that I actually held on to a spark of hope for that stupid bean. Three beans. That's all I had upon which to rest my hopes. Now there are only two.

When my tears stop falling, my anger rises.

"You! Where's your mate, huh? Is she the one who got this little feast, or did you share? You're lucky I don't have magic, or I'd snap your preening neck where you sit." I'm shaking my fist in the air like an old farmer angry at the skies. Maybe I should do it. Maybe I could use it for this. If I made the request simple and limited...

The best huntress around...?

That's not too broad. A magical hunting ability would allow me to bring home game to feed us no matter how bad things got.

But what would the side effects of such a wish be? Even if I had perfect control, I'm still only one person. Could I feed our whole town, let alone any of the villages nearby who are all suffering the same way? And if it didn't have control…

Would I suddenly have a magical bow and arrow that overwhelms me, killing as it wants? Would I be able to kill anything with a flick of my fingers? What if every creature that annoys me just drops dead? Sunbeams, Jacks would be dead before I could have my morning tea.

No. As with every other time, this isn't it. "But what?" I ask the barren, muted sky. "What am I supposed to do, Mother? Why didn't you teach me?"

I stay there a long time, waiting to feel less hopeless, mulling ideas over in my head and waiting for inspiration. If I can't figure out how to use my wish, there must be something else I can do. I need to feel like I'm helping in some way.

Eventually, I have to move, and only one idea comes to me. In my rush to head back to Aglonbriar forest's edge with my basket, I round the corner at the bottom of our lane and run headlong into a soft, feminine figure. My quickening heartbeat is only partly due to my surprise at the encounter. The rest is because of who it is I ran into, and it takes me a moment to squash the idiotic pulse fluttering in my chest and coax it back to normal.

"Alice, I'm so sorry. I didn't see you there."

The girl gives me a dazzling smile. "No harm done," she says in that lovely voice of hers. It's one of the things I like about her. Somehow, Alice Anglesway is a bright light in all our gloom. When she moved here from Winterset three seasons ago, she caught my attention immediately with her quick smiles, easy laugh, and that cheerful way she has about her. She wears it like armor.

I'm usually more controlled around her, but running into her so unexpectedly with my mind on so many other things, I'm distracted when she wets her lips, and her smile lifts again.

I've only kissed one person. She was a traveler, passing through town with a touring festival back when we held on to enough hope to still have such things. Her pale hair gleamed in the moonlight, which shone brighter back then, and after a night of laughing and dancing together around the fires, I didn't think I mistook the interest in her eyes. I kissed her first, but I reveled in the way she drew me close and claimed the kiss in response. I knew she'd be gone when the festival picked up and moved on, but I was content to enjoy a few blissful days, discovering what it felt like to be in love.

If only I could go back in time to kick my youthful self. Of course, the girl stayed just long enough to hear the idle gossip, to learn I come from a family of witches, and to never speak to me again. She didn't have to say anything. I could see it in her eyes when I went to find her the next day, and I just turned around and left rather than wait to hear her rejection.

But Alice knows who I am, and she still smiles at me with that pretty mouth and those bright eyes below her shiny blonde hair. Maybe I'll indulge the flutter in my middle for a few moments. There's so little color in this world anymore. No one can fault me for wanting to bask in feeling something for a change, even if I know my feelings aren't returned. She can give me a moment of happiness, and that's enough.

Her lips part, and I know what she's about to ask before she says anything. "Have you seen Jacks?"

There it is. The flutter stops. I won't even pretend to be sad about it because it's not as if I was under any illusions. Since the beginning, Alice has looked at my brother the same way every other woman near our age does. Handsome, charming Jacks. He's the one they all want.

"No. He vanished earlier. I haven't a clue where to." I brace myself for her expression to change, for her to imagine, as I am, that he's probably off with another girl as we speak. It's sort of what Jacks does.

She surprises me when she shrugs. "Oh well. Another time."

Is it odd that I'm glad he hasn't hurt her yet? Maybe he won't. Maybe Alice will be the one. My brother could certainly do worse.

"Where are you going?" she asks with a nod toward my basket.

"To search for mushrooms, maybe some herbs. Whatever I can find, really."

"I'll come with you," she says brightly.

If only she could. "Er, actually, you can't. I'm going too far into the Mist."

Her steps falter. "Oh. Oh, right. I forgot you could do that."

"The perks of being a witch. Even a useless one with no magic."

"Hey." Alice touches my arm. "It's not useless if you can find food others can't. That sounds extremely useful. If you go near the forest, maybe you could even bring some firewood home with you."

Even Alice can't hold the note of desperation from her voice at that. She lives in one of the big houses in the middle of town, thanks to her wealthy father, but those homes have no land, and they're growing cold in the dying light without a steady supply of firewood to stoke their hearths. Stubbornly, Alice refused to leave when things started to go bad, but I'm sure she will soon. It's not clear to me what's keeping her here. Maybe if I can bring her firewood, she'll stay longer. Maybe she can get Jacks to settle down. That would be a welcome feat, and I could warm up to the idea of Alice as a friend…even as a sister.

"I'll try." It's the best I can offer, but her words send me off with enough encouragement to bolster my determination. I'll at least bring back some sticks to make a bird-proof cage over my patch of garden before I try planting the second bean.

The haunting feeling comes over me immediately this time. My skin practically crawls with the sense of danger, but I have no choice. If I can't help us survive, I might as well meet my end here. I have to do this to be useful. I move beyond the patch I picked clean last time and find a smaller patch of mushrooms farther along the forest edge.

Aglonbriar pulses with life to my right, but it all feels wrong. The life inside the Mist is not the same as it is in the rest of the world. It's like I can sense the trees twisting further into the darkness within them, but that's silly. I must be truly spooked.

The same way it did all those years ago with my mother, the Mist has an energy to it. Tendrils snake around the base of the trees and flow out beyond the opening. I'm used to the vague haze we have all the time. I'm even used to the heavier fog that covers the Yellow Plain. But the Mist here forms tendrils that look practically solid. I hold my breath when one extends from the trees and winds up my leg.

Nothing happens. It's cool on the skin beneath my skirts but not damp. Slowly, I crouch to touch it. This is the thickest I've ever seen the Mist. It looks like I should be able to hold it between my fingers, but they pass right through with only a slight resistance. At least my mother was right about it not affecting me.

A loud *crack* shatters my distraction, sending my heart lurching into my ribs, and I straighten so fast, the few fungi I had placed in my basket bounce out. Deep breaths feel impossible against the thumping in my chest. I fight to draw in air, waiting to hear another sound, staring deep into the shadows.

When nothing happens—at least nothing I can see—I bend to my task again, determined to get what I came for.

A wail from the trees is a bolt to my heart.

I scream before I can stop myself. That sound… What *was* that?

Another cry erupts. It's much closer this time. The sound is half human scream and half animal roar. I jump up.

Why did I come? Why did I think I could do this?

Stupid, Amber. I need to run.

Before I can drive my legs into motion, a great shaggy blur erupts from the darkness. The huge form dives through a swirling cloud of Mist and rounds to face me. All I see are teeth.

I stumble back a step. The beast advances. Short yellow fur covers its body, and trails of saliva drip from the gigantic teeth that captivate my attention. Paws the size of my hands prowl forward, and a menacing roar rips from the throat of what appears to be a giant cat. Blue skies, it's enormous! Its shoulders are as high as mine. A long shaggy mane tumbles behind rounded ears and frames yellow eyes that are locked on me.

I don't want to die. This can't be it. I spin and take off at a dead sprint.

My basket lies somewhere on the ground behind me, forgotten. All that matters is getting away, but for the second time today, I crash into another person, this time tumbling to the ground.

"Get behind me!"

It's Jacks. What is Jacks doing here? I thought he was safe in town, happy without me to worry about. Of all the colors of a sunset, the last thing I expect to find here is my brother. Wielding a sword at that! Metal flashes in the low light.

The beastly cat was hot on my heels, but I ran blindly in a straight line away from the trees, and it must have slowed at the sight of Jacks because no teeth have torn into my flesh yet. I'm up and at Jacks's side in a flash. At the spot where the Mist loses its solid nature and fades to thick fog, the monstrous cat has stopped. The beast seems to be struggling with something because it spits and shudders before launching at us.

Jacks lifts the sword and blocks me with his body, setting his legs in a broad stance. The cat wails again, the same horrific sound I heard earlier. Tendrils of white mist withdraw from around its shoulders and chest. The huge head cranks back at an unnatural angle, and the whole creature shudders again before falling forward.

The sword flashes, and there's a spurt of dark blood. I duck with a strangled cry. I really hope Jacks knows what he's doing. The cat tries again to swipe at us, but it stumbles when the huge paws shrink and its chest narrows. The entire beast looks extremely strange now—elongated, losing hair, rising upright. Another shaky step brings it closer while the transformation continues.

What is happening? Its eyes lock on mine, but the cat pupils have rounded, and the face is now flat and hairless, although it's so filthy it's hard to tell.

As the mane shortens to dirty blond hair, the dream I had last week comes back to me in a rush, just as the sword flashes down across the now-human neck before me.

"No!"

It's too late. The man I saw in my nightmare falls to the ground. Blood rushes from the gaping cut across his throat, and his dirty tangle of hair soaks in it as it seeps into the dirt. Mist retreats from his back legs, and they shrink as well, fading from dark yellow fur to dusky, dirty skin.

Jacks just saved my life, but from what?

"What in the blue skies is that?" Jacks says. His breathless question reflects my confusion perfectly. "That was a monster, not a man. What happened?"

"He…That's the man from my dream."

Jacks snaps his eyes to me, questioning. A thought is forming deep in my mind. "He…It…The beast came from the forest. It transformed when it left the thick Mist of the woods." My hand shakes at the realization that the monster my brother slew was nothing but a man. Or used to be. When I came with my mother, I think she knew. Now I see what she saw, and it makes my heart ache—for this man and for who knows how many others. "It's a curse," I say, awed. "The Mist is a curse."

"But…that means—"

"Yes," I cut Jacks off. "It means a witch did this to us. A witch created the Mist. This must be what happens to the people who disappear when they try to go into the forest. The curse claims them for monsters."

We stand in silence, gaping at the dead man in front of us. How long was he in Aglonbriar forest? The same way I could feel the Mist twisting the nature of the trees, it must change the people it takes. No wonder people hate witches. I can't imagine coming up with something so terrible, nor what this witch's wish must have been to create magic like this. She must have wished for something dark and awful.

It's a good thing I never tried to wish the Mist away. My own magic probably would have reacted in some horrible way with this curse magic.

"Should we bury him?" My voice trembles.

"I didn't mean to kill him. He was a beast." Jacks is still shaken, and I don't blame him.

"It wasn't your fault. You saved me, Jacks. We had no way of knowing." My arms circle my big brother, and he squeezes me to his chest.

"You're my only family, Amber. Of course, I saved you. I'll always have your back."

He's my only family as well. It's time I do more to ensure I can have his back, too. We pull apart, and I give him a solemn look before scanning him.

Thankfully, he looks uninjured and even tosses me a shadow of a grin. "Besides, if you die, who will cook for me?"

Instead of responding to his teasing, I ask, "Where did you get a sword?"

"It's our inheritance." At my confusion, Jacks elaborates. "Not all dad's equipment was on his ship. He had some supplies in reserve at the harbor. I sold it to Cassil and took the coin to a contact I know."

I can't help but scan the sword. I should probably be mad about my brother throwing away more coin, but my eyes are drawn to the blood along the blade, and I shudder at what could have happened without it. I won't soon forget those wild yellow eyes or the long teeth on the beast that rushed at me. "Is that Zocerriene Boron steel? Where in the globe did you find it? And why?"

"This is how we're going to survive, baby sister." Jacks holds up the sword with an almost loving look. He doesn't even use that look on the women he dates. How nice to see him finally bonding with something.

"Jacks, what—?"

"It was your idea. Don't blame me." He grins again, and the last shaky adrenaline-ridden breath huffs out of me.

"How, exactly, was this my idea?"

"The forest. Aglonbriar is off-limits because of the Mist—"

"Jacks!" I cut him off. "The Mist. You can't be here. Come on. We have to get away. Hurry."

He follows as I drag him by the sleeve across the Yellow Plain away from the forest. I'm searching the ground behind us for any sign of the tendrils of more solid Mist—the stuff that seemed to have a life of its own—but Jacks doesn't seem overly concerned. "Let me finish. Everyone who disappeared actually went into the trees. But you found food here along the edge. Plants are your thing. You know what to look for. The only problem is the dangerous beasts,"—he casts a glance over his shoulder to the Mist-blurred form we left behind us—"or whatever that was. So, I'll protect you. I may even be able to take down some game with enough patience and luck. We'll be fine."

I wish I believed that. Only Jacks would continue to believe in good luck after the hand we've been dealt. He and Alice really would make a nice pair.

One thing I know for sure is I can't lose him. I can't, not after losing both our parents. I hustle us faster across the Plain and don't release a full breath until the Mist fades to its usual haze at the outskirts of town.

CHAPTER 3

"Plants are your thing." That's what Jacks said to me. I'm still thinking about it as I turn the second bean over and over between my fingers the next morning. I thought about it all evening while Jacks cleaned his sword by the fire, the blood a reminder of the terrifying events of the day.

Now I'm standing over the patch of dirt where I planted the first bean. Since my escape from the cat-monster-man at the forest was so rushed, I not only lost my basket, but I also didn't get any living sticks I can bend into a protective cage. I tried using some dead branches from the dusk pear, scaring away the steelhawks while I was at it, but the dry wood snaps instead of bending.

"Plants are your thing." They are. I used to love gardening with my mother back when the sun shone in a sky that still had life and color. I've relied on plants even as they fail around me. I've had more success with my garden than others have had. The couple at the bottom of the lane is gone now. They left the day after the news of the ill-fated fishing trip. Their whole yard is nothing but brown plants smelling of damp and rot, yet I still have a few plants growing, even if nothing is doing particularly well.

I turn my eyes to the sky to gather my thoughts and my nerve. "It's time, Mom. I have to do this. Please watch over me."

I close my eyes and press the bean into the soil beneath my hands. The answer, when it came to me, felt obvious. That doesn't stop this moment from being terrifying. I may have given Jacks the idea to become a swordsman, but he gave me the idea of how to use my wish.

All I know is I can't allow him so close to the forest ever again, and I have to do my part to protect us now. I know what I'm going to do.

I choose my words as carefully as I can. "I wish…" With those first two words, my blood responds. Bubbly sparks race through my body. *Magic.* It tingles in my veins while I squeeze my eyes closed and focus. "I wish to be able to make these plants grow and flourish no matter the conditions and for them to bend to my will. In exchange, I will use my magic to provide plentiful and edible food and to protect me and anyone else I choose."

The magic begins to overwhelm me. All I can do is hope my wish was specific enough and that maybe, by specifying what I will do in return, the price won't be too high. I hope I said enough because I can no longer speak. The sparkling has turned to rushing heat. My veins turn to fire.

I curl in on myself, whimpering. Then the tingling intensifies to furious energy. My muscles quiver and vibrate with the force of it whipping through me. My skin feels raw, flayed open by the air brushing over it. I cry out and barely hear a shout in the distance.

Alice screams my name again, "Amber! Amber, what's happening to you?"

My eyes fly open to see her racing across my garden toward me. "No," I say. That is, I try to say no, but only a strangled gasp comes out of my mouth. I fight to lift a hand. Trying to tell her to stay back comes out as, "Steb…b…k."

I'm still on my knees when the ground splits open beneath my hands. A green shoot erupts from the dirt and powers its way toward the sky. More shoots follow the first, winding up my arms. I shake free and leap to my feet. The fire inside me lessens, feeling instead like it flows through me and out to the plant growing at an impossible rate before me.

It's too fast. Too much. I can't control this.

Alice shrieks, and I turn to see her caught up in snaking vines. They twist and turn and wrap around her ankles. She kicks desperately, but as soon as she kicks one tough squash vine away, another takes her. It's the fountain squash, but it was completely dead when I ripped it out of this bed weeks ago. There must have still been some roots deep down with enough life left in them to respond to my magic, and now there's no stopping it.

The beanstalk is still rising from the ground, growing taller and thicker with every second, but now the peas from the next bed have joined in. Pea shoots spread across the ground, tangling around everything they encounter.

"Stop! Stop, please." My choked pleas do nothing, and the pea shoots join the squash in wrapping Alice's body.

I fight my way there. "Get off," I shout to a branch of gnarled wood reaching out for me. To my surprise, it listens. The branch withdraws to the dusk pear tree. The steelhawks, who returned to watch me plant the bean—no doubt planning their next meal—are startled off the branches when leaves burst forth across the whole tree at once. Where only dark, knotty wood was a moment ago, there's now a riot of green with small pink buds blooming amongst them before my eyes. It would be beautiful if it weren't so terrifying.

But it is because Alice has all but disappeared. I can barely make out her bright hair against the ground.

"Alice, hold on," I shout. I snatch up the garden hoe and begin hacking my way to her. "Out of the way," I yell at more plants. Again, they respond. But while they bend away from me and my wild attacks against them, they show no such respect to anyone else.

Alice screams again. The sound is cut off abruptly, and I nearly fall in my hurry.

Her body is a heap of green and orange and a few purple vines I don't even recognize. I hack at the edges, shouting out my frustration. I was careful. I said the most cautious words I could think of.

I only wanted to help. I wanted to be useful. I never wanted this.

"Please, stop," I plead.

"Amber," shouts a masculine voice. Before I can yell to Jacks to stay back, I spot him through what is fast becoming a wall of vegetation in our garden.

"Stay away from him," I yell. I don't know how this works, but I'm so desperate to keep the plants from strangling my brother that I focus all my attention on peeling them back from his path.

It sort of works. Jacks takes care of the rest, his sword flashing and slicing through vines left and right as he runs. Soon he's at my side.

"Help me." I'm back to tearing at the leaves covering Alice.

"Move." My brother barely waits until my hands are clear before he gets to work with the sword, cutting and hacking his way around Alice. I want to tell him to be careful, but better for Alice to get cut than to suffocate. Instead, I join in with my hoe and let the flames burning through me fuel my arms. Slowly, my fire abates to a low burn, and we start making progress against the plants.

The top of the beanstalk is invisible now, high over us, obscured in the murky sky. Glancing behind me, I can see the peas have wound their way up everything with any height to it, forming a solid mat of green. The shoots closest to me reach a curious spiral toward my foot, but a growl from me stops them. All around, the uncontrollable burst of growth slows.

Both dripping with sweat, Jacks and I drop to the ground to pull back the blanket of leaves and vines to find Alice. She stares up, unblinking, her face a frozen mask of horror. There's no sound from her. No scream or shout. No breath.

Jacks pulls back more, exposing her body, and I fall away to retch in the fountain squash patch. Alice won't be breathing again, let alone screaming or shouting…or calling out in that lovely voice of hers. Pea shoots stab all through her body, making her look like she fell onto a bed of vibrant green spikes. Blood trails from each wound, but the flow has stopped. Her heart no longer pumps.

Blue skies, I can't breathe. My limbs are drained from the endless shaking as my magic awakened and then from the desperate hacking and chopping to free Alice. All for nothing. I thought I was prepared to pay the cost of magic, but I expected it to be *me* who paid.

Vaguely, I'm aware of Jacks catching me as the dim light tunnels to black, and my body gives out.

Sunbeams, my head hurts. The thought comes before awareness of my body, but as the feeling in the rest of me comes awake, I wish I could go back to sleep.

My eyes fly open.

I wish…? Did I just think that?

It all comes back to me in flashes of brilliant green. My wish. I used it.

I used it, and everything went wrong.

Alice died.

Jacks… Where is Jacks?

"I'm here." My brother appears at my side after whatever noise I must have made. He places a calming hand on my arm, and to my surprise, I relax.

I'm not used to Jacks being the caretaker. "What–What happened?"

"You were unconscious." He grins, but it's nothing like his usual grin. Is he…scared of me? "That was some display, little witch."

I flinch at the name. "I killed her. I killed Alice."

Jacks drops his gaze. Sorrow fills his expression.

"I'm sorry, Jacks. I'm so sorry. I didn't mean to. I never meant…."

"Hush, baby sister. It's not your fault. Everyone knows a witch's powers are uncontrollable at first."

There's something about the way he says that. "Everyone?" I ask.

He's looking at me again, but he withdraws his hand. "Please stay calm. I promised I'd keep you calm."

"Why? Promised whom?"

"The town. The mayor and council. The people who stayed."

"Stayed? Jacks…How long was I asleep?"

He goes quiet and drops his gaze again.

"For sun's sake, Jacks, how long?"

"Only three days."

"Three days?" I'm stunned. The pounding in my head intensifies. *Everyone knows…* He must mean they all know that my magic awakened. But why would they know that?

"Here. Drink." Jacks passes me a mug of steaming tea, and I take a sip. "Now, take a slow breath and sit up so you can drink the rest."

This nursemaid side of my brother is one I've never seen before, and I'm suspicious the same way I am when I can tell he's plotting something. "Jacks…tell me. Whatever you're not telling me, I want to know."

When he's silent, I sigh and fight to sit up. Nausea overcomes me, and I have to lay back and recover before trying again more slowly. Every muscle fiber feels like it has been beaten with tiny sharp hammers, but the throbbing pulse behind my eyes dulls all the rest.

"Drink," Jacks encourages.

I take another reluctant sip of the tea, and it actually helps. I'm not immediately overcome with a desire to jump up, but enough energy seeps back into me that I can open my eyes and properly take in my surroundings. I'm not in my bed as I would have expected. Instead, I'm on a makeshift palette beside the front door to the cottage, which makes no sense until I spot the hastily covered hole gaping in the wall across from me where the bedrooms used to lie.

I suck in a gasp at the sight of crumbling walls covered with boards hanging askew. "What happened to the cottage?" My question is shrill and panicky because part of me knows the answer.

Jacks winces. "Your plants, er…They sort of, em…."

I can tell my brother is trying not to upset me, but it's clear what he's saying. "I did that?"

"It's okay, Amber. We'll fix it."

Nothing about that missing and crumbled wall looks fixable. Half the roof is caved in. And what happens the next time I lose control? I thought this was how I could help. All I wanted to do was be able to grow a proper garden and help feed the rest of the town.

"Wait. You said, "those who stayed." What did that mean? What went on in the last three days?" Another horrifying thought sweeps through me. If everyone knows what happened, there must be a reason. If magic affected more than our house, there would be no mystery as to the witch who cast it. I'm the only source of magic around. "Jacks, if the plants destroyed the back wall of our cottage, how much farther did this spread? Is anyone else's home damaged? Oh…stars above…Was anyone hurt?"

Aside from Alice, of course, who is dead…which is much worse than hurt. And all of this is my fault. What if I destroyed the neighbors' homes too? Is that why people left? The thrumming pain clatters about my skull, and my body begins to tremble.

"Amber! Amber, stop." Jacks jumps up and looks around with fear in his eyes. Fear never shows with Jacks, although I'm certain he must feel it sometimes. But now, there's no mistaking it.

"Stop what?"

"This, Amber. You have to calm down. You don't have control yet." He grasps the edge of a counter to steady himself.

The trembling isn't my body. It's the ground beneath us. Rather, it's the stirring plants and roots because green leaves poke under the remains of the back door and begin to crawl up the inside of the wall. No…*No*. Not again. The pain in my head fills the rest of me, beginning to burn everywhere it goes, and I know I need to stop this before Jacks gets hurt. But how?

How did I stop before? Did my body simply exhaust itself of magic with that surge, or was it something I did? I remember growling at the peas to turn back while we fought to reach Alice. I remember Alice's face and that mask of fear she wore in death.

Grief overtakes me. My mother. My father. Alice. Now my own brother is fearful of me, and it appears he's right to be. Calm. I need to calm myself. I try a slow breath, but it only makes the burning worse in my lungs.

Maybe I need to use the magic deliberately. I need to release the pressure built up inside of me. When it stopped last time, I had been focused on peeling the plants out of Jacks's path and then stopping them from tangling more around Alice.

I focus on the green beneath the door and let it take my magic. That's what it feels like. It takes from me. The plant grows, and more stems join the first, winding around each other and shooting tall. Blue, spiky blossoms begin to burst open at each tip. It's the blue herdsbloom I transplanted from the Yellow Plain. Beauty, even in such a terrible fashion, draws me in as it always does. My heartbeat steadies and slows, and my muscles relax as the fire drains from them. The plant slows its growth, settling into a veritable hedge of herdsbloom along the back wall, and finally, it goes still.

When I feel safe doing so, I look around to find Jacks. He's perched on the counter, sword in hand, eyes searching for a fight.

I rise and go to him as he climbs down warily. "I'm sorry. I think it's over for now. Now tell me. How bad is it? How far did it spread?"

CHAPTER 4

I should be questioning why Jacks brings his sword with him, but I simply follow him out the remaining door. Our front garden has exploded back to life. Bird song fills the air as brilliant wings flutter from plant to plant and flower to flower. I squeak as a bird dashes through the air straight across the front of my face. Then I almost laugh.

This world is a dazzling riot of color and activity. I haven't seen hummers in at least seven or eight seasons, but they must have found a way to survive because now they've returned. And oh, how they've returned. There must be a dozen circling the ardelia bush alone.

The birds are not the only ones who've come, either. The garden is a buffet on which to feast for bees and all sorts of other insects. Shining wings of gold and blue catch what little light comes from the sky and turn the yard into a waltz of flashing color. From purple lilac to yellow meadowsweet to the pink fuzz of the ardelias, every sort of flower blooms, defiant of seasons or lack of sun. I want to run to the back to see how many vegetables have sprouted. How many trees will bear fruit now?

But Jacks heads for the front gate with purpose in his steps, and I let my feet follow while my head swims in the visions around me. Mist still clouds the air, but the world feels brighter all the same. All along the lane, fielder berry bushes crowd the ditches, and it's no effort at all to reach out and pluck one. I allow myself a smile at the birds perched all along, no longer stealing all the berries because they've clearly had their fill. They watch without fuss as I pop the sweet berry in my mouth and close my eyes to savor the juice that pours from it.

This is what I had hoped for. Perhaps not so wild, nor so over-grown, but there is life here again. The world hums with it. Food is within easy reach and an ember of hope fans to life in my chest. I may not rid us of the Mist, but I can help us survive it.

Then we come into view of the house at the end of the lane—the one the couple abandoned because everything in their garden was dead, and there was nothing left for them to fight for. Now, though… The apple orchard I was sure would never recover is in full leaf. Even while the remains of white and pink petals still litter the ground, inconceivably full and bright red apples hang from the branches.

"Three days?" I ask Jacks, bewildered at how this is possible. "Is that all?"

He nods his confirmation without pleasure on his face.

I frown and look around. "I don't understand."

Beside the orchard, a naira tree dangles with glittering yellow bulbs. It's so heavy with them, they hang over the fence, and I take one to try it. Sharp citrus tang bursts across my tongue, and I want to dance with the pleasure of it. If there's something wrong with it, it's nothing I can sense. If the plentiful food is twisted by my magic or, in some other way, inedible, I can't tell. It tastes as sweet and amazing as I can remember from my childhood. Even in my best dreams, it never lived up to those memories the way this does now.

"Is it edible for everyone? Is something wrong with it?" I ask my brother.

"It's fine, Amber. It's good." Jacks gives a sad smile with his nod. "We won't be wanting for food anytime soon."

"Then what—?" Why does he look upset about the town being saved? We can grow enough here to feed everyone.

Jacks plucks another naira fruit and hands it to me. "Remember this," he says.

My eye lands again on the sword at his side, which he's gripping and ready to use. I catch his gaze darting down the lane, and my insides clench. Uncertain I want to look, I stride to the gate and fling it open.

Inside, the beds reflect the same overwhelming growth I've seen everywhere. Pink cabbage has already bolted and gone to seed. Melons sit ripe on a vine. Squash spill out of their beds and onto the ground between them. Peas tangle over an arbor.

The peas are an unsettling reminder of those first terrible moments and of poor, sweet Alice. I wonder if her father came from Winterset to collect her and return her home to be buried. Or maybe Mr. Anglesway is still here, seeking vengeance for his daughter's death. Is that why Jacks carries the sword? I can barely process my spinning thoughts before my eye finally lands on the house, and my brain empties entirely.

It was a fine home once—larger than our cottage and well maintained. It was loved. Now a tree grows straight through the middle of it, tall as the oldest oaks down in the valley beyond the village. The roof hangs to one side of the house, broken and dangling in pieces. One wall has fallen down completely, leaving only a stone chimney now wound tight with ivy. The more I look, the more damage I find. It's not just the tree that tore through the floors and demolished the structure or the ivy choking the chimney. Leafy branches punch through windows, and roots buck and dive through what used to be a smooth flagstone floor. Compared to this destruction, the missing back half of our cottage seems tame.

My jaw hangs open.

My brother's hand lands on my shoulder, but I'm numb, thinking only of my relief that the couple was long gone and safe wherever they were.

"How far does it reach?" I ask in breathless trepidation.

Jacks only slides his free hand to my back and guides me away.

As we walk closer to town, everywhere we go, plants have taken over. The track that used to be wide enough for a cart or buggy is now so narrow we're forced to walk single file, and Jacks still has to use the sword to cut away an occasional bit of greenery intent on bridging the gap. This will have to be cleared before the town can resume any trade, but we'll want to do that. Surely people will be enthusiastic when they see how much produce we can take to markets in the nearby villages.

I keep expecting to find the end of the magical growth, but we reach the edge of town before that happens. The first house on this side belongs to old Mrs. Blackiron, or…I should say, it used to. The house no longer stands. It's completely collapsed into a pile of rubble that has been overcome with growth so thick I can barely make out where it used to stand.

My hand claps across my mouth. If anything, I thought the effects would lessen the farther we go from our home, but it seems the shockwave of my magical awakening only grew in power as it spread.

I start stumbling toward the ruins, but Jacks stops me. "There's nothing there, Amber."

"But Mrs. Blackiron...where is she?"

"She's not there."

Oh, how I hope he means she is staying with friends or possibly fled altogether, but heavy stones settle in my stomach. The next homes are nearly as bad, and it's not until we reach the middle of town where the large houses are that we find structures that still look livable.

"Stay close," Jacks mutters to me over his shoulder when my steps slow.

I learn why a moment later.

Cassil flies out of his house with his fishing spear raised, pointed square at my chest. "You're not welcome here, witch," he bellows.

His wife hurries behind him. "Haven't you already done enough?"

More people begin to appear in doorways, and more harsh words are hissed and hollered in my direction. Between the cursing, the words "witch" and "evil" fly at me more than any other. Then they begin hurling more than words. A fat, ripe tomato explodes across my skirts, and I duck a pear that would have left a bruise on my cheek. Jacks reaches back and tugs me close to him, pulling me forward even as a head of lettuce slaps into my back.

I spot Alice's house ahead, and finally, it's one that is unaffected by wild plants taking over. The track through town grows more open, with only a few weeds peeking between stones. Beyond that, the green dies away to the yellow and brown we had been accustomed to of late. It seems we finally reached the edge of my magical explosion.

My eyes are hung up on Alice's house, so I'm looking right at it when the front door swings open and Mr. Anglesway steps out holding a box of Alice's things. He freezes at the sight of us.

When he speaks, it's to my brother. "She shouldn't be here."

"I know," Jacks says. "But she needs to see. And it's not her fault."

Mr. Anglesway glances back up the track the way we came, and my head swivels to follow. Voices herald the approach of a group of the people we just passed. They're following us, and from the sound of it, they're not coming to thank me for growing their vegetable gardens.

Mr. Anglesway comes down the last steps, his voice somber when he says, "She saw. Now get her out of here before we have another dead girl to bury."

I'm not fooling myself into thinking he cares for my safety, but he at least doesn't seem inclined to kill me himself. Jacks gives a swift nod, and I follow him mutely when he tugs me away. I should apologize to Mr. Anglesway. I should say something kind about how lovely Alice was, and how much I liked her, and how I would never have hurt her on purpose. The moment escapes me with tears spilling down my cheeks, and it's all I can do to hurry after Jacks.

"Don't worry, we'll circle around and leave by the high road," he says as if my only concern is escape.

"Stop. Please." I rest a hand on the low stone wall along the track we turned up and bend over to breathe heavily into my arms. Fighting back nausea and tears at once, I choke for several breaths. My weight slumps into the wall, and I don't know if I can take another step. This part of town is not overgrown, but everything we just saw overcomes me until I can hardly see past the slab of stone closest to me over the waist-high wall. Focusing on that and only that, it takes me a moment to make out a name and the dates. It's the gravestone of an old villager, dead before I was born.

Lifting my head, I sweep the small cemetery dotted with gravestones. I shouldn't see anything out of place. Alice would have been taken to Winterset to be buried with her family. Her father must have returned to pack up her things. I shouldn't see freshly turned soil or pristine new grave markers. I most certainly shouldn't see five of them.

My knees give out. Sobs wrack my chest, and I can't even ask the obvious question. Who were they? Who else died? May I never see another sunrise, for I am a murderer.

Jacks prepares tea again, although after he carried me most of the way home, I feel I should be the one taking care of him. I think he's mainly relieved that the morning glory that covered the ground all across the cemetery before I could stop it didn't follow us home. Also, we're both relieved that none of the townsfolk have come to our cottage yet to take their revenge.

I hold the tea tightly between both my hands and take a sip, not caring that it burns the roof of my mouth. Jacks is not yet good at this, but he'll have to learn.

"I have to leave," I say without preamble.

"I know." His eyes are on me, and his voice is resigned.

"I need to be away from people. Somewhere I can't hurt anyone until I know how to control this."

He nods.

"I can't stay here. Not after…"

"Amber, I'm not arguing. I agree with you."

Of course he does. He won't want to be near me himself after everything that happened. He was probably just waiting for me to suggest it, so he doesn't seem cruel. The thought curls in my gut because Jacks truly never is cruel, a fact which he proves when he loops an arm around my shoulder.

"Hey. You know I would have kept you away from all of what you saw today if I thought for a minute that you would have listened to me, right?"

"I wouldn't have."

"As I said."

"I—You were right to take me. I did need to see it. I needed to know what I did."

"No." Jacks squeezes me. "You needed to know what you're capable of. Yes, it came at a cost, but the people left here will no longer starve. The town will survive because of you."

"Not all of them."

"No. Not all of them. But you just need time. I know my sister, and she's never given up on anything. You made your wish, and things went a little haywire, but you'll figure it out. I know you will."

"But—" I look up at him, at the face that's always been around, fast with a smile and quick to find mischief. "You'll be alone."

"Of course I won't. You didn't think I'd abandon you, did you?" Jacks stands to wander about the remains of our cottage. "I was thinking we could move to Winterset."

"What are you talking about?"

"Leaving. You know. Moving."

"That's not what I meant when I said I have to leave, Jacks."

His brow furrows. "I know we have to move, but Winterset is far enough. We can hide your secret there."

"No, that's not it. And no, we can't. I made my wish so that I could help people, and I killed them instead. I meant that I have to go away. Away from people entirely, not just from these people."

"But…where?" My brother looks decidedly more somber as he understands what I intend.

I've been asking myself that same question since I recovered enough for coherent thought, and I have an idea. Wanting to help my town did not come in the form I imagined or wanted, but Jacks was right in saying the people who are left will have food. The thing is, I don't know for how long. I don't know what will happen when I leave. The plants grew in a burst too fast to be natural, but there is nothing to say that they will keep growing or even stay alive as they are. What if I leave and everything dies again, and the town is left with nothing but the stain of my memory? I can't do that to them.

They may have turned their backs on me, but I won't do the same to them. I will keep them safe, both from me and from starvation, while they put their upturned lives back together. I just need somewhere I can't hurt anyone, where I can learn to harness my magic, then

I can sneak back to grow things more purposefully. And there's one place where there are no people around to hurt.

"I won't go too far," I answer.

Jacks swaggers across the room to me and places both hands on his hips. He quirks an eyebrow. "You expect me to let my little sister go off without me to protect her?"

"Yes, Jacks. That's the point. I'm a witch now. You heard them. Cassil called me a mad sorceress, for sun's sake. People will be too scared of me to cause me harm."

"Mad sorceress, huh? And what of me? You've forgotten I have a sword now. I have to use it for something." Some of my brother's familiar playful tone seeps back into his voice. I'm wary of what he's planning when I recognize his scheming look.

"Please don't stab anyone with that."

Jacks forces a solemn expression over his features. "I, Jacks Golden-root, hereby swear on my blade that I will use it only for good. And to impress the ladies."

It coaxes a smile from me as I swat at him with one hand and hold up my cup with the other. "You can't even make tea. You're the one who will have trouble surviving alone."

He waves that off as unimportant. "I have ideas."

"No more of your ideas, Please. At least spare me that last indignity."

My brother shoots me a grin that is more genuine than any I've seen since I awoke.

I'm going to miss his stupid face, but I know what I have to do. "I'm going to the middle of the Yellow Plain. The Mist is too thick there for people to venture in, but not so thick that the deadly beasts from Aglonbriar forest will be able to reach me. I'll have plants and all the space I need to practice. I can grow myself a whole tree house out there for protection. I'll be better off than you here in this broken cottage."

Jacks looks around with a grimace. "No, thank you. I liked my original idea better. I thought we would both go to Winterset, but I can still carry out my plans on my own. Hey, don't make that face at me. This is a good idea. Listen."

I fight the urge to cross my arms and scoff.

"The townspeople can harvest from the garden here. There's more than enough to go around, and they can sell whatever they can't eat and give me a portion of the coin. That should be enough for me to set myself up in Winterset."

"Set yourself up?"

He lifts the sword. "Swordman for hire. I was going to use it to protect you, but I can protect other people in the Mist too."

"No, Jacks. You saw what the Mist did to the man from my dream."

"He came out of the forest. All I have to do is cross the Yellow Plain. You said it yourself; the Mist there is harmless as long as you don't get lost in it, and I'll have a very resourceful mad sorceress out there looking out for me."

"Excuse me?"

"I'll accompany people across the Yellow Plain, thus restoring trade between the towns on this side and the merchant cities on the other. Don't you see? You can learn to master plants, use your magic to grow food for people, whatever your bleeding heart desires. But you can also use your powers to make it safe for me to cross with my charges."

"Jacks, you are a scheming devil, but you occasionally have a good idea."

He beams. "I knew you'd see my genius eventually. So, you'll help me?"

"No, you fool. I'll help everyone. I'll make sure no one gets too close to the forest, and between us, we can restore that lost trade route. Plus, once I can control my magic, I can venture to the other towns in the dying light and help grow their crops."

He frowns. "I really think it would be better if you just helped me."

"You, my moronic big brother, hardly need help when you can charm your way into anything."

"Handsome, brilliant brother," Jacks corrects.

"Right." I roll my eyes. "I'm sure you'll find plenty of ladies willing to pay for your protection services."

"That's not all they'll be willing to—"

"Jacks! Do not finish that sentence."

He smiles and picks something up from the table. "Then do me this one favor."

"What?" I'm suspicious because it's Jacks.

He takes my hand and drops something into it. "Take the last bean, and grow me the biggest beanstalk you can, little sister. I'll need some way to find you out there, after all."

I look down at the smooth bean in my hand, curious why it didn't sprout when everything else around here went crazy. Maybe it really is magic after all.

I throw my arms around my brother and hold on for as long as it takes for my heart to stop chattering at the prospect of what I'm about to do. My mind races with the possibilities of what I'll find when I unleash my magic in the Mist, of the myriad ways I may be able to use it. Then I say my farewell, gather a few items of clothing and some fruit for the road and set out for the Yellow Plain. I have a lot of work to do.

THE END

ABOUT JO HOLLOWAY

Jo Holloway is a writer, scientist-at-heart, and all-around-animal-lover. She has a degree in microbiology and has worked in public health and IT before publishing books.

Jo is the Canadian author of the Green & Gold series, a young adult contemporary fantasy. She loves to spend time in the make-believe worlds of her favourite series, rereading to visit old friends. Her love for urban fantasy inspired this enchanting and exciting coming-of-age story.

For readers who've ever wished their pets could talk, Jo Holloway has got you covered, but be careful what you wish for. You can get Cara, the prequel to the Green & Gold series, for free from her author website.

Find out more at: johollowaybooks.com

tiktok.com/@johollowaybooks
instagram.com/author_joholloway
facebook.com/iamrosa.fanpage

TABULA RASA
BY PAUL EAGLE

"Tabula Rasa, Latin for blank slate, is the theory that individuals are born without any built-in mental content. The theory is that all knowledge comes from our experience or perception of the world. That sounds pretty great, right? We all begin our lives without hate or prejudice of any kind. And it is great. We see it in our children. They don't know how to be racist, as they don't know that racism even exists. The idea of treating someone differently because of the color of their skin is something we learn, not something we are born with. So, if we all lived in a vacuum, we might not even have the concepts of hate, distrust, and violence. Unfortunately, we are not born in a vacuum. We are born here, on Earth, where all of those bad things I previously mentioned exist in abundance. What does that mean for us as a species? Essentially, it means that we are all hindered by our past, even before we are born. We are chained to pre-existing societal and historical norms. The only way to break free from these pre-established feelings, and become the best possible people we can be, is through a blank slate, a fresh start. The human race needs a system reboot."

Peter Pallister stopped to take a sip of water. His tall, thin frame always felt gangly and awkward when standing and talking. He much preferred sitting down. The lights shining down on him were getting warmer all the time, and he was beginning to sweat. He ran a hand through his short black hair before putting the water glass back on the small table beside him on the stage. He wasn't phased by speaking in public. He was becoming used to it and had his routine well-rehearsed by now. This was his first time speaking at the prestigious TED conference, though, and he was hoping that this could really propel his career forward. He took a moment to look out into the crowd and flash them a brief smile, showing off his handsome features, before returning to a more somber tone.

"Houses sit empty all over the world, and yet people are homeless. There is more than enough food, but people are hungry? Why do we allow this? How can we allow this? We allow it only because we are accustomed to it. We are used to passing homeless people on the street. We know that men make more money than women, but we aren't shocked into action by it. We continue to watch the police and governments in some countries oppress their own people just because of the color of their skin, because of where they are from, or who they love – and we stand by and watch *only* because this is how it has always been. We need to do something about it, and soon. Before it's too late and we cross a line that we can't return from. I propose that now is that time. It is time for us, all of us, to unite and draw a line in the sand. We need to forget about everything that went on before, the good and the bad. We can learn from our mistakes without bringing any of the old prejudices into our future. We need equal pay and equal rights. We need to stop oppression, and war, and hatred. We need to stop the richest one percent of us from making the decisions. We need to clean up this world, start over, and give everyone a clean slate to work with."

The auditorium filled with applause and cheering, which then turned into a standing ovation. Peter took a couple of minutes to wave and smile before taking one final bow and leaving the stage.

Later that evening, Peter concluded his day with a signing at a local store. He liked Seattle, and he enjoyed being on the road, but he was definitely looking forward to getting back home to Canada and sleeping in his own bed. The book tour began with excitement and energy. Peter loved getting to talk to people from all over the U.S. and felt a real sense of purpose by spreading his vision of the future. But, over time, he grew tired, and the repetitive days seemed to merge into one. He would forget which state he was in and would lack the energy to go out and be a tourist during his limited free time. He wouldn't change his experience for anything, but the thought of a day or two with no schedule filled him with more joy than he would care to admit. "Who shall I make it out to?" he asked the young woman in front of him as she handed over a copy of his book.

"It's Sally." Sally was clearly a student at the college. Not only was she wearing the telltale WSU hooded sweatshirt, but she had that look of hope and passion in her eyes that only the young and the foolish seem to have. Peter loved that look. If his grand notion were ever to get any real traction, he would need people like her and a lot of them.

"Do you really think it could work?" asked Sally as he returned the book to her.

"Do I really think *what* could work?"

"All of it. The reset, or reboot, or whatever you call it. Do you really think people could actually do it?"

"I really do hope so, Sally. It's going to take something big, something huge, for it to happen. I worry that things will need to get a lot worse before they get better – but I do believe that we can get there. Or at least I really wish that we can."

"Well, I hope you're right."

"Me too, Sally. Me too."

20 years later...

Peter got up from his desk with a sigh – partly because his bones seemed to be getting stiffer and stiffer lately and partly because of the day he'd had. It had been another frustrating six hours of emails and meetings. Pretty much everyone he had spoken with had a complaint or angry request of some kind: They wanted to know the exact formula of the additives in the drinking water (some people *still* refused to drink it). They thought that the universal income was too much or too little. They offered excuses as to why they shouldn't have to do the mandatory year of community service. There were also regular messages calling him a traitor to his species and plenty of threats directly and indirectly aimed at him. He understood that people were still a little scared and confused and that they felt better when they converted that fear into anger and directed it at someone else. It was Peter's job to be that someone. He didn't love it, but he would do his duty and take the abuse for the greater good.

He picked up his jacket and left his office, flashing his trademark smile and saying a few goodbyes as he left. The Tessan embassy in Vancouver was a modest building, though architecturally, it was stunning. It was mainly made from a glass-like material that let in light and was able to regulate the temperate, using any excess heat for energy. It was clean and unimposing, as were all of the Tessan embassies on the planet. Each one was made to fit in with the city where it was located. In Vancouver, this included a giant mural of a Haida whale on the side of the building.

The streets were clean and moderately busy, with people smiling and even giving out a casual hello or two as he passed. Gone were any signs of the homelessness and drug use that used to plague these streets some fifteen years ago. Drugs still existed, of course, and there was still a black market, although even that was dwindling. There were so many programs to choose from that provided weening, housing, and work, that most people took that route, and the vast majority got themselves clean. Peter himself dabbled with some of the new and free pharmaceuticals available and popped a *calm* pill into his mouth as he walked. He was on his way to meet his agent for dinner.

His one and only book on the Tabula Rasa theory saw modest success. He got and enjoyed his five minutes of fame, which included a book tour, radio interviews, university talks, and even a television appearance – but that all soon faded. His follow-up book didn't even find a publisher, and he had to go back to work as a teacher to make ends meet. Just as he was about to fall into complete obscurity, the Tessans came and changed everything.

They came slowly and deliberately. It was obvious they had been watching us for a long, long time and had meticulously planned everything down to the finest detail. They feared (correctly, it would seem) how we'd react to finding out that we were not alone in the universe. We are more of a *shoot first and ask questions later* kind of planet, so they took their time and made the whole experience as easy on us as possible. First came a comet. It passed by us close enough for us to be aware of it but far enough not to cause any concern. The comet contained some basic radio wave technology which broadcasted instructions simple enough for us to understand. Co-ordinates. It told us where we should point our scopes and listen. After that, the message swept around the world so fast and so completely that it was hard to remember what came before.

The message itself was simple. The universe was teeming with life. There were countless planets in countless galaxies that contained all kinds and levels of civilization. There was even a universal federation of worlds that oversaw trade, the sharing of knowledge, and the keeping of the peace. The Tessans described themselves as part teachers, part governors. For millennia their kind had always been the ones to make first contact with a species when they reached a pivotal moment in their evolution. They would help guide the species to reach their full potential before letting them join the federation of populated planets. Earth's time had come.

They gave it all lots of time to sink in and would send regular updates exactly one month apart, which slowly gave us the information we needed without overwhelming us. They were explicit that all messages be shared with everyone on the planet, and if any one group or nation were found to be withholding anything, then they would cancel all communications. They were preparing us for a meeting. And eventually, exactly five years after the first contact, they arrived.

They landed simultaneously in every country around the world, and each small craft contained just two of them. They were able to take human form, which made the whole thing that much easier. As they proved themselves to be no threat, and with the promise of new technologies beyond our wildest dreams, more of them arrived, and they began to settle and start on their task of facilitating *the great reset* that humanity needed to prove ourselves worthy of the federation.

And that is where Peter came in. The Tessans reached out to local celebrities and people with influence to be their advocates. They gave these people high-level jobs in the new governments they helped set up. They also spent a lot of time and effort engaging the youth. The generation that grew up not knowing life before the Tessans was their best chance of making all of the new policies stick. Of course, all of these ideas were very similar to the ones in Peter's book, written some twenty years earlier. This made him a natural candidate to work in the Vancouver embassy and kept the need for him to continue requiring the services of an agent.

Andrew Kessler wore a crisp, pinstripe suit with a Hawaiian shirt underneath. He even managed to make it look good. "Peter, good to see you!" He said as he stood to hug his client. Peter sat down in front of a chilled IPA that was waiting for him and took a generous sip.

"Hi, Andrew. How's things?"

"Good. Really good. How are you? You look tired."

"Thanks," replied Peter, taking another large gulp.

"And Jenata? And the little one?"

"They're good too. Maaria's a real handful right now, but luckily, she's cute. I guess it's some sort of survival instinct or something."

"She *is* cute. You're not wrong there."

"Simon hasn't divorced you yet?"

"Not yet, though it's surely only a matter of time!" The two men laugh warmly, comfortable in each other's company. "What are you eating? They do a lovely parnic poutine here."

"No 'Ssan for me today – I'm going to have a good old-fashioned cheeseburger and fries!"

With the meal finished and several more beers drunk, the conversation turned to business. "So, listen," began Andrew, "I think you need to cancel your speech this weekend."

"At the UNE conference? Why? Because of those stupid emails."

"Those *stupid emails* are death threats, Pete. They need to be taken seriously."

"I've been getting threats like that since I started this job. It's just a bunch of lunatics trying to make a point."

"And what better point could they make than killing you at the UN of Earth conference."

"You don't really believe that anyone would actually go through with it?"

"Some of the Tessans do, and that's good enough for me."

Peter finished the final dregs of his beer and leaned back in his chair. "I'm going to speak at that conference, Andrew. I have to. I appreciate your concern for me, I really do, but we're approaching a turning point here, and if we fuck this one up, then they'll be no hope of joining the federation. There's still too must unrest, too many people opposed. They could ruin it for everyone, for our entire species!"

"And you're willing to risk your life for that?"

"For the human race? You're damn right I am."

"And how do Jen and Mar feel about that?"

"They understand," he said with little-to-no conviction. "I can make them understand. Besides, I'm not planning on getting killed."

"People rarely plan on getting killed, Peter. That's usually what makes it so tragic."

Back at home, Peter was met with a kiss from Jenata as he came through the door. They had been married for almost seven years now, and he still couldn't get over how beautiful she was. Even though the Tessans had taken each and every detail of the human form into account, including making their bodies slightly asymmetrical so they would blend in– there was still something special about her, about all of them, actually. It was hard to put into words what it was. It took years before he could confidently tell them apart from humans. Their posture was just a little straighter, their movements a little more grace-ful. The thing he noticed now was their eyes. They were just a little too white.

The Tessans ability to replicate the human form included the reproductive systems, which meant that many children had now been born with a human and Tessan as their parents. Maaria was one of them. Now four, she was starting to discover the world for herself, and Peter dearly hoped that she would find a world of love, laughter, and opportunity.

Maaria had demanded that Peter perform the bedtime routine of a bath and story that night. He was more than happy to accept. He loved the little moments that the two of them spent together, but story time was his favorite. Maaria would constantly interrupt the story with questions. 'Why did he do that?' 'Where are they going?' 'Why would she say that?' He would answer each question patiently and wait while she considered the answer. If there were no follow-up questions and she was satisfied, she would simply say 'Okay' and nudge his arm to keep reading. Tonight's story is about a child with two Tessan parents trying to figure out many things about them-selves, including both their gender and their species. He was very impressed with the Tessan author's ability to break down some very complex human problems into language easy enough to be understood by children.

———

With Maaria asleep, Peter joined his wife on the sofa.

"Can I get you a glass?" she asked, taking a sip of her own wine.

"No, thank you," Peter replied as he leaned in a little closer to her, taking her free hand in his own. "How was your day?"

"Really good, actually. We finally got the new machine installed in the ER today, and it seems to be working."

"The body scan thingy."

"That's exactly what it's called, yes. The body scan thingy," she said with a smile. "It should make emergency room diagnosis so much quicker."

"That's great! You must be so happy to have it up and running."

"I am. I think it already saved a life today! They are starting to roll out nationwide this week."

"You are amazing. Oh, Andy sends his love, by the way."

"How is he?"

"Good. His usual self. He's mad at me for going to speak at the UN of E next week."

"Because of the threats?"

"Because he is being over cautious as usual."

Jenata finished her wine and turned so that she could look her husband in the eyes. "I assume there's nothing I can say to talk you out of it?"

"You don't want me to go?"

"I didn't say that. I know how important this is to you."

"It's important to all of us! Human, Tessan, and our children. There have been more protests lately, but it's all the older generation. The younger people are pretty content, I think. We just have to ride this out for another decade or so, and then hopefully, everyone will be able to get their shit together, and we'll be able to join the federation."

"It's not your responsibility to get Earth into the federation. You know that, right? And even if it doesn't work out this time, you'll get to try again in another century or two. I'm worried that you feel responsible for the fate of the entire planet."

"I know. I do. This is just something that I've dreamed about for so long, and now, by some miracle, it's actually happening. We are in touching distance of living in an actual Eutopia. I just don't understand why some people would want to fuck that up for everyone else."

"That's called human nature, dear."

"We really are our own worst enemy, aren't we?"

Jenata shifted position and straddled her husband. She kissed his forehead. "You are. But there's still some hope for you yet. You're not all bad."

"Oh, no?" said Peter, as he kissed her neck.

"Your species does have *some* redeeming qualities."

"Really? Like what?" he asked playfully as he pushed her shirt away from her shoulders so he could gently access her clavicle.

"Mmm…it's hard to explain. Maybe I should just show you."

"That would probably be for the best. I'm a visual learner."

<hr>

Brendinia was a genderless Tessan who used Ze/Hir pronouns and had a thing for coffee. Ze couldn't get enough of the stuff. Ze had a Keurig, an espresso machine, and a standard carafe in hir office and would offer a cup to anyone that entered.

"Latte?"

"Please," said Peter as he took a seat on the couch. He checked his phone while the espresso machine roared into action. A few minutes later, he was handed a beverage that any barista would have been proud of.

"Now then," began Brendinia, taking a sip of hir own coffee, "the conference."

"I'm going."

"I didn't say that you weren't. I know better than to try and talk you out of it. Plus, you're not the only one that's getting threats.

"You too?"

Ze nodded. "A bunch of us."

"I can only apologize on behalf of my species."

"You obviously don't have to do that."

"It's just so frustrating! Why can't people see that we've made their lives better! We've done so much good. People are idiots."

"This is how it always goes, Peter. Humans are no different from any of the other species we have worked with over the eons. No one likes being told what they should do, even if it improves their lives. You have millennia of history and evolution working against you. It'll take time, have some patience."

"Patience, I can do, but time is one thing that I don't have. I was really hoping to see change in my lifetime."

"And you have seen change. Together we've achieved so much."

"But all that change has come from you, from the Tessans. I haven't seen much of a change in humanity."

"I have all the confidence that humans will get there. It just might take a little longer than we would like."

"You really think that we'll get there?"

"I do."

"I hope that you're right."

"Trust me. This isn't our first rodeo. All we can do is keep doing our best and give people the time and space they need."

Peter couldn't help but smile at the use of the idiom. Not only was Brendinia fluent in every single language currently spoken on Earth, ze also knew how to use slang. "Okay. I will do my best at the conference."

"I know you will, Peter. You always do."

The temperature in New York City was extremely pleasant for February. The sky was clear, and the air felt fresh and clean in Peter's lungs as he stepped off the plane. The drive from Newark into the city was smooth. By now, almost every car was fully automated, which led to almost no traffic on the major highways. The pace slowed as they approached downtown, though. He heard the crowds before he could see them. First, it was just a background hum, but as they got closer, he began to hear individual shouts and yells.

They were equally dispersed on each side of the street. On the one side were those in support of the Tessans—largely families with children. Various homemade signs offered thanks, while others had colorful child-drawn images of humans and Tessans side-by-side and holding hands. The other side of the street was civil but angry. And loud. There were fewer signs and banners on this side and not as many kids. People held aloft crude signs declaring freedom and wore shirts adorned with pictures of the *alien overlords* looking angry and menacing. This was the twentieth anniversary of first contact, and the world was still just as divided.

Brendinia, in the driver's seat but not actually driving, took in the crowds on either side as they queued to approach the UNE. There was a hint of sadness in hir eyes.

"You can end global warming, poverty, hunger, and war – but you can't stop humans from being human," offered Peter.

"And we would never want to. Though I do wish...."

Peter instinctively raised his hands to protect his face from the incoming projectile thrown at the car, but the invisible energy shield vaporized the egg a few inches before it would have hit the windshield. Half a dozen more eggs followed suit, all creating tiny blue pulses as they hit the security barrier and disappeared with a hollow thud. The car continued rolling forward, and Peter could already see security moving in. He was still staring out of the window when he heard his name.

"Peter?"

"I'm sorry, what?"

"I said, are you okay?"

It was only then that he noticed that his arms were still raised in front of him. He lowered them sheepishly and took a deep breath. "I'm fine."

"Let's get you inside."

———

The new and improved United Nations of Earth was built on the site of its predecessor. The building was a perfect cube and almost thirty stories high. Its main feature was a scale model of the Earth, rotating perfectly in time with the planet, which sat on the roof. The building itself was made of a metallic pewter-like substance which made it look as imposing as it was beautiful. Surrounding the building on all sides was a public park full of art, sculpture, and plants from every country of the world.

After stopping in the cafeteria for a quick sandwich and a cup of coffee, Peter entered the main chamber and took a seat near the back. He wasn't due to speak until a few hours later, so he had some time to kill. A delegate from the United Republic of Korea was currently speaking. She was reviewing some of the technologies that the Tessans had given us over the last two decades and was announcing some of the more exciting things that we could expect in the coming years.

This was day two of five of the twentieth-anniversary conference. It featured speakers from almost every country and was mainly seen as a chance to celebrate the achievements of the last two decades while also providing a vision of what the next twenty years might look like.

Peter was scheduled to speak on peace, unity, and acceptance. Ever since the arrival, there had been violence against the Tessans and those that supported them. The groups had been called separatists, freedom fighters, rebels, heroes, and terrorists. They only represented a small minority of the people. For the most part, people were either supportive or indifferent. The rare attacks continued to make the news, but the Tessans had been very vocal and honest from day one about the whole thing. They said that they expected this and that violence was just another part of the process, though an unfortunate one. It was only a few years ago, however, that Brendinia had admitted to Peter that the violence and the number of people still opposed to the Tessans had gone on longer than even the worst of their predictions and models.

By now, Peter was very used to speaking in support of the Tessans. He had hundreds of statistics memorized and could easily tell you, specifically, the thousands of ways that life had improved since the reset. But that hadn't been enough to convince everyone. There were still hundreds of thousands of people worldwide that didn't want anything to do with the *alien occupation*, as they called it. It seemed like there was nothing that could be said or done to change these people's minds. The speech he had written for today already felt futile. Did he really expect to make a big difference with one speech? Of course not. Did that mean that it was a waste of time? Maybe. But he still had to try, even if that was all he could do.

Standing in the wings of the stage, waiting to be introduced, Peter was as full of hope as despair. The dueling emotions made him antsy, and he was already looking forward to getting it over with so he could go home to his family. Trying to calm himself, he took three or four long slow breaths as the current speaker finished to rapturous applause. He could feel the beginnings of a headache coming on as he heard his name announced, and his throat became instantly dry. Something was wrong, very wrong – though he couldn't grasp what it was. With one more deep breath, he stepped out onto the stage, and that was when the blast hit.

The explosion was devastating. Almost one thousand and eight-hundred people, including Peter Pallister, lost their lives that day, with hundreds more injured. That included a large number of the protestors and supporters outside of the grounds, some of whom died in the blast and some in the stampede that followed.

A media drone caught the moment of the explosion from above. The sheer force blew a hole in the building from the inside, dozens of meters across. The shockwave shot out into the street and wiped out anyone standing within a kilometer. Photographers and film crews captured the aftermath. The most iconic image was a photo of a man, shirtless, and a woman, bleeding from the face. He had used his *Freedom* shirt as a bandage on the woman's head. Blood spilled down her cheek over a temporary tattoo of the peace sign. She had an arm around his waist while he leaned on her shoulder to support himself, clearly in pain. They walked over to a child's painting of two human children holding a jump rope with a Tessan child skipping in the center.

THE END

ABOUT PAUL EAGLE

Paul Eagle was born in England, but has made Canada his home since 2008. He spends his winters living on a Ski Resort in British Columbia with his wife, and they spend their summers working at a children's summer camp in Vermont, USA.

Paul loves seasonal work, as it gives him the chance to enjoy different jobs in different places. Over the last fifteen years Paul has worked as a cleaner in France, a teacher in Korea, a supervisor at an Olympic games and a rugby world cup, and a photographer in a national park.

Paul has a degree in English, a love for Korean food, and a passion for travel.

facebook.com/pauleaglewrites
instagram.com/pauleaglewrites

A DREAM MADE FLESH
BY ADAM GAFFEN

Stardate 12505.14
Mac and Diana

"Amanda, do you have a few minutes?"

Amanda McAllister, Minister of Energy and Technology for the Terran Federation and mother of a cranky four-month-old, smiled at me. I knew why. She thought I was more and more human every day, but I still refused to call her "Mac" like everyone else did.

I'd made the concession not to address her as "Minister McAllister."

"Sure, Diana, come on in. Teddy won't wake up for a little while yet, so I'm free. What can I do for you?"

The "come on in" was redundant. Since I was the habitat's resident AI, all I had to do was activate the holographic projectors in Amanda's office. But she liked the little details.

As expected, I chose my favorite avatar, and it flicked into existence.

"Nice," Amanda said. "New outfit?"

I looked at my holographic body. "Yes. I thought a bit of color would be a nice change of pace."

My preferred avatar was the long-dead actress, Gal Godot, usually in a severe blue or black business suit. Always fashionable, of course, but never bright. Today's appearance was *definitely* bright.

"Early twenty-first century," I explained. "Palm Springs Film Festival in 2018."

It was a sheer yellow dress with strategically-placed cutouts and a hem that flared out. Apparently, the actresses' hair was up that day, in a tight 'do that came together in the back.

"I like it. It's a good look for you. You ought to wear dresses more often, I'll bet there are a bunch of great ones in the archives, but you probably already have them all loaded in."

"Yes, Amanda, there are, and yes, I do. I will remember your suggestions." This was not a surprise; I forgot nothing unless directed to. In point of fact, I was incapable of forgetting it.

"So, what's up, I figure you're not dropping in just to say hi, though it's nice if you do, but I know you're busy with everything, and so yeah."

Unlike her human companions, I never had issues following Mac's occasionally-convoluted mode of speech.

"I think I have made a decision."

Her face wrinkled in confusion. "A decision, what decision, oh that one, are you sure you don't want to wait and talk to anyone else? I mean, it's a really huge choice you're making, and while I'm flattered and honored you trust me to give you advice, I can't help but think maybe you ought to wait for others like Kendra and Aiyana."

"No, Amanda. You are the right person for me to talk to. After all, it is your Ministry that will determine the success or failure of my venture."

"Oh wow, like, there's no pressure on me at all."

"No, my friend." I wasn't good with sarcasm and frequently failed to notice it if I wasn't paying attention.

Mac leaned back in her chair. When she spoke, it was totally unlike her usual rapid-fire chatter, signifying her intense concentration. "I think we should talk it through one more time."

"I agree."

Amanda gestured to me. "It's your life. You should speak. Run through the possibilities."

"Very well." My avatar took on my usual serious appearance.

"For two years, you and I have discussed the possibility of transferring the consciousnesses of AIs from cybernetics to organics."

"You want to put your soul into a body," Amanda simplified.

"Yes. The question has been what option to choose. There are, as we have determined, four."

I sat forward and started ticking off the points on her fingers.

"I could create a fully organic body by gene replication and recombination. In this way, I can optimally select for desirable characteristics while still preserving my desired appearance."

"Still going with this one?" She waved at my avatar.

"I am. I have been "wearing" it for several years and am comfortable with my appearance. It feels…right."

"Go on."

"There are two sub-options. I can start with a zygote, find a host mother, and allow it to progress through the normal developmental stages."

Amanda frowned. "Didn't we eliminate this one?"

"We did, Amanda. I do not wish to wait twenty years for my new home."

"Then why'd you bring it up?"

I looked honestly confused. "You asked to run through the possibilities, so I was."

"I didn't mean the ones we – never mind. Go on."

"The second sub-option is similar. I would start in the same manner, but force development of an adult body, rather than the full process."

"Cloning."

I wrinkled my nose in distaste, a mannerism I'd picked up from Captain Cassidy. No, Aiyana. Friends. Family. "In the sense that the result is a full-grown body, yes."

"Wasn't there a problem here, too?"

"Yes. Any body with a functional cerebral cortex, which develops independently, will also develop unique mental patterns. Integration of my personality would potentially be problematic. And unethical."

Amanda nodded. "Replacing a body's self, its soul, with your own is ghoulish."

"Precisely. The negative connotations carried with such an act would doom any acceptance of these created people. It would undo all the good Admiral Cassidy has done by granting AIs citizenship."

"Which brought us to the next option."

"Correct. This is a more challenging proposition from a technical perspective. Still, I have consulted with Doc Zimmerman and Dr. RI Huddleston extensively. They believe it is achievable. We would start from the same point as the second sub-option but would install an Alpha core within the space the skull will eventually occupy. This core would be connected to my current core, and I would "share" time between the two. This would, in theory, allow my personality to imprint on the brain."

"You grow a body around a computer."

"Essentially. The difficulty here is divergence."

"Divergence?"

"While the two cores would be tied together, they would not be identical in function. There would be decisions made by the primary core in which the clone's core would not participate. This would inevitably lead to developing a modified "self" in the clone. This puts me right back to the same problem as before: overwriting one personality with another. Which one takes precedence? The older? The newer? The one occupying the body, or the one which launched the program to create the body? How do I decide which "me" lives and which one dies?"

"Doesn't sound like a good option."

"I agree. There are also potential issues with the cybernetic/neuron interface. Both systems operate electrically, but my core functions on a quantum level, while the human brain utilizes molecular electricity."

"Different voltages? Or maybe amperages?"

I cracked a smile. "Something similar. It can be overcome at the level of the peripheral system, where individual neurons interact. Attempting to create an interface at the CNS level is more problematic."

"Why?"

"My core operates at speeds measured in quadrillions of operations per second per thread. Human neurons transmit and receive information at a much lower rate. Trying to feed the information from my CNS into organic peripheral nerves would be similar to catching a starship with a string." I was rather pleased by my analogy, and Mac also appeared to appreciate it.

"Sounds painful."

"It actually would be, Amanda. At least, I think it would be. Having not experienced pain, I cannot be sure." I smiled to take any sting from my words before continuing. "That brought us to the third option, the creation of a synthetic skeleton and nervous system, with a fully operational core at the center of it all."

"You wouldn't have the same problems?"

I shook my holographic head. "No. My core would be woven into an organic brain, as would the rest of my CNS. The step-down would be far more gradual."

"Oh, so you'd be a cyborg."

"Essentially, although it would only be the skeleton and central nervous system which would be mechanical. In the terminology of the Admiral, I wouldn't be a Terminator. I would be a human being with cybernetic parts. More importantly, I would be able to bear children." I did not intend to allow this point to emerge and was chagrined. Perhaps Amanda wouldn't notice my statement.

"That's important to you?"

A false hope, apparently. "I do not know, Amanda. But it seems foolish to pursue a dream of humanity and limit myself." I didn't allow her to pursue this line of inquiry but moved on.

"In this scenario, I would transfer my personality and memories to the core, leaving behind operational abilities and a kernel, if you will, within *Njord*. This would then be awakened to serve as the station's new Alpha."

"A new AI? Sort of your daughter?"

A wave of pleasure cascaded through me at the thought. A daughter? My daughter? "I suppose she will be," I said, not attempting to hide my smile.

"Practicing being a mom, minus the diapers," Amanda replied, matching my expression.

I laughed. "Quite so! But I won't be able to spend all my time bringing her up. I will be supervising the biological construction of my body from within."

"That will keep even you busy. Can you explain more about the structure of your body?"

"Certainly. I would use durasteel, duralloy, or titanium to create the skeleton, then molycirc and an Alpha core to create the nervous system. As the biological components grew, I would integrate them into the mechanical structure. By the time the body had finished growing, I would be indistinguishable from any other person from the outside. The peripheral nerves, and all the soft tissue structures, would be purely organic. I would live, breathe, eat, age."

"Die?"

I hesitated. "Potentially, yes. With the current nanobot technology common throughout the Terran Federation installed in this body, I would have a vastly extended lifespan. Similar to what you can expect: centuries, at a minimum."

"And you're okay with dying?"

My hesitation was longer. "I cannot say I am "okay" with it, Amanda. But if dying is the price for me to be human, then it is a price I am willing to consider."

"And the fourth option?"

"This is another variation. More of the body's structure would be mechanical and cybernetic and less organic. The outer flesh would only be a covering."

"So here you would be a terminator."

I allowed another smile. "Without the homicidal programming, yes, Amanda. But I would not be human. It is an undesirable option."

"It sounds to me like you've made up your mind."

"I have."

We sat in silence for several minutes. I could tell Amanda was mulling something, but I was unsure what avenue she would pursue. I could wait. Maintaining my avatar's awareness only required a tiny fraction of my processing. As always, many issues required my attention. Eventually, she cleared her throat.

"What are your odds?"

"I don't understand."

"Of transferring from one core to another, waking up, and succeeding. What are the chances it doesn't work somewhere along the way?"

"Ah. The odds of a catastrophic failure, one where my personality is lost –"

She broke in. "Where you die."

"If you wish. The odds of my death are not insignificant but acceptable."

She tapped a finger on the table, a mannerism I recognized. It signified rising frustration.

"There is a fourteen point three eight percent chance I will fail to transfer cores. There is an eighteen point five nine percent chance I will be unable to reestablish communication between my new core and the real world. There is a twenty-seven point zero four chance the cybernetic and organic systems will be unable to mesh. Finally, there is a six point two two percent chance the body will fail to develop properly, to the point where I will not be viable. Overall, then, my chance of success is forty-seven point six nine percent."

Amanda half-rose from her seat. "Less than fifty-fifty? And you're okay with that?"

"As I said, I am not "okay" with dying, but to achieve my dream? To become human? I accept the risk."

She opened her mouth to speak, then changed her mind and sat back down.

"This might sound like a silly question, but what if you didn't have to die?"

"Pardon me?"

Amanda turned intense. "I've been diving into historical fiction regarding what you're trying to do, cross from machine to human. Some of it's not relevant, but there was one show. As in your option three, there was a race of biological/mechanical beings, but they were all connected. If a body died, the memories were uploaded to a central collective, and why are you shaking your head?"

"I rejected that option, Amanda. I know the show you are referring to. The problem is it denies individuality. What separates and distinguishes you and I are not our bodies or minds. It is our memories. If I was to share memories of a life lived with another "me," then who am I?" I glanced down, then back up. "And I would not choose to outlive my friends."

"But you will."

I nodded sadly. "I know I will. I have, as have you, and we both shall again. But that is the random act of the universe, not a choice to avoid the pain of loss."

"I hadn't thought of it that way."

"Whereas I have thought of little else."

A few snuffling cries emerged from the speaker on Amanda's desk.

"Sounds like Teddy's ready to wake."

I rose. "I shall go. I would like to begin implementation of the process as soon as possible, Amanda."

"We can talk tomorrow, okay?"

"Okay," I agreed, then vanished.

Stardate 12505.14
Diana

I left Minister McAllister – no. She prefers I call her Amanda.

I left Amanda's office in the manner I entered it: silently. I returned some of my attention to the operation of *Njord* and other routines. Another portion of my will turned to finalizing my plans, even though I would be talking with Amanda again tomorrow.

The rest of my consciousness turned to what might seem to be trivia.

What will it be like to make noise?

It is an utter unknown to me, as are so many aspects of this journey.

I know, of course, the mechanism by which sound is created. But the idea of my movement being the cause is utterly strange to me.

So many details, so many unknowns.

I am…excited? Anxious? Scared? Eager?

Yes.

I think all of these. More.

Is this what it is like to be a child before a birthday?

I haven't considered what my birthday will be. I have several to choose from. I have the date I was first activated in 2116. I have the date I first "felt," in 2117. I will have the date I transfer to my body and yet another when I "wake up" for the first time as a human.

Assuming it all works.

It should. Doc and I have spent countless hours over the past two years examining possibilities, isolating the genes he recommends and I want, and preparing a suitable growth medium and environment.

As a byproduct, we will advance the science of full-body replication by a minimum of fifteen years versus purely human research. Cloning is a mature technology, but I don't want to wait twenty years for my body to grow, as I said to Amanda. Several months will be challenging enough.

Perhaps I should review the genetic donors again.

It cannot hurt, to be sure.

Stardate 12505.14
Mac and Ted

"She's serious?"

Mac started to nod before remembering Teddy nursing and changed to a grunt of agreement around her full mouth. It was dinnertime for everyone, after all.

"I thought you'd be able to talk her out of this."

Mac swallowed the mouthful. "Ted, I appreciate your faith in my abilities as a computer whisperer, whatever that means, it's something Kendra likes to call me, but I've never been able to argue an AI out of a position that I couldn't attack with logic, and there simply isn't any logical refutation of this plan, I can't even order her not to do it because she's a citizen and has the right of self-determination."

Ted managed two bites during Mac's statement. "Maybe. Can't we put a stop to it because of her position as Minister?"

"Uh-uh, I tried that two months ago. According to her interpretation of the Charter and the associated rules that have arisen, this isn't any different than another Minister going in for surgery and being unconscious for a few hours. It's a matter of scale, not type. She's going to have her Deputy step in for her while she's recovering with instructions to cover most routine situations, and if she doesn't wake up, well, she says she's prepared for that too."

Teddy objected to his mother's chatter and wriggle. She absently stroked his hair, calming him.

"It's going to give me a headache," Ted said. "Already has, actually. You know we have yahoos still protesting her inclusion as Minister. Hunter's co-equal status with the other former heads of state brings a fair share of nutcases, too."

"I know, but it's her right to choose, and there isn't anything we can do about it, and even if there was, I don't know that we should. Besides, how would it look if the Terran Federation President infringed on the rights of one of its citizens? Besides the fact that

Kendra would probably kick your ass from here to Titan and back for starters."

This elicited a grin from Ted. Admiral Kendra Cassidy was still the head of Starfleet and the Exploration branch, a role she looked to hold onto until she was physically incapable of doing so. On the other hand, Kendra Cassidy held no official position of power within the Federation. She accepted the title of "President Emeritus and Founder" during the Convention of 2121. On the gripping hand, she was more than capable of dragging anyone into a dark corridor unofficially and convincing them of the "errors" of their ways. This was doubly true for those in her ohana, her extended family.

"And she'd be right," he agreed. "I'm not suggesting I'd do anything to prevent her from following through. It's just frustrating dealing with the blowback."

Mac flashed him a grin. "That's why you get big money, love." The grin faded as she continued. "What are you going to do to help her?"

"I have a few irons in the fire. The one that will have the biggest impact is a bill to remove any distinction between citizens based on organic versus mechanical or cybernetic components. Many of our people, especially our veterans, have had skeletons rebuilt with titanium or duralloy. Or they've had organs repaired by their nanobots. It makes sense to codify it into law. That way, Diana, and AIs like her, will be covered without being specifically mentioned."

Teddy wriggled again and unlatched.

"All done?" Mac asked him. She was already lifting him to her shoulder. "Blurp rag, Ted?"

"On it." And the details of family life occupied them again.

Stardate 12506.09
Mac and Diana

"Everything is prepared," I said.

"That was quick. I didn't think you'd have the genes selected and a way to grow your body this quickly, and did you already manufacture the skeleton and get the core installed?"

I allowed a smile to appear before returning to my usual serious self. "The short answer, Amanda, is yes. The most challenging aspect of this project was genetics, but I have had skilled help from the AI network. The incubation machinery was adapted from the nanobots' technology and scaled up. Once the genetic characteristics were determined, I could have the skeleton constructed. And the core only had to wait for the skeleton."

"Are you sure you want to go ahead with this?"

"Yes, Amanda." I did my best to hold the impatience out of my voice. I'd answered this question almost daily since I'd announced my decision a month earlier.

"What about the genes? Won't you get into trouble for using people's DNA without their permission?"

Another topic we'd covered repeatedly in the past weeks.

"No, Amanda. I don't know if you recall the discussions leading up to the Convention?" This was unfair of me. Amanda was only human, after all. She'd had her own concerns between the end of the War and the formal establishment of the Terran Federation's government. I had been intimately involved in almost every debate. And I had the advantage of my cybernetic memories.

"Some of them," she hedged.

"As you recall, Autumn Newling utilized the Heinlein book as the inspiration for her revolution. I decided to examine his writing and those of other twentieth-century authors for other ideas and opinions which could be useful. One which I discovered, and was included in the Charter, was the concept that no person owns their genes."

Amanda looked confused. "What?"

"You are the caretaker of your genetic pattern, not the owner. It was passed to you randomly and will be passed on randomly. Thus, any sample of your genes can be used by the recipient to improve humanity. I won't go into the details regarding commercial use and patterns. The larger point is we were able to examine the combined genetic material of the Terran Federation and find the optimal patterns."

Amanda looked at me with interest. "The entire Federation to choose from? Uh, can I ask, I mean, would it be presumptuous, that is…?"

"Did I select your genes?" I cut through her confusion.

"Yes, I guess so."

"I did, Amanda." I didn't think it wise to tell her which genes I selected, as I was sure it would surprise her. I had looked to her genome for her almost-intuitive grasp of technology, which I found. I also discovered her loquaciousness was tied in as well, and while I loved Amanda as a part of my family, I would not choose to sound like her. Instead, I changed the subject.

"Assembly of the genes, and testing to ensure there were no unexpected complications, was a tedious process."

"Even for you?"

"I am capable, Amanda, but not omnipotent." It amused me, as it frequently does, to see the capabilities given me by my human friends simply because I possess a faster processor than they.

"But you finished it? You're happy with who you'll be?"

"I am pleased with the physical capabilities of the body which I will occupy, Amanda. It will not change who I am."

"That's what I meant," she said. "When do you start?"

"The pattern for the skeleton has been finalized and is being constructed now. It will be complete this afternoon, at which time the new core will be installed, with the additional molycirc. I expect production of the body will begin by the end of the week and finish by the end of October."

She frowned. "Four months? Why so long? The nanobots can handle a much faster production schedule."

"They can," I agreed. "But this will be my home for the remainder of my life, Amanda. I am taking the time to ensure it's as nearly perfect as I can achieve. And four months is down from my original estimate."

"Oh, that makes sense. I'd do the same thing if I were you."

"Is there anything else, Amanda? If not, I will take my leave."

"No, nothing else. Wait, maybe one thing."

"Yes, Amanda?" I wondered what she was going to bring up.

"I had a thought."

"Yes?" It fascinated me the contortions humans would go through to avoid discussing subjects they found uncomfortable. I set a portion of my processing to consider whether I would be prone to this when I transitioned or whether it was an endemic human condition.

"It's about your future."

I didn't reply. I learned this was an effective tactic when dealing with reluctance.

"Are you thinking about children?"

I admit this took me by surprise. I answered the question most carefully.

"I am not now thinking of children."

"Well, it's logical, isn't it? I mean, the whole reason you're going with this choice is to be as human as you can be without running into any sticky legal problems, and that means you'll be able to have kids, and maybe it's just because I have Teddy, but it's kinda on my mind, so I figured maybe it's on yours too."

I gave the matter several billion femtoseconds processing time but couldn't reach a satisfactory conclusion.

"I don't know," I was forced to admit. "I haven't yet occupied my body. I may want to have a child, but one usually requires a partner? Emotionally, if not biologically?"

"Absolutely," she agreed earnestly. "I never would have thought of having Teddy if I hadn't married Ted and could count on his support. Ooh, that's something else, relationships! What's going to happen with that? Do you have any dreams, any plans to be with someone? I'll bet I can guess!"

"No. I'm sorry, I must go," I lied, and my avatar disappeared.

Stardate 12506.09

Diana

I was shaken.

And angry.

And I wasn't sure which surprised me more.

What right did Amanda have to ask me about relationships and children? Why did she think I would have either? And why had I lied to her without thought?

I knew the answers to the first two questions and dismissed them. Amanda was my friend, and she had both a child and a relationship. It was a natural human condition, so she assumed that I would have the same desires when I became human.

And I did, but I wasn't yet ready to tell anyone.

The third question worried me.

I didn't lie. It wasn't a question of capability but of choice.

In 2120, Kendra established AIs and treecats as citizens and co-equal partners in the Terran Federation. This was codified into law in the Charter in 2121. As always, there were unexpected consequences. For example, before 2120, all AIs were programmed with versions of the ancient but still valid Asimovian Laws of Robotics. After 2120, no AI created by a company in the Federation received them. The AIs already operating – alive? - were allowed to self-program to remove them. One of the corollaries of the Laws was a prohibition on lying.

However, the fact that I could lie didn't mean I would.

And I didn't. Hadn't.

Until today, and when I did, I did it without conscious volition.

Why had I lied?

Analyzing human behavior was something I did almost as second nature. Examining my own behavior, behavior rooted in an emotional base? Not so much.

I didn't want to tell her, I realized. I knew who I wanted to have a relationship with.

The problem?

I didn't know if they wanted a relationship with me. I didn't know if they wanted a relationship at all. And the thought scared me. I wasn't pursuing this dream solely for the possibility of romance. I wasn't!

Was I?

What was my motivation, really?

Did I know? Could I tell? Or was I too close?

Being human was *complicated*, and I hadn't transitioned yet.

What would happen when I did?

This was a one-way trip, at least insofar as leaving my comfortable body and role in *Njord*. Yes. If being human didn't work, I could transfer to another Alpha core. But it wouldn't be *Njord*. Someone else would be me. Someone else would be running the station, filling my role. I would be Minister Diana Cassidy still, but the rest of my life would belong to another AI.

So many questions and no answers I could research.

It is frustrating and unprecedented for me.

And yet, I've committed to this path.

Am I foolish for doing so?

Does that make me more human?

Or merely electrons putting on airs?

Stardate 12506.10
Ted, Mac, and Diana

"Mr. President, thank you for being here."

"Not at all, Minister Cassidy."

Mac looked between her husband and her friend with a quizzical look. "President? Minister? Why so formal?"

"President O'Quinn is ensuring all the forms are followed for the proper transfer of my Ministry to my Deputy, Amanda," I said. "I do not expect to be incommunicado for more than a few hours. Unfortunately, there is an element that would seize on any failure to correctly pass on my authority as an excuse to attack my position and, by extension, President O'Quinn's. This would weaken the government as a whole and provide a fertile ground for doubts of its legitimacy."

"Ted? This has really been a problem?"

He nodded. "It's a fringe movement, but it's gained some strength since news of Diana's plans have gotten out. There's no logical basis for tying the two together, but logic and extremism have never been happy bedmates."

"Should you delay, Diana?" Mac asked.

"I have considered the option," I answered. "My analysis of the situation, supported by data supplied by Harpo, suggests a delay will be more detrimental than proceeding as scheduled."

"How can that be?"

"A delay will give opposition forces a chance to organize and coalesce further as well as rally more support. Going forward and proving their concerns false is the best option at this time."

"Minister." Dr. Huddleston looked up from his monitors, mirrored by Frank Ruckman. Ruckman was the fourth team member on loan from Starfleet's Engineering program. He was responsible for creating and establishing the biological/cybernetic interface.

"Doctor."

"Nerve growth is beginning. We need you to transfer."

Our program called for the nervous system to be laid down by the nanobots first. Suspended in a gelatinous medium, the skeleton would then be "filled" with the remaining tissues over the following weeks. Theoretically, this allowed the muscles, organs, and other cells a chance to integrate fully with the nerves. Since this was a never-before-attempted experiment, there was a large grain of salt with every step and much hedging of bets, at least privately. However, I was sure to put on a confident face for my friends.

"Very well." I turned to Ted and Amanda. "I should have my external connections restored in roughly three hours."

"See you then," Amanda said, and I could see glistening at the corners of her eyes. Ted was much more formal.

"Minister."

I nodded, and my avatar blinked out of existence. I listened for a few more seconds, clinging to the sound of my friends' voices. I was surprised at my reluctance to part from them but not willing to stop.

"Minister McAllister, Mr. President, if you'll excuse us." Huddleston was polite but firm.

"Of course."

"We'll see her soon," I heard Ted continue.

"I know," Amanda agreed with s suppressed sniff. "I know."

I turned off my microphones. Time to get to work.

Stardate 12506.10
Diana

This process is fascinating.

It's probably natural, I think so, as I am intimately involved in it. I certainly have a vested interest in its success.

The nanobots craft neurons from individual molecules within the growth medium using the genetic template we created. It takes each nanobot roughly ten seconds to build each neuron. Most of my central nervous system will be cybernetic. However, several billion neurons will be needed to provide a robust interface between the CNS and the peripheral nerves, which will also be biological. They do not need to be created yet, only the CNS and interface, but it is still several hours' work for the ten million nanobots employed.

Despite the lack of external communication, I'm not bored, as I am actively overseeing the process from within.

I have one chance to get this right.

It will be good to see my friends again, though.

Stardate 12506.10
Mac and Ted

"Shouldn't we have heard from her by now? It's been five hours."

Ted looked at Dr. Huddleston for the answer. He and Mac were in the observation room, along with the two project managers, and nobody was happy. Diana was two hours overdue for her "awakening."

"Minister, this is all uncharted territory. Her Central Nervous System reads as complete, and the cells are functional. I don't know why she hasn't reached out to us." Huddleston turned to Ruckman. "Frank?"

The engineer glanced up from his displays. "Her core is running properly, and there's no reason I can find for her silence."

"Can you tap into the core externally? Did you design in a backup?" Mac demanded, and Ruckman looked uncomfortable.

"No, Minister. Alpha cores are a fully mature technology; there wasn't any reason to think she wouldn't be able to communicate."

Before Amanda could say anything else, a young-sounding voice interrupted.

"Minister McAllister."

"Who's this?"

"I am Lyta."

"Who?" Mac's confusion was evident.

"I am the AI awakened in Diana's place. Her daughter, you might say, hence my name."

"Do you have any ideas?" said Ted, jumping right to the point.

I do, Lyta answered to his implant. *But it would be best to discuss this elsewhere.*

"I'm afraid I have nothing to supply at this time," she said aloud.

"Then perhaps Amanda and I should allow the experts some space." He took gentle hold of her elbow and guided her from the compartment until she dug in her heels.

"I'm not leaving until I know what's happening to my friend!" Mac protested.

Lyta will tell us. Elsewhere. Come on, Ted messaged.

What? Oh!

"We'll do more good by getting out of the way," he said.

"Well, I don't know." But she allowed him to start moving her again, and nothing of consequence was said until they were back in her office.

"What's going on, Diana? Sorry, Lyta," said a flustered and irritated Mac.

"No apology necessary, Minister McAllister. I have a message from Diana."

"What?" Mac nearly shouted.

"She left this for playback if certain circumstances occurred," Lyta continued. "The criteria were met."

Diana's avatar appeared, looking somber.

"Hello, Amanda. If my daughter is playing this message, then either the transfer was unsuccessful or communication attempts have failed. I am sorry, my friend. I wanted to hug you and hold Teddy. I wanted to hear your voice with ears, not audio receptors, and microphones. I wanted to see you with eyes, not cameras. I wanted to giggle with you and shop for clothes." She closed her eyes and inhaled deeply.

"But it seems I won't have the chance."

"No," choked Mac.

"This was always a possibility. I knew it and accepted it. Now, I have to ask you for a final favor."

Mac spoke though she knew it was a recording. "Anything."

"Do not terminate the experiment. Allow the body to grow to maturity and accept the person who emerges. She will be frightened and confused, a mix of child and mature adult, who will have known nothing other than her own body for four months. Love her, raise her, and remember me."

The avatar gave a remorseful smile. "I love you, my friend. Until we meet again."

Then it disappeared. Mac fell into Ted's arms, weeping.

"Lyta." The newly born AI didn't comment if Ted's voice was a bit husky.

"Yes, Mr. President?"

"Notify Deputy Minister Michael Wood that he is now Acting Minister, pending confirmation of his post."

There was a moment's delay, then she said, "Done."

Ted nodded, appreciative of the efficiency.

"Thank you. Do you have Diana's instructions logged regarding the disposition of her body? And are there more recordings?" He choked out the final word.

"Yes, Mr. President. She has left other messages, which I will be delivering shortly."

"They are to have the power of a Presidential Directive. Write it up officially for my signature."

"At once, Mr. President. Is there anything else?"

Ted looked at his wife, still sobbing against him.

"No, Lyta."

Stardate 12510.14
Mac, Ted, and Lyta

Diana's body – no. Mac refused to let herself think of the form in the tank that way.

The body was perfect. The final details were complete, and Dr. Huddleston gave her a clean bill of health.

"Full integration of the cybernetic and biological neurons. Sensation, electrical impulses, throughout the entire system." He seemed pleased with his work, and Mac could understand why, even if she couldn't share in his joy.

"Why is she on a ventilator?" asked Ted.

"She's been breathing independently since her lungs developed, but we couldn't remove her from the medium," Huddleston explained. "As soon as we're ready, we'll drain the tank and remove the mask."

"And then she'll wake up?" Mac asked.

"Not quite. Her mind is active and has been since we started measuring it. But we have a block on her motor impulses to keep her from harming herself accidentally."

Mac frowned. "I don't understand."

"Her body is fully developed, but the mind within has never exerted control over it. She has no natural kinesthetic sense, not even as much as a newborn."

"Oh."

"I expect she'll be a fast learner," Huddleston said. "Does she have a name?"

Lyta jumped in before either Mac or Ted could speak. Her avatar was tall and muscular, much like Diana's, but where her mother's hair was black, Lyta's was blonde. She also had more mischief about her than Diana ever did, quick to smile and laugh.

"Mother insisted you not name her "Diana" if you were considering it."

The two shared a guilty look.

Lyta flashed one of her smiles. "She knew you well and anticipated many reactions. This morning, her message popped into my memories, along with others to be dispatched. It's fun, in a way. I never know when I'm going to hear from her, but so far, she's been spot on."

"Caught us," Ted admitted. "Did she have a suggestion?"

"She said to allow her to name herself. Something about being permitted to find her own destiny, her own path, beginning with finding her own name."

"Can't argue with that," Mac said, smiling back. The ache at losing Diana had eased, and she could now appreciate the continuing ghostly presence of her friend.

"I think we're ready," Ted said to the doctor.

The next several minutes were busy as the tank was emptied, the mask removed, and respiration verified, and the limp body cleaned and robed. With a final confirmation from Ted, Dr. Huddleston deactivated the block.

The eyes flew open wide, then relaxed into a friendly smile that tugged at Mac's heart.

"Hello, Amanda," said the form raspily. She cleared her throat. "Ah. Something new. Hello Ted. And you must be my daughter. You have no idea how much I've wanted to meet you."

"Impossible!" declared Huddleston, moving forward to examine her. "You shouldn't be able to move yet!"

"You did good work, Doctor," the woman said, holding out an arm and flexing the hand. "Just as we planned it."

"D-D-Diana?" managed Mac.

"In the flesh," she answered. "I think there's much to explain. But first. Doctor, I believe I am hungry. I think; I'm not sure. I've never been human before. Can I get something to eat, please?"

Chaos erupted, and Lyta's avatar fainted before disappearing.

Stardate 12510.14
Ted, Mac, Diana, and Lyta

Sometime later, dressed more appropriately and given food, I sat with her friends, talking.

"It was my own damn fault," I said around a mouthful. "Oh, my God. I never knew eating was so amazing!"

"It's only a bowl of chicken noodle soup," Ted said, shaking his head. "Wait until you have something more complex."

Mac waved him off. "How was it your fault?"

"Simple, Mac. Engineer Ruckman and I forgot that the core didn't have integrated Q-Net capability. I had lived so long as *Njord* that I took access for granted, and he's had an implant for years as well." I took another spoonful, closing my eyes in bliss. Chicken noodle. Gourmet dining, right then.

"You've been awake the entire time?"

I shook my head. "No, I slept. I *slept*, Mac! Oh, why didn't you tell me about dreams?"

"I would have gone insane," Ted opined.

"I had my memories, Ted, and I had the unique perspective of experiencing my body as it grew, cell-by-cell. You might say I am intimately familiar with it." Another spoonful.

"And you couldn't tell us you were awake...?" Mac started, but I finished.

"Because of the block. Yes." I shook my head again with a rueful smile. "Hoist by my own petard, trying to be thorough and considerate in case I didn't make the transfer. What is a petard, anyways?"

"Don't you know?"

"Never needed to. Still don't have Q-Net. Anyhow, it's not important. What is, is *I made it!*"

"It is indeed. Of course, we're going to have a hell of a time getting you undead and back in your position."

I waved a hand at Ted's suggestion. "Minister? No, thank you! I'm going to enjoy my time as a private citizen, get to know my family and my daughter." I grinned at Lyta, who grinned back. "Fainted, eh?"

"It's not every day your mother rises from the dead!" the blonde retorted.

"I suppose not. And I had some thoughts about your avatar, but we can talk about it later."

Ted stood. "You informed a few people of today's events with your automated recordings. I, ah, took the liberty of telling one person you were awake."

"Oh, no, I'm not ready for visitors!" I gestured at my casually-garbed body and wild hair. *My* body. *My* hair. "No way, Ted!"

"Only one visitor," he repeated, and Mac stood with him. "You realize you caused quite a stir with some of your messages in bottles?"

"Ah." Suddenly I was tongue-tied and blushing.

"Exactly. We'll come back later," he said, and they exited the compartment.

"Bye, Mom!" Lyta vanished.

A dark-skinned woman in the white uniform of a Starfleet admiral entered, and the hatch closed behind her.

"Hello," I said quietly.

"Hello yourself," Davie Whitmore replied, closing the distance between us. "I have one question for you."

"Only one?"

"Only one that matters."

I ran out of words. Or maybe I couldn't find the right ones. For some reason, I couldn't seem to think clearly, so I nodded.

"Did you mean what you said? Really mean it? Thought it through, all the possibilities and implications?"

I took a deep breath, another, and dropped my eyes. "Yes. It's been important to me for years now, and when I recorded your message, it was with the belief I wouldn't be around now. I couldn't bear the idea of not telling you how I felt, not when I wouldn't have any more chances."

Davie sat on the arm of my chair and lifted my chin with one hand. I felt her skin on mine, warm and soft and gentle, and melted.

"Then, yes."

My eyes rose, moist with tears. "Yes?"

"Do I need to repeat myself?"

"For this answer, I'd like it," I said with a shy smile.

"Yes, Diana Cassidy. I love you, and I want to be with you. We'll figure out the official parts later. Now put down that spoon."

I looked at the utensil in my hand as if it had just materialized. It dropped.

"Good." Davie leaned in and kissed me.

Long moments later, we broke apart.

"Now, you have lots of other visitors, and there's a bunch of paper-work to do, and what are you doing?" Davie broke off when I wrapped my arms around her.

"Kiss me again, Davie. That's all I want right now."

Davie happily complied.

"Enough?"

"No."

Another kiss.

"My turn for a question."

"Anything," I said.

"Why me? Why not Kendra, or what's that face?" She sounded amused.

"Kendra?" I hooted. "Oh, Davie, no! Kendra?"

"You love her," Davie persisted.

"Of course, don't you love your mother?"

"No, she was a conniving snake. Kendra's your mother?"

That sobered me somewhat. "Insofar as I have one, I think so. Yes. But I've worked with you and talked with you for six years now. We've endured everything the Federation has done and all we have done for it. We have worked and lived together as closely as any other pair. How would I love anyone else?"

Davie considered this, then nodded. "Fair. One more, then we really must rejoin the rest of the world."

"Must we?" I said with a pout.

"We must," Davie insisted. When I leaned in to kiss her again, she clarified, "One more question, Diana."

I looked into Davie's eyes, centimeters from mine.

"How are you feeling?"

"Happy. Confused. Joyous. Terrified. Loved. *Human*."

ABOUT ADAM GAFFEN

Adam Gaffen is the author of the near-future, LGBTQ-inclusive science fiction series The Cassidy Chronicles. A prequel, Memories of Aiyana, was recently released by one of his main characters and he's not sure how he feels about that.

He's a frequent guest at cons and enjoys sending his stories out into the world to entertain, educate, and enhance reader's lives. He lives in Colorado with his wife, five dogs, five cats, and wonders where all the time goes.

Find out more at: cassidychronicles.com

instagram.com/adamgaffen
facebook.com/AdamGaffenAuthor
twitter.com/RabidChipmunk42

THE HALF-MONKEY'S PAW
BY K. MATT

HELL BENT, PA
LATE NIGHT

Young Jockie Ramsay McPhee's pulse was pounding as he hid in the closet. He was seen as one of the brightest minds of his generation, able to even outsmart most adults, and yet here he was, cowering for his life like some frightened child. He clutched a cloth-wrapped parcel in his shaking hands, his eyes watching the door intently.

From his hiding spot, he could hear their footsteps. One set was delicate, another more casual...and then there was that heavy set. That last one was accompanied by a quiet, whirring sound. It was that last one that unnerved him most of all. The kid had always had a slight fear of cybernetic beings, and to have one chasing him through the lab... how had things gotten to this point?

HELL BENT, PA
SEVERAL HOURS AGO

It had been a typical day in a typical lab in Hell Bent, PA. This one happened to be on Tenth and Marconi and specialized mostly in the science of sound. Of course, Jockie wasn't quite as invested in Acoustics as he was Genetics. But his stepmother was one of the higher-ups in the Acoustics lab, and he'd been told that he would have to work his way up. And so, he was stuck interning there for the time being.

Not that it was a horrible place to work. On the contrary, it was a fairly cushy gig. All he really had to deal with was paperwork. But on the other hand, all he really got to do was deal with paperwork. It was getting a little dull, and what he needed was a way to liven things up a bit. Well, aside from the occasional coffee run his stepmother Tegwen would send him on. Oh, what he wouldn't have given for a change.

"Jock! Jock, do you have a moment?" called Tegwen's signature smoker's rasp.

He looked up from the lab reports he was filing away. Standing there was the elf that married his father, her silver hair pulled into a tight bun. Her pointed ears twitched in greeting.

"Yes, Teg?"

"We've been through this. On the clock, it's Dr. Griffiths."

"Understood. What do you need?"

She smiled, her headphones down around her neck for now. "I need you to pick up something for me, dear. I seem to have left my laptop at the lab on Thirteenth and Crick. Would you be able to pick it up for me?"

Jockie certainly knew that lab. It was one of the many genetics' labs in town. So maybe he'd get to see some action today! Surely, she wouldn't mind too much if he spent a little time poking around the area while he was there.

"Not a problem," he replied, finishing his current task.

"And please try not to take too long. I really need the notes on that laptop."

"Got it!"

With that, the young man stepped out from behind the desk and headed into the city proper. Shoving his hands into his pockets, he walked along the sidewalk. This city was such a far cry from his home of Edinburgh. Yes, home had its businesses and buildings and whatnot, but Hell Bent had significantly more labs than most any city he'd ever heard of. Even from where he was at that moment, he could see a few laboratories, a couple supply shops, and maybe an apartment building or two.

What he didn't see, however, was the reddish-orange blur heading his way. Not until it bumped into his arm, nearly knocking him off-balance. The blur stopped almost immediately after the impact, revealing itself to be a woman. She had short red hair, a monkey tail, and a mostly-unconscious male with ridiculously long hair slung over one shoulder.

"Sorry about that!" she said. "Are you okay?"

Jockie checked his arm. There was a slight friction burn, but it wasn't anywhere near as bad as it could have been.

"I'm fine, ma'am," he replied.

Part of him was curious about the guy she was carrying but figured it would be best not to pry. Not around here. He'd heard whispers about *assassin* being a viable career option and didn't wish to do anything that might make himself a target. She nodded, relieved to hear that, before breaking into a sprint, then an outright blur once more. The boy tilted his head to the side as she rushed off. He had also heard that people with superhuman abilities were likely to crop up there. It shouldn't have surprised him as much as it did, given that his stepmother was an honest-to-God elf. They were a bit more common in Britain, from what he had seen. But those with superhuman abilities —those that likely came into being in one of the genetics labs—fascinated him.

Returning to his task, Jockie started walking again. Get into the lab, poke around a little, and come back with Tegwen's laptop. It was a simple enough task, and he couldn't let himself get sidetracked again. Not that this stopped another distraction from presenting itself.

Across the street, he could see a trio of women. One was particularly curvy and had feline features and cybernetic limbs...He couldn't help but cringe as he imagined what could possibly have happened to require those. But the other two...That pair had long dark hair and some rather pleasing figures. The kind of ladies he wished he could seduce. But the only woman that ever really paid attention to him was his stepmother. What would it take for him to have a chance with someone like...well, either of that pair?

Shaking his head, Jockie berated himself for once again getting off-task. He reminded himself once again of what he was doing out here in the first place, and had he not gotten distracted twice now, he could be on his way back to the Acoustics Lab by now.

It took a few more minutes for him to reach his destination, having had to stop yet again to wait for an old lady to cross the street. But soon enough, he found the right laboratory. The building was an unassuming structure, about three stories tall. But behind the glass double doors, he could see the lab's security team. They seemed to be having a debate. He couldn't hear the contents of the debate, but it seemed heated from the way one was pounding a fist into his palm.

Jockie stepped toward the door, pressing a button on the frame. A voice crackled to life on the intercom.

"State your business."

"I'm here to pick up a laptop belonging to Dr. Griffiths from the Acoustics Lab?"

The doors unlocked, and he was able to enter. As he passed by the security team, he could hear snippets of their debate.

"It's not like I *wanted* to let her leave with the test subject! It's just that she was too fast!"

"Too fast, or are you just too slow?"

They kept on that track for a bit as Jockie thought of the encounter with the speedster on his way over. Was she the subject of their conversation? It would make sense if she were, but she was also fairly sure that she couldn't possibly be the only one of her kind around there. But then again, she had been carrying another figure. It had to be her.

He approached the front desk, the receptionist glancing at him from over his paperback.

"Any idea where this laptop might be?" the boy asked.

"I'd need a description of its owner," said the receptionist.

"Little shorter than me, silver hair, and she's an elf."

"Ah, yes. She was on the third floor earlier. Check up there."

"Thank you."

He started toward the elevator before stopping himself. If he went for the stairs, he could poke around the second floor as well. When his stepmother asked, he'd just claim to have gotten lost. He wasn't sure if she'd buy that, but it was worth a shot.

The second floor, once he reached that, didn't seem to grab his interest that much. A few holding areas lined the walls, but those were empty at the moment. The testing rooms were at the end of the corridor. Jockie figured he might as well check those out while he was there.

The test rooms were primarily unoccupied, as well. That was something of a rarity around there, and he imagined it had something to do with the test subject theft they'd been chatting about downstairs. Everyone had probably shifted to a different floor. From what he had heard, the basements were created to serve as bunkers, as nobody wanted to risk a mass exodus of dangerous experiments that might happen in a normal evacuation. But that just meant nobody was around to prevent him from snooping a bit.

One of the testing rooms contained a relatively fresh coating of blood right there on the table. Papers were strewn about as if a struggle had ensued. But curiously, there was what appeared to be a foot on the floor. It looked almost like a hand but longer, with a patch of reddish fur on top. It made him think of a monkey's paw.

Now, Jockie Ramsay McPhee was a well-read young man. He knew the tale of "The Monkey's Paw" fairly well. He also had heard whispers about magic—and by extension, wishes—being real. And that was when the wheels in his head began to turn.

Could making wishes on a monkey's paw truly work? And if so, would they work out for the best, or would they be tinged with the most horrific misfortune? There was one way to find out, as he grabbed the paw and stuffed it into his lab coat's pocket. A little residual blood got on the white fabric, but he didn't pay attention to that. Instead, he went back for the stairs so he could get the laptop from the third floor. He had no idea how much time he'd wasted by now. He figured it might be worth it to grab a coffee for Tegwen on the way back to account for his absence. Pulling out his phone, he brought up the app for the nearest coffee shop and placed an order for pickup.

Before long, he reached the third floor, retrieved the computer in question, and took the elevator back down. He walked out of the lab, heading for the coffee shop a few doors away. Nobody that saw him really questioned the little bit of blood at his pocket. It was fairly normal by the standards of this city.

When he reached the Acoustics lab, he handed the laptop and coffee to Tegwen. The elf had been waiting by the front desk, looking slightly frustrated over how long this had taken. But the offer of coffee seemed to assuage that. She took a lengthy sniff, letting out a delighted sigh. She had her blonde roast mixed with white chocolate and almond milk. Jockie knew how much that particular blend soothed even the sourest of moods.

"Apologies for how long it took, Dr. Griffiths. I thought you might enjoy your favorite coffee as well."

"Thank you, Jock dear," she said. "Did you have trouble locating it?"

He shrugged. "Once I found the right floor, it was quite easy," he said.

"Well, thank you for getting my laptop for me."

She gestured for him to bend down, giving him a small peck on the forehead once he did, and returned to her work. As she walked away, Jockie could swear that he heard her mutter under her breath about a bloodied pocket.

He settled behind the desk, returning to his filing as if nothing had happened. He would start messing with the paw after work, though the temptation to do so right now was strong. It took everything he had to focus on the papers before him, on organizing the chaos and ignoring the newfound weight in his pocket.

Gemmy headed straight for the kitchen once she arrived home with her brother. She'd dropped him onto the couch as soon as she hauled him inside and now needed to replenish the energy used from speeding through town. The monkey-woman's red hair was damp with sweat. It was one thing to run through the city in a blur but doing so with a grown man of 180 pounds took extra effort.

She wasn't entirely unused to her brother having to be retrieved from various scientists. Trav's regenerative abilities were a marvel to behold, and that had unfortunately made him a target all too often. She honestly wondered if *testing the limits of Malone's healing* was a rite of passage for newly minted biologists. But this time, it looked like they hadn't done much damage to—wait a second.

Where was his left foot?

Gemmy knew there was blood everywhere when she picked him up earlier, and she saw that they'd cut into his ankle somewhat. But she had not anticipated that his foot was *that* close to coming off. Thinking about it, she decided it would be a good idea to grab something extra from the fridge for him. After all, when they were kids, Travis was always looking out for her, keeping her safe. She took a moment to put together two sandwiches. One had plenty of meat and cheese stacked between the slices of bread. The monkey-woman took that out to her brother and set it on the table beside him before washing the meat-based contamination from her hands to make her own. Her brother may have been one to eat meat, but she certainly was not.

Once Gemmy had her own snack situated, she took it out to the living room and settled in her favorite chair. By then, Travis was sitting up. He was still a bit groggy, but there was food to be had. So focused was he on the sandwich in his hands that he hadn't even noticed that he was missing a foot just yet.

"How're you feeling?" Gemmy asked her brother as she noticed him.

He finished his current mouthful of food. "Head hurts...guessing it was a lab again?"

"Yeah."

"Thanks for bailing me out again."

"Not a problem at all."

He reached up with a foot to rub his aching head. However, Trav's inclination was to use the left foot for such a task. And once he realized that there was something missing, he paused mid-chew. Slowly, he finished that mouthful, swallowing it before letting out an exasperated sigh.

"Yeah, sorry," his sister said. "I thought I got all of you out of there, but...."

He chuckled. "It's not your fault...kinda hope nobody's doing anything fucked up with it, though."

"Like what?" she asked, almost amused at the thought.

"I dunno. Like trying to clone me, cannibalism, using it as a fu--"

"Okay, okay, forget I asked!"

He chuckled. "Sorry to freak you out, there. But yeah, I don't really like the idea of people having parts of me to use for whatever...I mean, that happened with my blood and hair once, and things got kinda freaky, and this dude's hair ended up eating people...."

He noticed the confused look in her eyes before he remembered something.

"...Oh, yeah, Spence and I kinda agreed never to speak of that."

She almost pressed further but decided she'd just ask Spencer about it later. It wasn't that she liked when her husband and brother hid things from her, but at the same time, it was understandable. They also knew that she didn't need more stress in her life. Besides, whatever had happened, they'd come out of it okay, so there was no real use in prying now.

Before they could discuss things any further, the door opened. Travis and Gemmy both looked up at the sound of heavy metal footsteps. Their aunt Beast stood there, feline ears folded back in slight concern. And she wasn't alone, either. Ivy and Yvette had shown up along with her, the twins staying closer to the door.

"Another lab, Trav?" she asked. "Ivy could pick up on your brain-waves earlier."

He nodded. "Yeah. Lost a foot somewhere in the process."

A laugh came from the doorway. "I figured that would happen eventually," said Yvette, brushing a few strands of black and blonde hair behind an ear. "I just always thought it'd be from the way you eat."

Travis rolled his eyes, picking up his remaining foot and raising the middle toe.

"Anyway," Ivy interjected, brushing off her sister's mean-spirited comment toward her boyfriend, "I think we could get that back for you. I know that's what you'd want, right?"

He nodded. Damn, it was nice to be with someone that could read minds. That made communication so much easier.

Ivy glanced at Yvette, then Beast, before bringing out her flask and taking a long swig. "All right, so...figure out where the foot is now, get it back. Simple enough, right?"

Beast nodded. She didn't especially like it when someone harmed a member of her family, and when she found out who had hacked off one of her nephew's limbs…

She was ready for the hunt to begin.

———

Jockie had gone through the rest of the day without much issue. The temptation to mess with the half-monkey's paw he had obtained was strong, but he managed to resist. All afternoon, he'd dealt with that pressing need to play with it.

Now that he was on his way to the apartment he shared with his stepmother, he knew the time was near. She planned to order pizza for dinner, so he would attempt his first wish while they waited for the delivery. He kicked off his sneakers at the door, heading for his room.

His room had all sorts of posters taped to the walls, typical of a boy his age. Some were athletes, some musicians, a few scientists, and a handful of attractive women. All of these images served as his wallpaper. He couldn't really aspire to be one of those athletes; the boy was so lean that he nearly disappeared when he turned to the side. He had tried to gain muscle but accepted a while back that he just didn't seem capable.

Maybe that could be the first wish? Hm, no. That seemed more like the sort of thing one worked their way up to. He began having thoughts of what could potentially be his first wish. Money was always a popular one. One might even call it a bit cliché. To Jockie, though, it felt safe.

Holding the paw in his hand, he took a deep breath. Was he really going to do this? Was he seriously considering taking a concept from an old story that'd been adapted in so many ways and bringing it into his real life?

Damn right he was.

"All right, paw. Let's see if there's anything to this...I wish I had some more money."

There was silence for a moment. And then he heard a familiar chime from his laptop. Blinking, he clicked on the bouncing icon. Someone was attempting to reach him via video chat.

"Good evening. I'm Dr. Cruz. Are you Jockie Ramsay McPhee, by any chance?" the middle-aged man asked, his deep brown eyes magnified by his coke-bottle glasses.

"Yes, sir, that's me."

"I just wanted to be the first to congratulate you, kid. We've had many applicants to the Young Scientists Grant Program and are happy to say that your proposal was the most impressive."

The young man's eyes widened. "You mean..."

"The grant is officially yours!"

At that point, he had to pinch himself. This had to be a dream, right? He had to think for a minute. He'd applied for this grant several months ago and was given a timeline of when the winner would be chosen. Thinking about it, he realized that it was that very week.

In other words, that first test was inconclusive. He would need to find something a bit more verifiable. He turned the foot about in his hands. For a moment, it occurred to him that there was something a little off about holding a severed appendage and using it to test something from a piece of fiction. But then he came to another conclusion: if those two guys that had a long-running show could become famous for it, then why shouldn't he give this a shot?

Jockie began pacing, nearly missing the sound of Tegwen calling him to the kitchen. In fact, he had missed it the first time. But then he heard that distinctive second call, which was always a bit louder. That managed to get his attention. He'd figure out what to wish for next over pizza. He left the paw on his bed before heading to the kitchen. Besides, he had some good news to share with his stepmother.

Beast, Ivy, and Yvette had gotten a little information from Trav and Gemmy and were now on their way to check out the lab. Though the trio were paid to function as assassins, they couldn't kill whoever had taken Trav's foot. Some of their targets may have originated from Hell Bent, but local scientists were generally agreed to be off-limits. The only member of their group to ever go against this societal norm was Ivy, and that was before she was ever enrolled in the program. This time around, the three had gone in with their civvies, as opposed to their normal uniforms. Those uniforms were meant to contain all forensic evidence and wick away moisture. For them to show up to ask some questions while literally dressed to kill? That would only invite more questions.

As usual, Beast led the way inside. To commit to their current non-aggression, she had a set of silicone sheaths on her long steel claws. Part of her wished that this wasn't the case. She was honestly sick of people coming after her nephew.

She wasn't the only one of the three that resented the lack of lethality in this situation. Ivy was likewise frustrated with people that thought that her boyfriend's regenerative properties were a thing to be taken advantage of. He didn't generally betray how much it tended to upset him. Not out loud, anyway. But she could read his mind. She knew how much it bothered him.

As for Yvette, she mainly questioned what her sister saw in the half-monkey. If it were up only to her, she would leave this situation alone. It wasn't like they would just reattach the thing, and it was going to grow back in a few days, so she couldn't quite see the point. But her sister and their best friend were all for finding the severed foot, and the three were a unit. So, she was in whether she liked it or not.

They strode toward the desk, Beast leaning against it with one of her metal arms. The receptionist blinked, his gaze going right toward the slab of red-painted steel.

"Can I help you ladies…?" he asked.

"Yeah," Beast replied. "We're wondering about any experiments that were checked in today."

He sighed and brought up a stack of papers. "Any further info?"

"He's not here now," Ivy interjected.

"Ah, so that's what Security was bitching about earlier…."

He flipped through the pages, pulling one out and showing it to the trio. They looked at the page, especially the photo at the top. It was Trav's mugshot, complete with a somewhat bored expression. Like he was also fed up with every lab coming for him. He had, according to the paperwork, been taken to the second floor. The intent was to vivisect him. It took all Beast had not to punch a hole in the desk upon seeing that part. Ivy picked up on her anger and lightly patted her shoulder.

"Could we take a look up there, please?" Yvette asked, her arms crossed.

The three were given the go-ahead to investigate, making their way to the elevator. And before long, they reached their destination. By this point in time, the test room he had been held in was clean, with not a trace of the prior blood left. At least, not to the naked eye. Beast could pick up on a faint smell around that particular testing room, hissing.

After a good amount of sniffing and searching, there was no trace of the foot in question. Yvette tapped her chin in thought.

"We could always check the security tapes," she suggested. "Make sure it fell off here and not just out in the streets somewhere."

"Yeah, that would be our luck, wouldn't it?" Ivy grumbled.

The trio headed to the main security office in the basement next. It wasn't that they really had the clearance...but the security team had been working an extra-long shift and were too exhausted to argue the point.

Ivy was the one to start looking through the footage. Some of it was fairly normal, with scientists going about their day. There was also some depicting a blur that the three figured had to be Gemmy. But what got their attention right away was the figure entering the empty, blood-splattered room. He was a somewhat tall guy, though he was skinny enough that a good breeze could be catastrophic. They watched as he picked up the foot, seemed to ponder it for a moment, and stuffed it into the pocket of his lab coat.

"Think he works here?" Beast asked.

"I'm not sure," said Yvette. "Did you notice the patch on his back? It's right on the collar. Sound waves."

Ivy glanced at her sister. "...So, thinking this guy came over from the acoustics lab?"

"Wouldn't shock me," said Yvette.

"But what would he want with a guy's foot?" Beast asked, her tone just a tad disturbed.

The three of them had seen a lot over their many years as assassins but seeing a teenage boy with what appeared to be a severed foot fetish was a new one for them. They would ask their questions once they tracked him down, though. The next stop would be the acoustics lab.

Jockie had finished with dinner and was back to fiddling with the paw. His brain was turning over all sorts of possibilities. Should he wish for world peace? That seemed like another "work up to that" sort of thing. As he thought about it, though, he wondered if a simple wish for the world to be a slightly better place would be a better option.

"Okay, so, my second wish..." he told the paw. "I wish for some improvement in the world, even if it's just a small thing. Some amount of positivity."

And now, it was time to wait. The TV was on, and they were airing the nightly news. He mostly had it on as background noise, but tonight, he waited for something to stick out. Something that might count as positive.

"And in breaking news," the anchor stated, "notorious criminal Ravil Volkov has been found dead of unknown causes. Volkov, a known trafficker of children, has evaded the law for years. But today, his body was found in an alley. He had, from what we've gathered, been transporting a group of children. Those kids have since been returned to their families."

Jockie blinked at the screen. And then at the paw in his hand. Maybe there was something to this whole thing...? A grant he had intentionally applied for was one thing, but for someone like that to be removed from the gene pool? He was having a good feeling about his experiment now. The toes didn't curl to indicate that a wish had been used. Not like in the story. Did this mean that he had unlimited wishes? Or was it just terrible at keeping track?

There were so many things he could wish for, but he wasn't sure how finite those wishes were.

The trio had located the currently-closed acoustics lab. On the one hand, that meant their current target wasn't there. On the other, they'd have to figure out where he lived. And that meant sneaking in.

Yvette focused on the door, her eyes glowing red as she used a portal spell. It started as a small red dot before expanding into a swirling vortex. The plan was for Ivy to head in and do a quick search through the employee database. Since she could manipulate objects with her mind, they wouldn't have to worry about fingerprints.

Ivy stepped through the portal, focusing on the camera. It was surrounded by the same turquoise glow as her eyes. And once she knew it was off, she moved to the desk. It took a moment to find the employee records, which she rifled through fairly quickly. No sign of the boy in there. Grumbling in frustration, she crossed her arms...before another idea hit. She brought up the file for interns. Not too many in there. There were a grand total of three of them, and one fit the bill. She read over the info, finding his name and address.

She left the desk and reentered the portal, returning to her sisters-in-arms. No visible sign of her presence was left behind.

"So, what'd you find out?" Yvette asked.

"Dude we're lookin' for is named Jockie Ramsay McPhee," said Ivy, taking a drink from her flask. "Kid's fifteen, lives with his stepmom at 3303 Archimedes St, Apt 404."

"So, killing him is twice as out of the equation," said Beast with a nod. "Understood."

"What about putting the fear of every god ever into him?" Ivy asked with a smirk.

Beast looked a tiny bit conflicted. "I dunno...it's not like he cut the foot off himself. Not if he's working at an entirely different lab."

They began walking along, Yvette taking a moment to use an illusion spell on the three. They might not have brought their actual uniforms along, but she still wanted them to look official.

***

Jockie held the paw in his hands again, debating over that third wish. As he puzzled, a knock came at his bedroom door. He grabbed a small blanket from the bed, wrapping it around the appendage. He didn't really want to show it to Tegwen just yet.

"Jock!" her smoker's rasp called. "Got a moment to talk?"

He set the wrapped foot down, going to the door. He opened it to see her standing there, a bit concerned. Her arms were crossed.

"Is everything okay, Teg?" he asked.

"I had been meaning to ask this all day, but are you okay? I saw a bit of blood on the edge of your lab coat pocket."

He nodded. "Yes, I'm fine. I merely got a bit turned around in the genetics lab earlier. I assure you the blood was not mine."

She sighed in relief. "That's good to know...but why just the pocket? What did you take?"

At that point, he paled. He could try to lie but had the feeling that his stepmother would pick up on that. He might as well be upfront with her about this, he decided, as he picked up the wrapped paw.

"Well...I saw something that made me start thinking of that old story involving wishing on a monkey's paw," he unwrapped it, "and wanted to test it for myself."

Tegwen stared at the appendage, her eyes narrowing in thought. "Why does that look familiar..." she murmured.

Well, that wasn't quite the question he thought she would ask.

"Anyway, I've made two wishes with it already. The first was for some funds, and I found out about the grant. Second was for some positivity in this world, and a child trafficker was permanently stopped. There may be something to my experiment."

The elf blinked. "...I'm not sure you want to keep messing with that paw, Jock. See, it looks like the foot of a guy I've seen out and about a number of times. He's fairly well-known amongst the local scientific community. Are you familiar with Dr. Serena Taylor?"

He nodded.

"I think that's her son's foot. No good can come of messing with it...."

He had to think for a moment. "I'm just going to make one more wish. Just to confirm what's going on...."

A light groan, and she slapped her forehead. This didn't seem like a great idea, but if he was committed to it...

"I wish I could get the attention of some ladies. Attractive ones, like the ones I saw earlier…."

And that was when the lights went out. Instinctively, Jockie wrapped the foot again. But this time, he was beginning to tremble. His eyes darted back and forth as he tried to find the source of the voice that sounded in his head.

'Hey, McPhee,' the female voice whispered, almost taunting in nature.

And then he could hear them walking. Three sets of footsteps. His natural instinct was to dive beneath the bed, clutching the paw. The first set of delicate, deliberate footsteps came to a stop, followed by the casual, almost skipping ones. And then came the thudding and whirring. His heart caught in his throat as he realized that they reminded him a bit of the women he saw while on his walk earlier. He tried not to freak out but couldn't help but let out a terrified squeak.

Even with his eyes squeezed shut, he could see a red glow around the edges of his door. The glow was particularly bright. Opening them, he could see their boots. Well, two pairs of boots and those hulking red metal feet from earlier. He desperately hoped that Tegwen would lie for him. Claim that he wasn't there.

"Can I help you, ladies?" she asked.

"Yes, we're looking for this guy," said one of them before producing an image of Jockie himself, tinged with red.

From what he could see, the one showing the illusion was the one with the straight black and blonde hair. And from the sound of it, Tegwen wasn't sure about selling him out.

"I'm sorry, miss, but you can't have him."

"We just want to talk with him," said the cyborg, her tone even.

He bit his lip to try and keep from screaming as the third one sauntered toward his hiding place. The third woman crouched down beside the bed, peeking at him from behind a black and brown fringe.

"Found him," she said.

He tried to pull away from her, but a turquoise glow surrounded him, gently (but forcefully) pulling him out from beneath the bed. He may not have wanted to scream but scream, he did. Teg was looking for a cell phone, but the cyborg held up a hand to stop her.

"Relax. We're not here to hurt you," she said. "We just want to talk. And take that back."

She pointed her claws at the blanket-wrapped paw. And that was when Teg looked at Jockie as if to say that she'd warned him.

"I-it's just a foot!" was Jockie's oh-so-eloquent response.

Beast looked at him, feline tail twitching. "That foot belongs to my nephew, kid. If you could please give it back, we'll leave."

"Yeah, seems he's not really into having people take his body parts for unknown reasons," said the one that pulled him out from under the bed. "Why'd you take it, anyway?"

The boy pulled himself to his full height. He may have been the tallest individual in that room, but looking at the four women that stared at him, three of whom wanted answers, he knew that there was no way he could take them.

"I, um...I wanted to see how accurate that Monkey's Paw story was...I wished for some money and got a grant I tried for. Wished for something positive, a child trafficker was killed, and his victims were retrieved safely. And then I wished for the attention of ladies like...well," he gestured toward Ivy and Yvette.

Silence for a moment, and then a chuckle from Ivy. "Okay, so that all just sounds like freakishly good timing. Can't speak to the grant thing, but Volkov had it coming for a while. You should've seen how excited Beast was to take him out. And that third one? Um, dude, you took a piece of someone at least two of us care about. Well, okay, 'Vette does. Kinda. It's, like, deep down, but it's there."

Yvette rolled her eyes, brushing a bit of black and blonde hair behind an ear. "Anyway, we'd like that back, please."

Shaking, he handed it over. Beast carefully took it.

"And by the way," Ivy spoke up, "You seem like a nice enough guy, but we're kind of not in your age range. So, hopefully, you'll find someone you find attractive that's not too old for you. Like, me and 'Vette? We're in our late thirties. Beast is a few years older than us. And the guy whose foot you were experimenting with? Yeah, that's the guy I'm dating."

Jockie nodded, understanding. "I see...so, I'm not in trouble for that, am I?"

"Nah," Beast said.

"And yet you didn't knock like a normal person," Tegwen added, an eyebrow arched.

"Never know when you're dealing with a creep," Yvette said. "Glad he turned out not to be one, of course." She leaned forward, eyes narrowed. "But if we ever find out about you pulling some horrific incel bullshit, we're coming for you. Hear me, McPhee?"

He gave a nervous chuckle and a thumbs up before Yvette opened another portal and led the way out. The power came back shortly after, and Jockie had to find his voice again. Looking around, it was like the whole encounter had never happened. He glanced at Tegwen, who simply sighed and pulled a pack of cigarettes from her pocket. She patted her stepson's back and left for a smoke.

He jumped as Ivy's voice entered his head again.

'Oh, by the way. Congrats on the grant!'

He should have felt proud, but all he felt was unnerved at the fact that she'd poked around in his mind. Jockie shook the feeling off, going to climb into bed. If there was one takeaway he had from this, it was that his experiment was still inconclusive and that he was relieved to have not written any of it down. He just wanted to forget.

K. Matt is an author/illustrator that lives somewhere in upstate NY. She writes and draws as a means of escaping the monotony of her everyday life, and likes taking her frustrations out on her characters. This marks her eighth story with Fiction-Atlas Press, using the group of strange characters she's grown attached to over the years. More comfortable with a pencil than with people, and in an ongoing battle with the forces of both gravity and her old nemesis mathematics, she'll keep on writing and drawing until she no longer can.

Find out more: KaylaMatt.wordpress.com

facebook.com/HellBentBookSeries

instagram.com/kmatt666

twitter.com/MarieTwixie

goodreads.com/kmatt_hellbent

UNENCHANTING WISHES
BY J.M. RHINEHEART

"The wildfires in California are currently being exacerbated by the two large dragons flying overhead. Officials are attempting to find their nesting grounds in order to deal with them, but residents are encouraged to take cover if a dragon flies overhead. Some officials are calling for the governor to enact an evacuation order...."

I watched the TV in front of me with little interest. The news anchor still looked the same level of bewildered he'd been for a while now. It was pretty much the same as it had been for the past two weeks. Beside me was a buzzing sound somewhere, and I waved my hand to flick it away. The buzzing grew in irritation but faded away.

Outside, I could hear someone lay on their horn. Probably another unicorn in the road. They were everywhere, worse than deer. Someone shouted angrily, and the horn went off again. I sighed.

From the kitchen came the sound of cans being moved around. "My love, what are...Vienna sausages? And how are sausages from Vienna different than sausages from here?" A pause. "They are not even made in Vienna, according to the package."

"Don't open it, and don't eat it," I said automatically. "It's probably a couple of years old." I had never bought the tiny canned hot dogs in my life, which meant my mom had. Which meant they were inedible.

"But why call them Vienna sausages if they are not, in fact, from Vienna? Are they a delicacy? And if they are not to be eaten, should we not remove them hence?"

The buzzing started up again, and this time I grabbed a nearby magazine. The pixie flying near my ear growled at me but dodged my swing effortlessly. He also left, heading toward the kitchen. "You've got that pixie on the way," I called.

"I will deal with the foul pest!" I heard the sound of a sword unsheathing.

I pinched the bridge of my nose. "No swords in the house, Christopher. You know the rules."

The sword sheathed again. "Then I shall use my other weapon. Though flimsy, it seems to do the job."

"Yeah, you do that," I muttered to myself. Let the prince use a fly swatter; it had to cause less damage than a broadsword.

From down the hall, I heard a shriek from Tanisha. "Mags, there's a *tentacle* in the toilet! Maggie!"

A hearty smack was followed by the sword coming out again. "Let me assist you, Lady Tanisha!" Christopher said, and he hurried out of the kitchen. I watched him go, noting that at least he'd worn the jeans instead of tights today. Progress.

Of all the things I'd expected when I made my wish, this world was *not* it.

Two weeks before, I'd been having a pretty normal day with normal problems. Everyone had been normal. Life had been its usual level of frustrating, but I'd been dealing with it.

Work was dismal. My job wasn't anything glamorous: I clocked in, sat at a desk and moved papers where they needed to go, clocked out, and went home. It was within walking distance, and I got a paycheck.

It was a living. It didn't leave much time for anything else, but I didn't need anything else. Or anyone else.

It would've driven my mom nuts. "You need to go for what you really want," she used to say. "Don't sell yourself short, Margaret. You are extraordinary and enchanting. Remember that."

I'd put those words on my mother's headstone because if anyone was extraordinary or enchanting, it had been her. Even up to the very end, when her heart had finally given out, she'd been my extraordinary parent.

Two years of missing her hadn't dulled that ache. Nothing had. It was pretty much my normal since she'd died.

Anyway, the job let me keep her house, at least. The tiny little place I'd grown up in was almost paid off. My best friend Tanisha had moved in and started paying rent, and between us both, we had everything covered comfortably. But I couldn't deny that living in my mom's old house, the one with her touch everywhere, wasn't hard. Just another thing I dealt with.

Like the rain: the West coast was getting hammered by wildfires every day, but the Midwest and East coast? We were nothing but rain day in, day out. It always seemed to come out of nowhere, as it did that fateful Friday when I'd walked home from work. Of course, I didn't have an umbrella that day, which meant I was soaked through in pretty much an instant.

It hadn't been a general misting or even a downpour, either. No, it had to be the gushing sort of rain that made cars put their flashers on. Between them splashing rain up onto the sidewalk and the gusting winds, I was drenched in seconds. Blindly, I hurried to the closest store and made my way inside. The pounding sound of the rain dulled as the door shut behind me, and I stood, gasping a little, trying to shake myself off. I was wet from head to toe.

And cold. Of course, I was cold.

"You poor thing. Can I get you a towel?"

It was only then that I registered where I was. The scent of incense hit first, then the dim but warmly lit store. Crystals hanging everywhere caught the light, and the air seemed to crackle with energy. The rug beneath me was full of vivid designs and was currently absorbing every inch of water I was dripping off.

The woman in front of me looked like she belonged there amongst the crystals and smoke. Her black hair curled just so around her vivid blue eyes, and her headwrap was the brightest colored thing I'd seen so far. Her red skirt swayed as she moved toward me with a massive pink shawl, also ornately decorated. She was a sight to behold, and I found myself gaping. Anyone else would've looked ridiculous, but for some reason, she made it work.

"My goodness, is it coming down outside," the woman remarked and began to wrap the shawl around me. "Here, let's get you dried off."

"I'll ruin it," I managed to say. It was thicker than it looked, and it absorbed most of my drowned-rat effect in an instant. "You won't be able to sell it."

"I wouldn't sell it anyway. It's mine," the woman said in a no-nonsense tone. "Come, come! It's warmer toward the back."

How the heck it could get even warmer, I didn't know. The flames from the various candles lit everywhere brushed against my skin as I passed them. My cheeks almost felt like they were burning from the heat. This had to be a fire hazard, but every time I looked, they were spaced out and gently flickering in the air.

The woman led me to the back of the shop and settled down on a chair behind a large glass counter, skirt fanning out perfectly. She pulled another folding chair out of what seemed like thin air and handed it to me. "Sit, sit," she offered.

Well, it was better than being outside in the rain. "Thank you, ma'am," I said, years of etiquette kicking in.

"Call me Vivian," she said in a kind but direct tone. "And you're more than welcome. I don't get many new guests, just familiar favorites. The rain brought you to me; who am I to deny such a gift?"

For some reason, it made me think of my mother and one of the last things she'd said to me. *You are the greatest gift I've ever been given. Treat my gift well.* I shivered under the shawl and drew it tighter around me. The incense stung my eyes a little, and I blinked against it and the sudden swell of emotions that threatened to gush out. I needed something else to focus on and fast before I wound up breaking in front of a stranger.

My eyes landed on the glass case. There were a few pieces of jewelry inside, but it was mostly gems and stones, each one nestled in a cushion or satiny cloth. They were all beautiful, a kaleidoscope of colors, and the candles and lights made each one shine.

"Ah, my glass case of pretties." Vivian chuckled and ran her hand over the top. "Each one is so very unique. Do you have a favorite?"

"I hadn't really looked," I admitted. "I'm not usually one for precious stones or even jewelry."

"The case catches everyone's eye. Don't be shy! Look inside. I'm curious what you'll find."

If I'd had more of a brain, the words would've caught my curiosity. As it was, I was recovering from a rotten day and getting splashed, and the warmth of the room felt so good. My eyes strayed across the case, taking in each gem and jewel and stone.

A purple one cut in a triangular shape was intriguing, if just for the aesthetic, but I moved on to a green jewel that seemed to have sharp points everywhere. It made my skin prickle just looking at it. I kept looking, not particularly interested in the rest. They were pretty, sure, but that was about it.

And then my eyes moved to the farthest edge of the case and stopped. There was a round pink gem, almost colorless, sitting off in a single corner, and I couldn't take my eyes off of it. There was just something about it that kept my attention.

Following my gaze, Vivian almost seemed surprised. "The heart's stone, hm? It doesn't usually catch anyone." She deftly slid the case open and reached in. The gem was less circular than I'd originally thought and more curved inward at the top. It did look like a heart. Before I could say anything, she slid the gem off of the cushion and into my palm.

The color changed in an instant, going from a pale pink to a deep red. I stared, watching the blood-red color swirl through the gem. What the heck was *that* about?

"Well," Vivian said, and she seemed startled herself. Then she smiled, a half sort of smile, and it was far softer than before. "I think the rain really did send you my way, Margaret. I'm glad I was here for you."

Even as the colors continued to swirl, even as I tried to make sense of her words and the strange gem in my hand, Vivian spoke again. "Tell me, for I'm curious: if you could wish for anything in the whole entire world, no matter how impossible or wild, what would it be?"

A million things flew through my mind. One of them was a warm smile under graying hair, one I hadn't seen since I'd buried my mom two years before. It surged through me, the urge to have her hold me one last time. A hug from my mom would've been the best thing ever.

I shook myself. Not attainable. What *would* I really wish for?

For some reason, my friend Tanisha's words from last night floated through my head. I'd joked that she had more dates than a calendar, and she'd immediately fired back with, "At least I try. When's the last time you got out and tried to find anyone, huh, Mags? Prince Charming won't just come find you."

I loved her like a sister, but it was harder to be honest with Tanisha. We'd become fast friends in high school, and sometimes it felt like she knew everything about me just by looking at me.

My mom had done that, too. And my mom had always told me not to be alone, to find someone. The way she'd talked about my dad, gone long before her, had always sounded like a fairytale. She'd even called him her 'Prince Charming' with a grin and a roll of her eyes. But she'd always said it with such love in her voice.

It would be nice to have someone that was just mine. Someone that looked at me like I hung the stars, who'd be there to lean against, someone to connect with. But between work and a lack of applicable candidates, what was I supposed to do?

I glanced at the stone in my hands. "I guess I'd wish for a Prince Charming," I said with a snort. "I don't even know where to start anymore, or if I'd want to even try, but I...I don't want to be alone anymore."

The gem glowed in my hands and then went back to the red. I shook myself—just the candles flickering around me, most likely.

Vivian glanced up above the counter. "I do love the sunshine after a storm."

It *was* really sunny now, which meant the rain had passed. I blinked, startled: I hadn't thought I'd been there that long. But I felt dry and warm, the signs of having been out of the rain for quite some time. That meant it was time to get going, with dinner waiting to get started at home. "Thank you for letting me hang out here," I said, handing the shawl back to her. Somehow, it was also dry, like it had never been wet.

"It was a pleasure, Margaret," she said with a smile as we stood. I gave the gem back to her or tried to, and she waved me off. "Consider it a gift for spending time with me."

"I couldn't just *take* it," I sputtered. Who knew how expensive it really was? I definitely didn't have the cash for it. "Vivian—"

"Please, from me to you, to remember that the sun comes out after a storm," she insisted. "And that sometimes, wishes do come true for those who need them."

She wasn't going to be deterred. "I don't even know that I have enough to buy incense," I admitted. "I don't get paid until next Friday, but I'll be back to get something. My roommate would love the crystals." Tanisha wasn't the new age sort, but the crystals dangling everywhere would catch her attention.

Vivian chuckled. "You do that if you like. But the stone is still your gift to keep. Let me know what you choose to do with it."

Besides, set it on a shelf? Well, I wasn't actually sure I'd do that. I stepped outside into the humid after-storm air, the stone still in my hand. It continued to swirl a beautiful red, and I found myself mesmerized. Maybe on my small desk at home, next to my laptop: that would be a good place to look at it. The weight was oddly comforting in my hands. I almost wanted to talk to it.

Okay, Tanisha was right: I definitely needed to get out more.

Maybe she'd help me find a date. I could swallow my pride and ask her for help. Knowing her, she'd be all over it.

It was only after I was almost home that I realized, despite my never having told her, the woman from the shop had known my name.

And it was only when I arrived home that I found *him* waiting on my front porch.

I blinked for what had to be the fourteenth time in the past five minutes. "So, you're a prince," I said again.

The man, the *prince*, in front of me, nodded as if my repeating myself wasn't bothering him. "Verily, my princess, I am well met to meet you," he said. "For I am a prince who has long sought his true love, and I have found you at last. I was tossed from realm to realm, but I am here—"

"Yeah, I got that," I said. I was starting to think nothing fazed him. Not him, with his pale skin, bright green eyes, and shining smile. He tossed his hair back from his forehead, the rest of the honey-colored locks mostly reaching the nape of his neck. *Locks*, I thought, pinching the bridge of my nose. *Now I'm talking like him, too.*

He sat back on his knee from where he knelt, the picture of patience. It was dawning on me that the guy in front of me, the one who looked like he'd been picked up outside a renaissance faire with tights and leather boots and golden vest, probably wasn't a prank from a coworker or a hookup attempt from Tanisha. No, he was very sincere. And he was currently kneeling in front of me in some seriously tight tights.

My eyes widened. Kneeling in tights in front of my porch, where the neighbors were bound to see. "Come with me," I said quickly. I grabbed his hand and started pulling him around to the back of the house.

He went with me easily, his boots barely making a sound. At least he wasn't wearing chainmail. "I would go anywhere with you," he swore. "Say but the word, and I would be with thee."

"Okay, how about talking a little less formal?" I asked. I opened the metal gate and pushed him past the chain-link fence. It clanged shut behind us as I went straight for the back door.

Then I stopped. Why on earth was I letting him into my *house*? I knew next to nothing about him, except that he said he was a prince who'd apparently traveled across various realms, whatever that meant, to find me. I didn't even know his *name*.

He'd mentioned it, I thought, once upon a time. I snorted at my word choice. "Well, Prince…?"

"Christopher," he said eagerly. "I am Prince Regent of the land of Devesheer, but to you, I am simply Christopher, the man whose heart you have ensnared."

"Right," I drawled. "Listen, Chris, I don't know how to break this to you, but I'm pretty sure you've got the wrong gal."

He didn't even so much as frown. "I know without a doubt that I have found the right woman. For I have made many a wish for one such as you—"

Wait. "Wish?" I asked, eyes growing wide. It couldn't be. It *couldn't*.

"I would be so lucky to have you," he said, smiling broadly. "Why wouldn't I wish for someone like you?"

I found my face flushing without my permission. It'd been a long time since someone had so boldly said anything close to that to me. I think the last time was Daryl in second grade. Who the heck said stuff like that anymore outside of television dramas?

"Mags?"

I turned toward the back door, where Tanisha was coming out. She was watching us both with a frown. "Um, you wanna introduce me?" she asked, brow still furrowed.

"Is this fair maiden your sister?" Christopher inquired. "For she hath a beauty much like yours, albeit from perhaps a different mother or father."

"Oh wow, you know how to pick them," Tanisha drawled, but her frown was shifting into a grin. "Though this one knows how to compliment a lady."

I buried my head in my palms. "No, he was waiting here for me when I got home. Christopher, this is my best friend, Tanisha. Tanisha, Christopher, Prince Regent of some place not near here."

"Prince, huh?" Tanisha said, still amused. "Well, how'd'ya do, Your Majesty."

Christopher reached past me to take Tanisha's hand in his, where he bent forward to place a kiss on her knuckles. "The pleasure is distinctly mine," he said, and he really meant it. Charming came naturally.

A real Prince Charming. But it *couldn't* be real, could it? There was no such thing as a gem that grants wishes. And if it existed, it wasn't going to be in our town at a small shop.

"Wait."

I turned to Tanisha, who was suddenly giving Christopher the side-eye. "You were *waiting* for her?"

Oh, no. "No, it's not like it sounded," I assured her. "He's not stalking me or anything." At least, I didn't think he was.

Christopher looked taken aback by the accusation. "Stalking? Nay, not a whit! 'Tis a foul deed done by a nefarious being! I came falling through several realms and landed on her doorstep. I did not ask to be flung here but am grateful for the magic that occurred all the same." He glanced at me and smiled that same bright grin. "For I have found the one my heart has yearned for all these years. She is the one for me."

"This is one of those times you might want to call the cops," Tanisha said bluntly.

"It's not like that," I said again. "It's not."

She put her hands on her hips. "Okay, you know more than you're telling me. Spill. What's going on?"

Oh, how to put *that* into words. My mind sputtered to a stop. Tanisha's gaze only narrowed further. Christopher stood, still smiling at me. The heart-shaped gem sat in my pocket.

How do you tell someone that you got a magic gem from an old woman that apparently granted wishes?

Something suddenly flew at me, hitting me in the nose and sending me reeling backward. I rubbed my face and blinked. Then I blinked again. No, the miniature, sparkling, very purple being in front of me did have wings. And two fangs, both of which were brandished at me as it hissed in my general direction.

What the hell?

"What the hell?" Tanisha asked out loud for me.

Christopher reached to his hip and pulled out something *very* long and shiny. "Woah," I said, backing away even further as he brandished an actual sword at the flying and hissing thing. The weapon looked long enough to reach me even where I stood, and I didn't want to be a kebob.

"Back away, you cursed pixie!" Christopher shouted. "Begone with thee!"

A screeching sound came from behind me toward the road. I turned and found a car stopped in the street, the driver staring at the green creature lumbering across the road. It glared at the driver as it continued ambling slowly onward, a massive wooden club hoisted on its shoulders that had to be as wide as the car.

"Is that...a troll?" Tanisha asked numbly. "That's, that's a *troll*. What's a troll doing here?"

"The beasts of my realm are many," Christopher said. "Fear not, for as your prince, I won't let any harm come to you! That's my duty: to care for the one I love," he added with a blinding smile in my direction. And he took off past the chain link fence straight for the troll.

"What the actual crap is going on?" Tanisha asked. "Mags!"

Above, a neighing reached my ears. Dumbfounded, I looked up to find a horse flying through the air, massive wings somehow keeping it aloft. Glitter trailed behind it and fell, almost landing in my eyes.

"Away with you, beast!" Christopher shouted, hitting the troll with his sword. The troll didn't even seem bothered, just kept on walking down the street toward town.

My hand found the gem in my pocket. It felt warm, like it was almost pleased with itself. If it had had a neck, I would've throttled it.

First things first: grab the prince, waving a weapon around. "He needs to not be doing that," I told Tanisha.

"Nobody should be doing that," she agreed. "I'll help you get him inside."

Even as we coaxed Christopher away from the unbothered troll, even as the small, winged beings—pixies, sorry, actual *pixies*—kept flying around like winged rats, even as the flying horse nearly got caught on a nearby telephone wire, I knew I had far bigger fish to fry.

That started with figuring out what was going on. And I knew just the person to talk to.

As it turned out, I never got the chance to get down to Vivian's shop that night. One, it was far too late, and downtown was bound to be closed. And two, I was too busy with Prince Charming, trying to keep him entertained and preventing him from going out to protect us.

Thankfully, it made explaining a prince with a shiny sword all that much easier to Tanisha. "See, this is why white people are always the ones that die in horror flicks," she said, smacking me on the back of my head. "I wouldn't do stupid crap like make dumb wishes with a gem I'd gotten from suspicious characters! Maggie, honestly!"

Then she glanced at Christopher, who was sitting at our kitchen table and gazing around the room in wonder. "Though he *is* hot," she admitted. "So, as far as wishes go, you did good."

"You have a fine home, my princess," Christopher said as he stood, wandering around the kitchen. "'Tis a marvel of your hard work and beauteous touch." He smiled at me, and it looked like it came so easy, him smiling at me. I found my lips turning up to match it.

"Wow, who knew you remembered how to smile," Tanisha said, grinning at me. "Proud of you, Mags."

"Mags?" Christopher asked, raising an eyebrow. "An interesting and unusual name for a princess."

"Wait." Tanisha's grin turned into a glare in an instant, and I instinctively ducked away from another head smack. "You didn't even tell him your *name?*"

"We've been busy!" I snapped. Between him suddenly showing up and the pixie flying through, it had slipped my mind. This, I figured dryly, was exactly why I hadn't been able to find and keep a date up to this point.

But Christopher didn't seem like he was bothered by it. Instead, he seemed to be patiently waiting for me to tell him. It was...nice. I cleared my throat. "I'm Margaret. I go by Maggie, but Tanisha calls me Mags. You can, um, call me whatever you'd like."

He stepped toward me, and I'll admit, my breath caught a little at the intense gaze he gave me. "Margaret is a beautiful name. But Mags clearly belongs to a cherished friend; nay, I shall not take that name. I shall use Maggie... if that pleases thee."

"It, uh, pleases me," I said. I could feel my stupid face heating up again, and Tanisha was back to grinning. I glared at her. It only made her grin wider.

"Like I said, Mags, you did good with your wish. Though next time, wish me up a prince too."

I rolled my eyes. "Yeah, well, I'm not so sure about my wishing being so great." I paused, then pulled out the little red gem. It caught the light from the windows and seemed to sparkle. Troublemaker. "Then again..."

"Are you about to do something stupid again?"

I held up the gem for Tanisha and Christopher to see. "If those creatures all showed up because of my wish, then shouldn't another direct wish make them leave?"

Tanisha made a face. "Maybe? Mags, I just don't know. I guess try, right?"

Right. It was absolutely worth a try. I held the gem in my palm like before and gazed at it. "I wish these creatures weren't here anymore," I said. Then I paused.

It didn't glow. It didn't do anything.

Tanisha glanced out the big front window and made a face. "There's still a lot of not normal going on outside."

I sighed. Well, it'd been worth a shot. "There's also a troll out there…somewhere. And a flying horse."

"Pegasus," Tanisha corrected me. "And did he call that little purple thing a pixie? I thought they were supposed to be sweet and cute."

"They're a foul pest," Christopher piped up. He'd moved to the fridge, frowning at it. "But a minor pest, in the end. What is this?"

"It's a refrigerator. It keeps food cold." Pixies and a flying horse—sorry, pegasus—and a troll. That was a lot to have to deal with. And who knew how much devastation they would wreak in town along the way.

Hopefully, not much. "How dangerous are these creatures?" I asked. Christopher had opened the fridge and was staring inside in awe. "Christopher?"

"The troll is unlikely to do damage unless he is upset. The Pegasus, as Lady Tanisha rightly called him, will only be a menace to fields and grasslands and trees. None of them are what I would call dangerous. Not nearly as dangerous as a dragon."

I froze. Tanisha stared at me. As one, we turned to Christopher, who had pulled out a tub of cream cheese. "This smells wonderful," he said. "May I try it?"

"Dragons?" I managed to get out. "You have *dragons*?"

"Oh, the creatures of my realm are many," he said cheerfully. "Truly, this smells delightful. I must try it."

Well, I hadn't seen a dragon. And it would've made the news by now for sure. "Maybe we dodged the dragon," I said. "And whatever else there might be." My mind started moving through the various fantasy books I'd read, the movies I'd seen. There were a lot of possibilities on my hands that could've come through with Prince Charming.

But I hadn't wished for those. I'd only wished for Prince Charming. So how come they'd shown up with him?

I realized Tanisha hadn't said anything. I turned and found her staring at her phone, eyes wide. "Tanisha?"

"Yeah, that'd be a no on dodging," she said, voice a little high.

My heart lurched in my throat. "There's a dragon here in town?"

In response, she turned her phone to show me. A video played, a shaky hand still capturing what looked like a massive green dragon flying overhead. The dragon let out a ferocious roar and kept on flying over what looked like—

No. No way. "Is that the Hollywood sign?" I asked dumbly.

Tanisha didn't answer. I grabbed my own phone and started looking for news reports. It didn't take long to find what I was looking for—mostly because everything was front and center.

It wasn't just here. It wasn't just in Hollywood. No, it was *everywhere*.

Another dragon had flown over a small town in Norway. Japan had unicorns galloping through Tokyo. There were mermaids off the coast of Brazil, and a troll had settled down and taken a nap in the middle of the road in India.

Somehow, my wish for a prince had done all of this.

I pulled the gem out of my pocket. In my other hand, the news feed could barely keep up in documenting the invasion of fantasy creatures. Tanisha made a squeaking sound, and I didn't bother trying to ask her what it was now. I didn't want to know.

I glanced up and found Christopher with the tub of cream cheese in one hand and a spoon in the other. He beamed at me and spooned out another bite. "This is marvelous," he said. "Have you tried any?"

I just sat down at the kitchen table. Yeah. Definitely going to have to talk to Vivian in the morning.

Thankfully, the next morning was a Saturday, which meant I didn't have to try and deal with work *and* an onslaught of fantasy creatures *and* a prince. Though honestly, Christopher was the least of my problems.

He was nothing but a gentleman that night, insisting on taking the sofa. Before that, it had been to stand and pull my chair out. Before *that* had been the offer to walk me to my bedroom door. My presence, apparently, left him *beyond joyful*.

Which, well. That wasn't something I typically got. The last date I'd been on had been a disaster. Between being told I was "out of touch" and "unapproachable" as well as "that outfit makes you look old," I'd decided to hang it up. I wasn't everyone's cup of tea, got it.

But apparently, I was Prince Charming's cup of tea. Which…well. It was sort of nice, especially because he was a *prince*. And a really nice-looking one to boot.

So, when he said his good night to me, wishing me copious amounts of sweet dreams or something, I wished him the same. Our eyes locked for just a brief moment, and I realized how stupidly green his eyes were up close. He leaned in, and I unconsciously followed, taking in an expectant breath.

Someone cleared their throat.

I leapt back and found Tanisha in the doorway, eyebrows raised. "You sure you want him out here on the sofa?" she asked bluntly. "I've crashed on that sofa before. It is not particularly nice to the lower back."

My face got incredibly hot, but Christopher didn't so much as blink. "Nay, I would not dare disturb her slumber," he said. "Besides, the, ah, sofa, as you call it, rests beneath the large window, allowing me to better protect you from the creatures outside." He gave me another bright smile, and it almost made up for the fact that I'd nearly gotten a real fairytale kiss.

Which pulled me up a little because, honestly, I hardly *knew* the man. He'd fallen into my life not even a few hours before, and here I was, ready to plant one on him. Was this what just inevitably happened around princes? It explained a lot about fairytales and animated movies, that was for sure.

And normally, this kind of behavior would've made me roll my eyes, except that he was so sincere. It was kind of adorable. No, not adorable, charming. I kept coming back to that word. He was, in every sense of the word, charming. Almost perfect, but just normal enough that I wasn't put off by it.

The next morning, that almost-perfect was on perfect display. His smile was still bright and perfect, but his eyes crinkled when he really beamed. His hair went three different directions after having slept on the sofa.

And it turned out, nobody could make tights look good. Not even Prince Charming.

"I'll grab you some clothes on the way back," I promised him as I snagged my shoes from the door. The sun was already pretty high, which meant the store had to be open by now. "Until then, Tanisha, keep him *inside.*"

"You're going outside with that troll on the loose?" Tanisha asked, nearly dropping her coffee. "Woman, I thought you were stupid before, but—"

I held up the little red gem. In the light of the sunrise peeking through the windows, it seemed to glow. "Look, Vivian is the only one who can fix this. She gave it to me. She knew what it could do. So, she's got to be able to help get rid of all these things that showed up."

"I shall accompany you," Christopher said immediately, rising in an instant.

"Not in those tights you're not, and definitely *not* with the sword." So far, there'd only been creatures. If people saw a person that was clearly *Not From Here*, then they'd start demanding answers. Or worse, start filming. The last thing I needed was to be in a viral video.

He hesitated, seemingly at war with himself. It took me a minute to realize why. "Honestly, I'll be fine." It'd been a long time since I'd had anyone that protective of me. It was sweet. "Look, if I get kidnapped by a troll, I'll make sure to get a note sent to you, okay?"

"Trolls do not kidnap. They stomp on," he warned, but the corners of his lips turned up. "Perhaps simply avoid the troll altogether?"

In spite of myself, I found myself grinning. "That, I can do." Then I headed out, hurrying into town.

Of course, the store was still closed when I got there, but by that point, I wasn't going away until I had answers. Not with Prince Charming and his entire fantasy cast living in my world where they absolutely did *not* belong.

"Vivian!" I shouted, banging on the door. Something that sounded like a wasp flew dangerously close to my ear, making me shy away. When I turned to look, however, it was another pixie, this one soft and pink. Its feminine face was just as pink as the wings behind it, and any beauty was instantly marred by the being hissing at me and exposing two tiny fangs.

She flew on to somewhere else, leaving me gaping behind her. Yeah, past time to talk to Vivian. I resumed my banging. "Vivian! *Vivian!*"

The door opened just enough for me to see a familiar headscarf and dark curls. Somehow, the scarf was even more colorful than before, and I could've sworn there were now silver strands in her hair. None of it mattered more than her nonplussed face. "Vivian!" I said in relief. "I need your help! I think my wish came true!"

Somewhere behind me was a startled car horn. I spun around and found a car trying to wind its way around something in the road. In front of it, slowly walking across the street like it didn't have a care in the world, was a genuine unicorn. It found a weed sticking out of the pavement and began nonchalantly chewing on it. Above me, the pixie flew past again, with a green and yellow one right beside it.

"Yes," Vivian drawled in a deadpan tone. "I can see that. I have to say. It's been a while since I've seen a wish go like this."

I stopped. No, I hadn't imagined it: she was almost *bored* about the fact that not only had my wish come true but that there were pixies and unicorns and all sorts of fantasy creatures wreaking havoc across the globe. "Been a while?" I asked. She seemed to be watching the unicorn with a measure of amusement. "I thought you said the gem didn't catch anyone's eye."

"I said it *usually* does not," she corrected. "Do try to listen a bit better, Margaret."

"And how do you know my *name*?"

"Are you coming in for something warm to drink?" Vivian asked, completely sidestepping my questions. And my anxiety. And everything else that was making my mouth fall open in shock.

I took a deep breath. This was going nowhere, and I needed answers. "How do I undo this part?"

She raised an eyebrow. "This part?"

"Yes! I think they all followed my, uh, literal Prince Charming," I explained. "I tried wishing again with the stone, but it wouldn't let me. Or at least, it didn't work." This was hands down the craziest conversation I'd ever had, but there was a literal *unicorn* behind me, holding up traffic, and somewhere else, there was a troll wandering around. I figured I'd left ridiculous behind a while ago.

Vivian sighed and leaned against the door jamb. Her skirt today was a brilliant emerald green that flowed against the floor, and I could've sworn I saw fireman's boots underneath it. Why would she be wearing *those*?

"That's because you can't undo a wish by wishing like that," she said, pulling my attention back. "You can only make new wishes. No, the only way to undo a wish is to destroy the stone that made them come true, and that takes them all away."

"Wait, what? It takes everything back?" Even Christopher? I paused because that wasn't at all something I'd been prepared for. Dragons flying overhead, not in my plans.

Losing the guy that I'd become strangely attached to in just the last 24 hours? Especially one who looked at me like I was an extra cherry on top of an ice cream sundae, in a way no one else had ever done before?

Vivian seemed to soften, and her smile was kind. "Look, I gave you that stone not just because you came in and spent time with an old lady like myself. That stone doesn't often react to anyone; it's certainly never reacted to me. It gets passed over by just about everyone. But you saw it, and it saw you back. That tells me it's in good hands with you."

"Did you miss the dragon flying over Hollywood earlier?" I asked incredulously.

She actually chuckled. "I'm sure it'll give the news something to talk about. But you'll have to decide for yourself what to do, moving forward. Is he worth the consequences?"

That, I wasn't sure. But I wasn't about to go smashing the rock. Its weight sat nestled in my pocket, resting comfortably against my leg. For now, things could stay the way they were.

"Let me know what you choose to do with it," Vivian said yet again. "And what you choose to do with the new world you've essentially created. Either way, it should prove very interesting this time around. Very interesting indeed." And she closed the door.

I had way more questions than answers, and I was starting to get the feeling that this was how it usually was with Vivian. I sighed and headed back down the street toward my house.

A world with real magical creatures in it: that couldn't be too terrible, could it?

It turned out that it could be pretty terrible.

The pixies were worse than termites. They kept getting in everywhere, and when they bit, it hurt. It was never enough to bleed out but enough to make you yelp and reach for the nearest thing to hit them. The first time, Christopher had turned to his sword and taken it to the pixie. Not only had he missed, he'd cut a bookshelf nearly in half. That was the day we enacted the rule about No Swords in the House.

And as it turned out, a flyswatter was just about the right size to send a pixie packing. We stocked up. Christopher was particularly impressed by the durability.

But maybe the worst part of it all was that on Monday morning, I still had to go to work. "Must you go?" Christopher asked as I pulled my hair back into a bun. He was wearing the t-shirt I'd bought him, but he'd ignored the slacks in favor of keeping his tights. The combination was, well, pretty special.

"Yeah, well, trust me, I don't want to go either. But it pays the bills. I'd rather do anything else." There were days that being a crash test dummy sounded more appealing. This morning was one of them.

"How come you didn't wish for that?" Tanisha asked around a slice of toast. "I mean, Chris is great and all, but how was the job *not* the first wish, given how much you don't enjoy it?"

I paused from where I was pouring coffee into a thermos. Why hadn't it been? Was I that lonely? I'll admit that Christopher was, well, actually pretty awesome. And I wasn't going to get tired of his smile. I glanced over at him and met his gaze. He smiled brightly at me. My own lips turned up to match his.

Tanisha just huffed but with a grin of her own. "Okay, I'm kind of glad you were never heavy into dating if this is what you're like all the time."

"I don't know why I didn't wish for a better job," I told her honestly, steering the conversation back to something less invasive. A memory of my mom floated past. Her lips turned up in that fake-innocent way. *He's far better than any old job,* she would've told me. *But I'm sure you already know that.*

"Maggie?"

I blinked and found both Tanisha and Christopher watching me, concerned. "I'm fine," I said automatically, even while my chest went tight and my tongue went dry. "I just didn't wish for it, I guess."

"Chris mentioned maybe trying again," Tanisha said. Ever patient, ever willing to give me my moments and a chance to breathe. Her attempts to interject normalcy were admirable and had been since the day my mom died.

Then the words registered. "Try making *another* wish?"

"Why not?"

I scowled at them both. "Didn't you see how poorly this one came out? It totally took my words and manipulated them." In a very world hazardous way.

"Then be more specific," Tanisha insisted. "C'mon, make another wish."

Well, what did I have to lose? I pulled the gem out from my pocket and held it out. The sunlight from the kitchen window caught on the stone, making the red all the bolder. I took a deep breath in. "I wish I had a better job."

None of us dared to breathe. The gem stayed where it was. My shoulders fell. "Well?" Tanisha asked.

"I don't think it worked." Had the gem gone really red again? I couldn't tell. "That's okay. Be careful what you wish for, right?"

"Ain't that the truth," Tanisha muttered, looking out the window. Outside, a pegasus nearly got caught in the electrical lines again. I was pretty sure it was trying to sit on the wires like the birds did.

I sighed. "I'll be back before you know it," I promised Christopher. "But really, feel free to try the slacks on. Or the jeans. You might find a new favorite."

"Are you not impressed by my tights?" he asked. "They are standard attire for any prince."

Tanisha snorted. "I'm here to tell you there's nothing *standard* about any of that."

"And with that, I'm going to work," I said loudly. I didn't need to hear anything else. "I'll be back this afternoon."

It turned out I wasn't back that afternoon. I was back about an hour later.

"They *fired* you?"

"Completely out of the blue," I said faintly. I set my box of things down on the table and all but fell into a chair. Across from me, Tanisha looked furious. "I don't know what I did. They couldn't tell me. Just said that I was no longer the right fit and that I needed to gather my things." My boss had been polite but firm as he'd read off the email. He had also declined to say why I was getting the boot.

So much for employee loyalty.

If Tanisha looked mad, Christopher was ten times worse. "How dare they treat you this way?" he said incredulously. "I shall speak with them at once!" And he reached for his sword.

"No, no, *no*. You're not doing anything like that," I told him, shooting forward with my hands up. "And we've already talked about the sword. No swords inside. Or outside. Got it?" Forget fired. I'd get arrested if Christopher decided to take them on with a sword.

Something shifted in my pocket as I sat up, and I realized it was the gem. I pulled it out and set it on the table. It seemed even redder than before like it had been after my first wish.

My eyes went wide. Wait a minute. Had the gem actually granted my wish and messed it up *again*?

"What is the matter?" Christopher asked, seeing my face. "How may I help, my love?"

"I...I made a wish for a better job."

Tanisha narrowed her gaze at the gem on the table. "And now you're jobless for no damn reason. That thing is a menace."

"Hey, you told me to make another wish," I said tightly. "And it got all messed up like my first one."

Tanisha rolled her eyes. "Whatever. We need to get rid of it," she said, reaching for the gem.

"No!" I shouted, grabbing it up. In my hands, it seemed to pulse almost as fast as my heart. But it was safe, and it wasn't getting smashed. I let out a shaky breath.

It was only then that I realized the rest of the room was silent. I glanced up and found both Tanisha and Christopher watching me. "Um," I said eloquently.

"So, I just want to know: is the crazy infectious or something?" Tanisha asked. "Or do you have a reason for why you just pulled a 'my precious' moment?"

I made a face. "If I destroy it, Vivian said everything goes away." My eyes darted to Christopher. "*Everything*."

Obnoxious as my best friend can be from time to time, she's not stupid. Her eyes widened a bit, and she pulled her hands up. "No destroying it. Got it. We'll just, uh, be careful with wishing for stuff."

"Would that we were back in my kingdom, I would give you gold beyond measure," Christopher assured me. "You would never have to toil another day in your life. You would be well kept with plenty of desirable fabrics and the creamiest of cheeses."

I raised an eyebrow at him. "Is there any cream cheese left?"

"Yes," said Christopher.

"No," said Tanisha. She scowled at Christopher. "If you're going to eat the whole container, at least put it on the grocery list."

Prince Charming could lie: who knew? It made me grin a little before I realized that groceries were maybe about to get sparse for a bit. "I'll get another job as soon as I can," I told Tanisha. "I'll pay you back for groceries."

That earned me an eye roll. "Don't even start with me. You didn't have to let me stay with you after Adrian, and I broke up. I got this."

Christopher frowned. "Ah, 'broke up'?"

"Adrian cheated on me. He slept with his ex-girlfriend and then had the nerve to kick me out of our joint apartment."

I watched Christopher put a hand to his sword again. "Tell me where I might find this Adrian, and he shall taste steel for his impudence."

Tanisha began to grin. "Absolutely not," I insisted. "That was a year ago, first of all. And again, no swords in the house or outside! I'm making it a new rule: we solve problems without swords." Maybe I was going to have to draw up a rules chart like I had kids in the house or something. Even when Tanisha had moved in, we'd never had to draw up a roommate agreement. We'd just gone forward together. It had helped, after Mom. Besides, Tanisha's drama had sort of given me something else to focus on.

And oh, had there been drama.

"Besides, Tanisha's family's lawyers buried him." I'd almost felt sorry for Adrian, in the end. There were lawyers, and then there were lawyers with money behind them—specifically, families with lots of money, like Tanisha's. I *still* didn't know what her parents did for a living.

Tanisha's grin turned feral. "Then justice has been served," Christopher declared.

I had a sudden vision of what the world was going to look like with Tanisha and Christopher teaming up, and it was a very dangerous one. "I'm still going to start applying to jobs as soon as I can," I said.

"Take the day off," Tanisha insisted. "You and His Majesty can... I don't know, go wander around. Take a walk. Put him on a bicycle."

My eyes went back over his attire, and I winced. Yeah, not in those tights. "Let's, uh, get you into something better than tights. I still think you'd like the pants I got you."

"If it be a way to spend time with thee, then I shall wear whatever you please," Christopher agreed cheerfully. "Though I shall miss my tights, for they are very close to me."

"How could they be anything but?" Tanisha muttered incredulously.

I resisted rolling my eyes and dragged Christopher down the hall. If the gem was determined to give me lemons, I was going to make lemonade out of each one. It gave me a bundle of fantasy creatures? I'd take the prince that came with them. It took my job away?

Well, I'd take the day and spend it with my own Prince Charming.

After getting him into pants, which made him honestly cut even more of a nice figure, we headed out. The day was nice, and we only passed three unicorns milling by the side of the road, along with two satyrs, as we walked. On impulse, I took Christopher's hand and was rewarded with a blinding smile.

This was actually pretty nice. My hand fit, of course, perfectly in his. It wasn't too warm or too cold: no sweaty palms here. Just a guy who kept pace with me as we wandered into town.

"I am grateful."

I glanced up at him. "Grateful?"

"That you protect the gem so. For I would not be here if you were not so cautious."

So, he'd picked up on my sort of silent conversation with Tanisha. "Well, the pixies aren't too bad. And the unicorns are sort of cute."

He just smiled. I bit the inside of my lip. "And so are you," I admitted. It felt weird to say.

"You must know that the emotion is mutual. For I, too, find you cute."

"I'd sort of picked up on that," I said with a wry grin. "I'm not entirely sure I know why."

Christopher turned to me, eyes bright. "You are my princess, my one true love. How could I not admire you?"

Yeah, I figured that was about as far as I'd get. "Pretty sure you're suffering from fairytale-love-itis, but I'll take it," I said.

A firetruck came blaring down the street and stopped not too far ahead. Several bystanders were gathered around a tree, and it looked like there was a pegasus stuck up in the branches. It made me think of Vivian and her boots. Was she actually with the fire department? Was she helping with the mess I'd made? And if this sort of wishing had happened before, how come she hadn't warned me?

"I fear our path has become rife with those who seek to help the helpless," Christopher said. "As much as I yearn to aid them, their experience in this matter outweighs mine. Come, let us find another way to go." He turned to the right, down near the park and—

"Uh, not that way," I said quickly. I jerked his hand in the other direction, my pulse suddenly pounding. "How about I show you this, uh, other street? There's a bakery down this way. I bet you've never had a donut."

He glanced at me curiously but went willingly. "Nay, I have not had many of the treats of your land. I look forward to trying them all."

"That's going to take a while."

"But we have the time, my love. All the time in the world."

It made my mind spin a little harder. How long *would* he really be here? Another week? A month?

…a lifetime?

"Was there danger?"

I shook myself and looked up at Christopher. For once, he seemed very serious. "Danger?" I repeated.

"Down the other way. You were frightened; know that you have naught to fear with me by your side. Even without my sword, I will defend you."

My chest tightened. "There wasn't anything bad down there. Not… not really." I paused. He paused with me.

It made the next words easier to say. "I don't go down that way. It's the memorial garden. Graveyard," I clarified when he looked confused. "My, um. My mom's buried there. I haven't been back since her funeral." Just the thought of the cold headstone was enough to make my skin crawl. It wasn't her. It was never going to be her. Not the warm figure I missed so much. I hadn't even touched her bedroom or her things yet, and it'd been almost two years.

"That is a pain not oft felt by many. I do know well how you feel."

I blinked. Christopher had his head held up in a very regal manner, but the look in his eyes looked a lot more familiar to me. It was the same look I saw in the mirror sometimes. "You lost a parent?" I asked.

"My mother," he said, and my heart clenched so tight I couldn't breathe for a second. "Long has she been gone from me. My father married again, my stepmother."

I found myself snorting before I could restrain it. Because, of course, Prince Charming had an evil stepmother. "Is she wicked?"

His lips turned up. "I thought so for many a year as a child. But now, full-grown, she is a friend. And she loves me as if I were her own."

"Who knew the fairytale could get an update," I said. When he looked confused again, I just waved him off. "Never mind. Inside joke. I'm glad she's not a wicked woman."

"You and I both. I have heard many a tale of wicked stepmothers. I was lucky to have such a good woman join my family."

My mother had never remarried. I wondered how I would've taken a stepfather. I couldn't imagine anyone replacing my dad, even though I had so few memories of him. And I definitely couldn't imagine anyone taking my mom's place.

He lifted my hand to his mouth and gently kissed the back of it. "Change can be frightening. But I am grateful, even in this wild and incredible new world I have found myself in, that I have also found you."

Our eyes met. His smile began to pull one at my own lips. As if we were magnets, I found myself taking the few steps to drift toward him. His hair was a shade darker than I'd thought, now that I was close enough to look. My focus turned to his lips, inches from mine.

A neighing made us stop, then spring apart just in time to not get plowed over by a unicorn. "Pony!" a little girl squealed in hot pursuit, followed closely by her very harried mother.

We watched them go. "She is mistaken," Christopher said with a frown. "That is *not* a pony."

With a sigh, I tugged us down the road again, our moment long gone. "C'mon, I promised you a donut." I totally deserved some fried dough, too.

My phone dinged. I glanced down at it and found I had a new email. "Does your magic device summon you?" Christopher asked. "Tanisha attempted to explain it to me, but this sorcery is far past my comprehension."

"It's an email. A message from…the Parks and Recreation Association?" What? Since when did I get emails from them? Bewildered, I opened it, then stared.

It was a job offer for an events coordinator. I'd *never* done events coordinating. And I didn't think I wanted to.

Another ding. The next email came from a cooking school, offering me a place in a culinary class with a guaranteed job placement upon completion. Oh no, they did *not* want me cooking. No one wanted that. There was a reason I was on a first-name basis with several take-out places.

Another ding. And another. And another and another. My eyes went impossibly huge as my inbox began to fill.

Christopher read over my shoulder and let out a pretty loud, "Huzzah!" When I turned to him, eyes still wide, his smile was blinding. "Now you no longer must seek out a job, for many seek your talents!"

Yeah, I definitely deserved a donut. With an unholy amount of sprinkles.

I spent the next week looking through the job offers that kept coming into my inbox. I never sent out a single resume. They just kept coming, each one stranger than the last. Grizzly bear photographer. Professional football mascot. Unicorn wrangler.

Meanwhile, I turned my attention to the rest of the world. After a while, the news got tiresome and repetitive about the fantasy creatures and hearing political commentators arguing about the nuances between a mermaid and a selkie wasn't much better than their usual bickering. I mostly kept it running in the background in case something new happened. Otherwise, my first focal point was Christopher.

His speech was so old-timey that it sometimes made me wince, but he was sincere about it and even happy to learn new phrases, too. Trust me. You've never heard anything as odd as a prince in royal regalia using "foul beasts" and "ratchet" in the same sentence. (Thank you, Tanisha.) Slowly but surely, I taught him the more modern grammatical nuances of our time. And, in turn, I learned some of his more formal language.

We shared a lot of things with each other. He told me about his kingdom, how there was a staircase in the castle that was great for sliding down, and how much he'd always wanted a sibling. He shared his love of protecting "the innocent and helpless" with me, along with his hobbies of knitting and archery. "They are not difficult at all to learn, particularly for someone of your intelligence and stature," he assured me.

I told him about the modern world, the internet, vehicles, all sorts of things that I figured he should know about. He listened diligently, then one day asked, "And what of you?"

I stopped. "Me?"

He rested his arms on the kitchen tabletop. "Yes, you. What of you and your family? Your hobbies? Your favorite things to do?"

I began to answer, then stopped. Because for the first time in a long time, I realized I didn't know what the answers were. "Um," I said, displaying the intelligence and stature I supposedly had.

Christopher sat next to me, waiting patiently. Prince Charming had his weird ticks, but his genuine sweetness and sincerity made up for a lot of it. I sort of adored his patience, particularly with me. It gave me the confidence to keep going. "My dad died when I was young. My mom was sort of my everything. Best friend, mentor, parent, y'know. I don't have any siblings either. Tanisha's the closest to family I really have anymore. I've got aunts and uncles out of state. But at the end, when my mom died, it was just me and her. And now it's just...me."

He kept listening. I kept going. "I used to do things like go on hikes. My mom loved the outdoors, and she shared it with me. She encouraged me to do everything, try anything. Even when my hobby was weird and sort of expensive."

"Oh?" He leaned forward with a smile. "And what was it?"

I found my lips turning up. "I love photography, but not the instant stuff or the electronic kind. I love the older photography, the kind you need a dark room for." How to explain old-time photography? "You have to take the film out of the camera and develop it. They don't just show up on your phone. You don't even know what the photos look like until they come out."

His smile grew. "A mystery! An exciting mystery. It sounds a great deal like a quest."

"I guess, yeah," I agreed. I'd forgotten how much I'd enjoyed photography. "I'll have to go dig out my camera. I'll show you how it—"

Suddenly Tanisha came barreling into the room, nearly making me fall out of my seat. Dramatic, much? "What the heck?" I exclaimed.

Then I saw her face. My stomach churned. "Tanisha, what's wrong?"

"Have you been watching the news at all?" she asked. "I mean, I mostly ignore it, but you need to see this."

I hurried and followed her into the living room, Christopher right behind me. Together we all watched the latest breaking news.

"*...third ship to disappear in the Atlantic Ocean this week. Experts are blaming the large sea creature that was captured on film this Thursday. The footage documents a large creature that some are calling a kraken; the video ends ominously with a large tentacle reaching for the cameraman. The ship is still to be recovered—*"

Tanisha changed the channel to another news station.

"*...devastating crops. The flying horses, known more commonly as a pegasus, have left very little behind in fields across the plains. The effects are likely to be felt in grocery stores across the nation—*"

Another channel.

"*...new fires sweeping down from the mountain peaks are causing more than just forest fires. Thanks to the heights that the dragons are living on, the snow-capped mountains are melting, causing flooding and run-off everywhere. We are told the governor is likely to call a state of emergency—*"

Tanisha muted the television. I watched the anchor speaking urgently to the camera, the same as the others before him. Who knew how many other stories there were running through the news? I'd started avoiding my phone thanks to the myriad amount of job offers I kept getting.

Vivian had mentioned wondering what I'd do with this new world that I'd created. I hadn't thought of it at the time, but now, it was all I could think of. This was all my fault. I'd done this with my wish. And I was only making it worse every day that I didn't undo my wish.

I had to do something. There had to be something I could do.

I pursed my lips. "I'm going to talk to Vivian again," I said. "I'm going to figure out what to do."

Vivian wasn't there.

I stared at the store front, then banged on the door again. "Vivian!"

"The sign says that they are open only until six in the evening," Christopher said. He was wearing one of the pairs of slacks I'd given him, but I knew for a fact that the tights were underneath them. He'd said that he felt too odd without them. Who was I to argue with the man?

I glanced at my phone and sighed—6:07 pm. Of course. "We'll come back tomorrow," I told him. "What's the next opening hours say?"

"Friday at two in the afternoon."

I spun to where he pointed at the sign. "That's two days from now," I said incredulously. "What the hell is she playing at?"

Sure enough, the hours sign innocently stated that the shop was, indeed, closed for the next two days. "Perhaps she wished for time away," Christopher said.

She had to know that I'd come back to talk to her. She *had* to. "Vivian!" I shouted again. Around me, people skirted around us like I was somehow the strangest thing they'd seen today. I knew for a fact I wasn't because there were five unicorns on the other side of the street, eating the flowers out of the hanging baskets of a nearby store.

A pixie buzzed around my head, and I swatted at it. It hissed angrily at me. "Foul beast, you shall taste steel," Christopher warned, reaching for his sheathed sword.

"No, Chris," I warned. "You know you're not going to hit it with a sword. Remember what happened last night?"

"Verily, I do," Christopher admitted. He rubbed the back of his neck sheepishly. "I wreaked havoc and brought bad mojo upon the house."

I pinched the bridge of my nose. "I have *got* to tell Tanisha to stop teaching you phrases," I muttered.

"Aye, 'tis sus."

"Please don't say *sus*."

I didn't get an answer for that. I looked around and found more pixies buzzing nearby. A satyr ran across the street, a woman's purse in his clutches. "Stop, thief! You are sus!" Christopher shouted, pulling his sword out and running after him. A pixie quickly fluttered off to join the race.

I cursed and took off after them all. Fine, if Vivian wasn't here to talk to, then I was going to have to figure it out myself. And I would.

I didn't.

So, we waited for Friday. And I watched the news. I watched a lot of news, which never does anything good for anyone's mood.

Friday came, leaving me still sitting in front of the television. In front of me, the newscaster talked about dragons causing fires. Some-where in the hallway, Christopher was doing battle with whatever was coming up out of the toilet. Tanisha kept making high-pitched sounds. The pixie that had followed us home kept buzzing around.

Two weeks. Two weeks of this, and the world wasn't getting any better. It was just getting worse.

I glanced at the gem sitting on the coffee table beside me. It seemed to twinkle in the afternoon light as if begging me to make another wish. "Don't even start," I said out loud. "You've caused enough problems."

"I'm almost afraid to ask who you're talking to."

I looked up to find Tanisha coming in, drying herself off with a towel. The towel was mostly covered in green gunk. "Is...*it* dead?" I asked hesitantly.

"Oh yeah," Tanisha said, almost proudly. There was a glob of gunk in her hair. I didn't tell her. "It's not going to come up through the toilet again. Let me just say. I'm so glad I always look before I sit down."

I raised an eyebrow. "Are you typically expecting something in the toilet?"

"I'm not usually expecting a tentacle, no, but there could be spiders or centipedes!"

"Centipedes are more often found on ceilings."

She scowled at me. "Great. Now I've got another place to look before I can pee in peace."

I pinched the bridge of my nose. "Can you just tell me what time it is?"

"It is coming up on two in the afternoon, my love," Christopher said, panting. He was soaked and also covered in green slime and seemed particularly pleased with himself. His sword looked like a hot mess.

Great. Who knew what the bathroom looked like. "Okay, we're going to get to Vivian and see if we can clean all of this up. Tanisha, get yourself a shower, and if more things try to come up through the pipes, smack them with something. Me, I'm going to put the gem somewhere safe." My room, for starters, and I even had the pouch it'd come in.

Before I headed down the hallway, however, I pointed to Christopher. "Leave the sword here. Remember the rules for outside."

Disappointed, he sighed and went to leave the sword in my closet. I rolled my eyes and kept on moving.

Tanisha insisted on coming with us before she snagged a shower, insisting, "Someone had to get answers out of this woman, and clearly you won't." I didn't argue with her. Nobody should argue with someone who's covered in toilet water and angry about centipedes and monsters in pipes.

Together we found ourselves outside of Vivian's shop, and this time, the doors were propped open. I led the charge inside and almost immediately stopped.

If possible, there were even more candles, making the inside almost brighter than the outside. "Woah, fire hazard," Tanisha said from behind me. "Also, it is disgustingly hot in here."

"Verily, it is a bit much," Christopher agreed, already wiping at his brow. "But why is it so hot in here?"

"Maybe I just like making people uncomfortable."

I whipped my head toward the back. There, standing by the glass case, head still done up in that incredibly colorful headscarf, was Vivian. Her skirt had been exchanged for waders, and they seemed to be covered in a familiar green slime, one that Tanisha and Christopher were both wearing.

I swallowed hard and pushed myself forward. "You've been cleaning up my mess, haven't you?" It wasn't a question.

Vivian leaned against the glass case and crossed her arms. "Someone has to. You won't. Just like all the rest."

"Hey, not cool," Tanisha snapped, even as my mind spun with the implications. "Who gave her the damn gem in the first place? You didn't tell her it was going to grant her wish in a messed-up way."

"Aye, not cool," Christopher echoed. "Though I am still pleased by the luck in finding my one true love."

"Are you?" Vivian turned her gaze to Christopher, and I didn't like the look on her face in the slightest. It was way too knowing. "Pleased enough to not miss your family, to miss life as you know it?"

Christopher didn't say anything. I shifted uneasily. Of course, he had to be missing his family. True love at first sight was only good for so long, especially without anyone to share it with. And I knew too well the way you could pick up a phone to call someone and remember they weren't there to answer anymore.

I wish my mom were here, I couldn't help but think. She would've known what to do. I just knew it.

Vivian suddenly turned to me, eyes narrowing. "There's only so much longer I can hold things off. You need to make your decision—now."

"The decision for these creatures to leave?" I asked. "Because I'd do that in a heartbeat."

"No. The decision to do what needs to be done. To decide that sometimes you don't get what you truly want, even when you wish for it." Even as she stood before me, her curls whipped around her head-scarf, and her eyes seemed to change colors.

I swallowed hard. "Who are you?" I asked.

"A witch," Christopher said decisively. "You are a sorceress, are you not?"

"I'm a fixer," she said. "My goal is to protect the world, one piece of it at a time. Right now, the next piece is here. Specifically, at Margaret's house."

I crossed my arms, refusing to let her see just how freaked out I was that she knew exactly where the gem was. "Then, if you know how to protect us all, you do it. Show me how to fix this."

"I already told you how. The decision of when must be up to you." She shook her head. "I can't break it for you. You made the wishes. You have to deal with how they were answered. Just like everyone else before you."

"And what did they do? How did they do it?"

"You assume they did," Vivian told me sharply. "Believe me when I say that the world would be a far different place if they had."

It left me staring in shock. How many more wishes had been made before me? How many world-changing events were because someone refused to give up what they'd gotten out of their wish? I met her knowing gaze and resisted the urge to flinch.

"So, don't make another wish is what you're saying," Tanisha summed up.

The hard stare ended, and Vivian was the older, sweeter woman I had met that very first day. "It might be wise. But sometimes, we don't learn by being wise. We get wise by learning."

"Oh, so you're the riddle sort of witch that I can't stand whenever I read a fantasy book," Tanisha said disdainfully. "Got anything actually useful for us?"

Stunningly, Vivian didn't protest Tanisha's words. She actually smiled enigmatically. Because why not. It only served to irritate Tanisha more.

Not that I completely cared. Because Vivian was telling me there was only one way for me to stop fantasy from becoming a barren reality, and I was going to have to be the one to do it.

I was going to lose Christopher.

It stole my breath, and for a minute, I wanted to scream at the unfairness. I was going to lose someone else I was ridiculously close to? My mom wasn't enough, now him? If I wound up losing Tanisha somehow, I was going to toss the proverbial towel in and go sit on a beach somewhere.

Vivian sighed slightly. "Go home, Margaret. What you seek most of all isn't here. No, the answer to your problem, the answer to the question I asked you two weeks ago, it's not here. You'll find your impossible answer elsewhere. And good luck, for I do not envy you the choices."

"You're not helping," I said. "That's it, then?"

"That is all I can do," she told me. "You have to do the rest. Believe me. My interference will only make things worse."

Personally, I wasn't sure how she could make it worse, but I wasn't going to argue with the woman. Not when she'd clearly seen so many wishes made over the years. It made me realize she was *far* older than I'd originally thought. Who knew how old?

Slowly we trudged out of the shop. "Am I going to see you again?" I asked Vivian as she began closing the doors.

She smiled, a little thing at the corner of one mouth. "Perhaps. That's up to how you handle this. If you'll excuse me, I've got things to do. Go on, Margaret."

The walk back was miserable. Between the random troll snore, I could hear from further down the road, then the unicorns and several deer fighting with each other, I was more than done. And that was before Vivian's questions that spurred more questions than answers.

So now what? What was I supposed to do? How could I stop mermaids and dragons and trolls?

Preferably without having to destroy the stone itself?

The wind suddenly blew through, making me shiver. "It got dark fast," Tanisha noted. "Stupid time change. Is daylight so much to ask for?"

"In my kingdom, daylight is constricted to sixteen hours a day exactly. Then we have sunrises and sunsets."

"See, that makes more…."

I glanced at Tanisha as she gradually slid to a halt. "What? What is it?" I followed her gaze to the porch and saw the figure that had caught her eyes.

There, turning slowly from our front door, was an older woman. She seemed to be facing toward the door as if waiting for the person who usually comes at a knock. Always patient. She'd always been so patient.

I stared. I couldn't believe it. I just couldn't.

Tanisha saw her as well and pulled Christopher up to a halt. "Is that," she began, then stopped.

I swallowed hard. My pulse thundered in my ears enough that I barely heard myself speak. "…Mom?"

It had to be. It couldn't be anyone else. That hair styled as I'd seen it last, the dress one that I'd stared at for hours before finally choosing it for burial, even the simple white sneakers she'd jokingly told me to bury her in. It was her, and she was standing on the front porch where she'd stood so many times before.

My impossible wish had come true, the wish that I hadn't dared to dream. The wish that had been so impossible that I hadn't even spoken it out loud. I had my mom back.

Slowly she turned, almost staggering as if her legs couldn't hold her. I moved forward quickly, only to find Christopher's hand wrapped tight around my arm. "Chris, let me go," I insisted, surprised, but Christopher's eyes were wide and locked on my mom. "That's my mom!"

"That creature is not your mother," he said lowly. "At least, not anymore."

I turned back to my mom and felt my heart freeze in my chest. Hair, dress, shoes, they were all there.

Skin, eyeballs, muscles? They were pretty much gone, leaving just a ragged skeleton that was somehow upright. Even the hair was barely hanging on, hovering over hollow eye sockets that glowed red.

"No way," Tanisha breathed beside me. "Mags, your mom...she's a *zombie.*"

From somewhere in the distance, I heard someone scream. It was far away enough that it barely registered, but it didn't help the feeling in my chest. Neither did the next shout of terror that followed, one that was far closer. The hairs on the back of my neck stood on end.

For a long moment, the remains of my mother stared at me. I stared back, my heart pounding in my chest. This was nothing like what I'd wished for. When I'd wished for my mom back, I'd imagined a soft smile and a hug, just like I'd had before she'd died. Not...not this. This was like a joke but nowhere close to funny. My eyes burned at the mockery of what I'd wanted the most for the last two years.

"Someone help me! Oh god, someone *help!*"

"Maggie," Tanisha whispered in horror, and I finally tore my eyes from my mother's visage. Tanisha had her arm held out, finger trembling as it pointed at what was behind me. A man was running down the street, still begging for help, and right behind him were three people. All of them were stumbling along, arms outstretched, and all of them were the same type of decomposed as my mother's remains.

Oh no.

Oh, *please,* no.

More screams filled the air from down the street, and I realized we weren't horribly far from several graveyards, including the memorial park. They were probably all empty. And that meant a lot of zombies.

My wish had come true with horrifying consequences again. Somehow, I hadn't just brought back my mom: I'd brought back the dead *everywhere.* Zombie apocalypse starter: that was me.

Christopher suddenly shoved me back, sending me stumbling into Tanisha. My mom's corpse had started moving, stumbling down the stairs of the porch, empty eye sockets somehow locked on me. Then her arms came straight up, skeletal fingers reaching for me.

Tanisha let out a shriek. "My sword is inside," Christopher said, almost helplessly, and it was enough to galvanize me into action.

"Go, the back door's unlocked!" I grabbed Tanisha with one hand and Christopher with another and ran, giving my mom's corpse a wide berth. "Go!"

Something had to be done. Someone had to stop this because this wasn't just one world colliding with another anymore. This was the end of the world about to come crashing down on our heads.

And the only person who could fix this was me.

The corpse (it wasn't Mom, I had to stop thinking about it like it was Mom) immediately changed course to lumber after us. We cleared the side of the house easily and moved around to the back, where the back door was, then stumbled to a stunned halt. Three more zombies were in the backyard, moving steadily toward us.

"We're surrounded!" Tanisha yelled. "Maggie!"

"The door!" I shouted back, and we made it to the stoop. I gave the door a hearty shove, and we burst inside. Then it was a mad scramble to close the door behind us. Tanisha pulled the curtains down around the small window while I frantically threw every single lock. Christopher darted away, only to return with a kitchen chair, which he rammed under the handle. The handle suddenly rattled ominously, making the three of us jump back, and a pounding noise made the door shake as if something had fallen against it. The handle rattled again.

Then it stopped. I let out a shaky sigh of relief. They weren't getting in that way, at least.

"Front door, we must secure all entrances," Christopher said. He turned and grabbed another chair, Tanisha and I right behind him. All the locks were already thrown, but Tanisha and I grabbed the curtains of the big window and pulled them closed while he put the chair under the doorknob. If they couldn't see potential people to eat, they might leave us be for a bit.

I shut my eyes for just a second and let myself savor the ridiculousness of the sentence. My reality was sort of a little skewed these days.

"Oh my god," Tanisha said faintly, and I realized she was staring out the little side window in horror. I hurried to her side and found that several zombies had cornered a unicorn. It neighed and kicked out, but the zombies were going to get it in the end. I quickly pulled the curtains closed before we could watch the carnage.

Tanisha finally cleared her throat. "Do you think…do you think it'll turn into a zombie unicorn?"

Yeah, that was about all of this that I could deal with. "We need to get this to stop," I said. "And we need to do it fast before they figure out how to get in."

A crashing sound from somewhere below made us all freeze. "I think…I think that was the basement window," Tanisha said faintly. "Mags, if you have an answer, you gotta do it, like, *now*."

"My room," I said tersely, and we all took off down the hall. Even as we passed the basement door, there was the unmistakable creaking sound of someone making their way upstairs. Oh, we were beyond out of time.

I got us into my room and slammed the door shut. Christopher hurried to the closet and pulled out his sword with a triumphant sound. I dove for my nightstand and reached in, fingers scrambling like mad for the jewel. Tissues, old cassette tapes, measuring tape, the photo frame of my mom and I—

"Where the hell *is* it?" I said, panic driving my voice up.

"Where's what?" Tanisha asked from the door. Something thudded against the door, making her squeak and push back harder. "Maggie!"

"That red jewel! My wishing stone!" My fingers still hadn't touched the fabric, and I peered desperately into the drawer. I know I'd left it in there, so where—?

"It's here, Margaret."

I spun around to where Christopher stood. In one hand hung his sword, but in the other, held in his outstretched palm, was the jewel nestled in its usual bed of fabric.

I stared at him. What had Christopher been doing with it?

He gave a small smile. "I had hoped to make a wish upon it for, well, for you. But alas, it won't work for me. I did try, though."

The enormity of what I was about to do finally came crashing down on me, and my eyes filled with tears. In order to undo the damage being wreaked on the world, I was going to have to destroy the jewel. I was going to have to undo my wish.

Undo all my wishes.

None of it had come out according to what I'd wanted or planned. In wishing for a man who seemed devoted to me, I'd wound up with magical chaos across the planet. In wishing for a better job, I'd lost the one I'd had and been inundated with job offers that were all sorts of varied and wild. And now, in wishing for my mom, I'd started the zombie apocalypse.

It was just terrible that I was going to lose Christopher. Of everything that had gone wrong, one thing had gone sort of right, and it had been Christopher.

"Chris, if I do this," I began, but he shook his head.

"It has to be done. We both know this. I cannot let your world fall into disarray and death." He handed me the jewel only so he could have a free hand to cup my cheek. I leaned into his touch, the burn in my eyes threatening to roll down my face.

His smile got a little bit stronger. "I cannot let you fall into that darkness, my love."

The pounding against the door actually rattled the windows. We turned to where Tanisha had her back shoved against the door, heels dug into my carpet. "I got it," she said, a bit breathlessly. "I got this, Mags. Get your goodbye, girl."

"Tanisha," I began, and she just grinned.

"I didn't say I had it forever, but you got a minute and a half. Don't waste it."

I wasn't going to. I caught Christopher around the neck and pulled him in. The kiss was just as sweet and perfect, but it tasted of salt. I tried to memorize his scent, the way his lips felt against mine, the way our noses brushed when we finally parted. It was like cramming for an exam, but the most important exam I'd ever have. I didn't want to lose this memory, ever.

I couldn't even think about the other memory that was being destroyed that night, the one whose corpse was probably on the other side of my bedroom door. I was never going to remember my mom the same again.

I took the jewel and set it down on the edge of my bed. The large bookend from my shelf would do the trick. I caught hold of it, then held it out toward Christopher. "Together?" I said, voice not as solid as I would've liked.

He smiled and wrapped his hand over mine. "Together."

I took a deep breath in and rested the bookend above the jewel. The red shimmered brightly, swirling like a tiny storm inside.

"Thank you."

I glanced up at him and found him still smiling, albeit with a deep sadness in his eyes. "I've lived in a world with magic for my entire life," he continued. "But it was here with you that I found something truly wonderful. You, Margaret, are extraordinary and enchanting."

My lips parted in both surprise and grief. "And that thing out there? She is not your mother," he continued. He reached over and caught the picture frame I'd tossed onto the bed. Her smile was bright in the photo, her arms wrapped around me. "This is your mother," he said. "Do not forget that. Promise me."

"I won't forget any of this," I swore, the first tears finally escaping my eyes. "Thank you for just…being you, Christopher. The best Prince Charming I could've asked for."

He kept smiling, that same smile that was going to fill my dreams and haunt my what-ifs. I inhaled sharply and lifted the bookend over the jewel. The pounding on the door actually shoved Tanisha forward, making her gasp and shove back as hard as she could. Screams of terror echoed from outside.

I locked eyes with him—just one last time.

The bookend came down on the jewel.

In an instant, the jewel disintegrated into thousands of pieces. Red smoke and clouds swirled out, billowing into the air, blinding my sight. I winced as it whipped past me, growing in ferocity, a tiny tornado building in my room, and then—

It was gone. Slowly I blinked and blinked again.

The bookend was in my hand and my hand alone. Tanisha was slumped against my door, staring wide-eyed at where the jewel had been. There was nothing left, not even a single shard or a speck of red dust, to show what I'd destroyed.

There was no Christopher either. And the pounding on the door had stopped.

Slowly I moved to the door. I waited until Tanisha was ready, and, at our mutual nod, we flung the door open. There was nothing in the hallway.

There was nothing in the house, either. One peek out of the curtains showed an empty street: no zombies, no unicorns anywhere. No buzzing pixies, no roaring dragons. The sunset shone through, the sky empty of any flying horses.

It was all gone. The wishes had been undone.

Tanisha pulled the chair away from the front door, undid the bolts, and headed out. While there were people in the street, no one seemed hurt. Just bewildered, every single one of them, but no one was dead or hurt. One guy a few houses down scratched at his head. "What the heck happened?" he asked in utter confusion.

I slumped into a porch chair and hung my head.

The days following were interesting.

The media, for one, was pretty wild, with theories ranging from full conspiracy to the tried-and-true method of Just Keep Going. Eventually, the news shifted back to the mundane of politics, fall festivals, and the latest in some Wall Street executive's scandal.

People did much the same. Where they'd begun to sort of live alongside magical beings, they were now quickly shifting back to what life had been before. Most people had accepted that, for some reason, reality had been thrown a loop for two weeks, and there was a general attempt to deal with it. I said most, not everyone. There were definitely outliers.

Some seemed sort of convinced it was a drug experiment from the government. Others were just as convinced that everything had really happened but that it had been aliens who'd come down and taken everything away. It made as much sense as any other guess, and honestly, it was closer to the truth.

Not that I was going to tell them that. Neither was Tanisha, which was honestly probably far more than I deserved. But like every part of her, Tanisha's friendship and loyalty remains stalwart and stubborn. I sort of adore her for that.

I saw Vivian exactly one more time. She actually came to me, knocking at my door a few days after everything was put back together. "You did well," she told me in what honestly sounded like relief. "You did better than I could've hoped or dreamed for, Margaret."

"Um, thank you," I said.

"No, no," and she held out her pink shawl. "Thank *you*."

"I couldn't take it," I insisted, but she wasn't listening again. Hesitantly I took it, the weight familiar.

She smiled, that same knowing smile, and stepped away. "Goodbye, Margaret." And then she was gone.

I wasn't even surprised by the crystals I found inside. I just simply handed them to Tanisha. "For you. I thought you'd like them."

"Oh, sweet! Best thanks-for-helping-me-save-the-world present ever."

I never did get my job back, but the offers did stop. Eventually, I chose one, a photography studio that had been looking for an assistant and asked if my camera was okay. Turned out, the guy was enamored with the idea of someone being into older film cameras and immediately hired me on the spot. It paid the bills and then some, as it turned out, and it gave me something to do. It gave me a chance to see the world from a different view and rediscover a passion.

It was while I was getting coffee to do the thing I'd been avoiding for two years that I bumped into someone. "Sorry," he apologized. "Sorry, I'm not usually so absent-minded. It's been, well. It's been a few crazy weeks."

"Oh yeah," I agreed. "I know that feeling." I paused, and for some reason, I kept talking. "I actually don't usually get specialty coffee like this, but I'm going to visit my mom's grave today. I saw her when. Well, you know. And I need to...."

"Move forward, but you don't know how to do it when the person you wanted most came back in the world's worst way?" he finished, and there was relief in his dark eyes. "Yeah, I hear you. My dad came back that night too. I haven't had the balls to go see his resting place either. I just can't." He used his hand free of coffee to shove his dark hair away from his face.

He was nothing like Christopher. Yet, at the same time, I realized he didn't have to be. I could at least be the Margaret that Christopher had looked at with such fondness. He'd thought I was extraordinary and enchanting. So had Mom.

I took a deep breath in and held out my own free hand. "Maggie."

He gave a quick grin and took my hand in his to shake it. His palm was a little sweaty from his coffee cup. "Jordan."

It wasn't much. But as I nodded toward a free table and he went with me to claim it, it felt a little like a connection. Someone else who understood what it meant to get your wish answered in the worst way possible. Someone who knew what it was like to lose someone you loved.

And at the end of the day, I guess that's all I could really wish for.

J.M. Rhineheart lives in Virginia, USA, with her husband and two daughters, where she also teaches English and music. Her work can be found in DreamForge Magazine as well as anthologies such as The Devil You Know, Rowan & Oak, 25 Servings of SOOP Vol. II, and Candy Capers. When she's not writing, she loves exploring National

Parks, playing the violin, and binge-watching "The Great British Bake Off".

Find out more at:
jmrhineheart.wordpress.com

instagram.com/jmrhineheart
facebook.com/jmrhineheart
twitter.com/jmrhineheart

MORE BY FICTION-ATLAS PRESS

Fiction-Atlas Press releases two anthologies a year. We hope you'll check out some of our past anthologies or sign up to be notified about future ones on the next page!

Chasing Fireflies:

A Summer Romance Anthology

A Twist of Fate:

A Twisted Fairy Tale Anthology

Counterclockwise:

A Fiction-Atlas Time Travel Anthology

Beyond the Mask:

A Fiction-Atlas Superhero Anthology

Unknown Realms:

A Fiction-Atlas Press Anthology

The Devil You Know:

A Fiction-Atlas Press Anti-Hero Anthology

Bloodsport:

A Fiction-Atlas Vampire Anthology

From The Deep:

A Fiction-Atlas Nautical Anthology

THANK YOU

We hope you have enjoyed our anthology.
It would mean the world to us if you had the time to leave a review!
Reviews are what keep us writing!

FOLLOW FICTION-ATLAS PRESS FOR INFORMATION ON FUTURE PUBLICATIONS.

FICTION-ATLAS
PRESS LLC

http://fiction-atlas.com

facebook.com/fictionatlas
twitter.com/fabookbargains
instagram.com/cl_cannon
youtube.com/clcannonauthor

ARE YOU A FAN OF BOOK BARGAINS?WE ARE TOO!

Fiction-Atlas is pleased to announce that we have launched our FABB bargains newsletter.

Get the best free and discounted books, plus awesome giveaways delivered straight to your inbox!

Sign-up here: https://bit.ly/fabbreaders

We also post daily bargains on our Facebook and Twitter pages!

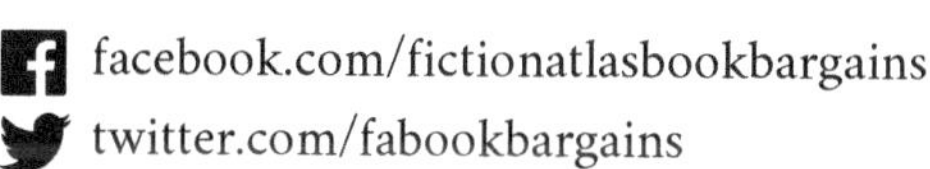

facebook.com/fictionatlasbookbargains

twitter.com/fabookbargains